DISCARD

of Eden

EVE ADAMS

ST. MARTIN'S PRESS
❧ *New York*

www.stmartins.com

Book design by Jonathan Bennett

Library of Congress Cataloging-in-Publication Data

Adams, Eve, 1946–
    The garden of Eden / Eve Adams.—1st ed.
      p. cm.
    ISBN 0-312-32363-8
    EAN 978-0312-32363-9
    1. Triangles (Interpersonal relations)—Fiction. 2. City and town life—Fiction.
  3. Forgiveness—Fiction. 4. Betrayal—Fiction. I. Title.

PS3553.O5796 G+
813'.54—dc22

                          2004051393

First Edition: May 2005

10 9 8 7 6 5 4 3 2 1

To the memory of
Jimmie Ryder Sr., and to Tommy, Hersh, Ellen, and Sarah

We are living in very strange times, and they are likely to get a lot stranger before we bottom out.

Hunter S. Thompson

The Garden of Eden

ONE

The road to Eden runs up the valley from the town of Indian River. All along its length are small farms, occasionally a large one, and, set back from the road in the edge of the forest, a few fine homes. Although the valley is wide, as valleys in that country go, the road is not the straightest and is only two lanes of asphalt. The centerline was repainted by the state not long ago, so that looks nice.

The village of Eden is twelve miles from Indian River. Due to some bureaucratic oversight the village still has a post office, a small brick building with an American flag on a pole out front. Old Mrs. Marple puts the mail up, sells stamps, and passes the time of day with anyone who walks in. She has been behind the counter in the post office for almost forty years, longer than many of her customers have been alive.

Across the road from the post office sits the primary business in Eden—well, the only business in Eden. The sign on Doolin's Restaurant and General Store is faded and the paint flaking off, but everyone in four counties knows it. The enterprise is owned and operated by Moses Grimes, who bought it from Doolin years and years ago and never got around to having the sign repainted. Doolin moved away after he sold out and may even be dead now—no one seems to know for sure.

In the general store Grimes stocks groceries, fresh meat, tools, nails, nuts and bolts, electrical and plumbing items, ammunition, fishing equipment, and a breathtaking array of over-the-counter medicines, beauty products, pots, pans, school supplies, etc. Out back in a cinder-block shed he keeps fertilizer, bulk pet food, culverts, charcoal and the like.

Every item in Doolin's General Store can be purchased cheaper in the county seat, Indian River. Most of the patrons tend to buy only things they forgot to purchase on their last shopping expedition in town. Grimes would probably go out of business if it weren't for the restaurant, where he features good, plain country cooking at rock-bottom prices. Packed three times a day, the restaurant is the social hub of the Eden community. The dining room is not large, so people talk to their neighbors at the other tables. Sometimes four or five of these conversations are in progress at once; since the volume can be awe-inspiring, it takes a trained ear to hear the remarks directed at you.

All this hubbub takes place before the worst mural ever painted, a stupendous outdoor scene that covers the largest wall. The grossly distorted perspective of this work is trendy enough, yet one suspects the artist was color-blind or had decided this wall was the perfect place to dispose of a large quantity of hideous green paint. Regular customers find that the food goes down easier if they avoid looking at the mural.

There are four houses in the village of Eden, nice old houses with two large rooms downstairs and two up, with chimneys on each end and fireplaces in every room. Three of the houses are in fair condition, and one is ready to fall down because miser Hardy, who lives there, never spent a cent on paint or nails in his life.

A village would be incomplete without a church. Fortunately Eden has one: the Eden Chapel, a white frame building with a small bell tower, surrounded by a graveyard brimming with past Edenites. The former preacher, the Reverend Mr. Henry Davis, just retired, lives in the house beside the post office with the good Mrs. Davis.

At the south end of the village is a schoolhouse, now abandoned, located between two county roads that lead away from Eden. The left fork goes off through the hills to Canaan and Goshen; the right fork goes to Vegan.

Although both forks are paved for the first mile or so, they are narrower and more twisty than the Eden road, and the state didn't waste any paint on centerlines. Once they pass through Eden, most tourists turn around in the old schoolyard and head back down the valley toward the town.

Tourists *do* visit Eden. The trees may not be straighter there, taller and more symmetrical, the grass greener, the sky bluer and the distant mountains more purple and majestic, but it often seems so. On fine mornings the locals like to tell each other that, indeed, God made this place first. While no travel or leisure magazine has ever done an article on the Eden country and probably none ever will, word-of-mouth keeps a steady, dripping trickle of cars driving slowly up the Eden road, visiting Doolin's and turning around in the schoolyard.

Today Trooper Sam Neely of the state police pulled his cruiser into the schoolyard and sat looking at the abandoned one-room frame structure with its peeling paint, broken windows and weeds growing in the playground.

He glanced back through the village. He could see past the chapel to Doolin's and the post office. Although the scene looked inviting, with huge old maples and oaks towering over everything and still in full foliage these first weeks of September, there wasn't another person in sight.

Sam Neely groaned.

He was just one week out of the state police academy and this county was his first assignment. This morning his sergeant told him the southern half of the county was his beat. His colleague, Trooper Tutwiler, with two years in the state police under his belt, got the northern half.

After the sergeant left to return to Capitol City, Sam Neely got into his police cruiser with the bubble-gum machine on top and drove slowly along the Eden road to see what he could see.

It was bad.

Oh, the houses were spiffy enough, the meadows mowed, the pastures full of hundreds of fat black cattle, the late-summer foliage lushly verdant, yet to young Sam Neely the place was as exciting as a postcard from Iowa.

He had joined the state police because he wanted adventure, and they sent him here! To this rusticated nowhere. The most interesting thing he would ever do here in the line of duty would be to chase a cow that slipped though a gap in a fence.

Neely turned off the engine of his car and listened to the wind in the leaves. Listened to his heart beat. Listened to his youth slip away. He felt like crying but didn't because he was young and tough.

He started the engine while he wondered if he should go on up the road to Canaan and Goshen, then maybe swing back through Vegan.

He decided against it. He could only stand so much of this excitement. He would leave that odyssey until tomorrow.

Tomorrow.

And the day after, and the day after . . . The days stretched away before Trooper Neely into an appalling, dismal haze.

He cranked the wheel around and aimed the cruiser down the Eden road toward town.

Rot. He would rot here watching the cows chew their cuds, rot while listening to these rustics prattle endlessly about the weather and hay and politely nodding, nodding, nodding . . .

Rot!

He, Sam Neely, a young man in perfect health ready for any adventure— a true American ready to put his life on the line to defend honest citizens and the American way of life when the clarion call of duty pealed once again— already had one foot in the grave. He could almost feel the slimy worms crawling over his flesh. He shivered involuntarily.

His pistol would rust from disuse. The twelve cartridges they issued him for the pistol were a lifetime supply. He would still have all twelve when he retired—in thirty years.

Musing along these lines, Trooper Neely didn't notice the driver of the car he passed just outside of Indian River headed up the Eden road. Even if he had, Neely had not yet met the man and would not have known who he was.

Mrs. Eufala Davis, the preacher's wife, was a mile behind Trooper Neely, and she saw the car and recognized the driver, Ed Harris, the banker.

That's odd, Mrs. Davis thought. Ed Harris should be at the bank on Wednesday afternoon. Why, Ed Harris was bragging just last week that he hadn't missed a day's work sick in ten years.

She made a mental note to ask Mrs. Harris, Anne, why her husband was going home at two o'clock on Wednesday afternoon.

What Mrs. Davis would later learn was really no mystery. Ed Harris was going home because he was indeed sick. Stomachache. He felt slightly queasy. Didn't think it would look right if he threw up in his office at the bank, so he had made his excuses and was on his way home.

He turned off the Eden road into his private driveway, which led across the meadows of the valley, past the huge sycamore that had been threatening for years to fall over. He steered the car carefully as the driveway wound its way into the trees.

The house sat a hundred yards back in the forest on a low hill. It was a big two-story with eight rooms. Ed and Anne had designed it themselves, valuing privacy more than a scenic view.

Ed pulled into the turnaround in front of the house and killed the engine. He sat staring at the car beside Anne's.

A Dodge.

Looks like Hayden Elkins'.

Naw. Couldn't be. Hayden was his friend, his best friend. Why on earth would Hayden be over here on a Wednesday afternoon? With Anne alone in the house? With Ruth away at college? With Hayden's best buddy Ed Harris at work at the bank?

Ed got out of the car, his nausea forgotten. He used his key to let himself in through the front door. He walked slowly toward the stairs, climbed them one by one. They were covered with carpet and didn't creak. Not one of them. He and Anne had built this house to last. Their house. Their home!

On the top of the stairs was one of Anne's shoes. And a tie. A short distance down the hall was a skirt. And a sports coat . . . and a man's shoes.

5

He could hear them giggling. The bedroom door at the end of the hallway was partially open.

Ed Harris turned around and went back down the stairs. He went to the den and sat in his favorite chair, which faced the magnificent ten-point buck's head hanging on the wall.

He sat staring at the wall, his thoughts tumbling over one another in no particular order.

Later he couldn't recall just how long he sat there or just what he thought about, but when he arose from the chair he went to his gun cabinet.

He selected a twelve-gauge shotgun from the rack and a box of shells from one of the bottom drawers. He shoved three shells into the magazine of the gun. Then he jacked a shell into the chamber and engaged the safety.

Here he paused. He took off his tie and tossed it on the desk.

Grasping the shotgun tightly in both hands, he strode for the stairs.

They were naked in bed. Anne was on top, her head flung back, her dark hair bobbing.

Hayden saw him first. He pushed Anne sideways off of him.

"Jesus Christ, Ed! Don't shoot us!"

Ed Harris held the shotgun across his chest, the way he did at the skeet range just before he said "Pull."

Anne turned and saw him, then swept the hair back from her eyes and looked again.

"Now, Ed . . . ," she said.

"For the love of Christ, Ed . . . ," Hayden pleaded. He was twenty pounds too heavy, Ed Harris noted objectively, and would be bald as an apple in five more years. In bed with his wife! Of all people . . . his friend— Hayden Elkins!

Anne lowered her face into her hands and began sobbing.

Hayden wanted to argue. "Now Ed, this isn't worth killing someone over. You don't want to go to prison, have someone's death on your conscience, do you? Of course not! My God, Ed, I *am* sorry. This just . . . *happened!* After all, we're healthy people and Anne loves you—you *know* how

6

much Anne loves you!—and this was just a roll in the hay, something to do on a Wednesday afternoon. We're not in *love*, not like Anne loves you. You *know* how she loves you—"

"Get out of bed," Ed Harris ordered. "Get dressed."

"Ed, it was just a roll in the hay, for God's sake—"

He gestured with the barrel of the shotgun. "Shut up! Get out of bed and get dressed. Both of you."

Anne was sobbing hard, with her hair down over her face. Ed got a glimpse of tears streaming down her cheeks. Oh, Christ!

They dressed quickly. He went out in the hall and kicked the shoes and skirt back toward the bedroom, all the while keeping the muzzle of the shotgun pointed in their general direction.

When Hayden got his trousers and shoes on, Ed gestured with the shotgun toward the closet door.

"In there," he said, "are her suitcases. Get them out. Pack all her stuff. All her clothes, her jewelry, cosmetics, everything. Quickly now."

"What are you going to do?" Anne asked.

"Do as you're told," Ed replied roughly, and backed against the wall so he would be out of the way and could watch them both.

Not that Hayden was going to try anything. Not with Ed standing there holding a shotgun. Hayden might be dumb enough to screw your wife on a Wednesday afternoon, but he wasn't crazy stupid.

Anne was crazy enough, and unpredictable to boot, but the shock of being caught in bed with another man had apparently taken the starch out of her, at least for a little while.

They opened the suitcases on the bed and Anne threw some things into them. Not all of her clothes, of course; it would have taken a small truck to haul all her clothes. Just the stuff she liked and wore often. One valise was for beauty paraphernalia and jewelry.

When the suitcases were about full, Hayden broke the heavy silence with a question: "What are you going to do?"

"Me? Nothing. It's what you and Anne are going to do."

The way Ed said that made Hayden queasy. "Now, Ed, you aren't going to shoot us. Please! The kids . . . *Please!*"

"Shut up, Hayden," Anne snapped. Her eyes were red, and tears were still leaking down her cheeks, but she had pulled her hair back out of her face and was biting her lip as she emptied her jewelry case into the small valise. "What are we going to do, Ed?"

"Pick up the suitcases."

They closed them, and Hayden hefted three and Anne took the two small ones. That left one medium-sized one that Ed hoisted with his left hand. He held the shotgun in his right hand, his finger outside the trigger guard, and followed Hayden and Anne along the hall and down the stairs.

In the driveway Ed pointed the shotgun toward Hayden's car. "In there."

Hayden loaded the suitcases in the trunk and on the backseat. "What now?" he asked when he finished, turning to face Ed Harris.

"Hayden, ol' buddy," Ed replied. He poked the barrel of the shotgun into Hayden's ample stomach. "Anne's all yours. You are going to take her home and treat her right and be a good husband to her. She's wonderful in bed, as you've found out. She can't cook very well and won't clean the bathtub or the toilets no matter how much you bitch about it. She's a little selfish, highly opinionated, mildly spoiled and appreciates the finer things in life. Likes vacations in the Bahamas and gold jewelry at Christmas and Valentine's Day. You are going to make her happy, Hayden. You are going to provide her with all that. I worked my ass off for twenty-two years doing it, and now it's your turn."

Hayden Elkins' chin worked; his Adam's apple bobbed up and down several times. Finally he found his voice. "I've got a wife, Ed."

"Now you have two."

Anne tittered, a touch hysterically, Ed thought. She wiped the tears from her cheeks with her hands.

"Ed, think of what you're saying," Hayden pleaded. "Give me a break!"

"You're a lucky man, Elkins. You've lost a friend and gained a wife."

"What on earth will I tell Matilda?" Hayden moaned.

8

"Your problem," Ed Harris said brusquely. He backed away from Hayden several steps. "You might start with the truth. Matilda is a strong woman. Gotta be—she's put up with you for a long time. Tell her the truth."

"I'll bet you're bluffing," Hayden said belligerently. "I'll bet that gun isn't even loaded."

Ed Harris pointed the gun to one side and pulled the trigger. The report was like a punch in the chin to Hayden Elkins. Then Ed worked the Remington's slide, flipping the spent shell on the ground at Hayden's feet.

When Hayden raised his eyes from the shell, Ed told him, "You had better treat Anne right, *amigo*. If I hear that you're not treating her as well as Matilda, if I hear that she's unhappy"—Ed leveled the business end of the twelve-gauge full in Hayden's face—"then this gun is going to go off again."

He lowered the gun. "Now get out of here. Get in the car and get out of here! Now!"

They went.

Ed Harris went back into the house and put the shotgun away. He poured himself a stiff bourbon and sat down in his favorite chair in the den.

As Hayden Elkins drove along the Eden road, Anne sobbed some more. "Matilda, what will she say?" Hayden wondered aloud. "The people at the courthouse, at the country club, all our friends . . ."

"He'll tell everyone," Anne put in. She wiped her tears away and looked at Hayden without sympathy. "We're in for it. You might as well face it."

Hayden brought the car to a stop. He lowered his face onto the steering wheel and began crying. "He might have killed us back there."

"He still might," Anne said, digging the needle in spitefully. "You heard him."

She dearly liked Hayden, but at times he was such a baby. So unlike Ed, who was all man all the time. Too much so, in fact. She needed a man who needed her. Ed was just so . . . well, he was Ed. Hayden's soft spots stirred her womanly instincts, although at this moment he could do with a little more backbone. That was all right—she was perfectly capable of providing some.

"Let's go," she said. "We might as well face Matilda and get it over with."

"I love her very much," Hayden declared bravely, fighting back the tears. "I'm not going to divorce her."

"I didn't ask you to," his second wife told him. "She may have something to say about the matter, though."

When they broke the news to Matilda she fainted, to Anne's disgust. Hayden caught her and chafed her wrists and kissed her and cuddled her in his arms until her eyes fluttered open. She started and stared around wildly. Her gaze fastened on Anne.

"You hussy, you home wrecker, you man-stealing tramp! You—"

"Now, dear . . . ," Hayden said soothingly.

"Let go of me, you bastard."

Matilda fought free of her husband's arms and got to her feet. She swayed slightly. "You tomcatting son of a bitch. I won't have this hussy in my house."

"Dear, we don't have a choice. Ed is crazy! He had a gun. He *has* a gun. He's crazy enough to use it."

"By God," his first wife declared, "if I had a gun I'd use it here and now. I'd shoot off your silly little weenie." Matilda shook her fist in Anne's face. "If your husband were a real man he'd have killed you both."

Anne kept her dignity. She bent over and picked up the two small suitcases. "I'll put these in the guest bedroom. Bring the others in, won't you, dear?"

Hayden had to restrain Matilda as Anne ascended the stairs. Matilda was in a fine fury, spluttering with rage.

When she had calmed down some, Hayden whispered, "I'm sorry, darling. You know how much I love you. I'm weak. It was just a flirtation that got out of hand."

"You and your damned peter!"

"Darling, this will all be over soon. She'll probably go home tomorrow when Ed cools off. Don't do anything rash."

"I want her out of my house. Take her to the hotel in town."

"Then everyone will know," Hayden wailed. He had seen the look on Ed Harris' face and was truly afraid of him, so now he grasped at this straw. "Let's keep silent and send her home tomorrow."

"Do you love me, Hayden?"

"Oh, of course I do, darling. You know how much! I am so *sorry*. I'll make it up to you, I promise. She'll be gone in the morning."

"Our son! He'll be home from school any minute—"

"Don't worry. I'll talk to him. He won't tell anyone. This won't get out."

"How long," Matilda asked acidly, "has this little thing between you and Anne been going on?"

"Today was the first time," Hayden said. "The very first time."

"If only I could believe that."

"Matilda, for God's sake. Let's not let this wreck our lives. Our marriage. We have to think of our son, of our position in the community."

"The community? I don't give a damn what the community thinks."

"Matilda! Darling! Don't be rash. We have to live here. Our son has to live here. Anne will be gone in the morning. This whole thing will be just like a bad dream that's forgotten in the morning. You'll see."

Matilda was in the kitchen fixing supper and crying, and Anne was upstairs, when Billy Joe Elkins came home from school. He was a senior in high school this year and drove his own Jeep. His father heard it skid to a stop in the gravel outside. He opened the door and met the young man on the porch.

"Son, we have a houseguest."

"Who?"

"Anne Harris."

Billy Joe's eyebrows went up toward his hairline. He drew back and scrutinized his father's face. "Anne Harris?"

"Anne Harris."

"What happened? Did her husband kick her out of the house?"

"In a manner of speaking, yes."

Billy Joe took another hard look at his father and snorted, trying to hold back the laughter. "What happened? Did ol' man Harris catch you in bed with her or something?"

His father sagged into the porch swing.

"That *is* it, isn't it?" the boy howled. "Dad, I can't believe you did this. Anne Harris?"

"It's not so damned funny. Quit that laughing."

"Oh man, this is so *far out!*" The boy held his hands to his head and danced around in a circle. "I can't believe this. My own *father?* What does Mom say?"

"Well, she's unhappy, but . . ." Hayden stopped because his son wasn't there anymore. The boy darted through the door and made a beeline for the kitchen, where he knew he'd find his mother this time of day.

"Dad and Anne Harris?" he demanded of his mother, who turned to face him with a large wooden spoon in her hand.

"She'll be gone in the morning, dear. Your father and I want you to say nothing about this outside the house."

Billy Joe couldn't believe his ears. "You think no one else will hear about this? On the Eden road?"

"She'll be gone in the morning, dear."

"She's upstairs, right?"

"That's right," his mother confirmed. "And you are not to disturb . . ." She was talking to thin air. Billy Joe's thunderous tread sounded on the staircase.

He knocked on the door of the guest bedroom.

"Come in."

He opened the door. Well, you had to give the old man credit, he acknowledged. Mrs. Harris was a dish. She still had a figure that would stun the guys over at school. Face wasn't bad, either. Mrs. Harris was unpacking and stood before him now with a piece of filmy lingerie half folded in her hands.

12

"Uh, Mrs. Harris, I didn't mean to cause you any distress or anything . . ."

"That's quite all right."

"I heard . . . you and Dad?"

"That's correct," Anne Harris said with simple dignity.

"Hoo boy. Whew!" This was *big*, the biggest thing he had ever tried to handle in his seventeen and a half years. "Awesome," he muttered, still staring at the lingerie in Mrs. Harris' hands.

"It must be a shock to you," Anne said. She was always practical. She hated that quality in herself, but it was useless to try to change it this late in the game.

"And you're leaving in the morning?"

"I don't know what gave you that idea. No. I'm staying. This is my new home."

Billy Joe was overwhelmed. He mopped his brow and fell into a chair. From its depths he stared at the woman standing before him, who finished with the nightie and began working on folding a dress. "Uh, Mrs. Harris . . ."

"Better call me Anne, since we'll be seeing quite a lot of each other, I imagine."

"Anne."

"Yes?"

"Uh, I don't . . . I'm not sure I understand exactly . . ."

"Well, I don't quite know myself. My husband caught your father and me in bed together this afternoon. There was quite a scene, of course. Very distressing and embarrassing."

"Oh, of course."

"No use lying about it. The truth is impossible to deny."

"Of course."

"It will undoubtedly be talked about."

"Of course."

"So I'm here for a while."

"Of course."

"You understand?"

"I understand. Of course." Billy Joe pondered that answer for several seconds. "Understand what?"

"Mr. Harris had a gun."

"A gun . . ."

"A shotgun."

"Un-huh."

"He said that . . ." Anne Harris sighed. "Well, it wasn't *what* he said. He implied that he would shoot your father if he didn't take me home and care for me."

"Care for you?"

"That's right. He told your father that he had two wives now."

The boy's mouth hung open.

"Close your mouth, Billy Joe," his father's second wife said.

The closing jaw made an audible noise. The boy opened his mouth several more times, closed it each time, scrutinized Mrs. Harris' face, her figure, the clothes she was folding and stowing in the dresser . . .

He stood, jerked open the door and shot through. He left the door standing open behind him.

Anne closed it and sighed again.

"Jesus H. Christ, Dad! How could you?"

"Don't use that kind of language to me," Hayden Elkins told Billy Joe. He was still sitting in the porch swing.

"Two wives!"

"Sssht! Don't say that where your mother will hear. You'll upset her."

"I'll upset her? *Me?* I'm not the one who was caught with his pants down!"

Hayden cringed. It was hard hearing those words from the boy. Very hard. "Son, you don't seem to appreciate—"

"You always told me to keep my pants zipped up. Don't let your peter rule your life, you said."

"I *know* I said those things."

"Don't do your thinking with the head of your dick, you said."

"I did say that," the father admitted.

"Should have followed your own advice, Dad."

"Son, there are complexities here that you don't seem to appreciate. True, I used extremely poor judgment with Mrs. Harris and—"

"Anne."

"Yes, Anne—"

"*Two wives*, Dad! *Two!* Boy oh boy oh boy oh. Am I a lucky ducky or what. Should I call them both Mom?"

"Young man, I—"

"See you later, Dad. I'm going over to Tommy's house."

"I think you should—" But the father found himself talking to the back of his quickly departing son. He drew in air to shout, then thought, The hell with it! Let him go!

The kid dived into the Jeep and spun the wheels getting it under way. Gravel flew into the yard. At the end of the driveway the boy turned right and shot off down the Eden road.

Hayden Elkins sagged back into the swing and lowered his face into his hands.

His life was shattered. How could Ed Harris do this to his very best friend? Why, Hayden wondered, didn't he just shoot me and get it over with?

Anne Harris didn't go home the next day. She arose at her usual hour and ate breakfast alone in the kitchen. One egg boiled, dry toast and tea. The house was quiet. Well, it *was* nine o'clock. After she washed her dishes and put them away, she ran some clothes through the washer and ironed several dresses that had gotten wrinkled in yesterday's rushed packing.

Last night Hayden had brought dinner to her room on a tray. He wanted to talk, but she refused, shooed him out. She had yet to speak to Matilda since the scene when she arrived.

She finished the ironing and was waiting for the dryer to complete its cycle when a car pulled into the driveway in front of the house and Matilda Elkins got out. She came into the kitchen carrying a bag of groceries, saw Anne and stiffened.

"When are you leaving?" she demanded as she placed the grocery bag on the kitchen table.

"I'm not, Matilda. Not soon, anyway. Ed is going to need some time to get over this. I appreciate your hospitality."

"Do you realize what people will say about us? Are saying about us?" She lowered herself into a chair by the table. "I was at Doolin's store. You should have heard them and seen the looks! I have never been so embarrassed in all my life. 'Two wives.' Amazing! Where that phrase came from I've no idea."

"Sharp tongues wagged by dirty minds," said Anne Harris with finality. She had never been concerned about what other people thought. Perhaps she should have been, but the truth was she just didn't care. "That's inevitable," she added as an afterthought.

"Don't play the plaster saint with me, lady," Matilda snarled. "I certainly don't think your going to bed with my husband was the right thing to do, and I haven't forgiven you for it. I don't know that I ever will."

"I apologize."

"Apologize? As if you sneezed in public? Seducing Hayden was a wee bit more than a sneeze."

"Seduced him? Hardly. He'd been eyeing me for years, flirting, stealing a feel when he thought no one was looking. I just . . . gave in. I wish I hadn't. Still, if you had given him some decent loving he wouldn't—"

"How dare you! To stand in *my* house, in *my* kitchen, and tell me to *my* face that it's *my* fault that you seduced *my* husband! Of all the nerve!"

"I'm not suggesting it's your fault. I'm merely pointing out that Hayden needs more loving than you've been giving him. That's as obvious as the nose on your face."

"Don't make cracks about my nose!"

"I am not talking about your nose."

"There's nothing wrong with my nose."

"I concur. There is nothing wrong with your nose."

"I give him enough loving."

Anne Harris raised an eyebrow.

Matilda Elkins collapsed in tears.

The other woman put her arms around her shoulders. "There, there, Matty. We must be brave. We're in this together."

"I feel like a good cry."

Anne's eyes were also tearing up. "So do I," she admitted.

"Well," said Mrs. Eufala Davis, the preacher's wife, that is, the wife of the retired preacher. "I don't like to talk, but they say Hayden Elkins just moved her in. She's there now."

"Oh, my dear. There's so much more to it than that," the widow Wilfred said breathlessly. She lived a half mile from Eden and often stopped in to see Mrs. Davis, her best friend. "Oh, my, yes. I just heard about it at Doolin's. Why, they say that Anne Harris and Hayden Elkins have been having a torrid affair for years and years. No one knows just how long. And poor Ed fired a shot over there yesterday. Tried to kill that wretched wife of his."

"I heard about the shots," Eufala said, squirming in delight. "My husband just called me from town. He had a dental appointment and heard the whole story there in the dentist's office. So Ed tried to kill Anne?"

"Of course. She was too quick for him, the brazen hussy, and is holed up with Hayden at his house."

"But poor Matilda!" Mrs. Davis cried. "What about her?"

"To have that shameless creature under her own roof!" the widow Wilfred wailed.

"You won't believe this, dear," Mrs. Davis said breathlessly. "The coincidence! Horrible. But I actually saw Ed Harris going home yesterday afternoon. He never does that. He must have stumbled onto Anne and Hayden in his very own bed."

"That must be what happened."

"What a horrific shock! Some men might have lost their minds, might have murdered both the guilty parties right in their bed of sin."

"Yes," Mrs. Wilfred agreed. "It's good that Ed didn't succumb to his animal passions." This remark was made without enthusiasm. She brightened, remembering the shots. A picture formed in her imagination of serious, austere Ed Harris chasing his naked wife with a gun, blasting away.

The widow Wilfred shivered deliciously and lowered her voice to a conspiratorial whisper. "I hear Hayden Elkins is going to keep Matilda and Anne as his *wives*."

Mrs. Davis twitched uncontrollably. This was really *too* much. Without a doubt, this was the most exciting thing to happen on the Eden road since they found farmer Williams making love to his son's pet sow. Poor depraved man—he was in a home now. And such a nice wife he had. The shock killed her, poor thing.

She shook her head to rid herself of farmer Williams and his pig. She focused on Hayden Elkins. The evil of it! "Men!" she said nastily to the widow Wilfred, who nodded knowingly.

"I'm going to see about this. It's sinful and wicked." Mrs. Davis rose from her chair and reached for her sweater.

"But what are you going to do, Eufala? What can you do?"

"I'm going to the police. I'm going to swear out a complaint."

"Oh, dear," Mrs. Wilfred said. "I better go with you. You realize, Eufala, that if you swear out a complaint, you must go to court and testify?"

Mrs. Davis stiffened. She drew back her shoulders. "Good people must raise their voices against depravity. It's our Christian duty. And I will answer duty's call."

"We had better hurry," said Mrs. Wilfred, the soul of practicality, "before someone beats us to it."

The two women found Trooper Sam Neely in his office in the basement of the courthouse, his half-closed eyes focused on a calendar picture of the

West, where Men could still be Men, where presumably honor and courage and straight shooting were occasionally still required.

Trooper Neely shifted his gaze to the two ladies before him and regarded them without enthusiasm. What on earth could they want?

"Yes." It came out so deadpan that he forced himself to say it again, with feeling. "Yes?"

"I want to swear out a warrant—"

"Make a complaint," the second lady said, correcting the first.

"—Against Hayden Elkins."

The trooper took a very deep breath, sat up squarely in his chair, and drew a yellow legal pad around in front of him. He clicked his pen and waited.

"He has two wives," Eufala Davis began.

"He's living with them," the widow Wilfred added. "At his house."

"He's a bigamist. Living in sin, living with evil and wickedness," Mrs. Davis gushed, "without shame, without remorse—"

"—In defiance of the laws of God and man," Mrs. Wilfred finished.

"Hayden Elkins?" Trooper Neely asked unbelievingly.

"That's right."

"Hayden Elkins, *the prosecuting attorney?*"

"That's right!" Eufala Davis proclaimed triumphantly. "He's the very one."

TWO

Trooper Sam Neely had two complaints duly signed and sworn, but he didn't know how to investigate them. His instructors at the state police academy had emphasized that when he had questions about an investigation, he should go to the prosecuting attorney for a legal opinion. Since one of the complaints was about that prosecuting attorney, that course of action didn't strike him as a good idea.

He got out his notes from his criminal investigation classes at the academy and went over them. Nope, nothing in there about how to investigate the prosecuting attorney. For bigamy.

But wait—those ladies had said that Ed Harris, the banker, had fired shots at his naked wife, Anne, in the yard of their home, attempting to murder her. They wanted to sign a complaint to that effect and Neely managed to dissuade them. They reluctantly agreed to sign an allegation of felony menacing instead, which was an allegation that someone was threatened with a firearm.

Neely had explained to the ladies that a complaint was merely a license to investigate. Any charges ultimately filed with the court would have to be based on evidence that established probable cause.

Felony menacing! There was a crime a fellow could sink his teeth into. Frivolous or not, the complaint had to be investigated. The obvious place to start, it seemed to Neely, was an interview with the alleged victim, Anne Harris.

He found her, of course, at the prosecuting attorney's house on the Eden road.

After he knocked on the door, he removed his service hat. Mrs. Elkins opened the door.

"Mrs. Elkins, I'm Trooper Neely, and I would like to interview Anne Harris. I understand she is here?"

Matilda Elkins glanced skyward and said, "Oh, merciful God, why did you do this to me?" Then she addressed the policeman. "Please come in. I'll tell her you are here."

In minutes Anne Harris was sitting in the living room across from Neely. She demurely adjusted her skirt down over her knees and smoothed her hair back from her eyes.

"Yes, Mr. Neely?" Although they hadn't been introduced, the letters on his name tag were unmistakable.

Trooper Neely was at a loss about where to start. "I'm here in an official capacity, Mrs. Harris."

"I didn't think you made social calls in uniform, Trooper Neely."

"No, ma'am." Well, he was making a fool of himself again, but there was nothing for it but to keep going. He cleared his throat and surreptitiously examined the victim. She looked mighty healthy, with no visible wounds.

"I find your scrutiny uncomfortable, Mr. Neely," Mrs. Harris said.

"Excuse me, ma'am. I assume you aren't wounded?"

"No."

"Did he hurt you in any way?"

"Who hurt me?"

"Why, your husband!"

"I'm quite unhurt."

"All the shots missed?"

"What shots?" Anne Harris started to ask, but then she remembered the shotgun blast that Ed had aimed off to one side, up into the air. And the spent shell had ended up at Hayden's feet. So melodramatic! Only Ed Harris could have pulled off a moment like that.

"There was only one shot," she said now, "which didn't hurt anyone."

Trooper Neely was visibly disappointed. He made a note, a large "1" with a circle around it, in his notebook. "So he missed?"

"He didn't aim at anyone."

"Not even the prosecuting attorney?"

"Oh, no. Ed just fired up into the air for effect."

"What effect?"

"He had just told Hayden to take good care of me."

"I see."

"I'm glad that you do."

Trooper Neely blushed. "I'm sorry that I have to ask this," he said, "but was this shot fired before or after your husband caught you and the prosecutor in bed together?"

It was Anne Harris' turn to blush. "After," she admitted.

"And you are now living as the second Mrs. Elkins?"

Fury swept over Anne like a wave. She almost came out of her chair after the twit. "Really, I don't see what gives you the right to ask these questions, sir."

Correctly realizing that he wasn't handling this very well, and at a loss as to how to do it better, Sam Neely retreated to the shield of duty. "I'm just doing my job, ma'am. Trying to determine if a crime has been committed. There was a complaint."

"By whom?"

Trooper Neely consulted his notes. "A Mrs. Eufala Davis and a Mrs. Twila Wilfred."

"Gossips. Two old biddy gossips with no firsthand information."

"Be that as it may, you see that I must do my duty, which is to investigate. It is not as if I have a choice in this matter."

"Ask your questions."

"Are you now living as the second Mrs. Elkins?"

"Yes." She said it with simple dignity. If they wanted something to gossip about, she was perfectly capable of giving it to them. Trooper Neely opened his mouth, but she signified that she had more to say. "Matilda and I will of course share the housework and shopping."

"Uh-huh."

"She will do the yardwork. I was never much good with plants. Except petunias. I've always had good luck with petunias." She managed to look pleased with herself.

Feeling that he must do something, Trooper Sam Neely, frustrated warrior for justice, made a note about petunias.

"But I will do the windows," Anne continued bravely. "Matilda has always loathed doing windows."

"I see." Neely bent to the task of making another note.

Anne didn't pause. "We will share the kitchen duties. We each have a few specialty dishes that we are quite proud of. For example, I do a terrific fried eggplant—it just melts in your mouth. The secret is the spices in the breading. Hayden loves it."

"Un-huh."

"However, we are still discussing the conjugal arrangements."

"Con-jew—?"

"Yes. Matilda wants me to use the guest bedroom and Hayden can just visit each of us every other night, but I think we should all share the master bedroom. The bed is quite large."

She leaned forward, which gave the young trooper an excellent view of her cleavage, and explained earnestly, "It's an antique four-poster with a feather mattress. Quite comfortable for three. So snuggly." She wiggled her shoulders, which made the front of her blouse move in a very interesting way.

Sam Neely tore his gaze from Mrs. Harris' jiggling blouse and wrote furiously on his notepad. When he finished and looked up, Anne gave him an angelic smile.

"Uh, uh, have any of you . . . has anyone . . . involved, so to speak . . . been to see about a divorce?"

"Really, Mr. Neely! I certainly couldn't comment upon that! Divorce is a civil matter—I thought you were investigating criminal conduct."

"Oh, yes. Yes. I am trying to. Still, perhaps it might have some bearing . . ."

"I can't see how."

"Umm."

"I think the three of us will be quite happy here."

"I . . . I hope so." Trooper Neely instantly regretted that remark, but those were the first words that came to mind, and they popped out before he had time to stop them.

"Thank you." Anne floated from her chair and came across the room, where she seized him lightly but insistently by the elbow. She steered him toward the door. "I'll relay your good wishes to Matilda and Hayden. Please come back when we have the open house."

"Open house?"

"We'll send you an invitation." She eased the front door shut in his face.

Ed Harris sat behind his big desk in his big corner office on the second floor of the bank staring at nothing at all. He felt like hell. After he awoke this morning he had showered, shaved and dressed, as usual, then wandered through the house touching this and that, listening for sounds that weren't there. The place was like a tomb.

Damn Anne! They had been so happy here. Then she ruined everything.

Were they happy?

Here in the office he worried that question yet again. Well, he had been happy. He had the bank and his friends, golf occasionally, fishing in the spring and summer, bird hunting in the fall, and of course he had Anne. Beautiful, vivacious, witty Anne, Anne with her gorgeous smile and droll observations, Anne who made every day an adventure.

And she had bedded his best friend, Hayden Elkins, and on that day—of all days—he had gotten a stomachache and gone home.

Hayden had insisted that incident was the first time. Ed Harris had been looking at his wife when Hayden said it, and he believed the man.

It seemed like something from a nightmare. Your whole life comes crashing down around your ears. Just shatters like old crystal into a million sharp little pieces. And you continue to shower, shave, and soldier on, smiling bravely at the world . . .

It doesn't matter. No, really, I'm fine. I'll just sit here and die quietly. I won't make a fuss. There'll be no unsightly mess. Trust me. Go on about your business, please.

He always despised people like that. So instinctively he had done just the opposite—made a huge mess. Sent Anne home with Hayden.

The only bright spot was the fix dear ol' Hayden was in. That jerk!

Maybe, Ed mused, he should have shot Hayden. A spray of birdshot right in the crotch. Put a dozen of those little BBs in that pecker that he was so proud of. Sitting here now, Ed Harris wished he had done just that.

The telephone rang. And rang and rang. He didn't even glance at it.

It had stopped ringing when his secretary opened the door without knocking and stuck her head in. "Your daughter is calling, Mr. Harris."

He waited until the secretary had closed the door, then picked up the telephone.

"Hello."

"Dad."

"Hi, kid." Ruth was a sophomore at State College this year. This was the first time she had called since he and Anne delivered her to the dorm the week prior to Labor Day.

"My telephone has been ringing off the hook, Dad. And I just got off the phone with Mom."

"Uh-huh."

"I can't leave you two alone for a minute."

"What's on your mind, Ruth?"

"Guess."

"I sent you money last week."

"Dad!"

"You're not coming home for Thanksgiving?"

26

"How could you, Dad? How on earth could you send Mom over to the Elkinses' at the point of a gun?"

"It seemed like a good idea at the time."

"You two have really stepped in the poop this time. I know it was a hell of a shock, finding Mom in bed with that puffed-up ass you call a friend, but still . . . Are you trying to kill Mrs. Elkins?"

"I don't give a hoot in hell about Matilda Elkins. She's Hayden's problem. He should have thought of her before he—"

"Oh, my God!" his daughter moaned. "At my tender age, before I even get a chance to have a life of my own, I have to cope with two senile parents who can still fuck."

"Life's unfair," her father told her. "Everyone has their cross to bear."

"So are you going to divorce her?"

"Haven't thought about it."

"You new moderns! Why didn't you think about *that* before you marched her off with a gun in her back?"

"It never occurred to me."

"Mom says the state police are investigating. With your luck you'll wind up in jail."

He made a noise.

"Well, have you given any thought to *why* Mom was in bed with Hayden?"

"She never liked to do it standing up."

"*Dad!* I'm serious."

"Do you think she's started through menopause?"

"For Christ's sake! I'm trying to have a serious conversation and you give me this crap!"

"Listen, Ruth. If I knew what goes through your mother's head we would not have lasted this long. And I'm not going to sit here scratching my navel meditating about why it's my fault your mother went to bed with Hayden Elkins."

"You're innocent as a newborn lamb," Ruth said, her voice dripping with disgust.

"Kid, I'm going to give you some good advice. Better drop psychology—you're going to fail the course."

Ruth hung up on him.

Now there was a knock on the door. The secretary opened it and stuck her head in again. "You have a visitor, Mr. Harris."

"I told you I didn't want to see anybody, and by God I meant it."

"Yessir. But this is a state policeman. Apparently about your domestic crisis."

He gave her an evil look. She didn't turn a hair. "Tell him to get a warrant."

"Mr. Harris! Really!"

"Okay, God damn it, send him in."

Trooper Sam Neely was very professional. He had been like a fish out of water questioning Mrs. Harris, but this was Man to Man. He told Ed that he was investigating a felony menacing complaint.

"At this point, sir, you are not a suspect, but you may become one during the course of this conversation. You don't have to talk to me and you don't have to answer any questions."

Ed Harris brushed that away as if he were shooing a fly. "What do you want to know?"

"What happened at your house yesterday afternoon. Everything you can recall."

So Ed went through it. The stomachache, the bedroom scene, the shotgun, forcing them to pack Anne's stuff, the shot fired at the trees, his comment to Hayden about taking care of Anne.

"Or the shotgun would 'go off'?"

"That's what I said, as near as I can recall."

"And the gun was loaded when you pointed it at Mr. Elkins and Mrs. Harris?"

"Of course it was loaded. It would be silly to point an empty gun at someone."

"You understand, I'm just clarifying."

"Clarify away."

"Would you have shot Mr. Elkins or Mrs. Harris if they didn't do as you instructed?"

"I don't know."

"Do you intend to shoot Mr. Elkins in the future if he doesn't do right by Mrs. Harris?"

"I have no intentions just now."

"But you might shoot him?"

"You are asking me to speculate. My answer is that I have no intentions at all at the present time."

"Could he have taken your remarks as a threat?"

"I don't know how he took anything. Ask him."

"Or your conduct? Do you think he perceived your pointing the shotgun as a threat?"

"You'll have to ask him."

"Mr. Harris, do you think a reasonable man would have felt threatened by your conduct?"

"What I think is my business and none of yours, Trooper. Now, I have better things to do than sit here listening to you argue the case to the jury. Scoot. Scram. Don't come back unless you have a warrant."

Trooper Neely left with dignity.

In the reception area the secretary gave him a huge smile. Neely decided not to return it. She might end up as a witness, or even a victim. This Harris fellow might be one of those ding-dongs who goes off his nut and runs berserk.

Well, he had the statements of two of the three people involved, so he might as well get the third one. Hayden Elkins. The county prosecutor. Being county prosecutor was only a part-time job, so Elkins had an extensive private practice. He maintained his own office in a fairly new building just across from the courthouse.

Elkins' secretary smiled at Neely and asked him to take a seat. He cooled his heels for fifteen minutes until an old man came walking slowly from the prosecutor's private office. The secretary told Neely he could go in now.

Neely went along the hall and entered the inner sanctum.

"Good morning, sir."

Indeed, it was still morning, only 11:45. The prosecutor looked as if he hadn't slept. His hair was rumpled, his clothes messy, and his beard blue on his pasty white face.

He grunted at Neely.

"Sir, I've come to interview you about a felony menacing complaint."

"Me?"

"Yessir. I understand that you and Mrs. Anne Harris—"

"*What?* Who made this complaint?"

"Uh . . ." Neely consulted his notes again. "Mrs. Eufala Davis and Mrs. Twila Wilfred."

"Those two crones? You listened to poisonous gossip from two half-wit busybodies who have absolutely no personal knowledge of a damned thing?"

"But—"

"Then you come bustling in here to question me about something that is none of your business? You get out of this office! Git! Scram! Out, you stupid, silly nincompoop!"

"Sir, there's a question of bigamy. Mrs. Harris says she is your second wife—"

Hayden Elkins looked as if he were going to have apoplexy. At a loss for words, he sat frozen, pointing at the door.

"I take it, sir, that this means that you decline to be interviewed?"

Recovering his voice, Hayden snarled, "God, you're quick. That's exactly what I mean. *Out! Now!*"

At a loss for what to do next, Trooper Sam Neely went to see the circuit judge. Investigating the prosecutor inevitably meant that certain irregularities were going to be necessary. It seemed to Neely that although he had the prosecutor's word that no crime had been committed, perhaps a less biased opinion would be in order.

The fog was thick for Neely. There might be a menacing charge lurking somewhere amid all that shotgun pointing, and bigamy did seem to be the word to describe Hayden Elkins' marital arrangements. A little legal light would help immensely. And if a crime *had* been committed, it would be nice to know precisely what it might be.

He toyed with the idea of visiting the sheriff. Naw. His sergeant hadn't had much good to say about Sheriff Arleigh Tate, and there was, of course, the usual professional rivalry between the state police and the county sheriff's department. If the prosecutor needed to be bit where it hurt, the state police should do the biting.

As he walked the wide, dark, quiet corridors of the courthouse, he tried to put his interview with the prosecutor behind him. He was still smarting from the verbal hiding Hayden had given him.

There was something soothing about the interior of the courthouse, which seemed an oasis of calm amid the human storms that raged outside. Here problems could be dealt with, disputes settled. Here, in this fine old cut-stone building that had been built to endure as the generations came and went. Neely's footsteps echoed on the polished oak floors. He found the judge's chambers, squared his shoulders in front of the door, then opened it and went in.

Judge Lester Storm was in his midsixties, with white hair and a booming, gruff voice. Rumor had it that he was an irascible curmudgeon. Since this would be the first time Sam Neely had visited him professionally, the newly minted state trooper was understandably nervous.

The outer office was empty. Neely crossed to the open door to the judge's office and saw the great man at his desk. He rapped on the sill.

"Come in, Neely," the judge called, loud enough to wake the dead. The jurist laid down his newspaper and gestured at one of the chairs. "How are you this fine day?"

"Okay, Your Honor," Neely replied as he dropped into the indicated chair.

Neely heard someone behind him and half turned. It was a woman, the judge's secretary. She also doubled as the court reporter. Her name was Audrey Something.

"Judge, you have a twelve o'clock hearing scheduled. Elijah Murphy."

Lester Storm glanced at his watch. "Lucky you're here, Neely. Have to do Murphy just now. Why don't you pop over to the county hotel and get him. Bring him over here. This won't take long—we'll tend to your business afterwards."

"Yes, sir." Neely went.

Elijah Murphy was in the big cell on the second floor of the jail. He was a dirty, bedraggled specimen with only half his hair and teeth. He held out grimy wrists for the cuffs and came right along.

Murphy's hands were slightly palsied, and he concentrated fiercely on putting one foot in front of the other. It wasn't until Murphy was seated in front of the judge's desk and Neely got a look at him in good light that the state policeman realized the man had the DTs.

"How is everything over at the jail?" Judge Storm asked the prisoner.

"Dry, judge. Bone dry."

Lester Storm chuckled. He reached into the bottom drawer of his desk and extracted a water glass, which he passed to Murphy. Then he removed a bottle from the same drawer and poured Murphy several fingers. Jack Daniel's.

"Here's looking at you," Murphy muttered, and tossed off the whiskey as if it were water. He set the empty glass back on the desk, shivered once, sighed, then sat waiting.

The judge had the file in front of him. He opened and perused it. "You are charged with indecent exposure. Aggravated. The aggravated part is why they sent it to me instead of the justice of the peace. Theoretically upon conviction I could give you a year in the can—the squire can only give out six months max."

Murphy just nodded. He glanced at Neely as if seeing him for the first time, then let his gaze linger lovingly on Audrey the stenographer, who was taking shorthand on a legal pad.

Neely was appalled. This wasn't like any trial he had ever heard discussed at the state police academy. He cleared his throat explosively and the judge looked at him over his glasses.

"Your Honor, is this Murphy's trial?"

"Yep. This is it," he was informed.

"Uh, what about lawyers? A defense lawyer, a prosecutor?"

"Murphy here doesn't want a lawyer. Never has in the past. Or do you?" The judge addressed this last query to the defendant.

"Nope. Can't afford no lawyer. Don't want a free one neither."

"But what about the prosecutor?" Trooper Neely objected. Really, this little *in camera* disposition was extremely irregular.

"Hayden? Why should the county pay to have him over here for this?" the judge asked. "My God, the taxpayers don't want their money squandered on misdemeanors and such. Now, if Murphy here thinks he didn't get a fair shake, he can always get a free lawyer who will appeal his case to the trolls on the Supreme Court in Capitol City. Isn't that right, Murphy?"

"That's right," Elijah Murphy acknowledged.

Neely wasn't convinced. "What about witnesses? Swearing to tell the truth and all that?"

The judge just grunted. He held up a sheet of paper and fluttered it. "Trooper Tutwiler did the investigation. Here's his report. As for telling the truth, Murphy will do that, won't you, Murphy?"

"Yessir. You bet."

Lester Storm cast a cold eye on Neely, which stoppered him, then glanced again at the police report. "Murphy, it says here that you exposed yourself to the widow Wilfred."

Wilfred? Wasn't that the woman who came to see Neely this morning? Iron-gray hair, glasses, a little plump—not a bad-looking lady.

"She was looking at me through field glasses, Judge," Murphy explained.

33

"Sitting up in her house looking at me through the window when I come outside on my porch. Been doing that on and off for months. A man can only take so much. So that morning when I went outside and seen her spying again, I just dropped my pants and showed her what I had."

"And?"

"Waved it at her a little."

"Says here you did more than wave it." The judge fluttered the paper again.

"Well," Murphy admitted with a glance at Audrey Something, "I did stroke it a few times to make her mad."

"You accomplished that feat. She called the state police."

"Yeah, and Tutwiler asked a lot of questions, then took me off to jail. Been over there a week. And a very dry week it's been, too."

"By any chance are you interested in the widow Wilfred?" the judge asked softly as he arranged the papers in the file.

Murphy was taken aback. "You mean . . . ? Why, no! Of course not."

"She interested in you?"

"Not that I ever noticed. Always spying to see what I'm up to, complaining to everyone about the junk around my shack, shouting at me to sober up and take a bath . . . why, if she's got romantic notions, I never heard tell of making 'em known thataway."

"You never know about women," Judge Lester Storm told the defendant. "Maybe you ought to try to be nice to her and see what happens."

Murphy sat silently contemplating the possibility that the widow Wilfred might have something on her mind besides making his life miserable. Neely could tell from his expression how unlikely Murphy thought that was.

Remembering Mrs. Wilfred and staring at Murphy, as unprepossessing a human specimen as he had yet had the misfortune to look upon, Neely concluded that the judge had a screw loose somewhere.

"Well, you've been in jail a week," Lester Storm said with a sigh. "Give you credit for time served. They'll let you out Saturday morning to make room for the Saturday night party crowd. Until then you can keep eating county food and using county toilet paper and sleeping in a county bed. Don't think you're doing right by your fellow taxpayers, Murphy. Honest, I don't."

Elijah Murphy bowed his head contritely.

"Nobody gives a hoot what you do up at your shack, except maybe the widow Wilfred—and I think you ought to explore that a little—but when you're down here at the county hotel living the high life, that's something else."

"I'm sorry, Judge."

"Neely will take you back to jail. Remember your fellow citizens the next time you get a wild hair."

"Yessir."

The judge nodded at Trooper Neely as Murphy rose from his chair. The prisoner led the way out, with the policeman following.

When Neely returned to the judge's chambers, Audrey Something was still there, seated in the chair that Murphy had vacated.

"What can I do for you today, Neely?" the judge asked as he adjusted his fanny in his padded swivel chair.

"Sir, I've got a highly irregular situation and I need some guidance on what I ought to do next. I tried to interview the prosecutor, but he declined to help me."

The judge sat up straight. "Hayden Elkins? He refused to talk to the state police?"

"Yes, sir. This matter involves him."

Lester Storm snorted. "Let's hear it."

"We received a complaint that he's living with two women."

"Two?"

"Yes, sir. Mrs. Elkins and one Anne Harris. I understand she's the banker's wife. Apparently Mr. Harris caught the prosecutor and Mrs. Harris in bed together yesterday afternoon and waved a shotgun around and fired a shot and told Elkins that he could just take Mrs. Harris home and treat her like a second wife. She's at the Elkins house, worrying about the conjugal arrangements . . ."

He got no further because the judge was laughing. He wasn't just laughing, he was roaring, a hearty belly laugh that made his face redder and redder. Finally he choked. Gasping for air, his face beet red, he jerked open the bottom desk drawer and got out a glass, into which he splashed some whiskey. This he tossed off neat.

When he got himself more or less under control, Lester Storm laughed some more. He looked at Audrey, who was blushing deeply and smiling, then went off into another laughing fit.

Trooper Neely lowered himself into a chair and made himself comfortable while the judge hooted and chuckled and giggled.

Finally the jurist said, "Okay, tell me all of it."

Trooper Neely complied. He used his notes. He told about Ed Harris' stomachache, the bedroom, the shotgun, and the threat.

The judge laughed so hard he almost fell out of the chair.

"Damn, Neely," he gasped, "you're gonna kill me. Is this true or did you just make it up?"

"I wouldn't make up something like this, sir," Sam Neely said primly.

"Hayden and Anne Harris! Second wife!" Lester Storm howled, then leaned back in his chair and laughed so hard that tears rolled down his cheeks.

When his mirth subsided this time, the judge asked, "Where did you get that information about conjugal arrangements?"

"Uh, I went out to Elkins' house and talked to Anne Harris."

"No!"

"Yes, sir. I did."

"She said . . . ?"

Neely consulted his notes. The judge howled over the featherbed crack and became incoherent when he heard the open-house remark. "By God," he exclaimed finally, "that is a *woman!* I wish to hell I were ten years younger—I'd go after her my own self."

After Lester let it percolate awhile, he asked Neely, "How'd you get into this, anyway?"

"I was investigating a complaint. Mrs. Wilfred and Mrs. Davis came into my office this morning and swore out a complaint against the prosecutor. They alleged bigamy. They also swore out a complaint against Ed Harris, alleging that he menaced his wife and Hayden Elkins with a shotgun. They wanted to file a complaint against Harris for attempted murder, but they alleged nothing to support that charge. These does seem, however, to have been a little criminal shotgun pointing going on at the Harris household yesterday afternoon."

"Neely, why didn't you throw those two women out of your office?"

"Davis and Wilfred? Why would I do that?"

"For heaven's sake, son! Those two women are in every other week swearing out complaints against somebody." Lester shook his head and chuckled. "But I am not going to say anything more about Harris and Elkins. Those two unhappy fornicators may wind up in front of me for something or other, like a divorce. Go see Arleigh Tate. He can tell you what you have there."

Trooper Neely rose and thanked the judge for his time.

"No. Thank *you*," Lester Storm wheezed. "My wife is trying to get me to retire. If I'd been sitting in Florida listening to old farts tell me about their diseases, I'd have missed this. They're going to have to carry me out of this office in a box."

He waved his hand, shooing Neely out.

Audrey dived out the door behind Neely. She made sure the door to the corridor was firmly closed and closed the door to the judge's office—Lester was still in there chuckling and snorting—and picked up the telephone. Her sister would *love* to hear about this! The banker, the banker's wife, the county prosecutor . . . Golly!

———

Sheriff Arleigh Tate was a short, fat man who chewed green horse-dick cigars. As he listened to Neely's tale, he giggled. Occasionally he removed what was left of his cigar from his mouth and spit into a brass spittoon beside his desk, but mainly he just giggled, which made his belly quiver. He reminded Neely a little of Santa Claus.

When Neely ran dry, Tate said, "Son, that there's one hell of a tale. Better told than when my wife related it to me an hour ago. That bit about con-jew-gal arrangements is a very nice touch. Fried eggplant, huh?"

"Yes, sir. She said the secret is the spices in the breading."

Tate giggled and spit some more. He rolled the tobacco mess around in his mouth as he eyed Neely with interest. "Why'd you question those people?"

"I told you. Mrs. Davis and Mrs. Wilfred—"

"They were just gossiping. If us cops investigate every piece of gossip that comes our way, we'll be busier than flies at a Labor Day picnic."

"Bigamy? Is there a bigamy charge against Elkins?"

"Bigamy requires two simultaneous marriages. You've got to marry the second wife before you get legally rid of the first one. Has Hayden taken Anne Harris to the altar?"

"Uh, there's no evidence of that. He's just living with her as his second wife."

"We'll have to use a couple of the larger counties as jails if we arrest everybody in this state who is living with a woman without the benefit of holy matrimony," Arleigh Tate declared. "Fortunately that still ain't a crime as of this morning."

"Felony menacing?"

"Waving a gun around ain't legal *if*—and this is a big if—if someone felt menaced. Who felt menaced?"

"Well, no one would admit it."

"Even if they did and we were fools enough to take this to court, no jury would convict Ed Harris of anything. He didn't shoot anybody, and he's got half the county laughing at the man who screwed his wife. Now that's pretty damned good, I'd say."

"I suppose," Trooper Neely said sadly, ruffling through the pages of his notebook.

"Don't feel bad, son," Sheriff Tate said. "Was this your first case?"

"Yes, sir."

"Don't worry. There'll be enough to keep you busy. The folks hereabouts don't lead quiet lives."

THREE

September mornings in the Eden valley are as good as life gets, Richard Hudson thought as he stood on his porch and inhaled deeply. Tendrils of fog wafted through the trees, responding gently to air currents that were undetectable here on the porch. The sun rising over the low mountain to the east would soon burn off the fog, leaving the morning crisp, blue and cloudless.

Three years ago Richard Hudson purchased this small farm near Eden and said a permanent good-bye to Manhattan. This morning he gave that decision five seconds of thought and concluded again, for the hundredth time, that it was the best one he ever made.

The garden looked pretty good, he told himself after a careful inspection. No aphids, only a few beetles, and not many weeds. Everything had done exceptionally well this summer. He went through the rows pulling an ear of corn here, a handful of beans there, picking three or four cucumbers and placing the produce in a bag. He had been eating from the garden for a month now and had lost ten pounds. And never felt better. He put the bag on the kitchen table and returned to the garden.

As he grubbed with the hoe, Richard Hudson's mind turned to the problems of Prince Ziad of Endor, who just now was engaged in an extraordinary duel to the death with Ka, the great champion of the bird warriors of Alpha Theta Four.

Richard Hudson arrived at a solution to Prince Ziad's current predicament before he finished hoeing the first row of pole beans.

Ziad's adventures were swashbuckler fantasy; Hudson could tap out two thousand words every working day in about two hours. The stories didn't take much thought, and the writing went fast. Then the publisher slapped a scantily clad, well-endowed beauty on the cover alongside the well-muscled prince in a heroic pose, usually holding his laser gun or sword at the ready, and the books sold like tickets to heaven. There had been four Ziad books so far—Hudson was working on the fifth. The gallant prince was making Hudson rich.

He had been a full-time professional writer of science fiction for twenty years, since he was twenty-two years old. Alas, Richard Hudson books had never sold very well. Only these last few years, after his agent twisted his arm and talked him into doing the Ziad series, had he done better than barely eking out a living. Before Ziad slashed his way through the hydra-infested swamps of Endor to rescue the exotic princess Calisto in his first adventure, Hudson's best year writing earned him a mere $24,000 even though he published three books that year. Still, regardless of the money, Ziad's adventures were only fantasy trash, so Hudson refused to let the publisher put his real name on the covers. He wrote Ziad under the pen name of Rip Hays.

Now that money was flowing like a river, he had abandoned Manhattan and was living the good life here in Eden. And when he finished the daily Ziad grind, he was writing serious stuff, sci-fi as good as he could write it.

Good sci-fi was designed to stimulate the imagination of the reader. Consequently the writer had to do a lot of thinking before he committed words to paper. The thinking was the part of the creative process that Richard Hudson liked the best. Making words appear on the computer screen, spell-checking and editing were merely clerk work.

Just now Hudson paused in his agricultural efforts and cleaned his thick glasses. With his glasses off the garden was a blur. It didn't matter. His mind was elsewhere. Years ago he had realized that the primary purpose of the neocortex in the human brain was probably communication with other human beings. He had expressed that idea in various ways in three of his Richard Hudson novels, but if serious scientists read them, they had given no hint.

What would be the consequences, Hudson asked himself now, if a species developed the neocortex to the point that they abandoned speech? Deceit and lying would disappear. What would society look like then? Would it be human? He turned these questions over carefully and examined them from several angles.

Ideas had always intrigued Hudson. In his younger days he had spent at least two afternoons a week reading scientific journals in the New York Public Library. His income now allowed the luxury of subscriptions. When he first came to Eden, old Mrs. Marple at the post office was stunned when he collected his monthly armload of magazines in their plain brown wrappers. No doubt she thought him some kind of pervert. She finally concluded, correctly, that he was a harmless eccentric.

His train of thought today wandered from his mercilessly honest society and lingered momentarily on the great men through the years who postulated the theories we call learning. He took comfort from the fact that most theories eventually turn out to be wrong. The universe was an extraordinarily complex place, he believed, and the quest for knowledge was not almost complete—it had just begun.

Hudson had little patience with the popular media cynics who were well paid to sneer at the human condition. That mankind was noble he had no doubt. Noble but ignorant. Yet how terrible it would be to spend a lifetime doing careful research and rigorous thinking, only to have later generations shake their heads sadly over your efforts. Noble efforts so often ended ignominiously.

He replaced his now-clean glasses on his head and critically examined the bean row that he had just finished. Something moving on the road, just beyond the fence, caught his eye.

Someone walking. A young man. Goofy. Carrying his cinder blocks. On his way to peep in a window somewhere, Hudson concluded.

The writer went back to his hoeing.

Aren't we all peepers? Really. We peep through any window, crack or mouse-hole we can find for a glimpse of some portion of the works, then announce loudly that we know what makes the whole thing tick. Don't we? Of course we do.

So what would human society look like if there were no curtains, no walls, no secrets, no possibility of deception about motives?

About the time he finished the beans, it occurred to Richard Hudson to wonder where Goofy was going today. He might have hit on the answer if something shiny had not caught his eyes.

There, in the dirt, something . . . gray, with a dull luster. He bent and reached for it. Part of it was buried and he had to pull to remove it from the soil.

An arrowhead! A huge arrowhead.

By the Lord Harry!

He sat heavily in the dirt, beans forgotten, and stared at the artifact in his hand. It was long, perhaps three inches, and so perfectly made that it appeared absolutely symmetrical. The edges were flaked with dozens of tiny serrations. He brushed away the crumbs of dirt, fingered the tiny indentations. And the point . . . he pressed a fingertip to the point. Needle sharp.

After all these years.

And the shaping of the stem . . . so perfect.

The craftsmanship—the hours and effort and skill that had gone into this—instinctively he knew it wasn't an arrowhead. Too big. Too heavy. A spear point? Or a knife blade?

Richard Hudson looked around, at his small house, the lawn and trees . . . and the Faraway Hills and Blue Mountains that formed the horizon. Then he looked up into the vastness of the sky. Three years. He had lived here three years. And he had never once suspected that this stone point was right here, in the dirt, a few inches under the surface, literally waiting for him to dig it up.

How long had it been there?

The firm coolness of the shaped stone set his mind racing. Sitting in the dirt with his legs crossed, suffused with a curious sense of well-being, he fingered the stone and contemplated the enormity of time.

Finally his thoughts turned inward. He felt good. Very, very good. In fact, he didn't know when he had ever felt better.

This stone blade was partially responsible for that. It was so perfect . . . and it was without a price. Money had not purchased it and he would not sell it. It was a gift from a long-dead craftsman, an artist in stone, reaching across the ages.

"Thank you," Richard Hudson told the sky, and meant it.

Trooper Sam Neely sipped coffee in Doolin's Restaurant, listened to the hubbub around him, and contemplated the mural on the wall. He had never seen anything quite like it. The overpowering green made beads of perspiration erupt on his forehead. He half-turned in his chair and put a hand on his brow, blocking the picture from view.

"Hey, whatcha doin'?" Junior Grimes, the son of Moses Grimes, the owner of the restaurant, dropped into the chair across from Neely. They had met several days ago. Junior was a few inches over six feet tall and had thin hips, a flat stomach and a broad chest that supported a well-formed head with a square jaw. His muscled biceps formed knots under the short sleeves of his grease-stained shirt. His forearms were brown and thick and ended in wrists that were twice the diameter of Neely's. He looked larger than he was and strong as a bull, which was no illusion. Just in case you forgot his name, the word JUNIOR was printed on a patch above his left breast pocket.

"Sitting here drinking coffee," Sam Neely replied, which made him feel a bit stupid. He had already heard this greeting from a dozen people and knew it wasn't a real question. Yet it sounded so strange that his first reaction was to answer it honestly.

"What are you doing?" Neely asked Junior, turning it around.

"Oh, nothing much," Junior Grimes said, and grinned. He had a good grin. He apparently took all his meals in the restaurant, but he lived in a house near his father's, Neely knew. Junior owned a wrecker service and a junkyard and from time to time sold used cars, but primarily he was an automobile mechanic. His thick hands bore the scars.

"How are you liking it here in Eden?" Junior asked heartily in another effort to get the conversation rolling.

"Okay so far," Neely said, and drained the last of his coffee.

"Uh, if you don't mind my asking, I hear you called on Anne Harris. Is it true she's . . . uh . . . permanently moved in with Hayden Elkins?"

Junior had a booming voice—he was perhaps the least subtle man you would ever meet—and Neely was instantly aware that the question had quieted conversation throughout the dining room.

"Nothing in this life is permanent."

"Not that it's any of my business, you understand," Junior said, trying to work some deference into his voice and actually managing to insert a detectable trace. "But people talk."

"Gossip, you mean."

"Call it what you like. There's sure a lot of it about Hayden and Anne. Something like that ain't gonna slide by unremarked. Around these parts it ain't every day a man loads up with two wives. One can usually dish out all the aggravation most fellas can handle."

Neely was weighing an answer when Mrs. Grimes, Junior's mother, shouted from behind the cash register, "Trooper Neely, you have a telephone call."

Neely was relieved. "Apparently Mr. Elkins has an unusual constitution," he told Junior as he rose from the table.

The telephone was on the counter behind the cash register. Junior trailed along behind the trooper and stood close enough to hear the policeman's side of the conversation.

"Neely." He listened a little bit, then said, "I can get directions here . . . Okay. I'm on my way."

46

When he hung up both Junior and his mother were looking at him expectantly.

"No wreck," he told them when he remembered that Junior had the only wrecker in the southern end of the county.

"Uh-huh."

"I need directions to the Carcanos'."

"Carcano?"

"Hmmm," said Mrs. Grimes, her eyebrows rising. She stared over her glasses at Neely for several seconds, then shifted her gaze to her son. "June, isn't that the new woman preacher that moved into the old Thorpe place on the Vegan road?"

"Why, I believe it is."

"Up the Vegan road, Mr. Neely, fourth place on the right."

"They're new around here," Junior said unnecessarily.

"Why do the Carcanos need the police?" Mrs. Grimes asked.

"Why would a preacher call the law?" Junior echoed.

Trooper Neely drew himself up to his full height. Half the people in the restaurant were looking at him, waiting for his answer. "No doubt they want to ask me what I'm doing today," he told mother and son and the assembled citizens of Eden.

"Preachers have problems same as everybody else," Mrs. Grimes said to Junior.

"I heard that," the affable giant replied, and grinned.

Neely smiled in spite of himself. It was impossible not to like Junior.

The state policeman laid a dollar beside his coffee cup as he went by the table. He consciously avoided looking at the mural.

As he left the restaurant Neely heard Junior tell his mother and everyone within the building, "He says Elkins has an unusual constipation."

The whole concept of women in the ministry made Sam Neely slightly uncomfortable. What kind of woman would get the call? It had been his experience that women were a pretty righteous bunch without clerical vestments, so giving one a pulpit from which to point out the failings of men looked to him like a sure way to make Sunday mornings extremely uncomfortable. Listening to some dried-up old prune thunder about the evils of the flesh, Neely mused, with the cross behind her and colored light from the stained glass windows playing across the altar, would be a religious experience that would rock you to your shoe tops. Just thinking about it made him shiver.

So it was with mild trepidation that he drove into the yard of the Carcano house this morning and parked the cruiser.

Mrs. Carcano—he took it to be Mrs. Carcano—was waiting for him on the porch. She wasn't a dried-up old prune. Far from it. She was a lovely woman still on the right side of forty, he guessed, with brown hair fluffed up. She was wearing a nice summer frock, a sweater and flat shoes. She stood with her arms folded across her chest as he came up the walk.

"Mrs. Carcano?"

"Yes. I'm glad you came, Trooper."

"My name's Sam Neely." He removed his Smokey Bear uniform hat and glanced around the neatly mowed yard, then turned back to her. "How can I be of service this morning?"

"He's around back." She came down the stairs from the porch and led the way toward the corner of the house. "I told him not to leave and he hasn't."

"What's he done?"

"He was peeping into my daughter's window. She is a remarkably level-headed young woman. She saw him and left the room, found and informed me. I went outside, told him to stay there, then I called the police. My daughter has already left for school."

The man in question was sitting on two cinder blocks, stacked one atop the other, under a window. He watched Neely and Mrs. Carcano approach without curiosity.

Neely came to a stop ten feet away. He had put his hat back on to have his hands free, but now he took it off again. He started to wipe his brow with his shirtsleeve, then thought better of it and fished in his pocket for a hanky.

"I think he's retarded," he muttered to Mrs. Carcano.

"I believe so," she murmured.

"Do you know him?"

"No. We're new here. Do you?"

"I'm new, too."

He stowed the hanky in his hip pocket and rearranged his hat on his head. He tugged at an earlobe. Finally he approached the man, who appeared to be in his twenties, with an angular face, heavy brows and clear, vacant blue eyes. His shirt and trousers were worn and soiled. His boots lay beside him on the ground, and he was barefoot.

"This lady says you were peeping in the window."

The man nodded slowly.

"Were you?"

His head bobbed quickly several times.

"Why?"

This question took a while to process. Finally a look of surprise crossed the angular face. "Girl in there," he said.

Well, it *was* a stupid question, Neely thought ruefully. He glanced at Mrs. Carcano, who wore a gentle smile.

"What's your name?"

"Goofy." He had to repeat it twice before Neely was sure he had it. The words were a bit slurred.

"What's your last name?"

This question puzzled the young man, who rubbed his arms as he thought about it. "Don't know," he said finally. "People call me Goofy."

"Where do you live?"

He gestured at the road. "Ice's." At least, that's what it sounded like to Neely.

"Why did you take your boots off?" Mrs. Carcano asked.

"Too hot."

The boots were heavy leather brogans. "Well, I suspect they would be," she said.

Trooper Neely walked away from Goofy. Mrs. Carcano followed. The sun had burned off the morning fog and the sun shown brightly.

Neely stopped and faced the minister. "Will you sign a complaint?"

"No."

"I can't arrest him for a misdemeanor that wasn't committed in my presence unless someone signs a complaint."

"I understand. Nevertheless, I will not sign a complaint against a retarded person."

"Where is Mr. Carcano?"

"Dead."

"Oh. I'm sorry. I didn't mean—"

She looked slightly amused. "He died in a traffic accident several years ago, Mr. Neely. The Lord was kind. He died instantly and doubtlessly didn't feel any pain. And if he were here today he would not sign a complaint, either."

"I see."

She brushed the hair back from her forehead. "It was a difficult thing, losing him like that. We expect life to be gentle to us, and we are sometimes surprised and very hurt when for a few moments life isn't gentle. I found that getting over the loss was the easy part. Continuing to live a life I had shared with him proved quite impossible. When I was offered a ministry here, I decided to accept."

Neely took off his hat again and turned it slowly in his hands.

"My daughter and I like it here. This is a good place, I think."

He nodded.

"A very good place."

"Even with Goofy?"

"Especially with Goofy. He is a harmless creature."

"Who peeps."

"Apparently."

"Why did you call the police, Mrs. Carcano? You knew when you saw

50

him that he was retarded and you knew you wouldn't sign a complaint. Once you made that decision it was no longer a police matter."

"I don't know who he is or where he lives, Mr. Neely. You must take him home, talk to his people. It would put me in a difficult position to do that."

Neely nodded. "I see."

"It would be nice if something could be done to prevent future incidents of this sort."

Neely put his hat back on and settled it at the prescribed angle. He was dubious. "Without a complaint . . ."

"It's been a pleasure to meet you, Mr. Neely." She offered her hand and a smile. "Perhaps I'll see you Sunday morning at the Eden Chapel."

"Perhaps."

Neely walked over to where Goofy was sitting. "You're going to have to come with me. Put your boots on."

Goofy didn't tie the laces on his boots. He stomped them on, then picked up the cinder blocks, one in each hand.

"Leave those here," Neely told him.

"They aren't mine," Mrs. Carcano said. "He must have brought them with him. I don't own any cinder blocks."

Goofy nodded. Neely shrugged. "Come on," he said.

"Wait," said Mrs. Carcano. She knelt and tied the laces on Goofy's boots.

When she straightened, Sam Neely asked her, "What time are services on Sunday?"

"Ten o'clock."

The trooper smiled. "It's been a pleasure meeting you, Mrs. Carcano."

Sam Neely made Goofy put the cinder blocks in the trunk. As he pulled out of the driveway he was unsure of which way to turn. He paused at the road and thought about it, then turned left and pointed the car toward Eden and Indian River.

In the sheriff's office he told Goofy to sit in a chair outside the counter.

Deputy Delmar Clay was doing paperwork at the desk and frowned at Goofy. "Hey, retard. You peeping again?"

"Yeah," Goofy said.

"Again?" Neely asked.

"Didn't they tell you?" Delmar Clay asked. "Ol' Goofy here is our local pervert. Ain't got enough brains to wipe his nose, but he's smart enough to always take two cinder blocks with him when he goes peeping because the windows might be too high and there might not be anything else handy to stand on. He did have the cinder blocks, didn't he?"

"Yes," Neely acknowledged.

He felt so exasperated and depressed that he dropped into a chair beside Goofy. Finally he roused himself enough to ask Delmar, "Sheriff in?"

"Nope. Went over to the drugstore to get some cigars."

Neely nodded.

Delmar Clay tilted his chair back and smiled broadly. "No use locking the retard up. They'll just let him go."

"You're kidding."

"Nope," said Clay, obviously enjoying himself. "Little moron can look into any window he wants. And he knows it, too. Isn't that right, Goofy?"

The retarded man's face lost its permanent half grin and brightened momentarily into a smile. It was there for a moment, then it faded.

"The sheriff will be back in a bit. He can tell you himself, so he can."

Neely couldn't wait. He stood, adjusted the heavy gunbelt and told Goofy, "You wait here. Wait right there in that chair and don't go anyplace."

"He won't. I'll see to that." Delmar Clay scowled at Goofy, who didn't seem to mind. His expression didn't change. He looked at Delmar for a moment, then gazed around the room.

Neely went upstairs to see the judge. Audrey ushered Neely into the private office where Lester Storm was reading a newspaper.

"Morning, Neely," Storm boomed. "How's crime?" The judge chuckled at his own wit.

Everyone in this county is nuthouse crazy, Neely told himself as he found a seat. "Got a peeping case for you, Judge. A fellow named Goofy."

"You brought Goofy in?"

"Yes, sir. He was looking in a window at the home of Mrs. Carcano, the new minister at the Eden Chapel, peeping at her daughter. She called the police, then wouldn't sign a complaint."

Judge Storm shrugged. "Nothing we can do," he said. "The boy's retarded."

"I understand that, Judge. But letting him go around peeping in windows doesn't seem right."

"Did you talk to Arleigh Tate about this?"

"Not yet. He's over at the drugstore buying cigars and I got tired of listening to Delmar Clay."

The judge nodded. He said, "I got tired of Delmar years ago—welcome to the club. Talk to Arleigh."

"Yes, sir."

"Even if someone signed a complaint, Goofy's not mentally competent," the judge explained patiently. "Goofy is incapable of forming criminal intent. No incompetent person is going to be convicted of a crime in this county while I'm on the bench."

Neely accepted that, reluctantly. "Maybe he should be sent somewhere . . ."

"To involuntarily commit someone, the law requires that I make two findings based on a preponderance of the evidence. First, that the person in question is incompetent. Goofy is, beyond a shadow of a doubt. Second, that the person is a danger to himself or someone else. Goofy is not dangerous. To anybody. Some of these women might think he's a pain in the ass, but dangerous? Nooo."

"A man going around spying on women doesn't seem right, somehow."

"In this country we don't lock people up for being a pain in the ass. Any woman who doesn't want Goofy watching can draw her curtains or do her primping on the second floor. Goofy doesn't carry a ladder."

"Just two cinder blocks."

"That's right. One in each hand. He's been toting those blocks and looking in windows since he went through puberty. Nothing you or I could do or say is going to make him less interested in girls or stop wanting to look."

Neely looked dubious.

"Believe me," Lester Storm added. "I tried it years ago." The judge waggled a finger at the state trooper. "You tell Preacher Carcano that there are some things in this world that we have to accept the way they are. All the prayer and good intentions and Christian salvation we can muster aren't going to change them."

"I think she knows that."

"Ain't a solitary thing wrong with Goofy's interest in women," Lester Storm said darkly. "Most natural thing in the world. It isn't *dirty*. Those Bible thumpers hoot and holler about sin and they don't know the very first—"

"Mrs. Carcano isn't like that," Sam Neely said with an edge in his voice.

"I sincerely hope so," Judge Storm thundered. He leaned back in his chair, adjusted his testicles and picked up his newspaper.

"Thanks for your time, Judge."

Lester Storm grunted from behind the paper. Sam Neely closed the door on his way out.

In the sheriff's office in the basement, Goofy was still sitting where Neely had left him. "Do you have to go to the bathroom?" Neely asked.

Goofy nodded.

"Where is it?" Neely asked Delmar Clay, who was leaning back in his chair with his feet on the desk. Delmar jerked a thumb. Goofy went.

"Sheriff's back. In his office."

Neely thought about it, then decided he didn't need to talk to Arleigh Tate.

"So you went up to see ol' Lester, huh?"

"Yep."

"Found out that the retard can peek in any window he wants and nothing anybody can do?"

"Yeah."

"I won't bother to tell you I told you so," Delmar said, and grinned slyly. "Guess you don't believe the stuff us old hands can tell you. Must be that state police academy education."

"Oh, can it."

"The only way that retard can be cured is for a bunch of us to take him out behind the barn and teach him a lesson that gets through to his pea brain."

Neely stepped over to the desk and looked down at Deputy Delmar Clay. "You ever lay a finger on that man, Clay, and I'll smear your nose all over your face."

"You and who else?"

"Clay, get your feet off that desk." Arleigh Tate was standing in the doorway of his private office. "I put three summonses on that desk this morning. Go serve them."

"Sheriff, I—"

"Right now!"

Clay went.

"You come in here, Neely. We need to talk."

"Goofy's in your bathroom, Sheriff. We better wait till he gets out."

"Okay."

When Goofy was back in his chair, Neely went in to see the sheriff. Tate unwrapped a cigar and stuck it into his mouth. He didn't light it. "Want to tell me about it?"

Neely did.

"Goofy lives with Verlin and Minnie Ice," Tate told the trooper at the end of his recital. "I think he's Verlin's illegitimate son. He's harmless."

"That's what everyone says."

"Don't want you threatening the deputies, Neely. A thing like that will get around and make it hard for them to do their job. And Clay works the southern half of the county, shares your beat."

"I'm sorry, sir. Clay is—"

"I know. Wish I could fire him, but I can't." Tate expectorated into his spittoon. "He married my wife's second cousin."

"Oh. Your wife likes him?"

"She can't stand the son of a bitch. It's politics."

"Politics?"

"The girl he married has fifty voting relatives in the northern end of the county," Tate explained. "She's sort of scatterbrained, and I can't say much for her taste in men, but she's a nice girl and he needed a job to support her. So I promised him a job and picked up fifty votes."

"But why do you have him working the southern end of the county?"

"Like I said, politics. If I sent him up north he'd hound his wife's relatives and I'd lose the fifty votes."

"Won't Clay cost you votes around Eden?"

"Luckily my wife is from Eden. Her relatives vote for me so I'll have a job to support her."

For the first time since he said good-bye to Mrs. Carcano, Sam Neely grinned.

"To survive as a cop, Neely, you must learn not to take yourself or your job too seriously. You aren't going to be able to save the world. Hell, for all I know it doesn't need saving. Just remember that there are good people out there. They get into trouble from time to time and that's where you come in, but these are your friends and neighbors. Always treat them as you would want to be treated if you were in their place. That's what Delmar Clay is too stupid to understand."

After a bit Neely asked, "Where does Verlin Ice live?"

"Past Eden, up toward Vegan. Goofy will show you. He showed me when I became sheriff."

56

FOUR

Billy Joe Elkins was thinking about sex. The fact that he had an erection most of the time didn't help. The darn thing was just semipermanently stiff. When he thought about sex, it got stiffer.

Unfortunately, these days he thought about sex during most of his waking moments. He fantasized, speculated about how it would feel, wanted to do it so badly that he didn't know how he was going to make it to the next minute.

Needless to say, he wasn't thinking about sex as an abstract concept. The minds of seventeen-year-old males don't work that way. He was thinking about sex with Melanie Naroditsky.

Melanie, with the long brown legs and golden arms and velvet lips and ripe, firm breasts . . . and those long brown lashes that stroked her cheeks when she lowered her head and batted them so innocently. Melanie, with the almost inaudible moan that escaped her when he caressed the small of her back, with the tiny beads of sweat that appeared on her upper lip when he brushed his fingertips along her thigh . . .

Melanie Naroditsky was driving him wild.

Of course she well knew the turmoil she was causing in this young male animal who hovered around her like a fly over a honey pot, and she took pleasure in it. Great pleasure. Seventeen-year-old males aren't normally very sensitive to the emotional state of females, but Melanie's receptiveness had penetrated to the testosterone-soaked brain of Billy Joe Elkins and given him some big ideas.

Tonight. Tonight was *the* night.

This Friday morning in old lady Salmaron's English class he reached that momentous decision. Melanie was at her desk, bent over her English book, following along in the text while Lath-Legs Salmaron read poetry, incomprehensible gobbledygook about some dude named J. Alfred Prufrock. This "poem," Billy Joe thought, didn't sound like any "love song" he had ever heard. Had he been writing it, it would have come out a lot different.

Now Melanie glanced over her shoulder and met his eyes. A zillion volts arced across the space between the lovers, then she lowered her eyes again to the text. Billy Joe gasped for air.

Tonight!

With his organ pressed firmly against the zipper of his jeans, he began making serious plans. The whole object of his campaign would be to break down her natural resistance. He assumed she would have to be seduced. She wasn't *that* kind of girl.

The realization that he would be ruining a virtuous girl to satisfy his primal lust caused him exactly two seconds of angst. He sneaked another glance at the object of his passion, still bent over her book, her hair obscuring her face, and the twinge passed.

Just thinking about it made Billy Joe's palms perspire. *Stop,* he told himself. Stop thinking about the payoff and figure out how you're going to get there.

He wiped his sweaty hands on his jeans and pretended to concentrate on the words on the page before him as old lady Salmaron droned on and on.

That a wonderful girl like Melanie might be interested in sex, *that she might be contemplating the prospect of sex with him,* were thoughts that had never once crossed his fevered mind, which was fortunate. Had he but an inkling about the true state of Melanie's emotions, the resulting priapic frenzy might have done his health serious harm.

When the bell rang, he gathered his books and timed his charge for the door to coincide with Melanie's arrival.

Out in the hall he grinned at her. He thought it was a grin, but it was a leer. Melanie didn't seem to mind. She gazed into his eyes with the sincere enthusiasm that makes youth golden.

"Wasn't that poem fantastic?" she asked.

"Oh, yeah. Sure."

"It reminded me so much of us. Every line. It was as if Eliot could see into our hearts."

"Who?" Billy Joe asked, slightly disconcerted. He sincerely hoped no one knew exactly what he had been thinking during English class. Just now he purposely held his books in front of his fly to conceal his loaded and ready condition.

"The poet. T. S. Eliot."

"Oh, him."

"Weren't you moved?"

"Of course," Billy Joe lied. Since he knew a thing or two about girls, he added, "Just looking at you moves me."

"You're soooo sweet," Melanie said, and flashed her lashes, which made his temples throb.

"Tonight, after the football game. Will you meet me outside the locker room?"

"See you then, lover," she whispered.

Melanie Naroditsky ran a finger along his chin, then dashed away down the hall. Billy Joe watched her go. When she was out of sight, he took a deep, deep breath and exhaled slowly. Ooooh, boy!

Matilda Elkins was in her bedroom sorting laundry when she heard Anne drive away. Last night Hayden and Billy Joe went to the Harris house to retrieve Anne's car. Anne asked them to go, so they did, without even glancing at Matilda.

This morning when she heard the car leave Matilda finished sorting the clothes, then went into the bathroom and locked the door.

She felt empty. Deep in her heart she suspected that Hayden's philandering was her fault. Just what she had done wrong, or more likely should have done but hadn't, she didn't know. She had worried about that, fretted it, and at last concluded that she couldn't identify her error.

Finally she realized that she herself was the problem. She had never been assertive. She was a woman who was content to follow her man through life, go where he leads, defer to his wishes. Her mother had been like that, and Matilda thought she had inherited her personality.

It was plain that Hayden expected her to acquiesce in this new arrangement, to tolerate Anne's presence in the guest bedroom. That was bad enough, but Anne Harris also expected her to accept it, and that was galling. She wanted to assert herself, to force Hayden and Anne to . . . to do *something*. But what?

Her instincts and experience failed her completely. She had no idea what she wanted to happen.

Hayden had betrayed her. Nothing could change that fact. It had been done and could not be undone. And deep within her she knew that if she were somehow different, that event would not have happened.

She examined her reflection in the mirror, looking for the flaw that had to be there. The familiar image stared back. The flaw was hidden, buried deep. Whatever it was, it was a latent defect, but a defect all the same.

Matilda had cried herself out. She had cried for almost three days in the privacy of the bathroom and now she didn't have another tear left in her. As she cried she had toyed with the idea of killing Hayden and Anne. God knows they both richly deserved it, yet she knew she wasn't capable of the rage that murder would require. Finally, reluctantly, she had abandoned it.

Hysteria had its attractions, too, and several times in the last few days she thought she was about wound up enough. But she knew she could never pull that off, either. It would be too transparent. To have Anne Harris see through her best hysterical fit and laugh would be mortifying, quite impossible to live with.

Suicide was an option. She was certainly depressed enough. Sleeping pills would do the trick, and there was a whole bottle in the medicine cabinet. Just swallow them down, drift gently off to sleep, never to awaken and have to look again at Hayden . . . or Anne. Never again feel like a cracked, empty vase.

Matilda rejected suicide when she realized that she would merely be smoothing the path for Anne. In five years everyone would forget the chronology and assume that Anne moved in after crazy, demented Matilda did away with herself and left poor Hayden devastated. Matilda had a keen appreciation of the length of her neighbors' attention spans and the quality of their memories.

When all other possibilities had been rejected, that left only divorce. A good, juicy divorce, with a team of piranha lawyers ripping the flesh off Hayden and relieving him of every penny he had or ever hoped to get.

Yet a divorce would merely throw Hayden into Anne's arms. *Here, I don't want him. He's penniless and worthless and he's yours.*

Not that Anne would care about the state of Hayden's wallet. After all, she owned half the bank. Ed's father, Lane Harris, left half the stock to Ed and half to Anne when he died two years ago. Poor Lane, he must have been crazy as a bedbug in his last years, to bequeath half that bank to that brazen tramp!

No. Divorce wouldn't work, either.

Matilda stared at herself in the mirror and wished she could cry some more.

The tears wouldn't come.

Verlin Ice's home was an ancient Victorian that desperately needed paint. In fact, it was difficult to tell from the weathered gray boards just what color the Ices might have favored back when the world was young.

The house sat well back from the road on a small knoll, across a creek with a dilapidated bridge that groaned a warning when Sam Neely inched across in the police cruiser. He parked in the yard in front of the porch.

A lithe, blond goddess came through the open doorway and stopped on the porch at the top of the steps. She was dressed in a simple frock, with bare legs and bare feet. The wind stirred her long, thick, golden hair and swirled it across her face as Neely approached the porch.

Sam Neely, twenty-three years old and fresh out of the police academy, couldn't take his eyes off her. It wasn't polite to stare, but he couldn't help himself. She was the most beautiful woman he had ever seen. *Ever*, even in the movies.

She used a hand to brush the hair back from her eyes, a futile gesture. Neely stood mesmerized.

She smiled gently. "You brought Goofy back, I see."

Neely gestured toward the cruiser and tried to talk, only to find that his tongue had the flexibility of a two-by-four. The thought tugged at his mind that he should tell this beautiful woman of Goofy's latest transgression. Standing in the grass looking up at Venus on the porch as the soft breeze pressed the dress against her body, he finally understood what Lester Storm had been trying to tell him—Goofy's peeping didn't matter.

"My name is Crystal. What's yours?"

Crystal Ice. Well, Crystal Ice, you and I—

"What's your name?" she asked again, her amusement obvious.

Name. Name! Get it out, boy. "Samuel Allen Neely."

"You want to see my father, I suppose?"

"Oh . . ." If he didn't find someone to talk to about something he was going to have to get back in the cruiser and drive away. "Sure. He around?"

"Out in the barn." She pointed.

Reluctantly Sam Neely moved in that direction. He took several steps before he managed to tear his eyes away from Crystal Ice and glance at the ground to keep from tripping.

Verlin Ice sat perched on a hay bale in the sun several feet in from the open door of the barn. His nut-brown, weathered face wore the stubble of several days' growth of gray beard, which matched the boards of his house. He was a smallish man, clad in tattered overalls and a faded blue shirt. As

Neely approached he was arranging a chew of tobacco in his mouth. With his mouth full, he held out the pack toward the state trooper.

"No, thanks. I don't use tobacco."

Verlin Ice rolled the quid around with his tongue, got it placed just so, then spit a dark brown stream of juice into the fine, dry dirt at his feet. Some of the juice dribbled down his chin; he didn't seem to notice.

"Don't trust a man who don't use tobacco," he said matter-of-factly. "Too uppity."

That wasn't very polite, Neely thought. Slightly irritated, he said, "You're working hard this morning, I see."

"Yep. Working hard at living, so I am. Come out here for a chew 'bout ever' day 'bout this time. Women don't like me spittin' in the house, so they don't."

"Most of them are persnickety that way," Neely observed.

"Funny that the good Lord made men and women folk so different."

"Yep."

"Guess He got a good laugh over it. If I'd been Him, I'd still be laughin'."

"Maybe He is."

Verlin Ice spit again. Juice dribbled off his chin onto his shirt and overalls. He concentrated on his chewing.

The barn smelled good, smelled of bovine bodies and manure and sweet hay. The foundations were of cut stone, the uprights and beams squared-up timbers that still wore adze marks. Neely tired of standing and lowered himself onto a hay bale. It was surprisingly comfortable. He sat studying the way the massive beams fitted together.

"I don't mean to rush you," Verlin said after a while, "but we done discussed philosophy and theology, so I guess we done our social visitin'. Have you worked around to what you came for yet?"

"I brought Goofy back."

"Thanks."

"He was over at Mrs. Carcano's house this morning, peeping in a window at her daughter."

"Carcano?"

"The new preacher at the Eden Chapel."

"Goofy does that now and then," Verlin said, and let it go at that.

After a bit Neely asked, "Has he got a last name? Goofy?"

Verlin puzzled on it. He worked on his chew and spit before he answered. "Figures that he does, but I don't know what it is."

"He's not your son?"

"Well, now, he is and he ain't. Didn't come blessed with wedlock, so to speak."

"I see."

"That's good. People rarely do."

"It's nothing to be ashamed about. Isn't all that uncommon."

"Yeah, I guess it's not," Verlin admitted. Then his voice strengthened. "Me and Minnie had a boy. His name is Jirl. He lives up the road, near to Vegan, so he does. Fine boy. He come exactly nine months to the day after me and Minnie tied the knot. Then it was nearly ten years before his sisters started being born."

"I see."

"It wasn't like me and Minnie weren't trying, you understand. That's just the way life worked out."

"Uh-huh."

"Jirl's got a wife and a good farm and near two hundred head of cows and works hard at it. Comes down from time to time and looks in on me and his ma, helps with the chores. Checks on his sisters. Tries to give them some advice ever' now and then on men. They listen respectful 'cause he's their older brother and they like him, but I don't think they pay much mind to what he has to say. None at all, near as I can tell."

The reference to the Ice girls and men intrigued Neely, but he refused to be distracted. "So when did Goofy come to live here?"

Verlin stirred the quid around in his mouth thoughtfully before he spoke. "Years and years ago. He was mighty small, I recollect."

"Why did you take him in?"

The answer came quickly this time. "Where else was he goin' to go? Just a little boy, and even then you could see he was gonna be simple. What else could we do?"

Neely couldn't think of anything more to ask. He had, he sensed, all the information that Verlin Ice was willing to give.

Flies buzzed pleasantly in the barn, birds chirped high in the loft, and a huge black heifer stared at him from her enclosure as Verlin chewed leisurely and spit from time to time. A cat wandered over and rubbed against Neely's leg. He petted it, scratched behind its ears.

Then a grizzled, flop-eared brindle hound wandered in. "Hey, Sam," Verlin said pleasantly.

With a start Neely realized the old man was greeting the dog.

The hound collapsed in the dirt. He stretched, then lay full length on his side and closed his eyes.

Verlin's sun-cured face crinkled into a gentle smile as he sat looking at the dog. Almost as if he could feel the man's affection, the dog whacked its tail three or four times in the dirt. Not another muscle stirred.

Verlin leaned back against a post.

"Dogs and women are a lot alike," he said.

The obvious similarity between Verlin Ice and his hound seemed to Trooper Neely more apropos, but he held his tongue.

"Now you take that ol' coon hound, there," Verlin continued. "To look at, ol' Sam ain't much, just a worthless, worn-out dog. But when I look at him I see the best coon hound that ever ran the woods on a misty summer night hot on a trail. He understands me and I understand him. We're in tune with each other, don't you see."

Verlin paused to give his chew some attention. "Minnie's a lot like that," he added finally.

"I haven't met your wife," Neely informed his host.

Verlin continued, "You look at her, you see an average-looking old woman who's been down the road and put on some years. Me? I see the prettiest girl who ever grew up in this Eden country. She's raised kids through good times and bad, she's spooned food into all of us when we were sick and wiped my bottom for me when I couldn't. She's worked hard for so many years I guess we lost count. She's everything . . . She's just the best human on the face of this earth, so she is."

Trooper Neely didn't know what to say. He wasn't accustomed to hearing such a fervid affirmation of love for a woman from another man. He scratched his nose to hide his embarrassment, which didn't seem to bother Verlin Ice an iota.

Finally Neely got to his feet and brushed bits of hay from his trousers. "Oh, my name's Sam, too. Same as your dog. Sam Neely. Nice meeting you."

"It's good to get to know you early on," Verlin replied, "seeing as how you'll probably be out here a lot sniffing around the girls."

Neely flushed.

"Nothing to be embarrassed about. Chased a few skirts in my time, so I did. Boys interested in girls and girls interested in boys is why humans ain't extinct, despite the preachers' best efforts."

"I don't think—"Neely began.

Verlin Ice cut him off. It was too nice a day to debate religion and he wished he hadn't mentioned it. "Minnie will want to know your intentions when she gets you cornered, but don't let that bother you none. She frets all the fellas thataway. She don't mean no harm by it."

Sam Neely didn't know what to say.

"Get along now, young fella. Go back to work. You're standing in my sun."

Trooper Neely went.

The day girl had just come out onto the porch to remove the lunch tray when Sarah Armbrecht heard a car laboring up the hill through the trees. The drive ran through the forest for a half mile and the sound carried.

Sarah could still hear well, which was, she thought, ironic. She had never enjoyed music, preferring instead the whisper of wind in the pines and the songs of birds, yet her second husband had been a professor of music and an orchestra conductor. He had ended up deaf as a post by the time he was sixty and had been dead for thirty years. At the age of ninety-five, she was still listening to the sounds of the forest. Amazingly, she could still hear a leaf caress a windowpane.

There wasn't much life left in her ancient body, she well knew, but what remained she savored.

"There's someone coming," she told the girl. "We'll have tea, I think."

The day girl paused as she checked that the edges of the blanket were tucked around Sarah's legs, listened for a moment, then shook her head in wonder. She fussed a little more over the shawl around the old woman's shoulders, then took the tray and pill dispensers back inside.

Lunch, Sarah reflected wryly, half a pear and a sliced tomato, and the occasion for the noon pills—all eight.

The car stopped in the parking area and she heard the door slam. Soon she heard someone climbing the stairs. A woman, by the sound of her tread. Then she saw her.

"Hello, Granny Sarah."

Ahh, Anne Harris, her grandson Ed's wife. "Hello, Anne. So good of you to come." She could make out Anne's face fairly well when she was seated in a chair only six feet away. "You look stunning this morning."

"Thank you. I felt I had to come see you. Ed and I are having difficulty, and you will undoubtedly hear about it. I wanted you to hear it from me."

"You don't have to explain your life to anyone, Anne."

"I know. Perhaps because you don't judge, I care about what you think. You are one of the few."

"Let's have some tea first. If you haven't yet had lunch, may I suggest sliced tomatoes on toast? Moses Grimes brought them to me from his garden. They are at their peak just now, and they are delicious."

"I didn't know you knew Moses."

"When he was a young man, he used to mow my lawn. Then one summer he eloped to San Francisco with a doctor's daughter who wanted to see

67

the bright lights. Apparently it came as quite a shock when she announced she was a lesbian. Ran him off and moved in with a famous woman novelist. Moses eventually returned to Eden."

"Moses Grimes?" Anne asked, stifling a laugh.

"Moses Grimes!"

A vision of solid, conservative, slightly overweight and balding Moses Grimes crushed by love amid the cutting-edge moderns of San Francisco stayed with Anne as she ate several slices of toast covered with slices of ripe, red tomato dusted with just a trace of salt. "This is very good," she said to her hostess with her mouth full.

After the day girl had removed the lunch tray and both ladies were sipping tea, the object of the visit could be postponed no longer. "Ed caught me in bed with another man."

Anne told the story rather well, she thought, covering the salient facts and not minimizing her guilt. Nor did she dwell on it. Granny Sarah would find sackcloth and ashes quite repugnant.

Sarah Armbrecht listened in silence. A few questions occurred to her, but she elected not to ask them. Anne was telling her what she wanted her to know, and that was enough.

When Anne fell silent, Sarah Armbrecht poured herself another cup of tea. It was just the way she liked it, strong and hot.

"Why did Lane give you half the bank?"

Anne's eyes reflected her surprise. Of all the things she thought Granny Sarah might ask, that wasn't on the list. "He never discussed it with me. I was as surprised as anyone."

"Lane was his own man," Sarah said. "I remember when he was a boy . . . oh, so long ago. I bore him when I was twenty-eight. I raised him, watched him grow, select a wife, attended his children's weddings, watched him build that bank into one of the three largest independents in the state, watched while he died of cancer at the age of sixty-five. His whole life was encompassed in mine."

The teacup almost slipped from her fingers as the memories crashed over her like a tidal wave. That was the thing about old age that was so disconcerting—you had so very many memories and they came flooding back whether you wanted them or not, whether you were ready or not. Memories of joy and pain, of hope and despair, of love and . . . No, the hate and bitterness of the past had died, leaving only the ache of love of something gone. For they were all gone now, all those people she had loved so very much, her parents, her brothers and sisters, her husbands, her sons. She was left here to mourn them all.

Perhaps she had loved them too much.

She *still* loved them, yet they were gone forever.

When Sarah could speak again she said, "Parents shouldn't outlive their children. Children should bury their parents, not vice versa."

She managed to raise the cup to her lips. The warm liquid helped. When she felt completely in control, she told her guest, "I thought Lane would leave all the stock to Ed, his only son. As you know, his daughter married and moved to California. She's comfortably well off, I believe. Never had any interest in the bank. So when Lane divided the bank between you and Ed in his will, I found that hard to understand. I thought I knew Lane, but he surprised me one last time."

She put the teacup on the tray and didn't pick it up again.

"I have seen so much of life. When I was young I never ever dreamed how it would actually be. I've played all the roles—child, young girl in love, bride, mother, widow, mother of the bride, mother of the groom, grandmother, great-grandmother, old woman, old, *old* woman. Some of the roles I've played several times. Courted, married and buried three husbands. Had five children, only one of whom is still alive, Martha. Jack died of typhoid when he was eleven. Two of the boys died in a car wreck on their way to their father's funeral. Lane died of cancer. I have eleven grandchildren and, so far, eight great-grandchildren.

"I have lived it . . . lived *all* of it."

"Grandmother Sarah," Anne said, "I'm sorry I brought you my troubles."

"Oh, no, child. Don't apologize. You are human, as we all are. I'm sure you did what you thought best. Continue to do that."

"But I don't know what I should do."

"Then do nothing just now," the old lady said gently. "Ponder on it. Eventually a course will become plain to you."

"I have hurt Ed."

"And Matilda Elkins."

Anne snorted. She thought Matilda's troubles were of her own making, and had no sympathy to give away.

"But hurting other people is inevitable," Sarah Armbrecht continued thoughtfully. "It is part of life. We must love, we must endure the hurts that loved ones unavoidably inflict, and we must continue to love. If there is another way, I don't know of it."

The day girl appeared in the doorway. "Mrs. Armbrecht, it's time for your nap."

Anne retrieved her purse and stood.

"Come see me again, Anne," Sarah said. "Think about why Lane left you half the bank."

"I'll be back soon," Anne replied. She kissed the elderly woman's cheek.

FIVE

September and October Friday evenings in the Eden country meant high school football. Home games of the Indian River High School Warriors were social events, and one reason was that anyone who wanted to could get in on the fun.

Any boy with all his body parts functioning more or less as they should could play on the team—the coach never cut anybody. Even better, the coach regularly made wholesale substitutions in the last quarter of the game, so every player got in the game for at least one series of downs. This policy didn't help the Warriors' won-lost record—which perennially hovered around .500—but it endeared him to the students and the parents in the athletic booster club, whose support translated into job security, always a consideration with football coaches.

Any student who could hold an instrument could play in the band. With spiffy uniforms provided by the band boosters and instruments from the school board, the hundred-strong band played a short pregame show and an extensive halftime extravaganza for every home game, rain or shine. As the students marched up and down the field in orchestrated drills that formed letters and locomotives and war bonnets, three students in wheelchairs sat near the director's podium on the midfield sideline and tooted lustily.

Ten majorettes in skimpy costumes strutted in front of the parade twirling batons and flashing legs clad in flesh-covered stockings as their friends in the stands threatened to drown out the music with cheering and applause.

During the game, the cheerleaders on the sidelines performed simple synchronized gymnastics and made as much noise as a dozen girls can, which is not a lot. Still, with hair streaming and legs kicking, they were fun to watch as they exaggerated the emotional ebb and flow of the game and tried to coax big noises from the crowd to sustain the mighty Warriors doing battle on the gridiron.

Despite the debate among the chattering classes in the big cities over the politically correct usage of American Indian names for sports teams, this high school team was still the Warriors. Was and, barring atomic war, always would be. Anyone suggesting changing the nickname would have been laughed at. Every year a new crop of students made posters that exhorted the faithful, BE TRUE TO YOUR SCHOOL—SUPPORT THE WARRIORS, and hung them in the hallways of the school building. It was high-schoolish, of course, yet the innocent fervor of youth kept it fresh and new.

For all these reasons, when the Warriors were playing at home on autumn Friday nights, the stadium at Indian River High was *the* place to be. With the exception of a few curmudgeons and elderly crocks who had forgotten what it meant to be young, the sick and shut in, and those behind county bars or in county bars, *everyone* was there.

Even Hayden and Matilda Elkins.

Not that they had a choice. Their son, Billy Joe, was the starting quarterback. Still, with their conjugal troubles the talk of the county, Matilda was sorely tempted to avoid the humiliation that thoughtless tongues would inflict and leave Billy Joe uncheered this night.

"Look what you've done to us," Matilda said to her husband.

"I'd like to stay home, dear, and I know you would, too, but we must go," Hayden replied. "I'm thinking of Billy Joe. He'll want us there."

Actually he was thinking of Ed Harris, who would undoubtedly go to the game to see if Hayden had the guts to show his face. Well, Ed gave his wife away and made everyone laugh, but Hayden intended to laugh last. He was going to make Ed beg to get his wife back, beg on his knees. He would show the bastard.

Talking to Hayden was like talking to a stone, Matilda thought. She tried to explain. "This is Billy Joe's last year of high school. The very last, of our only son. We'll ruin it for him if we sit in the stands like two felons while everyone whispers and giggles and points."

"We're going. I'll go upstairs and get Anne."

Several seconds passed before Matilda recovered sufficiently to say, "You must be crazy!"

"No. She'll want to go, too." He darted up the stairs.

Matilda sat in a chair and put her head between her knees. He was going with Anne Harris whether she went or not. She could feel the walls closing in, threatening to crush her.

She heard Anne's voice in the upstairs hallway, heard her coming down the stairs with Hayden. "How chilly will it be tonight? Will I need a jacket?"

Matilda's last ray of hope faded. The darkness was total. She felt herself sliding slowly into the abyss.

"Come, dear." Hayden was at her elbow, lifting her from the chair. "You'll need a jacket, too. It'll get down into the fifties by the last quarter."

Matilda didn't know how she managed, but she got to her feet and navigated across the living room toward the door with her husband at her elbow. He snagged her jacket from the closet on the way by.

Out in the driveway Hayden got a shock. His sedan was gone. Billy Joe's Jeep was sitting in its place.

The boy hadn't asked permission to borrow the car, which irritated the father. The kid was taking liberties. He made a mental note to add this transgression to the list.

"We'll take the Jeep," Hayden said calmly to his ladies.

"You must be joking," Anne Harris declared. "It has no roof. My hair will be a mess. We can take my car."

Matilda almost revolted right there. It was bad enough going with Anne, but in her car? When she opened her mouth to protest, no sounds came out.

Hayden steered her toward the car with a firm grip on her arm and stuffed her into the right front seat.

Nothing was said on the journey toward Indian River. Nothing. We're three condemned prisoners going to our own execution, Matilda thought. Driven into the outer darkness by our wanton lust and sin, unrepentant and unable to save ourselves, we stagger blindly toward the gallows.

"What a lovely fall evening," Anne remarked cheerfully.

As they neared the stadium several people recognized them and waved. Matilda dug her nails into the palms of her hands.

After Hayden parked the car, they walked toward the main gate. A shrieking noise grew in Matilda's ears. The cries of souls in torment grew louder and louder with every step.

Anne Harris was paying no attention to the noise or gawking people. She walked along preoccupied with savage thoughts that had nothing to do with football. She had agreed to come tonight because the unexpected invitation gave her a golden opportunity to set tongues and eyebrows wagging furiously. Ed's object, of course, in ordering this living arrangement at the point of a gun had been to embarrass her, humble her, shame her. He was not going to succeed, she told herself again for the twentieth time. She was not going to knuckle under.

That shotgun blast had been a declaration of war.

Up to that moment, I could have forgiven him. He could have forgiven me. But when he pulled that trigger the die was cast. He chose war, war against his wife, the woman who loved him. So war it shall be, war hard and terrible, war unto the last drop of blood, war until the very stones shriek for mercy.

I'm tough enough, she told herself. *And I can fight—I can thrust, parry, cut, slash, stab and kill. I'm smart enough and tough enough to weather whatever comes, to endure, to triumph! When the blood stops flowing and the bodies are counted, I shall be the victor.*

The evening was damp. Minutes before the sun set, thin, gauzy tendrils of fog wafted across the ground in the open end of the football stadium nearer the river. Still, the band marched up and down the field blaring loudly as the players of the two teams milled on their respective sidelines. They whacked one another on the shoulder pads and smacked one another on the butt.

On the Indian River sideline Billy Joe Elkins took time from his male bonding duties to watch Melanie Naroditsky strut her stuff. She was a majorette, second one in on the left side.

Melanie could really strut, Billy Joe thought. Her knees came up waist high with every step; her head was back; those two magnificent breasts thrust forward and cut the air like the twin prows of a catamaran as her baton flashed up and down in perfect rhythm with the other girls'. And she was smiling. As she passed the bench Billy Joe caught her eye and gave her a little wave. She waved back with her free hand and her grin widened, displaying dazzling teeth that had cost her dad five grand in orthodontic bills.

Despite the gridiron warfare looming in his immediate future, Billy Joe felt a flutter in his loins.

While Melanie and her fellow majorettes led the band from the field, Billy Joe's eye wandered over the gathering crowd. He saw his parents making their way through the crowd with Anne Harris trailing behind, climb into the grandstand, clamber past the earlier arrivals and settle onto their roost, his dad in the middle between the two women.

Boy! You gotta hand it to the Old Man, Billy Joe mused. Bringing your wife *and* mistress to a football game—that takes balls!

Not once in the past seventeen years had Billy Joe gotten an inkling that his father had a performance like this in him. Dad had been staid, conservative, almost colorless, the prosecuting attorney for six or eight years, a serious man people treated with deference and respect. Just goes to show, Billy Joe told himself. You never can tell.

For several seconds Billy Joe wondered how his mother was taking all this. She was a quiet woman who usually had little to say. Looking at her in the grandstand, Billy Joe realized that he didn't know her very well.

Billy Joe was handling The Situation just fine. Of course, he had taken some kidding and would probably get some more, but it had been gentle, not intended to hurt. After all, it wasn't as if he had walked into algebra class with his fly unzipped, which would be a major mortification. Kids are a pretty tolerant bunch, most of them. Too many have to deal with difficult situations at home. While they mercilessly apply peer pressure over trivialities like clothes and haircuts and earrings, they are quite protective when one of their own has parent problems.

Billy Joe waved at people he knew. There was Junior Grimes, along with his buddy Arch Stehlik, Moses and Lula Grimes, ol' Verlin Ice . . . friends, acquaintances, all making their way in or cheering the band, pointing to friends, talking, laughing . . .

Billy Joe was still waving when the coach came up behind him and spoke. "Time to get your mind on business, Billy Joe. Those guys are big and tough. Remember the game plan."

"Sure, Coach."

Up in the stands Hayden was searching for his former friend, Ed Harris, while trying to look like he was merely watching the local team prepare to take the field. This activity involved keeping his head pointed toward the field while doing some serious scanning out of the corners of his eyes. Alas, he didn't see the man.

Don't tell me that cockroach didn't come!

Finally he whispered to Anne, "Do you see Ed?"

"I haven't been looking" was the ingenuous reply. "I couldn't care less."

Her answer peeved Hayden more than a little. Most women, in his experience, were extraordinarily curious about all aspects of the relationship between the genders. That curiosity was essential to their femininity. And Anne Harris didn't have it! The possibility that she was lying to him never crossed his mind. A wave of self-pity washed over Hayden, clouding his eyes with tears. He had picked an android from Planet X for his first—and last—extramarital fling. It just wasn't fair.

As quickly as the self-pity swept over him, it passed, leaving a bilious residue. His eyes swiveled to Anne. She sat smiling blandly, the third member of this happy *ménage à trois,* as if she hadn't a care in the world.

"I care," Hayden snarled at his second wife. "Start looking."

"No," she replied sweetly and waved to Billy Joe, who waved back. She leaned around Ed and said to Matilda, "There's our son. He sees us."

How she kept from exploding or dying of stroke right then and there, Matilda Elkins never knew. With iron self-control, she stood and turned to push past knees to the aisle.

"Where are you going?" Hayden hissed.

Her self-discipline deserted her. Matilda spoke in a loud voice that could be heard for twenty feet. "I'm going to pee, darling. If you will excuse me."

And she went. Past a half dozen sets of knees, down the aisle to the walkway, left turn and march toward the gate, then through and out of the glare of the lights into the foggy darkness.

As the damp night enveloped her, tears began flowing.

At least she could still cry!

The new minister of the Eden Chapel, Mrs. Carcano, saw her in the glare of her headlights, a woman staggering along, racked by sobs. She halted the car and told her daughter, "You can walk from here. The stadium is up ahead—you see the lights. I'll pick you up here in two hours, after the game."

"Yes, Mama."

Mrs. Carcano eased the distraught woman into the front seat of her car, then turned the vehicle around. She drove back toward Eden as Matilda Elkins cried and cried.

When Hayden and Anne arrived home after the game, the house was empty. No Matilda.

Hayden was beside himself. All during the game he had wondered where she disappeared to. Home, he told himself. Then he stewed because she went off and left him sitting alone with Anne Harris in the middle of thirty-five hundred people, every damned one of whom was pointing and whispering. He was a quivering mass of cold fury when he unlocked the front door and charged into the house. And she wasn't here. It didn't compute.

Where could she be?

A slimy worm of suspicion began to gnaw on his mind. She wouldn't. No. Not Matilda. She wouldn't pull a dirty trick like that, would she?

He seized the telephone and dialed. One ring, two—

"Hello."

"Harris, you bastard, is my wife at your house?"

Silence. Then, "This is not the stray wives' shelter. If you've lost one, you might call Hayden Elkins and ask if he has her."

Hayden slammed down the phone. He was so furious he shook.

He mixed himself a drink, hoping the alcohol would calm his nerves. He got halfway through a Bloody Mary before he again wondered what had happened to Matilda.

Like many young men, Billy Joe Elkins carried a condom in his wallet. He had purchased it for seventy-five cents eighteen months ago from a vending machine in a service station restroom, one decorated with a cartoon-quality color picture of an extraordinarily endowed, naked young woman in the throes of sexual ecstasy.

The artwork didn't sell the condom. Nor was the price important—he would have willingly paid ten times that amount. That was merely the first opportunity he had to make the purchase. Teenage boys can't select a package of Trojans or French ticklers in the local supermarket and toss them on the conveyor belt at the checkout counter for the female clerk to ring up. Nor are there many drowsy drugstores still extant with a worldly-wise male druggist manning the counter and no female customers in sight. Not in America these days.

Of course, some of his friends just shoplifted their condoms, but Billy Joe's father was the prosecuting attorney, which made the faint possibility of being arrested for shoplifting a condom too hideous a fate to contemplate.

It was only after he had the condom that Billy Joe realized that he could have merely approached Junior Grimes, who would have filched one out of

Doolin's for him and slipped the money in the register. Some of his friends obtained their condoms this way. When he needed another—he fervently prayed that day wasn't far off—he intended to get it with Junior's help.

Ownership of a condom created its own set of problems. Where to keep it? After much deliberation he did as so many others had before him—he stowed the weapon in his wallet, which transformed the wallet into a glowing, radioactive time bomb that would blow up in his face if he was the least bit careless. One of his friends, Jimmy Druckett, had had the thing fall out of his wallet at a movie theater concession stand when he was fishing in there for a dollar. That was a freak accident, tragic but probably unavoidable. The greatest danger was a snooping mother. Joe Bean's mom found his when he left his wallet lying on his dresser while he showered. Mothers snoop: Any boy who didn't understand that verity and take proper precautions was about to have a very bad experience.

Mothers never understand the significance of the condom to their teenage sons. A boy didn't get a condom because he had a willing female lined up and ready. Oh, no. He got it because he was interested—obsessed—with sex and was trying to convince himself that if an opportunity ever presented itself, he could handle it.

Girls were obsessed with attractiveness. Could they get the right male interested? They studied magazine articles on makeup and hairstyles and fashion, listened to pop music about "love" and preened endlessly, instinctively seeking to acquire the tools necessary to attract that male. They constantly reassured one another—"you look so good, your hair is perfect for you, what a stunning outfit, I love your lipstick"—because they needed constant reassurance.

Boys, on the other hand, were concerned with performance. Fear of failure was the nightmare that haunted young men. The condom in the wallet was their tangible, perpetual assurance that when the moment came, they would succeed.

Tonight Billy Joe Elkins and Melanie Naroditsky were going to slay their dragons.

Melanie was waiting when Billy Joe came out of the locker room after the game. In Hayden's car she held his hand, fluffed his hair, batted her eyelashes and rubbed his leg as they drove along regaling each other with the adventures of the evening. She was still in her majorette outfit, a tight sweater and a tiny pleated skirt that showed off her figure and legs. Her cheeks glowed, her eyes flashed, two-hundred-proof life coursed through her veins.

Billy Joe got the message. Yes.

He drove through Canaan and turned off into the driveway of an abandoned farm he knew about. The headlights seemed out of place on the one-lane dirt track running through the forest, but the happy lovers were oblivious to the incongruity. Billy Joe parked in the weed-choked yard of the crumbling old house and turned off the engine and headlights. Melanie flowed into his arms.

Yes, yes, yes.

The petting got heavy quickly. Soon they were both moaning softly. After only a minute more, they were undressed and ready as only two healthy teenagers can be. That was when Billy Joe retrieved his wallet from the pocket of his trousers, which were now on the backseat of the car, and extracted the precious condom.

As Melanie panted, Billy Joe tried to open the foil packet. Strange as it may seem, gentle reader, he had never before been tempted to open the packet and examine the device that would vault him into manhood. After all, a rubber is a rubber. "Just peel that tire down over your tool and have at it," his friends had told him in one of those long-ago male info sessions.

Now, in the darkness, with Melanie ready and willing and hot enough to melt, he couldn't get the foil packet open. He tried to tear it with his fingernails and that didn't work. What if his frantic efforts damaged the condom? Desperate, he threw caution to the winds and used his teeth. The foil tore.

Now he had the thing in his hands. He felt it hurriedly to ensure it wasn't damaged, then placed it where it was supposed to go and tried to peel. His efforts got it rolled down about an inch. It would go no farther.

Damn!

"Oh, Billy," Melanie moaned. "I can't wait much longer."

"I'm trying, darling," he told her, his frustration growing exponentially. He just couldn't get the damned thing on. "I think I got it on upside down or inside out or some damn thing," he confessed to his lady love.

The car was dark as a tomb. Melanie was a practical girl. She used her fingers to examine the situation.

He was panting and Melanie was buck naked and bent over his male organ working on the condom when a brilliant light flashed.

The flash stunned and blinded Billy Joe, but he instinctively knew what it was. A camera!

"You two just hold that pose and let me get another." A male voice, from outside the car.

Melanie screamed.

The camera flashed again.

"You son of a bitch," Billy Joe roared. He disentangled himself from Melanie and jerked at the door handle. The dome light in the car came on as the door opened, then an irresistible force slammed the door shut against him.

"Whoa, there, stud. You stay inside while I look this situation over."

Billy Joe went limp. In the two seconds the dome light had been on, he had gotten a glimpse of uniform and badge. The law!

A flashlight came on. Melanie was sobbing and trying to cover herself. Tears welled up in Billy Joe's eyes as the beam played over his face, the top of her head, her bare arms and legs.

"Well, well, well, if this don't beat all. Billy Joe Elkins and the Naroditsky girl. Ol' Frank Naroditsky is going to have a cow when he hears about this."

Billy Joe recognized the voice.

Delmar Clay.

"Clay, you son of a—if you—"

"Don't start with the bad mouth, punk. You're the one who's bare-ass naked. Now I suggest you two get yourselves dressed, then drive on out of here."

"Those pictures—why'd you take those pictures?"

"I said get dressed, then get out of here. Unless you want to go to the sheriff's office and watch me call your parents. Maybe your dad will bring all his wives with him, Billy Joe, when he comes to take you home."

Clay laughed at his own wit and kept the flashlight beam on them as they dressed.

"I gotta admit, Billy Joe, that there is one prime piece of ass. She looks like she can really fuck. You'll get some of that one of these days, I'll bet. But not here. Not tonight."

Melanie was near hysteria. Billy Joe bit his lip, but still the tears leaked down his cheeks. He kept his face down so that Delmar Clay wouldn't see him cry.

When he had his pants and shirt on, he turned the key, gunned the engine, and pulled the automatic transmission into drive. The glow of the deputy's flashlight was lost behind them in the darkness as the car threaded its way into the trees.

When they reached the safety of the Canaan road, Melanie put her head in his lap. "There, there, darling," he murmured, stroking her hair and trying to comfort the distraught girl.

His embarrassment leaked from him quickly, leaving in its place a sublime tenderness toward Melanie and a profound sorrow that anyone would ever hurt her. The bitter rage he felt toward Delmar Clay, however, grew with every sob that racked Melanie's body.

Although he didn't realize it then, and probably never would, Billy Joe Elkins had just taken a giant step into manhood.

SIX

Just knowing the country had Crystal Ice in it made it look different somehow. Sam Neely drove along at forty miles per hour with his left elbow out the window, looking . . .

He was feeling terrific that Saturday morning when he stopped into Doolin's for breakfast. Three tables had people at them. He nodded at everyone and selected the table farthest from the door.

He was examining the menu when Junior Grimes came through the door. He stopped at every table. "Mrs. Davis, you're looking mighty fine this gorgeous morning, so you are. Hello, Mrs. Wilfred. I declare, I like that dress. And how are you, Frank . . . Bob . . . Harry . . ."

Junior pulled out a chair at Neely's table and sat down. "What are you into today, Sam?"

"Fighting crime."

"That's the ticket. It sure needs fought and I'm glad you're wearing the gloves, ready to wade in."

They were giving their orders to the waitress, whom Junior addressed as Alva, when Moses came out of the kitchen and joined them. "Cook didn't come in today. I'm in there doing the damage. Neely, better try the ham today. It looks almighty good."

Sam Neely ordered ham and eggs.

Moses didn't smile as much as Junior, but he was the type of man people instinctively trusted. If Moses said something was so, then that was the way it was. Several large firms paid him retainers as a consultant, and about once a month he received a telephone call from out of state, someone wanting advice. It was common knowledge that Arleigh Tate consulted him on political questions, and occasionally Judge Storm invited him to drop by the courthouse for a visit. In short, Moses Grimes was somebody.

This morning he kidded his son a little, then addressed Trooper Neely. "I hear the Barrow boys are getting out of prison."

"That's right," Neely replied. "Sheriff Tate mentioned it this morning. They'll be out in a few days. What were they in for, anyway?"

"Lester Storm sent them up for burning down some houses. But they've been into about ever' sort of meanness there is, stealing, trashing cars, getting drunk and shooting up Indian River, pounding people. They're two bad ones."

"Prison was the best place for them," Junior declared. "Someone is gonna shoot 'em one of these days. Three or four people were looking to do just that for burning houses when the law snagged them and sent them off. Lester Storm probably saved their lives, so he did."

"They'll never thank him," Moses said.

"Ain't got it in 'em," Junior agreed. "Damn fools got into me bad up in the junkyard. They love to go up there at night and strip cars."

"Maybe you should give them a job in the garage," Neely suggested. He was feeling mellow this morning and even had a little excess human kindness to spread around on trash like the Barrow boys. Of course, he had never met them.

Junior was all out of charity. "Then they'd have to do an honest day's work," he said sourly. "They've made it this far without ever breaking a sweat. I doubt they're in the mood to give it a try. And I'm not going to stand over them forty hours a week like a prison guard to make sure they don't steal nothin'."

At the schoolhouse Neely had a decision to make. Should he take the left fork or the right? The right fork toward Vegan, he decided after a tenth of a second's deliberation. Maybe wave at Crystal if she was out in the yard or garden.

Alas, Crystal was nowhere to be seen around the Ice palace. Oh, well, he and Crystal would cross paths again soon, and the day was gorgeous. The trees were donning their autumn colors, so the hills were a riot of yellow, orange, and every hue of red, all under a golden sun shining down from a deep blue sky.

Sam Neely whistled as he drove along with his left elbow out the window.

He knew when he arrived in Vegan because a road sign proclaimed the fact. The village sat on top of a low ridge, with an excellent view toward the distant Blue Mountains to the east. Vegan also had an abandoned one-room schoolhouse and, directly across the road, a dilapidated little church with a hasp and padlock on the door. Around the church were at least a hundred graves.

Neely parked the cruiser and walked through the cemetery looking at stones. He sat on the fence and surveyed the Blue Mountains and inhaled the spicy, cinnamony aroma of sweet shrubs. The shrubs around the church were full of bees. Their humming seemed almost a song, one with a lilting melody and a rich harmony.

A fellow could get used to this.

Here, he thought, in this place, with these people, he could be content. If Crystal . . .

"Don't put the cart in front of the steed, young fellow," he said aloud. "Better let life unfold one day at a time."

Vastly pleased with himself for being so wise, Neely strolled back to the police car and aimed it toward Goshen and Canaan.

After passing through Goshen, he stopped to watch a farmer mowing hay in a meadow that covered the top of the low, wide ridge. The tractor moved at a stately pace as the sun rose toward its zenith and the sweet scent of freshly cut grass enriched the breeze, which was noticeably stiff here on this ridge.

Neely leaned on a fence post and took it all in. There was paperwork awaiting him in the office, but it was Saturday and he wasn't in the mood. Monday would be soon enough. He sucked in lungfuls of the laden breeze and watched it ripple the tops of the tall grass.

After about five minutes the man on the tractor stopped it, killed the engine, and walked through the grass to the fence where Neely stood.

"Anything I can do for you this morning?"

"No, sir," Neely said. "I'm just enjoying a look at paradise. You won't charge for it, will you?"

The man chuckled and pulled a pipe from the pocket of his overalls. "If somebody charged for looking, I'd have been broke all my life."

They introduced themselves and were passing the time of day as the farmer puffed his pipe when a black sedan pulled to a stop behind the cruiser. A big, German-made car, Neely thought, the first one he had seen in the Eden country.

The driver was a short, pudgy fellow. He nodded at the trooper, then addressed the farmer on the other side of the fence. "Are you Jared Kane?"

"Yep."

"My name's Richard Hudson." He offered his hand. Neely also introduced himself.

"Moses Grimes said you might be available to do some plowing," Hudson told Jared Kane.

"Yessir. Charge by the hour. Got a garden you need turned over?"

Hudson's face flushed slightly. "Well, it's not much of a garden. Just a patch, really. I want you to turn it over and do another ten acres or so besides."

"Going to plant some corn next spring, are you?"

"Haven't thought that far ahead. No, Mr. Kane, I'm plowing for arrowheads. Found several in my garden and I'm hoping there are more of them." He pulled two from his pocket and passed them across. Neely scrutinized them carefully; he had never before held one in his hands. After a careful examination he returned the artifacts to Richard Hudson.

"Guess I ought to show you my lucky arrowhead," Jared Kane said, and

86

produced it from an inside pocket. "Found this when I was just a boy and carried it ever' day since."

The flint was leaf-shaped, about three inches long, delicately made, exquisite. Hudson and Neely oohed and aahed over it as the sun warmed their faces and the breeze played with their hair. Richard Hudson held it the longest. He returned it to its owner reluctantly.

"I once showed it to a professor of archaeology," Jared Kane told them. "He said it was at least five thousand years old. I take it out and look at it when life gets to bogging me down. Helps me keep things in perspective, so it does. Reminds me that I'm only here for a little while, just a visitor passing through."

"So it does," Richard Hudson echoed fervently.

The old car sat under a giant oak near the road. When Neely rounded the curve, there it was, not ten feet from the mailbox.

Sam Neely pulled the cruiser off the road and looked it over. Most of the glass was gone from the windows, large splotches of rust scarred the hood and fenders, and there were weeds up to the door handles. It was only after he looked for a bit that he realized the car was sitting on the ground. No wheels.

Beyond the car was a neatly mowed lawn, and beyond that a small, well-kept white house. The name on the mailbox was J. S. KLINE.

Neely backed the cruiser up, then turned into the driveway and parked.

The driveway led to a garage behind the house. A man was visible through the open door working at something on a bench. Neely stood in the doorway of the garage. The man at the bench never looked up.

"Good morning," Trooper Neely told the man's back.

"What do you want?"

"I'd like to talk to you a minute about that car out front, if I might. It's Mr. Kline, isn't it?"

"The car ain't for sale."

"I don't want to buy it."

Now the man turned around. If he was surprised to see a state trooper in uniform standing there, it didn't show on his face. "Junior Grimes send you?"

"Junior? No. He didn't."

"Humpf." The man turned back to the bench. He was sharpening a lawn mower blade with a file. He had the blade clamped in a vise and was working the file back and forth across the cutting edge.

Sam Neely took off his hat and looked around the garage, taking everything in. The place doubled as a workshop. Tools hung along every wall. Every tool had its own place.

He wished he hadn't stopped. He'd turned to go when the man said, "Say what you came to say."

"About the car." Neely twisted his hat in his hands. "It's an eyesore. Looks like it's been sitting there a lot of years. I'm sure your neighbors would be grateful if you'd junk it or at least haul it around back of the garage here, where everyone wouldn't have to look at it."

The man laid down the file and faced Neely. He was at least seventy, Neely realized with a start, perhaps older. "You looked that car over careful, have you?"

"Well, I saw that the windows were broken and the wheels missing."

"You a collector?"

"Ah, no."

"A car nut?"

"No. I was just thinking about the way it looks, rotting there by the road."

"That car is a 1967 Camaro Z-28, with the 302 engine and a Muncie gearbox. Chevy claimed 290 horsepower for that mill, but it made an honest hundred more than that. It's sort of rare. Chevy only made six hundred Z-28s in '67."

"Too bad nobody's taken care—"

"That one's got a grand total of twenty-eight miles on it. Ordered it for my boy and it arrived at the dealer in Indian River two weeks before he was due home. From Vietnam. I went down and paid for it, drove it home, washed it and waxed it and parked it out there under that tree. He never came home. It's been sitting there ever since."

"I see . . ."

"Was sitting on the porch looking at that car when they brought the telegram. On the twenty-third day of June, 1967, so it was. Said he was missing in action."

Sam Neely waited for the old man to say more, but he didn't.

"Long time ago," Neely finally said.

The old man didn't seem to hear. He stood looking through the open garage door at the trees bathed in sunlight. At last he said, almost to himself, "It was foggy that morning. Then the fog burned off and the sun came out. That evening it clouded up and rained."

He took a deep breath, then glanced at Neely. "He had a girlfriend waiting for him. She waited a year or so, then started seeing another guy. Married him. Lives up near Detroit, I hear, has three or four kids."

After a bit he added, "Her kids must be grown by now, with children of their own."

Neely nodded and looked at his feet. Why on earth did he stop? He was going to have to learn to keep his nose out of other people's lives.

"His mom didn't want me to buy that car," J. S. Kline continued, speaking slowly, remembering. "Said it was too much. Said we couldn't afford it. Said it wasn't *right*."

"Well, I don't think there's anything wrong with—"

"She died about ten years ago. Don't think she ever got over not knowing. Wondering. If he was alive or dead or a prisoner or tortured or starved or crippled or out of his mind. Toward the end there she went out of hers."

Sam Neely kept his mouth shut and stood rooted.

"I ain't selling that car. I ain't gonna junk it and I ain't moving it. Not a goddamn solitary inch. It's gonna sit right there until that boy comes home or they put me in the ground."

"I'm sorry."

J. S. Kline turned back to the blade in the vise. He bent down to examine it. Over his shoulder he said, "It was in pretty good shape until one night a couple of years ago when the Barrow boys stopped by. They stole the wheels because they're thieves and smashed out the windows because they're mean bastards."

Sam Neely settled his hat on his head at the angle specified by state police regulations and took several steps toward the large open door.

Kline straightened and pinned Neely with his gaze. "I hear they're getting out of prison. You tell 'em for me, if you see 'em. If I ever see 'em within fifty feet of that car I'll kill 'em. Both of 'em. Keep a loaded rifle right there in the house for that very purpose."

"It's against the law to—" Neely began, then bit his lip.

J. S. Kline looked him straight in the eye. "I shoot 'em, I'll call you. Don't worry. You'll be the first to hear."

Elijah Murphy walked slowly up the dirt road that led to his shack at the top of the hollow. Delmar Clay had brought him out from town and stopped at the turnoff from the hard road. "You can walk from here," the deputy said. "Exercise will do you good."

Murphy got out of the car without a word. He wouldn't ask a favor of Delmar Clay if he were dying of thirst.

He was perilously close to that condition just now. Fortunately he had half a bottle of whiskey stashed under the bed at home, and that would take the edge off. And there was a six-pack of beer in the refrigerator. If he hadn't drunk it. He tried to remember.

The problem with being a drunk was that half your life was a daze that you couldn't remember in the other half. Or maybe that was the advantage.

As he hiked up the road Elijah Murphy thought about being a drunk. He had been one for a lot of years.

It would be nice if he had an excuse, some sort of traumatic experience that he could use to justify his addiction to the bottle—maybe a woman who betrayed him or a fortune squandered or great ambitions turned to ashes, something along those lines. Alas, Elijah Murphy had no colorful failures in his past. There had been no great loves, no squandered fortunes large or small, no ambitions, burning or otherwise. He was a humble man who had always lived pretty far down. His life had been hard, dreary work, long nights, and the bottle.

He thought about that past now, about his old man, who had been a first-class worthless son of a bitch, and about his mother, who died when he was thirteen. He hadn't seen the old man in forty years, at least. No doubt he was dead, and good riddance. Come to think of it, he couldn't even remember what he had looked like.

No, Elijah Murphy admitted to himself now, he was a drunk because he enjoyed it.

Ol' Judge Storm, now there was a character! Saying the widow Wilfred might have some romantic notions about him, Elijah Murphy. Why, it was laughable. Widow Wilfred?

Not that she wasn't a fair figure of a woman. She was no spring chicken, of course, but she wasn't all that bad. Mature, fiftyish, pleasant face, always dressed nice and neat, probably a good cook when she took the notion . . . and armed with a tongue sharp enough to shave with. But all women have sharp tongues. Elijah Murphy had never met one who lacked a whetted appendage.

Widow Wilfred gave him a hard time because he irritated her. And he irritated her because he enjoyed seeing her irritated. That was the truth of it, he acknowledged to himself as he rounded the turn in the road and his shack came into view. Two steps farther on he saw the widow Wilfred's house, a hundred feet from his. She wasn't in sight, and her car wasn't there.

He trudged up the path to his place, crossed the porch and opened the door. The door wasn't locked. There was a lock on the door, all right, but if there had ever been a key Murphy had lost it years and years ago.

Once inside he headed straight for the bedroom. Got down on his hands and knees and reached under the bed. There were enough dust balls under there to decorate Oklahoma, but no bottle.

Murphy lowered his head to the floor and looked. No bottle.

Damn.

Did he drink it?

He got into a sitting position and tried to remember.

That whiskey bottle was under that bed the afternoon Trooper Tutwiler took him to jail; he was sure of it. And it was at least half full.

Well, it wasn't there now. That was a fact.

The beer.

He went to the corner of the main room with the sink and refrigerator. Flies hovered over the sinkful of dirty dishes. Murphy ignored the flies and opened the fridge.

No beer.

He closed the door and closed his eyes. He stood there swaying, breathing deeply, in and out, in and out . . . Then he opened the door again.

Still no beer.

He slammed the door and wandered out onto the porch and sat heavily on the edge.

Saturday morning and he was sober as a judge. Sober as Lester Storm. Probably more sober. Lester kept a bottle in his desk that he could nip on from time to time, whenever he got a little dry. Of course, the judge never suffered from the raging thirsts that afflicted Elijah Murphy.

Murphy sat on his porch racked by sobriety as the sun climbed to the zenith and thought about the injustice of it all, how fellows who didn't get thirsty but once a week had access to oceans of whiskey and fellows who were so desiccated they were in danger of blowing away didn't have a solitary drop to dampen their tonsils.

Finally his gaze came to rest on the widow Wilfred's little white cottage. Wilfred . . .

Was it possible? Had she been over here? Could she have taken the whiskey and beer? Not to drink—the very idea was ludicrous—but to deprive him of it?

Naw.

Yet the notion didn't go away. Lester Storm was nobody's fool, Murphy reminded himself.

The judge had planted a seed in Elijah Murphy's mind. Now that seed germinated and began to grow.

Matilda Elkins came downstairs with the brunch tray that Mrs. Carcano had taken to her room about ten. "Mrs. Carcano, I don't know how to thank you." She headed straight for the kitchen with the tray, her host following behind. She wanted to wash the dishes, but her host wouldn't let her.

"All that talking we did last night, and I never learned your Christian name."

"It's Cecile." The minister poured coffee, and the two women sat at the kitchen table to drink it. The sun shining through the window made a bright square on the floor.

"The temperature fell to thirty last night," Cecile said after a while. "We'll have another frost tonight."

"Cool nights, foggy mornings, sunny days with the leaves turning, this is the most beautiful time of the year," Matilda said wistfully. "I am wasting it fretting over this mess."

"How do you feel this morning?"

"Much better. I guess I really needed to talk to a woman about my troubles."

"Occasionally we all need someone to listen," Cecile Carcano murmured.

"You didn't judge me. I appreciate that."

Mrs. Carcano sipped her coffee and remained silent. She was a good listener, which is a rare quality in any age.

"I hope you like living here in Eden," Matilda said.

"I'm sure I will."

"A fine welcome I offered you." Her lips twisted sourly.

"Will you be offended if I offer some advice, Matilda? I learned long ago that the most worthless commodity on earth is an opinion about how someone else should handle their problems or live their life. Having been the recipient of too many unwelcome gifts of that sort, I try to refrain from bestowing them upon others. Alas, I am human, so occasionally one bubbles up and begs to be voiced."

"Please do."

"I think you should stop blaming yourself for the situation you find yourself in. Nor is it productive to blame your husband or Anne Harris."

"That's it?" Matilda asked incredulously. "All that buildup for that little thought?"

"That's it," she was assured.

Matilda Elkins patted the other woman's hand. "Cecile, you are a rare treasure. One way or the other I will survive this, and I hope that then I can be your friend."

"You already are."

"I made a decision this morning. Up in your guest room. I want you to be the first to hear it." Matilda finished the last of her coffee, then continued. "I'm going to let Hayden and Anne stew in their own juices. I am going to do as you so wisely suggested—stop blaming myself—and let them wrestle with an impossible situation created by their own foolishness. The mess is their fault. Whether I blame them or not, they created it. They are going to have to clean it up."

Junior Grimes was removing a transmission from a wrecked pickup that Saturday afternoon when Billy Joe Elkins found him. Junior's friend Arch Stehlik was sitting on a nearby fender nursing a beer and lending a hand when something needed to be held.

Of course, Billy Joe had visited the junkyard many times before. Here in the splendid isolation of Junior's junkyard on a low ridge above Eden, the intricacies of the human dilemma could be discussed man to man, free from inhibitions created by the presence of women.

For women rarely came here, and when they did, they didn't stay long. The hundreds of junk cars tastefully arranged around a mountain of worn-out tires in this garden of weeds seemed to create angst in feminine hearts. Or maybe it was the numerous snakes that inhabited the place. Whatever, here teenage boys could drink beer and smoke cigarettes and talk dirty and tell lies about their sexual exploits free from the possibility of being spied upon by members of the opposite sex. For some reason most males needed places like this, and in modern America they were getting harder and harder to find.

"Whatcha doin'?" Arch asked Billy Joe as he settled onto a nearby fender.

"Oh, nothing much," Billy Joe replied.

Junior poked his head out from under the pickup to see who Arch was talking to. "Hey, Billy Joe. Whatcha doin'?"

"Nothing much. What are you doin'?"

"Nothing much, and that's a fact. Hey, Arch, how about holding this wheel here for a second while I pull these bolts."

Arch Stehlik winked at Billy Joe and climbed down off his fender. He flipped away his cigarette and handed Billy Joe his can of beer. Billy Joe took a swig.

As usual, Arch looked dirty. He did small logging jobs for a living and apparently every stitch he owned was hopelessly impregnated with oil, grease, and dirt, for Billy Joe had never seen him in clean clothes. His hands were always grimy, too. His hair was long and unkempt and he wore an equally well groomed beard. When he ate at Doolin's, as he often did, the occasional tourist usually looked at Arch with misgivings and tried to stay out of his space. One day a year or two ago it had dawned on Billy Joe that Arch probably enjoyed their reactions.

"Lift up a little more, Arch."

"Takes two experts for these delicate operations."

"Seen this one on *General Hospital.*"

"That's what we are, a couple of brain surgeons."

"You did real good in that game last night, Billy Joe," Junior said from under the wrecked pickup. "That last pass downfield was as good as I ever seen anyone throw a ball, and I mean that."

"That was a hell of a fine throw," Arch agreed. "Right on the money. And the Blankenship boy caught the ball, too. Usually he drops the long ones that come right at his numbers, so he does."

"Seems like if the ball goes over ten yards in the air he has too much time to think about it," Junior said, his voice slightly muffled.

Billy Joe laughed. Yeah, it was sure good to sit here in the junkyard with Junior and Arch. They always knew the score.

Out of the corner of his eye he saw something brown, something that moved. A doe. She came ambling toward them, stopped once to look them over, then came up to Billy Joe and sniffed his hand. Flecks of orange paint were visible on the ends of the hairs on her flanks, but other than that, she was a big, healthy doe in the prime of life.

"Junior, Mary is here and wants a treat."

"There's a couple of Snickers bars in the cab of my roll-back," Junior said from under the pickup. "Give her one."

Billy Joe unwrapped a candy bar as the doe stamped her feet and twitched her tail. He fed it to her bite by bite and rubbed her big soft ears as she chewed.

"She's looking real good, Junior."

"Mary's my sweetheart," Junior declared. Arch grinned at Billy Joe.

One spring night several years ago when Junior and Arch were running the roads, a doe had jumped in front of Junior's pickup. The pregnant doe was eviscerated by the impact. As a devastated Junior bawled like a baby, Arch freed the unborn fawn from its birth sac and blew air into its nostrils. Fed milk from a bottle and cared for like a human baby, the fawn survived. And thrived. And developed a taste for candy bars.

Due to the unusual method of its arrival—"an immaculate reception," Junior called it, although the birth had been a bloody mess—when he was pondering names he wanted something biblical. Alas, his knowledge of the Bible was confined to a few poorly remembered, garbled stories from Sunday school. He settled on the name Mary.

When Mary was grown, Lula Grimes insisted she go to the junkyard. The deer liked candy and made a royal commotion in the store every time she managed to get in, which she did on a fairly regular basis. When an unsuspecting person opened the door, she would dart inside, charge straight for the candy display and gobble candy, wrappers and all, as humans fluttered and tittered nervously, unsure of just what to do, until Lula arrived to shoo the deer out.

The flecks of orange paint were the remnants of last fall's racing stripe. Afraid someone would shoot the doe, which had no fear of humans, Junior painted an orange stripe completely around her body parallel to the ground.

"You're going to have to freshen up this racing stripe," Billy Joe said as Mary munched candy.

"Yeah. Gonna get to that pretty soon."

Billy Joe petted the deer and the men talked about football while Junior finished the transmission. Billy Joe helped them inch it from under the pickup and put it on Junior's roll-back. Then Junior produced more beer from a cooler in his truck cab. After checking for snakes, they found places to sit. Mary accepted a good petting from each of them, then wandered off.

At an appropriate place in the conversation, when they were ready for another subject, Billy Joe got around to the reason he came looking for Junior. "I had a little problem last night after the game," he began.

"Oh," said Junior.

"Huh," said Arch.

"Me and my girlfriend, Melanie Naroditsky, were parked up on the Canaan road and engaged in a little romance."

"Getting some, were you?"

"Trying to. Then ol' Delmar Clay came sneaking along."

"That Delmar . . ."

"The son of a bitch sneaked up on us. We were heavily engaged when all of a sudden camera flashes started going off. He said, 'Hold that pose,' and took a couple of pictures."

"I'll be damned," Junior said. "Never heard of anything like that. Delmar drives up on people all the time at night and runs them off, like it was illegal to get laid, but I never heard of him taking pictures before."

"Junior, he really embarrassed Melanie. Made her cry. Shamed her. It was a damned mean thing he did."

"That it was," Arch agreed.

"That isn't the worst part. He recognized Melanie. Said something to the effect that her dad would have a cow when he heard about this. And he had just taken pictures. So she's scared to death that he will send the photos to her father."

"He won't," Junior said. "He knows better than that."

"You think?"

"Delmar hasn't got the guts. I know Frank Noroditsky. He'd be ticked at Melanie, all right, but when he heard the whole story he'd go after Delmar Clay with his fists. Beat him within an inch of his life. Maybe kill him."

"So he would," Arch muttered.

"I don't want him to find out about it," Billy Joe said fervently.

"Don't sweat it. Neither does Delmar. He wants to keep living."

"So what do you think he'll do with those pictures?" Billy Joe asked.

"I'll tell you what I think," Arch said. "I think the bastard will have them developed and look at them and not show them to a soul. If he shows them around, Frank will hear about it eventually, and then Delmar won't be able to run far enough or fast enough."

"Forget the pictures," Junior said, nodding his agreement.

"Tell Melanie she has nothing to worry about," Arch advised. " 'Course, that won't do much good, but it's about all you can do."

After a bit Billy Joe said, "Boy, I'd sure like to get even with Delmar Clay. Lay one on him."

"You aren't the only one," Junior said. "He doesn't have a friend alive."

"Except his wife," Arch noted.

"Can't figure her," Junior mused. "What does a nice girl like her see in Delmar?"

"There's no telling about women," Arch declared. "For some reason the girl must have figured she couldn't do no better. Maybe one of those inferiority complexes. There's just no way of knowing."

"Arleigh Tate told Dad that the only reason Delmar's a deputy is politics," Junior told his friends. He explained the voting power of Mrs. Clay's relatives.

"Still, there must be a way to teach Delmar a lesson," Billy Joe insisted.

"Let's think on it," Junior advised. "Maybe me and Arch can come up with something."

Billy Joe left a half hour later. Arch and Junior helped themselves to another beer. As they sipped, Junior lay back in the weeds and stared at his mountain of old tires.

"I gotta get rid of those tires, Arch. Near as I can figure, I got eight thousand of the damn things. I'm running out of room and a fellow from the environmental has been sniffin' around askin' questions."

"Haul 'em to the landfill."

"I tried that. Loaded up a truck and hauled 'em down there, but they wouldn't let me dump 'em. Said they didn't want me filling up their landfill with old tires."

"Eight thousand tires. That's a lot."

"That it is."

"I hear there's companies now that melt them things down and make rubbers out of 'em, or some such. Why don't you call one of them outfits?"

"Going to. On Monday. I saw a couple ads in a mechanic's magazine and wrote down the phone numbers. I gotta get rid of them tires before the environmentals haul me into court."

"Who'd have ever thought that tires would be a problem?"

"Well, I never did!" Junior stated emphatically. "I've been taking them off cars for years. Been lettin' people come up here and just throw 'em on the pile. Been picking 'em up outta cricks and offa hillsides whenever I see 'em and hauling 'em up here. Never charged anybody a nickel, and now the gover'ment is after me. Don't seem fair, so it don't."

"Life never is," Arch told him.

They were each working on their fourth beer when Junior asked Arch, "Where do you think Delmar will get those pictures developed?"

"He ain't got a lot of choices. There's Doolin's——"

"We send 'em away. And any tit shots would be commented upon by the developer people, and my mom would raise holy hell. Remember Tom Saperstein? Took an artsy shot of his ol' lady buck naked and Mom told him he ought to be ashamed. Told him to get his dirty pictures developed someplace else."

"The food stores in Indian River send them to the same lab your mom uses," Arch continued. "I know the guy who drives their pickup and delivery route around here."

"That's right."

"But Benny Modesso at the Indian River Drugstore offers two-day service. I think he sends film to a custom lab in Capitol City. 'Course, he costs more."

"Benny Modesso . . . ," Junior mused, and reached for another beer.

SEVEN

On Sunday morning the sun rising over the Blue Mountains made the frost glisten on the blades of grass and leaves. The sunlight made the white crystals sparkle like diamonds and worked a magical transformation—the frost turned to heavy dew everywhere the sunlight touched it. The long shadows protected patches of white crystals for a few more moments.

Cecile Carcano walked slowly through the frost, feeling it crunch ever so slightly under her boots, pausing occasionally and looking back at her tracks. She climbed the low hill behind her house and stood in the old apple orchard watching the sun work its magic.

Another perfect morning. At Doolin's they assured her that nature had arranged this fantastic weather to welcome her. It wasn't true, of course. The foggy mornings and afternoon thunderstorms of summer were over, and the autumn rains would soon come. In a few weeks drenching rains would pound the last of the leaves from the trees and saturate the earth for the coming winter. That was the cycle, as old as the planet.

"Savor the Days." That was the title of this morning's sermon, her first as the new minister of the Eden Chapel. And of course, Cecile Carcano had a slight touch of nerves.

She had originally intended to deliver her best sermon, a tautly written little masterpiece about man's relationship with God that she had slaved on for months at divinity school. The professor gave her an A+ on it.

The Reverend Mr. Davis, the retiring minister, had assured her all would go well her first Sunday. He avoided commenting upon her sermon and merely bestowed a variety of platitudes and comforting words, which did nothing to quiet her anxiety.

Moses Grimes, one of the trustees, had been thoughtful when she talked to him earlier in the week. "They'll be looking you over," he admitted. "They want to see what kind of minister you're going to be. If you use the pulpit to advance your social concerns, you won't make it here."

"I have social concerns, Mr. Grimes. I care about people. That is one reason I became a minister."

"I understand. But the pulpit is not the place to tell people how to vote or what they should want their congressman to do. These people come to church to hear the word, to sing the old songs, to spend a few moments in the graveyard with their folks who've gone on before them." Moses Grimes searched for what he wanted to say. "For these folks, church is a link with the past."

"And a covenant with the future," Mrs. Carcano said softly.

She solicited advice from another member of the board, Verlin Ice, when he stopped by on Saturday afternoon. He sat in her porch swing and spit tobacco juice over the rail. If Cecile Carcano was appalled, she didn't show it.

"I'm not a preacher, never had the itch," Verlin Ice told her. "Don't know the first thing they teach in preacher school. But I've listened to preachers in these little churches all my life. I suggest you give 'em the word and let them figure out how to apply it. Don't preach down to 'em. If you preach politics, you're going to find the pews mighty empty after a few Sundays. That's my advice, for what it's worth."

"Thank you, Mr. Ice," Cecile said.

"One other thing. Occasionally ol' Davis would bring in some visiting divine who would thunder about hellfire and eternal damnation, the wages of sin. Those services were always poorly attended. Were I the preacher, I'd avoid racy descriptions of the fires of hell. Never met a preacher yet who claimed he'd been there."

"I'm not an evangelical."

"These Eden people sort of suspect hell looks a lot like New York City and Washington, D.C.," Verlin added, which made Cecile smile.

A little later he commented, "This congregation is yours to win, Mrs. Carcano. I believe you can do it or I wouldn't have voted to invite you here."

The trustees of the Eden Chapel had been remarkably unconcerned about matters theological, and for that Cecile was thankful. She suspected God didn't pay much attention to theology, either. Had she been asked, she would have stated that theology was the invention of professional Christians in musty offices filled with musty books who had little else to think about between Sundays. God created all living things, but man created dogmas and doctrines that threatened to fossilize organized religion. She had stated this opinion when interviewed for an associate minister's position at a large suburban church near Boston and had been politely shown the door.

God had brought her here instead, to Eden, given her this flock.

This morning in the orchard she gave thanks, asked for strength and wisdom, and walked back down the hill with the gentle rays of the morning sun caressing her face.

"You'll do fine, Mom," Jeanine Carcano told her mother as they walked the half mile to church.

When they came out of the house they automatically headed for the car. Cecile had the driver's door opened before she realized this wasn't the way she wanted to travel to *her* new church. "Let's walk," she suggested to her daughter, who was agreeable.

Now, walking along the road with the wind in the autumn leaves above their heads, Jeanine sensed her mother's tension and reassured her.

"Thank you," Cecile said. "But no matter what the congregation thinks, I hope you like the sermon."

"I'm sure I will," Jeanine said loyally. "But I wish Daddy were here this morning to hear it, too."

"Dearest, your father will be with us today."

"Like God?"

"Yes. I can feel God's presence and your father's. He loved us very much, and love abides forever."

"Yes," Jeanine agreed, "but I wish he were physically here. Walking beside us."

"So do I."

"Do you think you'll ever marry again, Mom?"

"I don't know, Jeanine. Perhaps if the right man comes along. We'll have to wait to see if that ever happens."

They rounded the corner and saw the church nestled under the giant maples flaming red in the morning sun. And they saw the crowd. Cars parked along both sides of the road, people filling the churchyard—the place was packed.

"Oh, wow," Jeanine said. "This is going to be like Easter."

As the small choir sang in the moments before the service, Cecile Carcano remembered that comment. When she got up to welcome the congregation, she told them about it. Gentle, warm laughter reached up to surround and envelop her.

After the service Lula Grimes paused at the door to visit. "You did well, Mrs. Carcano. I'm going to look forward to Sunday mornings."

"Thank you. By the way, I've been meaning to ask you: I noticed that there are three little girls buried in one corner of the graveyard, all named Grimes. Are you related?"

"They're my daughters. All stillborn. Something about positive and negative blood. I didn't think God wanted me to have any babies, then Junior was born alive."

"That must have been a difficult time."

"Junior sure was difficult, but sometimes I miss the girls something terrible. I never really had them, and yet I did. If I could just reach out and grab what might have been . . ."

Verlin and Minnie Ice came out of the chapel together. Both were dressed in their Sunday best, which in Verlin's case included a wide tie of the kind that went out of fashion twenty years ago. "You did fine, Reverend," he said. "I do believe I might have taken to spreading the gospel if I had had just one sermon like that in me." His eyes twinkled as a hint of a smile crossed his weathered brown face.

Minnie seemed the female version of Verlin, slightly smaller, same weathered face, work-hardened hands. "You'll bring new life to this church and this community," she told Cecile. "You did very well. I never thought I would see the day that a woman would be in that pulpit—and the men would *like* it."

Reverend Davis, Mrs. Davis, and the widow Wilfred came out together. The women fluttered and the retired preacher beamed. "The Eden Chapel is in good hands," he declared to everyone within earshot.

One of the last people to leave the church was Trooper Sam Neely, in civilian clothes. He murmured his "well done" to Mrs. Carcano, then lingered until everyone else was heading for the car, visiting graves in the cemetery, or chatting with each other under the giant maples. "Mrs. Carcano, I met someone yesterday who I think might enjoy a visit from you. I don't know how busy you are or if he even belongs to this church."

"I'm sure I could find time to call, Mr. Neely."

"His name is J. S. Kline. He lives near Canaan."

"I'll find him. Thanks for suggesting it."

A family came over and pressed a cold-chicken box lunch on Mrs. Carcano, so Sam Neely drifted away even though he hadn't told the minister why she should see Mr. Kline.

Then he smiled. Cecile Carcano didn't need any explanations. Of that he was sure. As he walked to his car he was whistling.

Sunday morning Elijah Murphy took a bath and shaved. Bathing was a lot of work since his shack lacked running water. He had to carry the water

105

from the well and heat it on the woodstove, then pour it into a washtub on his back porch. Keeping the fire stoked, carrying the water, adjusting the temperature—it was so much work that he rarely got around to it when he was drinking. This Sunday bath was even more startling since he had a bath just three days ago while he was in jail. Still, he decided this morning to do it anyway. With the tub full of water, he stripped off his clothes and lowered himself into it.

Shaving usually involved heating a pan of water on the stove—a lot less effort than a bath but a lot of work nonetheless—so he normally accomplished that chore only once or twice a month. Today, since he was in the tub half submerged in hot water, he arranged a mirror against a table leg and scraped on the whiskers.

Clean as a new penny, wearing underwear that he had laundered last night and dried on the porch rail, he went hunting his old toothbrush. He found it in the kitchen cupboard. He didn't look for toothpaste since he knew beyond a shadow of a doubt he didn't have any. However, he did have some baking soda, so he poured a dab on his toothbrush and scrubbed at his teeth.

He had one clean shirt left in the closet, the last survivor of his spring laundry day. No tie—he didn't own one. He combed his hair, then brushed out the old blue suit he had acquired years ago at an estate sale and put it on. He finished the job by rubbing his leather boots with a rag to get off the worst of the dirt and give them a bit of a buff.

Then Elijah Murphy sat in the rocking chair on the front porch and treated himself to a cigarette. The tobacco in the pouch was pretty dry, but he resolved to smoke it anyway. His hands still shook a little, but not too bad. He got the tobacco onto the paper and the cigarette rolled and sealed without spilling more than two or three small crumbs.

He rarely got a cigarette because he was usually too drunk to roll one and there was no way he was going to squander his drinking money on store-bought weeds. He was philosophical about it. The fact that he couldn't smoke drunk was probably the reason his shack hadn't burned down.

On this happy thought he went into the house for a kitchen match to light his smoke.

He had been sober for ten days; ten long, long days. He had conveniently forgotten the drink the judge gave him.

He tried to remember how many years it had been since he had spent ten days cold sober. Well, it had been eleven years. Eleven years and four months, to be exact. The occasion had been three weeks in the county jail. He positively recalled that he had done that stretch in April, but he was a little hazy about the year. No. It had been twelve years and four months since he did that dry three weeks. Normally Judge Storm only gave him two or three days in the can: Storm was always worried about the county's jail budget.

He could use a drink right now. Damn, would he like a drink!

But he wasn't going to go to Doolin's to buy a case of beer. No, sir. He wasn't. Not this morning. He was going to sit here until the widow Wilfred came home from church, then he was going to call. Going to see what's what.

That wasn't to say he wasn't going to fire up his old pickup and motor to Doolin's this afternoon. He didn't know. He was honest enough to admit that he was taking this sobriety experiment a minute at a time. Sitting on the porch puffing his cigarette and watching the breeze play with the treetops, he tried to think about something besides beer and whiskey.

His eyes finally came to rest on the mounds of junk and trash strewn all over his yard. He had what—four old cars? And an eclectic variety of engines and large major appliances, parts from bulldozers and sewing machines and hay bailers and Lord knows what all. Whenever he was working and someone wanted to get rid of some junk he always took it, brought it here and dumped it in the yard. The junk had been converted into a small stream of whiskey through the years—an old starter here, a few odd bolts there, that kind of thing. Fellows would bring a bottle, and Elijah Murphy would sit on his porch and drain it while they mined his junk.

I should do something about this mess, like clean it up.

That was a crazy thought, and the very fact that it just went flashing through his head startled him. He was really sober.

Elijah Murphy knew that he only got these weird urges when he was tombstone sober, without the slightest amount of alcohol anywhere in his system. Urges to move, to be doing something, to get *things* accomplished.

Of course, he tried to fight the urges. The fact is, all work is useless, like washing clothes. It really doesn't matter; the world keeps turning whether you get the work accomplished or not, whether your shirt is dirty or clean.

He finished the cigarette and carefully stubbed out the butt.

Where was that woman? He had heard a car come up to her house this morning, then leave, while he was building a fire in the stove. No doubt she had gone to church with someone.

The sun climbed higher and higher. The sitting was very difficult.

Murphy desperately wanted to do something, anything, but he knew just about anything he attempted would get himself and the suit dirty and ruin this morning's efforts, so he made himself sit through sheer force of will.

After a while he rolled another cigarette. He had it half smoked when he heard a car laboring up the grade.

He recognized the car when it came into view. Preacher Davis bringing the widow home. Thank heavens Mr. and Mrs. Davis merely stopped in the front to let her out. She waved good-bye as the car turned, then went inside as it drove away down the road.

Murphy gave her fifteen minutes, then went inside and brushed his suit again. He checked his reflection in the piece of mirror near the washstand. He was no youngster, that was for certain, but he was clean and polished enough for a funeral.

He went out on the porch, squared his shoulders and adjusted his suit coat, then went down the stairs, threaded his way through the junk and headed across the field.

The widow Wilfred answered the door the second time he knocked.

"Why, Mr. Murphy," she finally exclaimed after she spent several seconds in silent amazement taking in the clean, shaved, obviously sober man who stood before her. "How nice of you to drop by."

"Morning, Miz Wilfred. Just thought I'd drop by and pass a few minutes."

"Please come in." She held the door open. He stood inside the house looking around. He hadn't been inside in years, not since before old man Wilfred was killed. Lordy, that had been ten, twelve years ago. Wilfred had worked in the woods and was crushed when a big oak log rolled off a truck.

The place was neat and clean as an operating room. And well lit. Little knickknacks stuck here and there, a photo of old Wilfred on the mantel . . . white lacy things on the stands and table . . .

"Will you sit a few minutes, Mr. Murphy? I'm making coffee."

Elijah Murphy eased himself into a straight-backed cane chair near the door.

"Oh, no, Mr. Murphy. Try this one. This is the best chair." His hostess indicated the big, overstuffed easy chair facing the fireplace, then fluttered off to the kitchen.

By God, Lester Storm was right! Here he was, Elijah Murphy, bold as Monday, sitting in the widow Wilfred's parlor while she made coffee like he was the new preacher come to call.

"We were down at the Eden Chapel, Mr. Murphy," she called from the kitchen. "This was the new lady preacher's first Sunday. The Reverend Carcano. She gave a wonderful sermon. She even impressed Reverend Davis."

"A lady preacher!" Elijah Murphy replied loudly from the depths of the overstuffed chair. "I do declare!"

In a minute or two she bustled from the kitchen carrying a tray with two cups of coffee on it, a sugar bowl, and a little ivory creamer. Elijah Murphy reminded himself not to spill any. Thank goodness his hands were not shaking much. The worst of the DTs were over. He grasped the saucer with both hands and put it on his knees. Then he spooned some sugar and poured a little cream into the cup.

Didn't spill anything.

When the widow had doctored her coffee and was seated opposite him in another overstuffed chair, Elijah Murphy took an experimental sip.

"Miz Wilfred, this is the best coffee I ever drank, so it is."

"Why, Mr. Murphy, how kind of you to say so."

They sipped coffee, visited pleasantly about the weather, and Mrs. Wilfred told him all about the church service he had missed. She never hinted at the recent unpleasantness that had passed between them and resulted in Murphy's extended stay at the county facilities. Fifteen minutes just flew by.

Murphy carefully put the cup and saucer back on the tray and stood. "Miz Wilfred, this has been very pleasant."

"Must you go?"

"I think I'd better." He paused at the door. "Miz Wilfred, I'm going to try to be a better neighbor from now on. Can't make any promises, but I'm going to do my best."

"That's the best news I've heard in a long time, Mr. Murphy. You look to me to be the kind of man who can do a thing when he sets his mind to it."

"We'll see how it goes, Miz Wilfred, so we will."

He was off the porch and crossing the yard when she called, "Mr. Murphy? Will you come to dinner tomorrow night? I thought I might cook a roast."

He turned and stood for several seconds looking at his neighbor framed in her doorway. She *was* a fine woman, without a doubt. "Thank you, Miz Wilfred. I'll be delighted. See you then."

"Thanks for stopping by, Mr. Murphy."

He lifted a hand, then turned and walked around the hill toward his shack. As he approached it he surveyed his junk collection. He couldn't do anything about that today, but he needed something to do. Well, the woodpile had shrunk to almost nothing and fall was here. He could change clothes, then chop some wood. That would raise a sweat and keep his mind off drinking.

"Mother!"

Anne Harris was sitting on a wooden bench near a stream behind the Elkins house when she heard the call. Her daughter's voice. Ruth.

"Back here, Ruth."

"Mrs. Elkins said she thought you were out here."

"How are you?"

Ruth was twenty, of medium height, with her father's eyes and facial features. The resemblance leaped at Anne as she looked at her daughter with the sun highlighting her cheekbones.

"Checking up on my parents. When are you going home?"

"I don't know." Anne shrugged. "Perhaps I won't. I just . . . don't know."

"Oh, Mother! I never believed this could happen to you and Dad, of all people. I thought you two loved each other more than any other couple on this earth."

Anne didn't know what to say.

Ruth sat on the ground near her mother. After a while she asked, "Are you and Dad going to get a divorce?"

"I don't know." Anne thought that answer a trifle curt, so she added, "We'll just have to wait and see."

Ruth stood, dusted off her fanny, then leaned back against a tree trunk facing her mother. "Wait for what?"

"Wait."

"I can't believe you were in bed with Hayden Elkins."

"What do you find unbelievable? That I was in bed with him, or that your father caught us?"

Ruth ran a hand through her hair. "Both, I guess." When her mother didn't reply immediately, she added, "Hayden Elkins, of all people. It's so tacky."

"Perhaps I should have chosen Junior Grimes?"

"Give me a break! I didn't drive over here from State to listen to nonsense."

"Why did you come?"

"To find out what is going on. Mom, why didn't you call me and tell me you were having trouble with Dad? Your marriage was so solid."

Anne Harris pursed her lips thoughtfully. "Every marriage has its ups and downs."

"Mom! Adultery with Dad's best friend is a little more serious than leaving the cap off the toothpaste. Why don't you treat me like an adult and discuss this frankly, woman to woman?"

"I don't know."

Sensing she had a momentary advantage, Ruth attacked. "If it's menopause, you could have discussed it with me. And with Dad. Every woman has to go through it. It's certainly nothing—"

"I am not going through menopause."

"Dad must have done something wrong. What?"

"Ruth, I don't know why I did it. It seemed like a good idea at the moment. I don't know that I will ever figure out why that was so. If and when I do, I don't know that I will discuss it with you. It may be none of your business."

"Don't stonewall me!" Ruth pushed herself erect and stamped her foot. "This is my family, too, just as much as it is yours. You can divorce Dad, but I'm your daughter until the day you die."

"A mother-daughter relationship has its limits. You must trust me to—"

"Trust you?" Ruth barked harshly. "Ha! That was Dad's mistake."

With that Ruth was gone, running through the trees toward the house.

"Ruth . . . Ruth . . . ," Anne called, but the child didn't return and Anne didn't go after her.

"Dad!"

"In here, Ruth."

Ruth Harris came into the den and reached for the light switch. "Why are you sitting in the dark?"

"I'm thinking," Ed Harris told her. Actually he had been dozing in the easy chair. "Sometimes that goes better in the dark."

"A beautiful autumn afternoon, and you don't have the sense to let some of it in." His daughter pulled the drapes open. Sunlight streamed into the room, illuminating the remnants of the Sunday newspaper strewn about the floor, several coffee cups, and a breakfast plate. "Look at this mess. You haven't shaved and you're still in your pajamas."

"What are you doing home, Ruth? You must be missing a rally at the university about saving the world."

"I decided to devote the day to checking up on my precocious parents. I've seen Mom, I've visited Granny Sarah, and now I'm checking on you in your den of sloth. You'll be delighted to hear Mom is not sitting in the dark contemplating her navel."

"She never has. Not once in her life."

"Men are so messy," Ruth declared.

"You're going to make some man a fine mother, Ruth."

"This situation is your fault, you know."

"I know. I should have picked up the newspaper and run the dishwasher."

"Dad!"

"Yes, Ruth."

"You are so difficult to talk to. It's like we live on different planets."

"Stop talking to me like an errant child. I find that offensive."

Ruth sat in a chair opposite him. She spent a moment gathering her thoughts, then said, "Mother is holding up well, I think." She didn't think that at all, but felt a lie might get this conversation flowing.

"Terrific."

"Granny Sarah doesn't have much time left. You should go see her."

He nodded.

"She is such a dear," Ruth murmured, her head bent so that he couldn't see her face. When she raised her head, her voice sharpened. "How do you intend to resolve this situation?"

"I keep reminding myself that you are only twenty years old."

"Mother at the Elkinses'—a *ridiculous* situation. It's a farce. How long are you going to let it continue?"

"What did your mother say to that question?"

"Don't avoid the issue. You sent her there with a gun at her back. Don't deny it."

"I'm not denying anything. And I'm not discussing my relationship with your mother with you. I never have and I never will."

"Mother should come home, and you two should work out this matter like mature adults." When her father didn't reply to that suggestion, Ruth said, "Civilization has certainly advanced beyond the quaint morals of the World War II era. No one gets a divorce today because one partner has a sexual liaison with a third person. Sex is sex and love is love."

What her father thought of this modern sentiment he didn't say. Ruth sat on the couch looking around forlornly. Finally she said, "Dad, I love you. And I love Mother."

"Your mother and I are living our lives and you are living yours," Ed Harris gently told his daughter. "You must come to grips with the fact that you are not responsible for your parents."

In the silence that followed she began to cry.

On top of everything else, now Ed Harris felt like a jerk. He moved over to the couch beside her. "It hurts when you see people you love mess up their lives, doesn't it?"

She put her head on his shoulder and he put his arm around her. After a while he whispered, "Your mother screwed up and I screwed up, and we're going to have to work it out, Ruth. If we can. When you love people you have to give them room to solve their own problems."

"What if you and Mother can't solve this one?"

"Then we'll have to live with that."

"Sometimes Mother has a difficult time understanding how other people feel."

"That's sort of a universal failing, isn't it? Don't we all have that weakness to some degree?"

Ed Harris loved his daughter desperately. Even at the age of twenty she retained a generous dollop of little girl that came out at odd times and captivated her father. Her favorite song, which she still sang when she thought no one was listening, was a ditty from a cartoon show entitled "Happy Happy Joy Joy." Those words repeated with feeling constituted the only lyrics.

Sitting with her on the couch he remembered that song, and so many other moments that Ruth managed to make hers with effortless grace. Just before she left for school, she mentioned a boy's name at the dinner table, one Aaron. Although he thought he knew the answer, Ed asked innocently, "Who is Aaron?"

Ruth drew herself fully erect in her chair, grinned widely, luxuriously, and announced with pride, "My new flame."

To have such a daughter . . . he and Anne had truly been blessed.

"Being your father is one of the greatest joys of my life," he murmured now.

They sat in silence. Finally her tears ceased to flow. She sat upright and reached for the box of tissues.

"You have a generous, loving heart, daughter. It takes courage to love. You have enough."

"I don't feel very courageous," she muttered, swabbing her nose.

"Oh, you are. You have it, believe me. The love in your heart proves it. Whether your mother and I are brave enough is another question." He rose. "Come on, let's see what's in the refrigerator. I'm hungry."

Sam Neely decided to go calling Sunday afternoon. His apartment in Indian River was too small and oppressive. He brushed his teeth again, checked to make sure his clothes were immaculate and his hair combed perfectly, and set forth in his own automobile, a ten-year-old Ford with only ninety thousand miles on the odometer.

He rolled down the driver's window and stuck his elbow out, inhaled deeply of that pure air, then dialed up some tunes on the radio. He hummed and patted the wheel. Ah, life is *so* sweet!

Junior Grimes was sitting on the bench outside Doolin's when Neely went by. Junior waved and shouted, "Hey, Neely."

The state trooper waved back, then at the schoolhouse intersection aimed the Ford up the right fork toward the Ice farm.

Crystal was sitting on the porch with two younger girls, her sisters probably, when Sam Neely whipped the Ford into the yard. He hopped out and strolled over.

She was reading a book, a paperback with a hunk on the cover, a bronze stud naked from the waist up, swinging a sword.

"Crystal, you probably don't remember me, but my name's Sam Neely. I'm the state trooper who brought Goofy home one day last week."

"Of course I remember you, Mr. Neely," Crystal said, laying aside her book. Both the younger girls giggled. They were junior high school age, Neely decided, but it's hard to be sure these days. From puberty to forty, they all look like the universal dream girl. These two sure did, healthy, tan . . . No wonder old man Ice commented on the parade of young males that continually marched by.

Crystal stood, a fluid, lithe motion, raised her arms to stretch, then fluffed her hair with one hand. She reminded Neely of an awakening cat.

"It's good to see you again," she said. The girls broke into peals of laughter, but she silenced them with a look and jerked her head toward the front door. Still laughing, they went inside.

"They are my brother's daughters," she said. "To see them carry on, you'd think they'd never seen a man in their whole lives."

"You look mighty fine this afternoon," Neely remarked, because he couldn't think of anything else and he sure didn't want this conversation to drag.

"Thank you. Would you like to sit down, or perhaps go for a walk?"

"A walk? That sounds perfect on a day like this."

Crystal came down the steps of the porch and started around the house. Neely fell in beside her. "If you told me where you're from, Mr. Neely, I've forgotten."

"Capitol City. And please, call me Sam."

"Okay, Sam," she said, and grinned, flashing perfect white teeth.

Sam Neely felt so good he thought he'd burst. As they strolled up the hill into the orchard exchanging small talk and getting acquainted, he felt as if he were going to float off the ground like a helium balloon. It was a curious feeling, and a new one. He had just never felt this good before in his life, he decided.

"It's certainly a perfect day for a walk," he declared at one point, which wasn't an original thought but one that needed commenting upon, and Crystal agreed. The leaves, the balmy temperatures, the pastel sky, the warm shadows—it was a day from a dream. And to be walking and chatting with such a beautiful girl . . . Who would have thought that life had moments like this to offer?

Finally he stopped savoring his own sensations and concentrated on the woman who walked beside him. They climbed into the forest and found a seat on a fallen log on the ridge. There was an old limb sticking up from the log that Crystal leaned back against.

It was weird, but she looked somehow different than she did a few days ago when he first saw her. Just how she was different he couldn't say. Still, he got that feeling, and it was a little strange.

The feeling passed, however, as he was warmed by the heat of the vibrant femininity that emanated from her. Life, he concluded. She radiated life.

A chipmunk came out to play in the nearby leaves, and they fell silent for a moment as they watched. When they resumed their conversation the chipmunk discovered their presence. He ran about ten feet, then stopped and stared at them. Finally he concluded that they were harmless and returned to his search for nuts and seeds amid the leaves.

After a while Crystal rose from her seat on the log. Neely popped up, too . . . and she slipped her hand in his. Cool and firm, her flesh gave Neely a jolt as if he had touched a hot wire. He managed to hang on anyway.

As she chatted and laughed and listened carefully to all the wise and witty remarks he made, she led him along the ridge, deeper into the forest.

He thought he could feel the earth spinning. He was lying on his back amid the leaves and she was on top nibbling on his ear and cheek. "Oh, Sam . . . ," she whispered, and he could feel the rotation of the earth, feel the spin as the planet whirled on its axis and threatened to throw them from the surface into that blue sky above the fiery leaves, toss them into the great black infinite depths beyond.

He pressed both hands against the earth, trying to hold on as Crystal unbuttoned his shirt and kissed his chest and her hair caressed his chin and the clean, piney smell of it filled his nostrils.

"We shouldn't," he said softly.

"Oh, Sam . . ."

She had been leaning back against a tree and her lips were so inviting, so irresistible . . . and he had been unable to help himself. Her lips parted to meet his and her arms came up around his shoulders and he was totally enveloped by her sensuality.

Now they were in the leaves, hearts pounding, her hands and lips stroking, moving . . .

She lay beside him afterward, her head on his shoulder, her fingers twining knots in his chest hair.

"It's getting dark," he said finally.

"I suppose."

"Crystal, I didn't want—"

She placed her fingers on his lips. "Don't spoil it," she said, "by saying something we'll both regret."

They got dressed and hand in hand walked back along the ridge as the shadows gave way to twilight.

As they came down through the orchard she said, "I would invite you in, but Mom may not have enough food fixed to serve you dinner, and I know she would want to."

"Another evening," he said.

"Yes. Another evening, lover."

EIGHT

On Monday morning Junior Grimes stood outside Elijah Murphy's shack surveying his junk collection. "Four cars, right?"

"Four."

"Give you fifty bucks for each of them, except for that Ford there—it's worth a hundred—and I'll buy the rest of this stuff by the pound. But you got to help me load it on my truck."

"How much per pound?"

"Penny."

"Okay."

"I'll be back tomorrow with the roll-back," Junior said.

When Elijah Murphy had walked into Doolin's an hour ago, he went by the beer display without even a glance.

"You're looking mighty fine this morning, Mr. Murphy," said a very surprised Lula Grimes. She had never seen the man scrubbed, without a stubble of beard.

"Thank you. Is Junior around?"

"In the garage."

Junior was busy on a transmission. He glanced at Murphy, then looked again. Even Murphy's clothes were clean.

"Whatcha doin', Murph?"

"Nothin' much, Junior."

"Goin' to a funeral?"

This oblique reference to Murphy's extraordinary toilet didn't cause him to flinch. "Nope. Came to do some business. Want to sell all that junk around my shack, get it hauled out of there."

Now, standing in Murphy's yard, with their business concluded, Junior decided to broach a matter that had caused him much grief. "I got a question, Murph. Don't think that I'm bein' smart, but whatcha gonna do with the money?"

"Don't know that that's any of your business, Grimes."

"You're right. It ain't, really. But you owe near to a hundred dollars down at the store, so you do. Remember all those times I let you have beer on credit?"

Each time his mother had been infuriated. She only let Junior mind the store on rare occasions, such as when she and Moses celebrated an anniversary or attended a viewing at a funeral home. Alas, Junior was unable to say no when confronted by a hard-luck story. And he liked everybody, including Elijah Murphy.

"Won't be any more of that, I hope," Murphy said solemnly.

Junior gaped. "You mean you're givin' up drinkin'?"

"Ain't saying that. I'm just trying to stay sober from one minute to the next."

"I gave up drinkin' one time," Junior said, trying to lighten the mood. It made him feel bad seeing Murph suffering so. "Twenty minutes later I was so thirsty I couldn't stand it."

Elijah Murphy was not amused. "I'm drier than a desert turd," he said forlornly. "I don't know if I can stand not drinkin'. All I can say is I'm tryin'. If I come into Doolin's wantin' beer, don't sell me any." Murphy's mouth worked some more, but no sound came out. God, he had been bold! Emotion overcame him and made his tongue too thick to speak.

"Want me to tell Mom that?"

Murphy took a ragged breath as the implications of that question sank in. If he fell off the wagon, Junior would still sell him beer on those rare occasions when he was behind the counter. Lula Grimes, never. Not even if he had cash to pay for it. While still trying to comprehend the ramifications of his first brush with glory, Elijah Murphy was being asked to commit himself further, to make his commitment absolutely irrevocable.

He had to struggle to get it out, but even then it didn't sound like his own voice: "Might as well."

There! He had done it! He had crossed the river of fire and burned the bridge behind him.

"Mom don't much care for drinkin'," Junior mused. "Only carries beer in the store because so many folks want it, but she don't hold with swillin' it."

Murphy pumped his lungs three or four times to clear his head, then remarked, "Women are like that, I reckon."

"Yeah. But what I'm askin' is, since you're coming into a little money here, what say you use some of it to pay your bill down at the store?"

"Don't know if I'll have enough."

Junior waited expectantly.

Murphy had to say it, finally. "I'm gonna build a bathroom in my shack. Gonna buy pipes and stuff and plumb it from the well. Already got an old pump on the back porch that I got some while back, and I think it works. Just need some pipe and taps and a john and a bathtub."

Junior received this extraordinary news without turning a hair. He merely nodded, then said, "Why don't you come over to the junkyard tomorrow and root through my stuff? I have a bathtub over there and a lot of water pipes. As I recollect, there's even a commode—just a little stained and chipped, perfectly serviceable—that you can have and it won't cost you nothin'. But I would sure take it as a personal favor if you could pay something on that bill at the store."

"Okay," said Elijah Murphy. The morning breeze swirled around him and played with his hair. He felt as desiccated as an autumn leaf, light, insubstantial, as if at any moment the wind might pick him up and carry him away.

———

Modern women have dropped screams from their repertoire. Those relics of a bygone era when men were men and women were women and everyone was happy with that arrangement are rarely heard these days. Consequently it had been quite a while since Lula Grimes savored a really good, first-class ear-splitter. She had hoped that someday fortune might allow her to enjoy another, so when a muffled, half-choked sob-scream—a sad effort, sort of pathetic, really—came floating through Doolin's, she sighed forlornly. Too short. Too spur-of-the-moment. Poor volume.

The sound came from the direction of the restrooms, just off the restaurant. Lula was at the cash register in the store. She automatically locked the cash drawer and pocketed the key, then came around the counter and headed for the restrooms.

She had covered about four steps in that direction when one of the best screams she had ever heard split the air like the whistle of a steam locomotive. It rose in volume and pitch simultaneously, quavered at the top three times, then dropped slightly and ended abruptly, leaving the listener stunned and gasping.

There are very few incidents short of a scalping that can induce a scream like that, so Lula broke into a trot.

The screamer was someone Lula didn't recognize, which made her a tourist. She was middle-aged and nicely dressed, and her face was white as a sheet. "The ladies'—" she gasped when she saw Lula hustling toward her. "A man—looking in the window."

Lula Grimes heard heavy footsteps behind her.

"Junior!"

"Yeah, Mom."

"The window of the ladies'. A man peeping."

"Yo," Junior acknowledged. He wheeled and headed out through the store.

Lula Grimes took the tourist's arm and steered her toward the restaurant. "There, there. That must have been a horrible shock."

124

"Oh, my God! I was washing my hands when I saw that *face* . . . leering . . ."

Junior circled the building. Goofy was still standing on his cinder blocks, looking in.

Junior slowed his pace. When he arrived he asked, "Whatcha doin', Goofy?"

The retarded man turned toward Junior. A moment passed before he got it out. "Nothin'."

"Nothin' much, you mean?"

"Yeah."

"Nothin' much," Junior repeated, helping Goofy with his social duties. "Why don't you get down offa there and come inside?"

Reluctantly Goofy stepped down and picked up his cinder blocks, one in each hand. Junior put an arm across his shoulders. "That was a hell of a scream, wasn't it?"

"Yeah."

"You just out doin' some travelin' today, are you?"

"Didn't mean . . . make her scream," Goofy said, on the verge of tears. At least that's what it sounded like to Junior.

"Some of 'em do that sometimes," Junior said with a frown. He was a little peeved at the female tourist for traumatizing Goofy. "Don't let it worry you none."

Goofy snuffled a few times and swabbed at his eyes.

"Hey," Junior said. "How about an ice cream?"

Goofy was sitting on his cinder blocks near the counter eating an Eskimo Pie when Lula Grimes marched into the store from the restaurant. Her finger shot out, pointing at Goofy. "That's the third time this summer, Goofy."

"Mom, he don't—" Junior began.

"Quiet, you. I'm not in the mood for any of your lip." She sighted along her digit at Goofy. "Peeping in windows at women going to the bathroom isn't right, Goofy, and you're smart enough to know that. You scared that woman in there half to death. I won't have it. You understand?"

Goofy cringed and kept chomping on the Eskimo Pie.

"I think you're a whole lot smarter than some of these geniuses around here," Lula told him as she glanced ominously at Junior. "You're smart enough to know better. And Junior always brings you in here and gives you ice cream. Does it every time. Won't you ever learn, Junior?"

"Mom, I—"

"I'm sick of looking at both of you. Junior, take Goofy home. And find something to do somewhere else. I don't want you around here for a while."

"Hey, I didn't peek in any window. And I got Lyle Samples' tractor in the garage and he wants—"

"Out! Get out! Lyle Samples can just wait. Get out of my sight. Both of you. Now!"

Goofy crammed the rest of the confection into his mouth, picked up his cinder blocks, and followed Junior out the door.

When Junior went by Richard Hudson's house, he slowed down. Someone was plowing the low ridge that ran parallel to the creek. It was a large field, perhaps ten acres. Someone else, it looked like Hudson, was trotting along behind the tractor looking down.

Junior whipped into the driveway. "Goof, let's stop and visit a while. That looks like ol' man Kane on that big John Deere tractor."

Goofy was, of course, agreeable. He had never been in a hurry in his life. As he got his cinder blocks from the bed of the pickup, Junior said, "We'll run you home after a bit. You won't need them blocks out in this field."

Hudson didn't look overjoyed to see them coming across the furrows, but that didn't bother Junior, who greeted Hudson with a hardy "Whatcha lookin' for?"

"Arrowheads."

Junior fell into formation two or three feet away and put his eyes on the ground. Goofy trailed along behind them and lowered his head, too.

"Found any?"

"A few."

"Today?"

"Yes."

"What do they look like? I never seen one."

Hudson looked wistfully at the tractor pulling away, then stopped and brought out several from his pocket. Junior took them in his hand and looked them over while Goofy watched over his shoulder.

Finally Junior brandished one and said, "Goof, what's this one?"

"Benton."

"What did he say?" Hudson demanded.

"I think he said 'Benton.' Did you say 'Benton'?"

"Benton."

Hudson didn't believe it. "You mean to tell me that Goofy knows arrow-heads?"

"What's this here one, Goofy?"

"Adena."

"Ain't that a marvel?" Junior asked Hudson as he returned the artifacts. "I wouldn't know an arrowhead from a crick rock, but last summer ol' Goofy worked with some perfesser on some kinda archo—archaeologic dig, and they say he got real good at figurin' out arrowheads. I guess the perfesser found arrowheads that went clear back to Adam and Eve. Goofy knows which is which and all that stuff, so he does. Don't you, Goofy?"

Goofy smiled vacantly.

Staring at Goofy, Richard Hudson decided that it might be possible. He knew from his research on the brain that some retarded people have normal capabilities in some fields, or even unusually well developed capabilities. Perhaps . . .

"Well, I swear, if this ain't one here." Junior bent down and came up with a point. "I found one! How about that!"

He rubbed it clean, looked it over, then passed it to Hudson.

Richard Hudson found himself on the horns of a dilemma. He wanted it, yet Junior saw it first. Courtesy won over greed. He held it out to Junior, who refused it.

"Wouldn't know what to do with it. Just another rock to me. You keep it."

Hudson pocketed the point before Junior had time to change his mind.

In a few moments Jared Kane brought his tractor to a stop and got off for a smoke. Junior passed the time of day while Jared puffed his pipe, then he and Goofy walked back toward the pickup. Kane dug in his pocket and held out a half dozen points to Hudson.

"I picked these up when it looked like they might get covered up on the next pass. This looks like a village site to me. There are lots of flakes, everywhere. And lots of points. Water right there in the stream, which runs all year. The Indians must have lived here occasionally for long periods."

"Don't you want to keep one of these points?"

"No. I found my arrowhead years and years ago. One's enough."

"Not for me."

"You haven't found the right one yet. You will, sooner or later."

Kane got back on the tractor and got it under way. The polished steel plow blades turned the earth as Richard Hudson followed along behind watching for flint treasures.

Diamond Ice was sitting on the porch swing reading when Junior turned the pickup into the yard. He got out and stretched and gave her a big "Whatcha doin' there, honey pot?"

"Nothing much," she said, putting down the book. She sashayed down the stairs and stopped with her feet apart and her hands on her hips. "Did you come calling today to propose?"

"Brought ol' Goofy here"—Junior jerked a thumb—"back from the restaurant. He was peeking again. Gave some woman tourist a heck of a scare, so he did."

"Won't do you any good trying to change the subject, Junior Grimes. I want to talk about marriage."

"You shoulda heard that woman scream. Like to curled my blood, so it did."

"Holy matrimony," the object of his past affections reminded him primly.

"That ain't exactly a new subject for you, Di. But I ain't in a marryin' mood this morning."

"Or any morning."

"Well, that's true so far. Just ain't ever got the itch to tie the knot." He reached out and took Diamond in his arms, picking her up as if she didn't weigh ten pounds. "On the other hand, I could do with a little lovin'. Would you happen to be in the mood for that?"

"Why buy a cow when milk's free?"

"Now, honey. You know how much I love you. But marriage is a big step. Just now I ain't in a financial position to afford a wife. I'm down in the barrel scrapin' goo off the bottom."

"Maybe you ought to be working instead of loving this fine morning. Then we'd be a few dollars closer."

"A few dollars one way or the other won't make no difference. And it's a fine, crisp mornin'. The feel of a real hunk of woman like you makes it finer, so it does. What say we stroll over to the barn and crawl up in the loft?"

"Well . . . ," Diamond Ice murmured, her resolve melting away. Junior was so big and strong, so darn *male*.

They were comfortably ensconced on a bed of hay when Diamond said, "Goofy may crawl up for a peek."

"He won't see nothin' he hasn't seen before."

Diamond giggled.

"It ain't like we're corruptin' the poor boy's morals, Di. What we oughta do is get that boy a gal."

"Hmm," Diamond said.

"Arch and me are workin' on it," Junior informed his lady love. "We figure that if he gets to do it for real, watchin' other folks will lose its attraction. What do you think?"

He never got an answer, and before very long, he forgot the question.

Goofy did indeed climb into the loft to watch, but Junior and Diamond never noticed.

Late that afternoon at Doolin's store Junior made a telephone call to one of the tire recyclers that advertised in a mechanic's trade magazine to which he subscribed. The call was long distance; Junior reminded himself to keep it short. So when the man at the recycling company answered, Junior skipped the social courtesies and got right to it.

"Hey, this is Junior Grimes over here in Eden. Twelve miles south of Indian River. I seen your ad that says you recycle tires and I got a bunch."

"How many do you have, Mr. Grimes?"

"I got eight thousand of the darn things piled in my junkyard, near as I can figure. Might be a few hundred either way. The gover'ment is after me to get rid of 'em."

"That many, we would need three tractor-trailers to haul the lot. We could send rigs next week. I'm looking at the schedule . . . next Wednesday. You load the tires, and we'll pay for the hauling. It's a dollar and a half a tire."

Junior was ecstatic. The tire problem was solved! He was going to be rolling in it. Wait until Diamond heard the news! She wanted so badly to get married. "Tell you what," he said expansively, "you come get 'em before that gover'ment man comes back, I'll let you have everything over seventy-five hundred tires *free*."

The man on the other end of the line chuckled. "I don't think you understand, Mr. Grimes. *You* pay *us* a dollar and a half a tire. Twelve thousand dollars. We'll need a certified or cashier's check for that amount when we arrive."

It took several seconds for the implications of that remark to sink in. When it did, Junior roared into his instrument, "Are you out of your mind? I ain't got no *twelve thousand dollars!* I run a junkyard, for Christ's sake, not a damn bank."

"I'm sorry, Mr. Grimes. But *you* pay *us*."

"You need a brain transplant, and you're goin' to have to finance it yourself," thundered Junior Grimes, and he slammed down the telephone.

Junior was so disappointed he felt half sick. He had to get rid of those tires. He tried the telephone number in another advertisement, only to be told that it would cost him $1.60 per tire plus freight to have his tires recycled by the experts at that company.

Disgusted, he threw the mechanic's trade magazine into a corner. Twelve thousand dollars! He had never had that much money at one time in his life. And Ed Harris at the bank was not going to loan him money to have tires hauled away. The bankers always said they needed "security" when Junior went into their quiet, decorated, carpeted offices to discuss the nuances of his balance sheet.

Was he ever going to have the money to marry Diamond Ice?

Arch Stehlik came into the restaurant for dinner that evening. Junior ate with him, then suggested they go see Benny Modesso. Arch was agreeable.

In the pickup on the way to Indian River, Junior told Arch about his conversations with the tire recyclers. "Arch, I don't have no twelve thousand dollars. And I ain't ever gonna get twelve thousand dollars unless I win the lottery, which ain't too likely since I never have money to buy lottery tickets."

"You're going to have to burn them," Arch said. That was Arch; he always went right to the heart of a matter and latched on to the only practical solution.

Not that Junior always liked Arch's solutions. "Dang, Arch, that's against the law," he pointed out now.

"I know it is. And there's no way to do it so no one knows about it. Eight thousand tires will make a pretty big fire."

"That new trooper will catch me," Junior protested. "Sam Neely is young and green, but he's not stupid. And Arleigh Tate is an ol' hound dog who's been around the mountain three or four times after the fox. Arleigh will be chasin' me ten seconds after he smells the smoke."

"Leave it to me," Arch said, the soul of confidence.

Junior needed more assurance than that. "I sure as hell don't want to wind up in front of Lester Storm again," Junior informed his friend. "Mom got mighty put out at me the last time."

"You worry too much," Arch said. "I'll take care of it. The less you know the better."

Benny Modesso's drugstore sat on a corner across the square from the courthouse. Junior paused at the door and inhaled the aroma of the place. He always thought he could smell the delicious odors of chocolate and the syrups they used to put in the sodas back when Junior was in grade school.

Benny was still making up prescriptions at the counter at the far end of the room. "Whatcha doin'?" Junior said.

"Nothing much, Junior. Arch."

"Your dad never shoulda taken the soda fountain out, Benny."

"We were losing money on it. People wouldn't buy sodas and malts when they could buy pop in a can for half the price."

"I guess," Junior agreed, looking around at the old fixtures and mirrors that adorned the walls. "Still, it was a shame."

"That it was," Arch echoed. One of the things he liked about Junior was his sentimentality, but the fellow could sure waste a lot of time mooning about what used to be. Before Junior could work up to a maudlin moment this evening, Arch said, "We came to see you tonight about some pictures, Benny."

"Oh," said the pharmacist, obviously perplexed.

"Yeah," Junior said, and leaned his hip against the counter. "Did Delmar Clay bring in a roll of film today to be developed?"

"I don't know. I didn't come in until noon. Why?"

"What time does the lab pick up and deliver?"

"Nine in the morning. Right after we open."

"Mind if we look at the stuff you've taken in today?"

132

"Well . . ."

"Look, Benny. We've been friends since the seventh grade. Have I ever done anything that caused you trouble?"

"Now that you mention it, Junior, yes, you did. I recall that time you told the girl I was dating that I had the clap. Judy Somerville. Remember that little incident?"

Junior chuckled. "About forgot. Truth is, I was sorta soft on Judy myself. I mean other than that?"

"Other than *that?* Jesus, Junior! You ruined my social life in high school. I couldn't get a date in this county until I was twenty-two years old, for Christ's sake."

Junior looked stunned, as if he had just taken a punch. "I'm sorry, Benny," he muttered. "I didn't know."

"I know you're sorry and you didn't mean to hurt me. That's the thing about you, Junior. You wouldn't intentionally hurt any living thing; everyone knows that. But all your projects don't turn out the way you think they will. You have all the best of intentions and still people get crushed under the wheels."

Junior didn't know what to say.

Arch Stehlik saw that Junior was done for the evening. He took over the conversation. "Delmar took some pictures of Billy Joe Elkins on Friday night after the game. Billy Joe and a girl were naked in a car, and Delmar caught them. He had a camera with a flash unit."

Without another word Benny Modesso got out the canvas bag that held the outgoing film envelopes. He dumped them on the counter. He and Arch sorted through them while Junior walked around the store with his hands in his pockets, his head down.

Benny found it. "Here it is," he said, holding it out to Arch.

Delmar Clay, one roll, twenty-four exposures. To be picked up Thursday.

Arch pried up the sticky flap that sealed the envelope and dumped the film capsule into his hand. The film was completely contained within the round metal housing, and he had no way to get it out without destroying the housing. He pocketed the roll and pointed to the boxes of new film that hung on the display behind the counter. "Give me one of those rolls, Benny. Thirty-five millimeter, twenty-four exposures."

Benny rang up the sale. Arch paid him, then opened the box. He pulled the celluloid completely from the housing, exposing it, then wound it back into the housing using a pencil. He dropped the roll into Delmar's envelope, sealed it, and tossed the envelope back into the bag.

"Thanks, Benny."

"Sure."

"Delmar come in here often with film?"

"One or two rolls a month."

"Why don't you talk to the folks at the film lab? Ask if they've developed any photos of naked people for Delmar."

"It's a Capitol City outfit, Arch. They think they're sophisticated moderns. Privacy and all that crap."

"Maybe they'll tell you something. I'd be curious to know if this is the first time Delmar pulled this stunt."

"Delmar Clay is a first-class son of a bitch," Benny Modesso admitted. "Okay, I'll ask."

Arch nodded. He turned to look for Junior. "Hey, amigo. Let's go."

Junior came over to the counter. "I'm sorry, Benny. I shouldn't have done that to you and Judy."

"It was years ago, Junior. We were kids then. I shouldn't have mentioned it. Forget it."

Junior lifted his big, meaty hands, looked at Benny and Arch with tears in his eyes, then turned and tromped for the door.

"Good night, Benny," Arch Stehlik said, and walked after him.

NINE

One morning thunderheads built on the western horizon and marched relentlessly eastward toward Eden. The trees whipped under the fury of the onrushing wind, and clouds of leaves filled the air. Then the rain came, at first a torrential downpour, slackening to a steady drizzle.

As the rain fell for the first time in weeks, Anne Harris got an irresistible urge to go home. She checked her watch. Ed should be at the bank, so why not?

She parked in the driveway. Rain pattered pleasantly on the umbrella as she sorted through her keys. With a click the door opened, admitting her into a silent, dark house. She put the umbrella in the decorator milk bucket by the front door to drain, wiped her feet on the mat, then walked slowly through the house taking everything in. She didn't turn on any lights.

She felt as if she were visiting a former life, and she wasn't sure she liked the feeling.

The kitchen . . . she went there first. Women always do that, Anne thought wryly. The kitchen is their room, the heart of their domain. Lord knows she had spent enough time in this one. She had coffee here in the morning, watched the morning shows on television, wrote letters and paid bills on the counter, sat here when she talked to friends on the phone, fried eggs and fixed dinner and made cookies and cakes—did all those domestic things, things that meant nothing in and of themselves and yet filled the days as the clock ticked mercilessly and the seasons swept past and lines appeared on her face and her figure thickened and her breasts sagged.

She hadn't spent her whole life here, of course, just the last two decades of it. When she was young she assumed as an article of faith that if she could find the right man, life with him would be perfect. Perfect! She knew she could love a man, love him totally with every atom of her being, give him a love so pure and perfect that it would become the central event of his life. And of course he would love her the same way.

The songs told her how it would be. Not the lyrics, for the lyrics were just words. The sensual rhythms and harmonies of the music made her soul resonate. *That* was what love would be—the song of the essence of life.

The reality of the boys she dated had not spoiled it. Gawky, awkward, with pimples and strong, quick hands and ropy, muscular bodies and lying lips—with them she had dabbled in love, sampled the tenderness and mystery. Alas, as her girlfriends reported one by one that they had found it—found *it*—she knew that she had not. Not with the boys of the groping hands and shuffling feet.

Just when she had begun to despair of ever finding love, there was Ed. Edward Morton Harris.

She had been a sophomore, he a junior.

They smiled at each other over Cokes; danced at little clubs, mostly to jukeboxes; held hands in the movies as lovers kissed passionately on the screen; listened to Elvis and Chuck Berry and the Four Tops . . . stood in the darkness near the women's dorm wrapped in each other's arms as the snowy wind howled and tore at their coats.

Oh, those had been good days, with the future stretching before them toward an infinite horizon. She had savored every moment, treasured it, because this was love and it was everything she hoped it would be. It made her laugh when she was alone, brought tears of joy to her eyes when she thought of him, made her a complete, total human being in tune with every living thing.

Standing in the house today surrounded by the artifacts of their lives, she remembered all that and wondered where they had lost it.

Lost it . . . as one loses the memory of a childhood friend or forgets the ecstasy of that first kiss. It slowly fades, then finally slips away as you go about the business of living. One day you reach for it and there is nothing there. Oh, an outline may remain, a shadow, a dim recollection of what once was, but the thing itself is irretrievably gone.

There was a spot of water on the counter near the sink, and without thinking she wiped it away with a dishcloth, then wrung the water from the cloth and draped it over the sink divider.

The dining room walls were decorated with framed photographs, photos of relatives, from way back when. Great-grandmother and great-grandfather, her parents, her husband's parents, Granny Sarah in her wedding dress, Ruth and a boy outfitted for the prom . . .

Anne took her time, looked at every photo, then paused to examine the silver and china in the china cabinet, the good stuff used only on special occasions. Well, there were very few of those. Most of this stuff needed washing; all the silver was tarnished.

She moved on. Inspected the laundry room, climbed the stairs and looked in each bedroom, each closet. The rooms were full of things, artifacts, gifts from twenty-two Christmases and dozens of birthdays and souvenirs from vacations and weekend expeditions. *Things!* Junk, most of it, absolutely useless junk of no conceivable value to any living person.

She felt hollow, empty. Her life was ready for the estate sale and she couldn't even cry.

After a while she found herself on the main floor again, by the front door. She was reaching for the umbrella, then drew her hand back.

The afternoon that Hayden knocked she had been in the kitchen. Heard the knocking. She came into the foyer and pulled the door open. Hayden had been standing there wearing an impish little grin.

He had looked better at that moment than he ever had before or since. Oh, he had flirted with her for years, and she guessed she had encouraged him. If she hadn't, he would not have shown up at the front door grinning and telling her he had a few hours.

And of all afternoons, Ed picked that one to have a stomachache.

Oh, well. She wouldn't have been very good at pretending it never happened.

It *did* happen. She had opened the door . . . like this . . . and Hayden was standing there. Hayden had never, ever come over to the house before when Ed wasn't home. And he knew darned well Ed wasn't home that afternoon.

He had smiled. She had greeted him. She could have merely told him to come back when Ed was home and closed the door. But she didn't. She stepped back and Hayden came in and she closed the door behind him.

Just like that. When she stepped back to let him walk through the door, she had known what was going to happen. A half hour later they were in bed together, as if it were predestined, an event that had to occur because they were trapped in roles the gods had written. So the earth spun on and the fools played out their parts.

Did the gods applaud? Or hiss? Or did they care?

Anne took note of the fact that the rain had stopped. She closed the door and walked toward the den, remembering.

Hayden had suggested a drink. The liquor was kept in the den. Here, in this cabinet above this tiny sink. This morning, since she was standing there, she got ice from the small refrigerator, put it in a glass, and poured a splash of bourbon on it. Just as she had that afternoon.

She stood sipping it, looking around the room. Ed's gun cabinet, the bookcases, the desk, that damned deer head . . .

She forgot about Hayden Elkins.

She sat on the sofa and stared at the trophy on the wall. The huge buck stared back with his brown glass eyes.

She hated that deer.

It wasn't because she had a Bambi complex or thought all trophies grotesque. It was *that* deer she hated.

Ed killed it the week his father, Lane, died. The first week of December, two years ago. God, what a week from hell that had been!

Dying of cancer, the old man signed himself out of the hospital and went home. Ed's sister from California fluttered about uselessly, unable to cook, unable to clean, unable to nurse, unable to cope. Ed's mother wandered around in a senile daze while the wind blew and cold seeped into the nooks and crannies of that old farmhouse and snow reduced visibility outside to a few yards. And she had to handle the whole damned scene by herself because Ed *went hunting*. From an hour before dawn to well after dark. Three days of that. The storm reached its peak on the third day, and that evening at dusk he had staggered in half frozen with news that he had killed the buck. His father died early the next morning.

She would never forgive him for leaving her in that drafty old house with his dying father and senile mother and drifty, snot-rag sister. Never.

To shoot a damned deer.

Lane had wanted Ed to go, of course. Wanted him to hunt that big buck Lane had seen earlier that fall, but why on earth did Ed ever agree? There's certainly nothing wrong with humoring a desperately ill person, within reason. But leaving your wife to feed and nurse and hold the bedpan for your dying father while you go hunting?

In all the years she had known Ed, he had never before hunted deer. Pheasants, yes, occasionally, in the fall with some fellow who had dogs. Hayden also went on those expeditions. But not deer. She hadn't even known Ed owned a rifle. Yet as his father lay dying he stalked the wily stag.

She finished the drink and washed the glass in the sink, dried it and put it away. She didn't want Ed to know that she had been here.

Then she changed her mind.

She got paper and a pen from the upper right-hand drawer of the desk.

"Why did you hunt that deer?" she wrote. She didn't sign the note or date it, just left it on the desk.

Anne locked the house on her way out.

When the big Mercedes sporting New York plates pulled in at Doolin's, Arch Stehlik was sitting on the bench out front visiting with Junior. "Looks like a cabin cruiser," Arch told Junior, who got to his feet to inspect the thing.

The driver was the only person in the car. He wore a snappy Frank Sinatra fedora, a blue silk suit with contrasting silk tie, and a rather extraordinary pair of alligator shoes. While Junior inspected the car, Arch eyed the shoes. Well, alligator shoes look just like they do on TV, he decided.

"I'm looking for Richard Hudson's home. I understand he lives nearby." With that accent, the guy wasn't from around here. Or anyplace close.

Arch gestured toward Vegan. "The right fork. Up about three-quarters of a mile on the left."

"You can't miss it," Junior tossed in. "They plowed the whole place up, and it'll be one giant mudhole after that storm this morning."

The stranger nodded. He glanced at the various signs that festooned Doolin's facade, then said, "I see that this establishment offers garage services. Are you gentlemen mechanics?"

"I am," Junior acknowledged. "This other gent is just passin' the time of day, though he does help out from time to time on a consultin' basis."

"When you screw something up," Arch added.

"Got a problem with this beauty?" Junior asked the stranger, full of interest. The prospect of raising the hood and looking her over real good was enticing.

"How are you on Mercedes transmissions?"

Junior instantly realized that the answer to that question would take some finesse since he had never in his life laid a wrench on any piece of hardware manufactured in Germany. He would certainly like to, yet chances didn't come along every day. Or year. Or ten years. Not in Eden. The only German iron in the county belonged to Richard Hudson, who took it to a dealer in Capitol City for servicing.

Junior was framing his answer when Arch let fly with "June, we watched that video last week, didn't we? Mercedes transmissions?"

Junior winced and launched into his oration. "Well, sir, truth is, we don't work on Mercedes stuff on a regular sorta day-to-day basis, so we don't. But we do see all kinds of stuff just comin' and goin', passin' through, like, with the usual little problems that afflict good machinery from time to time. I got the Triple-A towin' contract and hook in stuff made just about ever'where—Italy, Japan . . . even had a car made in Korea in here last week, one of them there Hun—Hunadays. Got it right back out there rollin' on down the Eden road in just under two hours, so I did. I'll be delighted to see if I can figure out what's wrong with your ride if you'd like to give me a few minutes with 'er."

While Junior was holding forth, the stranger in the silk suit was eyeing Arch, really getting a good look at the scraggly beard and hair and the clothes soaked with diesel fuel and grease.

"The ol' gal probably just needs a tender tweak and a pat here and there, so to speak," Junior added, in what he sensed was a lost cause.

"It's got me this far," the stranger said. "Maybe it will get me home. Thanks anyway."

"That there Hunaday had a transmission problem," Junior said wistfully, with a last covetous glance at the Mercedes.

"You can get anything on video these days," Arch said to no one in particular.

The stranger got behind the wheel of the big car.

"Nice-lookin' ride," Junior called as the engine came to life.

The Mercedes accelerated away up the Vegan road.

" 'Watched the video'. . . Thanks a *lot*, Arch."

"I couldn't resist. Did you see the look on his face?"

Junior giggled, then he laughed. Arch joined in.

"Let's rewind that video on Mercedes trannies and watch 'er again," Arch hooted. "Maybe we'll learn something this time."

The big man at the general store was right, Morton Sciata acknowledged when he got a look at Richard Hudson's estate. It was indeed a giant mudhole.

141

In fact, Sciata didn't think he had ever seen so much mud in one place in his life.

He parked the Mercedes in front of the house. As he surveyed the denuded landscape he spotted a familiar figure sitting about a hundred yards away, right in the middle of the war zone, on the crest of a low ridge. Short, thick and balding, that had to be Hudson. There was someone with him. The two of them were *sitting* in the mud!

Sciata waited patiently for several minutes for Hudson to look his way. He didn't. Finally Sciata waved. Then shouted. Hudson and the other person didn't seem to hear him.

He was going to have to wade through that mud in these good shoes, the only ones he brought.

He took a deep breath and started. The mud looked worse than it was. Only the top one or two inches was goo, but it stuck to his shoes and coated the bottom few inches of his trouser legs within the first five steps.

Damn!

Ten yards into the field he stopped, raised one leg and examined a shoe. Unbelievable! He placed the shoe, and the shod foot it contained, back into the mud, looked at Hudson's wide back, still hunched over examining something, and swore softly. Taking care not to let his feet slip out from under him, Sciata waded on.

Hudson turned around and looked at Sciata as he approached. The man was literally covered with this brown muck. His clothes were coated; it was on his hands and face, even in his hair. And he was *sitting* in it! So was the man with him.

"Richard, what in hell are you doing?"

"Hello, Morton. I'm hunting arrowheads. Goofy, show him the one we just found. Morton, this is my neighbor, Goofy. Goofy, this is Morton."

Sciata merely nodded once at the retarded man and glanced at the offered stone. He didn't reach for it.

"I've been calling you all weekend and leaving messages on your answering machine, Richard. You didn't call me back."

"I haven't checked the answering machine in a while. I'll get around to it eventually."

"This won't wait. I've negotiated a movie package for Prince Ziad. I need your approval."

Richard Hudson nodded, then took the arrowhead from Goofy's hand, adjusted his glasses and examined it again.

"Perhaps we can go down to your house and I will explain the offer," Sciata said testily. "I've had a long drive down from New York and I'd like to sit on something dry."

Hudson handed the arrowhead back to Goofy and struggled to his feet. He started walking toward the house. "This morning's rain was a godsend. The flint really glistens in the mud." The words were just out of the writer's mouth when he stopped, bent over and reached for something. He picked up a stone and displayed it to Sciata. "See!"

"Terrific," Sciata replied acidly. He marched on toward the house while he struggled to keep his temper under control. Halfway there he glanced back over his shoulder to see if Hudson was following. He was moseying along with his eyes down.

Hunting for arrowheads! By all that's holy—

Sitting on the back porch—Hudson didn't offer to take him into the house since both men looked like professional gravediggers—Sciata got right to it. "A Hollywood producer"—he named him and noted that Hudson's face didn't register a glimmer of recognition—"has offered a million for the right to make one feature-length film, with options for sequels at a million each and a television series at a hundred thousand per episode. And I got you one percent of the gross receipts."

"Fine."

Sciata started reciting the producer's credits from memory, but Hudson cut him off with a wave of his hand. "That's fine, Morton. You're the agent. If you negotiated the deal and are happy with it, I'll sign it. Do you have the papers in your car?"

"Yes."

Hudson got up and led the way around the house to where the car was parked.

"Don't you want to read the contract?"

"No."

"Don't you want to know who the producer plans to cast?"

"No."

"Casting is very important, Richard. If they put the wrong actor in the lead role, the value of Prince Ziad as a property will be seriously damaged."

"I don't watch movies or television. I wouldn't recognize a single name." Hudson stopped by Sciata's car and turned to face the agent. "Do whatever you think we should do, Mort. I trust your judgment."

"Richard! You are sitting out there in the middle of a Mayberry mudhole with a congenital idiot looking for worthless rocks when there are millions of dollars at stake!"

Richard Hudson pulled a shirttail from his trousers and used it to clean his glasses. "Goofy's retarded," he said, "but he knows projectile points. He worked with Professor—"

"I don't care if he dug up King Tut!" Sciata roared. "Look at yourself, man."

"What is your problem, Mort? You think I just shit ideas on demand? You must put something into a brain before you get something out. *This* is my life—*this* is what I do. I sit in the mud dreaming up stories; you sit in an office in New York selling them. Don't tell me how to write them and I won't tell you how to sell them."

A car drove into the yard while Hudson was summing up. The driver, a woman, parked it beside the Mercedes and got out. She was in her early twenties, trim, fit, and gorgeous. "Is Goofy here?"

"He's up in the field, Diamond."

She smiled. "I'm Crystal."

Hudson was a bit embarrassed. He had lived here long enough to tell the girls apart. Of course, he wasn't wearing his glasses. He resumed polishing with his shirttail.

Crystal critically examined the mud on the two men. She winked at Sciata.

"Crystal, this is Morton Sciata," Hudson said. "Morton, Crystal Ice."

"Hello," Morton said, and despite his churlish mood a smile split his face. Beautiful women always had that effect on him.

Richard Hudson finished the job on his glasses and put them on. He left his shirttail hanging. "I think we have a village site up there," he said to Crystal. "Lots of chips. Oodles. The earth is literally impregnated with them. And we've found bits of charcoal from ancient fires."

Crystal nodded.

"The creek is right on the other side of that low ridge, so they were close to water and yet high enough to avoid the danger of floods."

"Has Goofy been a help?"

"A big help. I'd like to come get him tomorrow, if I may. And I want to pay him for his assistance."

"You'll need to talk to Dad about that. I came to take him home so he can get cleaned up for supper." She raised her voice and called to the figure still sitting in the mud on the ridge.

While they waited for Goofy to come down the hill, Crystal said to Morton, "You're from New York?"

"New York City, yes."

"What kind of work do you do?"

"I'm a literary agent. I represent Mr. Hudson."

Crystal Ice turned toward Hudson and stared into his face. "Richard Hudson . . . ," she breathed. Her eyes widened dramatically. "*The* Richard Hudson. Oh, my God! And all this time I thought you were just some doofus who inherited money. I never made the connection." She slapped her forehead. "I never even dreamed . . . *the* Richard Hudson."

A sick look crossed Hudson's face. "You know my work?"

"Do I? Ha! *Sand and Stars, The Arrow of Time, Forbidden Planet* . . ." She rattled off four or five more titles before she paused for breath, then said, "But my very favorite was *The Survivors*. That is the best book ever written."

"Didn't sell many copies," Hudson muttered. "Even the libraries didn't buy it."

Goofy arrived and used Crystal's car bumper to scrape the worst of the mud off his boots. Then he sat on a newspaper that she arranged over the passenger seat.

Crystal was so excited that she couldn't contain herself. She bounced up and down, just clearing the ground each time.

"Richard Hudson. Here! In Eden!"

She grasped Hudson's hand and pumped it vigorously, looked at him full face one more time, then threw herself into the driver's seat of her car. She leaned out the open window. "I'll bring Goof back in the morning. And I'll bring the books for you to sign. I think I have them all."

The two men stood watching in silence until the car disappeared around the curve, going toward Vegan.

"I didn't know that no one around here knew you were a writer," Sciata said.

Hudson gestured helplessly. "Somehow what I do for a living never came up."

"Wait until they find out that you're Rip Hays and write Prince Ziad."

"They had better not find out," Hudson said forcefully. "I'll bet Crystal is the only person in the Eden country who has ever read a Richard Hudson book—the publishers couldn't give the books away. Don't tell me you've forgotten! How frustrated we used to get? For heaven's sake, the prison libraries refused to accept them as *donations*."

"I always liked your stuff."

"You were the only person in the industry who never lost faith."

"Those days are behind us, Richard. We need to—"

"I'll sign any contract you send me, Mort. You're a good literary agent, maybe the best. I'm just a scribbler who finally got lucky. The money hasn't transformed me into Stephen King. I'm still the little fat nerd who 'writes weird stuff for the intellectually challenged.' Remember that review?"

"I remember," Sciata acknowledged.

"You do the deals and I'll sign them."

"I'm sorry I told that girl who you were, Richard."

"You didn't know. Nothing to apologize for. But don't come back."

A frosty silence had the Elkins household in its grip. The adults spoke to each other only when necessary. Young Billy Joe was striving manfully to fill the void; he chattered incessantly, first at one adult, then another, always full of questions.

"You're really enjoying this, aren't you?" his father snarled at him one evening.

"What kid wouldn't?" Billy Joe chirped. "Two moms. Wow! Situations like this don't happen every day. In fact, none of my friends has ever even *heard* of another family like ours. I want you to know how grateful I am. Very few fathers would expose themselves to the public ridicule necessary to make it happen. That mine would makes me a unique young man, and I deeply appreciate it."

We will skip Hayden's reply, which, unfortunately, was surly.

So when Hayden arrived home from the office this evening, he was shocked when his first wife told him, "Don't put on your grubby clothes, dear. We're having guests for dinner."

"Are you joking? Guests?"

"Henry and Eufala Davis are coming over. I invited them."

"The Davises? Have you gone mad?"

"I have always managed this family's social duties. We ate at their home last month. We owe them a dinner."

"Are you aware that that poisonous witch Eufala swore out a complaint against me for bigamy?"

"That sounds like Eufala," Matilda acknowledged serenely. "She was always so enthusiastic." She glanced at her only husband. "You might wish to change that shirt, put on a fresh one."

"Is Anne going to attend this production?"

"I believe so. I mentioned it to her this afternoon, and she just nodded. Of course, she knows the Davises quite well, too."

That certainly sounded like Anne the ice queen, Hayden told himself as he stormed up the stairs to his bedroom. But what in the world had gotten into Matilda? Even as this question zipped through his synapses, he dismissed it. Really, he didn't understand either of the women in his life. Who the hell could?

Luckily he had a bedroom to himself. It was almost as if the gods on Olympus took gleeful note years ago when he told the architect that he wanted four bedrooms in the house, not three. Now they were making sure that little wart Hayden Elkins needed all four.

Yes, Anne Harris was the ice queen. That was her attraction. *Do you have what it takes to warm her up?* So he had tried, and tried and tried and got nowhere. For years. Then . . .

That irony he understood. You always want it until you have it, then you don't want it anymore. They ought to engrave that on the lintel of the Capitol in Washington.

When Eufala Davis got the call from Matilda inviting her to dinner this evening, she initially refused, making some inane excuse. Five minutes later she got a call from the new minister, Cecile Carcano. After a long, long conversation with Cecile, she called Matilda back and accepted her invitation. Then she called her good friend the widow Wilfred with the news.

"Henry and I are going to dinner tonight at the Elkinses," she said firmly.

"Oh, my heavens, Eufala!"

"It's our Christian duty, Twila. I've just had a long talk with Cecile Carcano and she is of the same opinion. We owe a duty of support to poor Matilda."

"My word . . . ," was all the widow Wilfred could manage.

"Henry doesn't know we're going yet—he's still loafing across the street at Doolin's—but I am sure he will agree."

"I see," said the widow Wilfred, who knew instinctively that Henry Davis would have no say in the matter. He was going and that was that.

They chattered on about how Matilda was bearing up under the strain and closed with comments upon the weather. Widow Wilfred didn't take advantage of this opportunity to tell Eufala about the wonderful dinner she had had Monday night with Elijah Murphy. She *knew* Eufala's opinion of Elijah Murphy.

It had been so long since Twila Wilfred had the opportunity to do for a man: fix the dinner, make the coffee, sit at the table afterward and talk about little things. She enjoyed every minute of it.

And Eufala would never believe that Elijah—she thought of him as Elijah now—had been the perfect gentleman all evening. He had praised her roast to the skies, said it was the best he had ever eaten. He had savored the coffee, eaten two pieces of cake and insisted on helping wash the dishes. After dinner he sat with her on the porch until it got too chilly; then he had built her a fire before he went home.

Eufala would never understand. She had Henry, and to hear her tell it, Henry Davis was the be-all and end-all in men. Even if he was, he was only one man, and Eufala had him.

Elijah—well, of course he had had a rough life. They hadn't really gotten into that Monday night, and the widow Wilfred was pretty sure she didn't want to get into it in the future, but she just knew. Underneath it all, he was a good man. That was as plain as the nose on your face.

The widow Wilfred relaxed on her sofa and sighed contentedly.

There was no contented sighing going on at the Elkins house.

Matilda was in the kitchen juggling pots and saucepans in a valiant effort to deliver everything to the table at the same time reasonably warm. She was calm, extraordinarily calm, the kind of calm that physicians usually see only after an overdose of tranquilizers. Yet she wasn't on medication. She was calm as only a woman can be who has decided on a course of action that will *settle the score*.

Had Hayden understood his wife's state of mind, he would have been even more upset than he was. As the dinner hour approached, he paced the den like a prisoner awaiting his moment with a firing squad.

Anne? She was in her room upstairs smoking a cigarette, quite unconcerned about the impending social crisis. She couldn't imagine why Matilda would want to spend two hours with Henry and Eufala Davis, who were at least as old as Matilda's parents and nosy prigs to boot. The Davises were precisely the kind of people Anne Harris purposely avoided. Since she didn't understand Matilda's reasons, she dismissed the problem. And Matilda.

Billy Joe had been sent to his room by his father when he arrived home from football practice. He put on clean clothes and sat looking out the window, waiting for the Davises to arrive.

Parents! Whooo boy!

The biology teacher had assured the class just the other day that parents were an absolute necessity, but you had to wonder. Was sex the only way nature could devise to bring the higher orders' next generation into the world?

Two weeks ago Billy Joe would have punched anyone for even suggesting that his mother and father could ever get themselves into a grotesquely embarrassing sexual fix. But it had happened. Which proved to Billy Joe that he really didn't know his parents very well after all.

Life is mighty strange, Billy Joe decided. The older you get the less you know.

When Hayden opened the door to admit his guests, he had a drink in his hand. Henry Davis gave him a frosty look of disapproval.

"Alcohol, counselor?"

Hayden had never particularly liked Henry Davis, who operated under the firm conviction that his particular brand of middle-class mores was dictated by the tenets of the New Testament. And he was in no mood for Davis' prudery tonight; he surrendered to a wicked impulse and said, "Haven't you heard, Henry? The Dead Sea Scrolls say that Jesus drank an occasional martini and enjoyed a good cigar."

The blasphemy was wasted on Henry Davis, who with his wife stood mesmerized watching Anne Harris descend the stairs wearing some diaphanous pink boudoir thing that Ed bought her years ago for romantic evenings at home.

"Good evening, everyone," Anne said gaily.

Hayden took one look at Anne and spilled his drink.

"Oh, darling, let me call Matilda," Anne gushed. "She needs to clean that up before it stains the carpet." She floated toward the kitchen calling, "Matilda . . . Matilda . . ."

"Jesus H. Christ," Hayden Elkins said.

"Will you return thanks, Reverend Davis?" Matilda asked when they were seated at the table in the dining room.

Henry Davis prided himself on his ability to rise to any occasion with an appropriate, impromptu prayer, not too long, not too short, but long and solid enough that all present knew they had been prayed over by a pro and God had probably paid attention. Yet Matilda's request was still hanging in the air tonight when he realized his mind was blank.

"Dear Lord," he began, trusting that something would come. It didn't. He racked his brain. Dinner . . . a dinner prayer . . . He was surrounded by flagrant, unrepentant sinners, and the whole situation was just too much. "Thank you," he managed, and finally, when he realized that going on was impossible, "Amen."

"That's the way I like 'em," Billy Joe remarked. "Short and sweet."

Eufala sensed her husband's agony and looked at him with sympathy as Anne said, "How perceptive you are, Billy Joe. That was an extraordinarily eloquent statement of the Christian message by the Reverend Davis. Never have I heard it summed up so well, or so succinctly."

Matilda's composure was unshaken. "I think you will enjoy these chops," she told everyone. "The recipe was my mother's and is Hayden's favorite." She asked him to serve the entrée. Once she bustled back to the kitchen to get more large spoons. Then she settled in to savor her meal with startling equanimity as the Other Woman flirted lightly with Hayden and Henry and doted on Billy Joe as if he were her pampered son.

Alas, Billy Joe was not on good behavior this evening. He called both women "Mom" and displayed horrible table manners. No one corrected him. Twice he reached across Eufala's plate and snagged something that he should have asked for. When he told Henry, "The kids at school call Dad 'the Legal Stud.' His adventures have done thrilling things for my social life," Anne laughed indulgently and patted him on the hand.

Hayden left the table momentarily and returned with a large drink in a water tumbler. He concentrated on his food, yet he ate little. His color wasn't very good, Eufala noticed.

Somehow—thinking about it afterward, the Reverend Davis was not sure just how—the subject of religion came up. Due to the tense social situation in which the diners found themselves, it was a wonder that they allowed the conversation to take this turn, but once it did, Anne Harris jumped in.

"Tell me, Reverend," she asked sweetly, "do you regard the Bible as allegory or literal truth?"

Only a person who rarely visited the Eden Chapel during his long tenure could have asked that, Reverend Davis reflected sourly. Sensing a pitfall, he weighed his words before he spoke. "The Bible is the revealed word of God." That statement seemed safe enough and had truth to commend it.

"I'm troubled by a story in Genesis," Anne said earnestly. "The Tree of Knowledge in the Garden of Eden. God put the tree there, and Adam and Eve, yet he told them that they could eat anything in the Garden except the fruit of that tree, which was forbidden."

"That is the story, as I recall," Reverend Davis said carefully.

"My problem," Anne said, making a deprecating gesture that didn't fool Davis for a second, "is that God comes off as terribly naive in that story. One is left with the impression that He was surprised that humans were attracted by the forbidden."

"Sin does seem to tempt people," Reverend Davis allowed, unwilling to address the question. He couldn't help himself—his gaze momentarily went to his host, who was staring morosely at the liquid in the tumbler in his hands.

"Surely He knew that forbidding the fruit to man was an absolute guarantee that it would be eaten," Anne stated, and jabbed the air with her fork. "As Mark Twain pointed out, the mistake was in forbidding the fruit. If He had forbidden the snake, they would have eaten that instead."

"The apple makes it a better story," Billy Joe noted, "with a certain Snow White flavor. Kids in Sunday school would gag over the snake, and the animal rights people would come unhinged."

"You are so perceptive," Anne murmured, smiling, then again took aim at Reverend Davis. "So we are left with two unpleasant alternatives: Either God is hopelessly naive, or the author of the book of Genesis horribly mutilated the revealed truth."

Before Reverend Davis could decide which horn of this dilemma he liked the least, Anne rolled on. "If God is as naive as he is portrayed in Genesis, then man is just a crude, flawed experimental prototype, created so God could learn how to improve him in the next iteration. On the other hand, if the Garden of Eden story is mangled, we must reexamine the philosophical basis for the concept of sin. What if God intended for Adam and Eve to eat the fruit? Expected them to eat it? *Wanted* them to eat it?"

"That story forms the basis for the entire concept of original sin," Matilda remarked, "and the traditional view of woman as temptress and man as morally weak when he surrenders to temptation."

"We humans spend our lives apologizing for and confessing to being human," Anne said to her, "and I am not sure that we should."

As Reverend Davis cast about for a graceful way out of this conversation, Anne continued, quite innocently, "I am sure God is wiser than that quaint old tale would have us believe. I think He knew Adam and Eve would eat the fruit. And when they did, I doubt that He ejected them from the Garden of Eden—to do so would have been equivalent to punishing a child for eating candy that one left near his plate."

"I have always been troubled by God's sentence for Eve's transgression," Matilda said. "As her punishment, man should rule over her."

"Obviously a translation or scrivener's error," Anne said firmly. "No man in history has been willing to accept responsibility for a woman's conduct, not even Adam. When God questioned him about eating the forbidden fruit, he blamed his wife."

"That was the only part of the story that struck me as probably true," Matilda said. Billy Joe joined his two mothers in laughter.

When she and Anne were once again more or less under control, Matilda suggested, "Perhaps we are still living in the Garden. What do you think, Reverend Davis?"

Eufala rescued her husband, to his intense relief.

"We know Billy Joe has homework, Henry has several shut-ins he must visit this evening, we don't want to intrude . . ." The Davises arose from the table and scurried for the living room to retrieve their wraps.

"Maybe He *should* have told them not to eat the snake," Billy Joe mused, scratching his head.

"It was so lovely, Matilda," Eufala called to the hostess, who was still extricating herself from the table. "Thank you." Then they dashed for the door.

As Henry Davis piloted his car down the driveway, Anne and Matilda stood on the front porch waving good-bye. Anne looked quite stunning with the breeze whipping the filmy material of her peignoir.

Back inside, Hayden Elkins faced them. "You two should be ashamed. Questioning the basis of that old man's faith—I find that offensive."

"His faith is pretty shallowly rooted if our comments can shake it,"

Anne retorted. "What *I* find offensive is the concept that men sin because they are weak and women sin because they are wicked."

She turned and ascended the stairs.

Eufala Davis called the widow Wilfred the instant she got home.

"Twila, you should have seen her. To suffer as she is suffering and yet never turn a hair . . . to endure what she is enduring and be unable to express any of it for fear of coming apart—never in my life have I seen such grace! I tell you, Matilda Elkins is a saint. A saint!"

TEN

"Honey baby lamb chop, you know I *love* you, so why not do this little thing for me?"

"You know I can't stand that creep."

"Yeah, but—"

"He'll put his hands on me. There's no way to avoid that, Junior. He'll grope me all over."

"Diamond, baby, I know that Delmar is a jerk. If he wasn't, I wouldn't be askin'. It's because he is a jerk that we have to fix his wagon."

" 'We'? As usual, you want help on a little project to improve the world."

"Delmar Clay's time has run out."

"Arch Stehlik thought this up, didn't he?"

Junior Grimes nodded.

"He's been getting you into trouble all your life, Junior. He never gets caught and you always do."

Junior didn't want to talk about Arch this morning. "I need your help, Di."

"Why me?"

"You're the only gal with the moxie to pull this off. And the guy has the hots for you. You've told me that yourself."

"He isn't the only one. There's a dirty old man who lives in Dismal Hollow who slobbers all over himself every time he sees me. Do you want me to encourage him?"

157

"Sweet thing, you know I don't. But Delmar wants to get in your pants. That's the hook. What do you want me to do? Advertise in the newspaper for women that Delmar Clay has the hots for?"

"Just what's in this for me, Junior Grimes? Are you going to seriously discuss marriage if I do this for you?"

"It's not for me. It's for Billy Joe Elkins and Melanie Naroditsky and Arleigh Tate and everyone else who's ever had a run-in with Delmar. Think of it as a civic duty."

"You're avoiding my question."

"You know I want to marry you, Diamond, but I don't have the money."

"A marriage license only costs three dollars, Junior Grimes."

"It's all the other costs I'm thinkin' about."

"So we can never get married? Is that what you're saying? We can never have a life together? Maybe you should get another girlfriend, one who wants to stay single her whole life. Or maybe you should get a real job that pays real wages."

Junior had had enough discord for one day. It was almost as if he were already married. "I've got a real job," he replied testily. "Now are you going to do this for me or not?"

"I'll have to think about it."

"I'm not asking you to have sex with the guy. Just get naked for a few minutes. No one will ever see your face in the photos. Then you can slap him silly. Bobbittize him and mount it on a walnut plaque—I don't care."

"Maybe I'll give him what he wants."

Junior got up from the table in the back of the restaurant and stormed off through the kitchen toward the garage.

Diamond Ice sat drinking her coffee. Her real objection to this scheme, which she had stated and Junior had ignored, was that Arch Stehlik thought it up. It was sly and a little wicked, both Stehlik trademarks. Junior had not a trace of either characteristic in his makeup, which was his charm. He was a good, decent, honest man who always said exactly what he thought. Yet all Arch had to do was suggest something sneaky and Junior was ready to climb aboard to drive the train.

Oh, well. Perhaps it was better for everyone that Arch had taken cards in this game. This way Delmar Clay wouldn't wind up in the hospital and Junior wouldn't spend very many days in jail.

Diamond Ice finished her coffee and left two quarters on the table.

A wave of anxiety swept over Richard Hudson when he heard the car pull into his driveway. As the sound of slamming doors reached him in his study, he looked longingly at the pleasant sanctuary where he had done his writing for the last three years. Somehow he had this feeling that this place would never again be the same.

No! He would not permit his privacy to be invaded. Would . . . not . . . permit . . .

A loud knocking on the door. He moved slowly, reluctantly, in that direction.

Through the glass he saw Goofy and Crystal, and they were staring in. Crystal smiled broadly and waved.

With a nagging suspicion that he was sealing his own doom, Richard Hudson unlocked the door and pulled it open.

Crystal charged in. Goofy followed. Each of them was carrying a shopping bag. "I brought eighteen books," Crystal announced, "which is all I had. I know you've written more of them. I want to get the other titles."

"Most of them are out of print," Hudson said listlessly, but Crystal wasn't paying attention. She was looking around as if this were the lobby of the Waldorf or Elvis' bedroom.

As Goofy dumped the books on his dining room table, Crystal Ice zeroed in on Richard Hudson. The dazzling smile, the perfect white teeth, the green eyes that took in every pore and pimple . . . he felt as if every spotlight on earth had hit him all at once and he had no place to hide. The lights were sizzling hot and he was perspiring.

She whipped a pen from somewhere and offered it to him. He took it reluctantly and faced the pile of books.

"Ooh, this is sooo exciting!" she declared.

He picked up the first book and turned to the title page. "To Crystal Ice, Best Wishes, Richard Hudson."

She watched over his shoulder as he wrote, watched from a distance of two or three inches. He could smell her scent, feel her body heat on his shoulder, feel the fire.

When he finished the first volume, he picked up another.

Instinctively he moved away from her. She followed. "This is going to take a while," he said. "Would you like some coffee? There's some in the kitchen."

"No, thanks."

"Pour me a cup, will you, please?"

That did it. She dashed away. He dropped into a chair and scribbled frantically.

He should never have published a word under his own name. It never occurred to him way back when that someday a problem might arise. He supposed that he must have had an inkling when he created Prince Ziad, some nagging sense that something might be lurking out there in the darkness, so—thank God!—he had had the sense to publish Ziad under a pen name.

He was marveling at his prescience when Crystal returned with his coffee and set it carefully near his hand, as if she were serving at a White House dinner.

She settled in on the other side of the table and stared at him.

He did another three or four books, then said, "You're making me nervous."

She tittered. "I guess I'm making a fool of myself. I'm so excited! If you only knew how you have delighted me through the years with your books.

And now, to see you in the flesh . . . it's marvelous! I feel as if I know you better than any other man in the whole world."

"You really don't know me at all."

"Oh, but I do! I know how your mind works, what you think. I know what you consider interesting, what you think droll, amusing, witty, sad, tragic, tender . . . I *know* you."

He stopped writing and forced himself to meet her gaze. "You know what I've written. But you don't know *me*. Open your eyes, Crystal. I'm a short, fat, ugly man who's well into middle age and losing his hair." He closed his eyes for a moment, searching for the words. When he opened them she was right there, her eyes boring into his. He felt like a butterfly pinned to a board.

"When I was a boy I wanted to grow up to look like Gary Cooper, but it didn't happen. I've always been short, fat and ugly. I'll always *be* short, fat and ugly."

Her gaze never wavered. "That doesn't matter."

"But it does," he protested. "It matters to me. I have to live with it. And I have learned how. I write stories. *This* is my life."

"I could live with it, too," she said.

He gaped. Where had this conversation come from? Where was it going?

He attacked the remaining books in a flurry of scribbling, dropping the Best Wishes from the formula in order to finish faster.

He pushed the last book onto the pile and rose. "Come on, Goofy, let's hit the dirt."

He left her sitting there at the table with her books. He galloped out the door and loped across fifty furrows before he stopped, turned and looked back the way he had come.

"She likes you," Goofy said when he caught up.

Richard Hudson could resist the pull of gravity no longer. He plopped heavily into the damp earth and sat staring at the house.

Crystal helped herself to the coffee that Richard hadn't touched and wandered slowly through the little house, taking everything in. She looked at this, fingered that, examined each item with interest. In his study she looked at the computer, the black screen, touched the keyboard where his fingers created the magic that moved her.

Finally she stood in front of the bookshelves, which occupied two walls of the study. There were all the Richard Hudson books. She counted—thirty-two. One by one she took down those she had never seen before and examined each carefully, then replaced it on the shelf.

Intuitively Crystal Ice understood one of the basic truths of the creative process: Richard Hudson was all the characters he had created, the good, the bad, the heroes and villains, the monsters and the victims, *all* of them. They lived inside of him and he put them on the pages to populate the stories that he wanted to tell.

If they weren't in him, if he couldn't give them life, the stories would fail. But they were . . . and he could . . . he had . . . so his characters, these little creatures from the living mind of Richard Hudson, walked and talked and lived and loved. They lived real lives and died real deaths between the covers of his books.

His best books were *The Voyagers* and *The Survivors,* an epic saga in two volumes about mankind's first attempt to colonize a planet of another star. Each ran to over three hundred thousand words.

She took the two thick volumes from the shelf and sat in the stuffed chair where he must sit, turned on the lamp and read snatches, refreshing her memory.

The Survivors was his masterpiece. The premise was that technology and civilization are inseparable. Mankind must have a critical mass of technological skills to sustain any particular level of civilization, and the ability to pass these skills to subsequent generations. If the skills could not be passed on, or if the number of people fell below the critical level, civilization would crumble. Human society would inevitably descend to a technological level that could be sustained, with an appropriate value system. In *The Survivors* the voyagers who had crossed the stupendous reaches of interstellar space had, in five generations, descended back into the age of unpolished stone. A scout ship that arrived from the mother planet two hundred years later found only a few scattered families of hunter-gatherers wearing skins, and no trace of the colonists.

The final twist—Crystal turned to the last chapter to read it again—was the most unexpected. The planet the survivors had colonized turned out to be Earth.

It was a dazzling twist, she thought. Very bold. If he fumbled the ending the whole novel would fail. But he didn't fumble. He pulled it off.

Indisputably the man who created this work was brilliant. Perhaps a genius.

Reluctantly she returned the books to the shelf. She stood at the window and gazed at the two figures hunched in the dirt on the ridge. Goofy and Richard.

She had spent her life surrounded by the ordinary. Met ordinary people, faced ordinary problems, ate ordinary food, worried about and solved ordinary problems.

Richard Hudson was not ordinary. Not by any stretch of the imagination.

She wandered back through the house. There was another bookcase in the living room; she stopped to examine the books that it contained. She adjusted a light so that she could see better.

Funny, there were some Prince Ziad books here. Her sister Diamond loved the Prince Ziad tales. Crystal had looked at them one day when she had nothing else to do, but they bored her. Strange that Richard should have these third-rate hunk fantasies on his shelf. Rip Hays couldn't hold a candle to Richard Hudson.

And here were some books in—what was that? Japanese. The covers were lurid versions of Prince Ziad. She opened one to the title page. Yes, this one was a Japanese translation of a Prince Ziad adventure. In fact, all the Japanese books on this shelf—there were a half dozen—were translations of Ziad.

And French translations, and Spanish, Italian, German . . . Chinese?

Why did Richard Hudson have all these foreign editions of Rip Hays' books?

An idea flickered, then ignited. Could it be?

She strode back to the study. Richard and Goofy were still up there in the mud. She jerked open his desk drawers and began going through his files. Bank files, investments, letters from his publishers . . . Morton Sciata, literary agent . . .

She scanned one of the Sciata letters. The one she randomly selected was a letter about publishing Prince Ziad in Poland. She read no further.

She put the files away, closed the drawers, and went to the window.

Richard Hudson was Rip Hays! Well, it made sense. He had told her several times that Richard Hudson books didn't sell. That certainly wasn't news. Obtaining them was always difficult. Many bookstores didn't even stock them and required you to place a special order.

Richard wrote Prince Ziad to make a living.

Crystal Ice smiled gently. Her genius had faced the wrath of the marketplace all these years alone, suffered for his art. Thinking how he must have writhed when the results of extraordinary effort were ignored by ordinary book buyers, she saw him in a whole new light.

Well, she had found him.

"It's going to be all right, Richard," she said aloud. "At last you've met a woman who appreciates you."

The Eden country looked good in any weather, but on a clear, crisp day with the autumn leaves at their peak, it looked superb. If you were also in love, the scenery was sublime. The air had a tangible sweet aroma, a taste like a kiss, and the breeze was a gentle caress. If you were in love.

Sam Neely was. He drank in the sensual sensations as he let the cruiser drift along the road through that Eden country.

It came as a surprise when he passed Richard Hudson's house and saw the love of his life coming down the porch steps into the yard.

Crystal!

He turned the cruiser into the driveway and killed the engine.

She was calling to the men on the ridge as Sam Neely floated toward her, his feet barely touching the ground.

"Lunch is ready!" she called.

She had a great voice, Neely thought, perfect timbre, perfect pitch, and it carried so well she didn't need to shout at the top of her lungs. He smiled broadly, unable to contain his joy.

She looked like Venus standing there with the breeze playing with her hair, looking at the men several hundred yards away. One of them raised his arm and waved.

Neely took several deep breaths, then said, "Hello, Crystal."

She glanced at him, said, "Hi," then climbed the steps to the porch.

He followed. "Just a hi? That's it?"

Now she faced him. "What did you expect? A big, fat 'Whatcha doin'?'"

Neely took a step back. His confusion showed on his face. "Well, I thought at the very least I'd get a pleasant smile, or something along those lines. After all . . ."

"I have soup on the stove," Crystal told him curtly. "Richard will be here shortly. He's coming now." She gestured toward the ridge and reached for the screen door.

"I didn't come to talk to Richard. I came to talk to you."

That stopped her. She frowned. "What about?"

"Well, about Sunday afternoon. I—"

"I was in Capitol City Sunday. There must be some mistake. Now if you'll excuse me, I must stir the soup or it will burn." She let the screen door slam behind her.

Sam Neely didn't know what to think. Sunday afternoon certainly wasn't a figment of his imagination. He was standing there at a loss for what to do next when Richard Hudson walked from the plowed ground onto the lawn. "Better wash your hands, Goofy," he advised his companion. Then he said hello to Neely.

Sam Neely was more interested in the house than in Hudson. Both men stood staring at the screen door.

"She made soup," Neely said.

"I didn't invite her to stay," the writer replied. "She's been in there all morning."

"Fine woman," the state trooper said warmly.

"Oh, sure," Richard Hudson acknowledged, never taking his eyes off *his* screen door, on *his* house. "Fine woman."

"One hell of a fine woman!"

"One of a kind."

"They don't come any better."

"I suppose not. But even so, I don't want her."

Trooper Sam Neely stared openmouthed at Hudson, who tried to explain. "I like the way I live. I need peace and quiet. You understand?"

Neely didn't. That was obvious.

"A woman would be an unnecessary complication."

Neely's mouth worked, but no words came out. He swallowed hard, then tried again. "They're complicated, all right. But I guess I don't—"

"When I was younger I wanted a woman. Wanted one rather badly, as a matter of fact, but she didn't want me. Wasn't the least bit interested. For me, then, the rejection was devastating. Now, looking back, I believe it was better for both of us that the situation worked out the way it did. She's married to a dentist now, I understand."

"Oh."

"Maybe I'm rationalizing. One can never be sure." He shrugged. "Not that it matters."

"What's that got to do . . . ?"

"I don't want this one." Richard Hudson pointed toward the house. "Can you get her out of there?"

"Ahh—"

"Without hurting her feelings?"

"No."

Hudson took the negative with good grace. He jammed his hands into his pockets. "I suppose not," he said, and slowly climbed the porch stairs. He opened the screen door, then disappeared inside. The screen slammed behind him.

Sam Neely took off his hat and scratched his head.

Goofy carried his cinder blocks to the kitchen window. He arranged them one atop the other, climbed up and peered in.

Crystal's voice split the still air. "Goofy, get in here and eat your lunch!"

Why did you hunt that deer?

Ed Harris found the note on his desk that evening after work. Anne's handwriting. The note was undated, so he couldn't be sure how long it had been lying there. He tried to remember the last time he was in the den. Well, Sunday, when Ruth was here.

So Anne had been here since. Poor Anne, poor lovely Anne who could never understand people.

Why did you hunt that deer?

He looked at the trophy on the wall, a magnificent buck, a once-in-a-lifetime deer. And his father died just twelve hours after the deer did.

Actually, he wished he had never killed it. He regretted pulling the trigger when he saw the animal dead and regretted it every time he looked at the trophy since. He had to kill it, though. Had to kill it so he could tell his father that he had.

But Anne hadn't asked that. "Hunt" was the word she used. *Why did you hunt it?*

He settled into the easy chair and went drifting back.

An early winter storm had blown in that week. Cold, sleet, snow, wind—those were the things he remembered most. A cold rain was falling when he and Anne had driven up to the house in the Faraway Hills, the afternoon the ambulance brought his father home from the hospital to die.

Up in his room the old man had whispered, "Eddie, I saw a huge deer this fall above Panther Lick—you know where it is. Take the national forest road on the back of the farm, about three miles up in there, up high. He's got a huge rack, beams as thick as your wrist. Big deer, big as a steer. Never saw one like it, not in my whole life."

He had coughed then, needing oxygen. When he could continue he said, "Ed, I've seen that buck three times this year. I was hoping that the docs could keep me going long enough so I could go after him."

A bit later he added, "Won't be easy. I figure he's five or six years old. Wily old cuss, he's made sure no one else has seen him. I listened to the hunting chat this summer and fall. If anybody had seen him up on Panther they would have talked . . . maybe the best deer ever grown in this Eden country . . . thing like that would be talked about.

"Get him for me, Eddie."

Ed Harris, banker, didn't want to go hunting. It seemed to him that he and his father should spend these last few days together. The old man had lived a long, full life, had fought in a war, had been a civic leader and built a bank, had fathered and raised children, had buried his own father . . . shouldn't they talk about all those things, about a life well lived, perhaps even about the future? Religion, God, the afterlife?

"Dad, I think—"

"Do this for me, Eddie."

"I'm not much of a hunter." That was a true statement. He hunted birds occasionally with a bank client who had dogs, yet he hadn't hunted deer since he was a senior in high school.

"Doesn't matter. Hunt him for me."

That night when they were getting ready for bed in the guest room, he had told Anne, "I'm going hunting in the morning. Dad wants me to."

She had stared at him as if he had lost his mind. Finally she said, "He won't live more than a few days, Ed. The doctors took out his IVs. He's lost seventy pounds these last five months. He's dying."

"That's why I'm going to do this."

"You don't have a hunting license. You didn't buy one this fall."

"I'll buy one tomorrow night at Doolin's."

"You'll buy a ticket when the show is over. That makes sense. What if Delmar Clay catches you hunting without a license?"

"He won't catch me. Listen to that wind! In the morning it'll be cold as blazes and spitting snow. Delmar Clay would be the last man alive I'd expect to run into in the Faraway Hills on a day like that."

"What if you get a deer?"

"Anne! I'm not going to get a deer. I'm going hunting! Because Dad wants me to go. So he can lie there thinking about how it was when he did it. There's not a chance in a hundred that I could get a shot at a buck in these hills in this weather. I'll be spending most of my time trying to stay warm and dry and not get lost."

"Ridiculous" was Anne's verdict.

The alarm rang at 5:00 A.M. He used a flashlight to dig his father's hunting clothes from a trunk in the attic. Long underwear, waterproof pants, two old sweaters, a waterproof coat and a wool hat with earmuffs. A wool scarf, two pairs of wool socks, a pair of heavy gloves.

His rifle was there, too. Still in the attic where he had left it all those years ago. It was a Model 94 Winchester, a lever action in .25-35 caliber, with an octagon barrel. In the glow of the flashlight he could see patches of rust. He worked the action three or four times. Well, he probably wouldn't be shooting it.

The rifle was older than he was. He had bought it from a man moving to Florida the summer he was fourteen. Paid forty dollars for it, money he had earned heaving bales of hay. When Dad inspected the rifle, he said it was made before World War II.

Two boxes of ammo lay on the shelf. That was good, since he doubted if anyone still manufactured ammunition of this caliber. He took ten shells and put them in his pocket. What was it Uncle Frank had once said when he saw him putting a whole box of shells in his pocket? "We're going hunting, Eddie, not to a war. Take enough for two magazine loads. If you can't get a deer with that many, you don't deserve to get one."

Ol' Uncle Frank . . . dead ten years now. He had loved to hunt. At least he called it hunting—sitting under a tree chewing a cigar with a rifle across his knees, watching the light and shadow as the sun moved slowly across the sky. He did two weeks of that every year and usually killed a nice buck. He always said that if a man could sit still long enough, eventually a deer would happen by.

An old pair of hunting boots lay in one corner. Ed Harris wiped off a cobweb and rammed his hand inside each of them checking for spiders as the wind sang around the eaves and sleet pellets rattled on the glass of the little attic window.

In the kitchen he made several sandwiches and wrapped them in plastic bags as the agency nurse watched. He also poured himself a cup of coffee and drank it greedily.

"He's finally getting some sleep," the nurse said.

"How'd he do last night?"

"About what you'd expect."

"You tell him I left before dawn."

"I'll tell him. He talked about that buck three or four times during the night."

Anne came down to the kitchen wearing an old robe with a sweater over it. She looked at the rifle and frowned. "It's very cold out there, Ed."

"Yes," he said, and kissed her cheek.

"You shouldn't go."

"I love you."

The wind hit him like a hammer. The invisible sleet pellets stung as they struck his cheek. He adjusted the ear flaps of the hat, got the coat collar up and the scarf wrapped halfway around his face, then trudged away into the darkness. The sleet on top of the wet earth made the ground slick. The temperature was about thirty degrees, he guessed, not cold enough to snow yet cold enough to kill you.

He got as far as the barn. He slipped inside out of the wind. The cattle sensed his presence and lowed several times.

This was crazy. Why in the world had he started before dawn?

Hell, he thought, *because this is the way we do it!* He could almost hear Dad and Uncle Frank telling him that. Dressing before dawn while Mom made a hearty breakfast, stuffing food into pockets for lunch, a kiss from Mom on the way out the door, Dad and Frank whispering in the yard as they loaded their rifles . . . yes, this *is* the way we do it.

But all that was past. Gone. He should have left at a decent hour. He certainly wasn't going any farther until he could see his footing. If he fell in the woods and broke his leg . . . he shook off the thought.

Standing in the dark barn, inhaling the aroma of cattle, listening to the birds in the rafters protesting his intrusion, he fought to keep warm. He was wearing only enough clothes to keep warm as long as he stayed moving. He thought about going back to the house for more clothes, then rejected it. The nurse might mention it to Dad.

He had played for endless hours in this barn when he was growing up. This morning in the darkness he was acutely aware of the other creatures in here with him, the cattle and the swallows and undoubtedly two or three cats. Spiders here and there, and probably, up high in the rafters where the cats couldn't go, an owl or two. Maybe a groundhog under the feedway, snuggled in his hole for the winter.

He had left this farm so long ago, off to college, then to banks in various cities where he accrued knowledge and experience. Seven years ago Dad had invited him to return to take over the bank here. He and Anne and Ruth had moved back to the town where he grew up.

The day came slowly, just a gradual graying of the world outside. When the visibility was thirty or forty yards, he went through the back door of the barn and started climbing the hill toward the forest.

He hit the old logging road at the top of the ridge and went along it for almost a mile before he came to the national forest fire road. This was the boundary of the farm. Soon to be his mother's farm. He thought about her, about how she would take her husband's death, as he walked along with the rifle cradled in the crook of one arm and his head twisted to avoid the sleet. She was already suffering from Alzheimer's and seemed to be in a constant slight daze, with almost no short-term memory. She could still remember what happened twenty years ago with perfect clarity but couldn't remember what you told her three minutes ago, or whether the stove was on or off. Someone was going to have to stay with her.

His mind went to the financial arrangements that would have to be made, then slipped on to the two big loans awaiting approval at the bank. Lawyers, mortgages, UCC filings, cash flow—he knew all those things so well, and yet there were times when the spreadsheets were less important than his sense of how a business was doing and whether the person borrowing the money was really good for it.

He was thinking of these things as he walked along the dirt road through the stark, black trees, higher and higher into the hills, when he realized that the wind was noticeably colder, with a velocity and biting cut that it hadn't had before.

Motion—he saw something moving quickly out of the corner of his eye. He fumbled to get the rifle up while he tried to see if the running deer had antlers. He couldn't tell. It gave a great leap and disappeared amid the black trees, swallowed by the gloom.

He heart was pounding, he was breathing hard.

He looked at the rifle.

He hadn't even loaded it!

Now he took off his gloves and dug into his pocket for the shells. He fed four of the cold, hard, shiny brass tubes into the loading gate on the side of the receiver, worked the action to chamber a round, then carefully lowered the hammer to half-cock. As he recalled, the half-cock notch on this old gun wasn't perfectly safe, so he squeezed the trigger while he held the hammer and made sure.

He had dropped his gloves into the wet leaves. He picked them up and put them back on.

Ready and alert, he continued along the dirt track through the forest.

Within minutes the sleet turned to snow and came furiously, almost horizontally.

ELEVEN

Every Thursday evening the Eden Lions Club met at Doolin's Restaurant for dinner. Many of the leading citizens of the area belonged to Lions; those who didn't belonged to Rotary. Sam Neely attended this meeting at the request of Sheriff Arleigh Tate, whose membership in the Eden Lions Club predated his political career by many years.

The principal of Indian River High was there this evening, as were two doctors, a dentist, several farmers and a variety of merchants. They were seated when Hayden Elkins arrived, looking as if he were in the early stages of recovery from a serious illness. This was his first appearance at a social function since the Friday night football debacle, and to tell the truth, he was praying no one would mention his female troubles.

All eyes followed him as he went to a vacant chair and collapsed into it. Then the eyes were politely turned elsewhere. The sight of a man in his condition was too painful.

Everyone here was male, Sam Neely noted with some surprise. He mentioned it to his host, Sheriff Tate, who informed him that the members of this club had long ago decided to welcome women, yet none had applied.

"Perhaps one of the reasons is that Junior Grimes is president of the club," Tate opined. "He gives our club a certain . . . tone . . . that's sort of unique."

Sam Neely nodded in amazement.

Had Neely but known, Junior had been elected president by acclamation. A Lion for over ten years, Junior was the most diligent member when it came to working on club affairs. No one in the county was more willing to devote time, effort and money—when he had it—to people in need than Junior Grimes. Still, everyone agreed, Junior had his faults. He had no education, cussed too much, and had little of the polish usually found on civic leaders. Indeed, some folks said he had no polish at all.

Polish or not, he looked like a fellow in command when he marched into the room tonight soon after Hayden Elkins, calling everyone by name. "Whatcha doin', Arleigh? Good to see ya, Harry. Hey there, Hayden. Glad you could come, Neely." Junior made his way to the head table and took a seat behind a Raging Lion statue. Nearby and handy was a wooden gavel.

After the invocation by the Reverend Davis, Alva began serving dinner, tonight meat loaf, mashed potatoes, peas and a roll. Junior was talking back and forth with all the men in the room regardless of where they sat—this was Doolin's—when he said to Neely, seated ten feet away, "Did I ever tell you about the first time I got the clap?"

Sam Neely's eyes went to Alva, who didn't seem to hear; she kept serving the heaping plates and pouring iced tea and coffee.

"It was down in Capitol City," Junior continued, loud enough to be clearly heard above the buzz by everyone in the room, if anyone had bothered to pay attention. Nobody did. The conversations continued at every table unabated. Maybe everyone else had heard this story before, Neely thought.

"We were down there for the races, and me and Arch went to the Sugar Shack. That's a titty club. You know it?"

Alas, Neely did. He, too, had once blown the better part of a twenty-dollar bill on overpriced drinks at that establishment while watching strippers bump and grind. But that was all of the entertainment he had purchased. Apparently Junior had bought a little more.

"Anyway," Junior continued, oblivious of the other people in the room, "as it happened I was wearing Dad's jacket that night, and when I got home Mom found a pack of Sugar Shack matches in the pocket. She ripped into Dad."

Moses Grimes was sitting across from Neely, and he *was* listening to the story. He nodded in amused affirmation of Junior's comment and Neely's searching glance.

"He told her he hadn't been there, and it was me," Junior said, chuckling. "Mom called me in, and I denied everything. Things were pretty tense around here for about three more days, then I started drippin'. Really made Mom mad, so it did."

In spite of himself, Sam Neely laughed. When he did, Arleigh Tate caught his eye and winked.

The last of the twilight was fading when Arch Stehlik climbed the ridge toward Junior's junkyard. He had parked his pickup in Skunk Hollow and walked about a mile cross-country through the woods.

He had been in the junkyard earlier that day, about four in the afternoon. That time he had driven up the driveway that led from the Eden road. There was no one in the junkyard then. Had there been, Arch would merely have made conversation, then left. Since he was alone, he poured fifty-five gallons of diesel fuel on Junior's pile of tires. He drained it from a tank of diesel fuel that rode on the pickup behind the cab, fuel that he normally used to service his bulldozer. He had only one five-gallon can, so the chore took a while. Then Arch went home for dinner.

Now he labored up the ridge toward the junkyard while trying not to trip over rocks and fallen trees. Here in the forest the darkness was almost total, and he couldn't risk a flashlight. He made almost no noise moving through the woods, only an occasional squish as a foot sank into wet leaves.

The yard was unfenced, so Arch didn't have to do gymnastics in the darkness. He paused on the edge of the clearing, listening and looking. Uh-oh! Voices!

Someone was across the yard, on the other side. Two men, it sounded like. Who in the world?

Using the carcasses of cars as cover, he crept closer. The two men were working on a car, no doubt removing a part. They talked in low tones, then paused to drink beer.

When one of them drained a beer bottle and threw it as far as he could, Arch recognized him. Of course! These were the Barrow boys, out of prison and broke.

Staying hunched over, hiding behind the cars, he made his way slowly back to the tire pile. After one last glance to ensure the Barrows weren't watching, he struck a kitchen match on a boot and lit a rolled-up newspaper he removed from a hip pocket. Then he stuck the flaming newspaper into a well-saturated area of the pile and made haste back the way he had come.

Diesel fuel was great for starting fires. Its low volatility made it quite safe to handle and slow to evaporate, but when it caught, it would really burn.

Arch was a hundred yards down the ridge going hard when he heard the low, rumbling *whoof* behind him. He glanced back over his shoulder and caught a glimpse of flames through the trees.

This was going to be a doozy of a fire. The volunteers of the fire department would be heading this way as soon as someone telephoned in the alarm. Arch wanted to arrive at the junkyard via the front entrance to assist the volunteers and, more important, ensure no one got silly and hurt himself fighting this thing. Consequently he hustled for his pickup in Skunk Hollow just as fast as he dared.

Alva came rushing into the back of the restaurant with a panicked look on her face. "Junior," she called loudly, getting the attention of everyone in the room, "somebody's on the phone. Your junkyard's on fire."

"*What?*"

"Come talk to them."

Junior charged for the telephone by the cash register. After two or three hurried comments, he hung up and dashed out the front door. His father and Sam Neely were right behind. Standing in the parking area, they could see a glow in the northern sky.

"That's the junkyard," Junior announced. "It's about three miles that way." Arch must have lit the tires, he told himself, a bit surprised that Arch had gotten around to this chore so quickly. It usually took Arch weeks to work up to anything requiring exertion.

"What the hell is there to burn up there?" Moses asked aloud.

"I don't know," Junior lied. "Something's on fire, though." He wondered if he was handling this right.

Alva stuck her head out the door. "Another call, Junior. About the fire." She looked at the glow on the northern horizon.

"You'd better call the fire department, Alva," Sheriff Tate said, after a glance at Junior.

"Okay." Alva disappeared into the restaurant.

By now half the Lions Club was standing in the parking lot. Junior tried to decide how he should act. Alas, he wasn't an actor and he knew it. In fact, Diamond always said she could read his face like a book.

Why did Arch light that dang pile with Sheriff Tate right here at the restaurant where he could watch me?

He felt guilty as a kid with a fist stuck in the cookie jar. He and Arch were probably committing a dozen crimes, not the least of which was arson.

He had better get up there. Fast. Make sure no one gets hurt.

"Lions Club is adjourned," Junior shouted, and trotted toward his pickup. He got it started and under way before anyone could get in the cab with him, but Sam Neely and several of the others leaped into the back. They couldn't see his face from back there, which was the only thing going right this evening.

Damn Arch. He should have told me so I could do this right.

179

Delmar Clay was tooling along the Eden road on his way to the Lions meeting at Doolin's, late as usual, when he saw the glow on the ridge. "What the . . . ?"

Fire! Wasn't Junior Grimes' junkyard up on that ridge?

He got an occasional glimpse of flame through the trees. Something was really burning! Delmar flipped on the cruiser's overhead flashing lights. He reached for the radio microphone, then decided to wait for a moment to call in the fire. Better make sure where it was.

He turned his attention to the road. The entrance to the junkyard was just around the next bend. He slowed and turned up the gravel road.

Delmar was a hundred yards up the junkyard access road when a car with its lights off careened around the bend ahead and came blasting toward him, threatening to hit him head-on. He aimed the cruiser for the edge of the road, then glanced at the other driver as the sedan roared by in a spray of gravel.

There were two men in the car, he saw that. The driver's face was illuminated for a split second by one of the cruiser's overhead emergency lights.

Coonrod Barrow.

Then the car was past him and accelerating down the hill toward the Eden road.

The fire was spectacular when Junior Grimes and the Lions Club crowd arrived. Flames shot from the monstrous pile of tires a hundred feet into the air and cast a brilliant, garish light, which reflected ominously off the column of thick, greasy smoke.

The fire truck arrived seconds after Junior did. "Where's the nearest water?" one of the firemen demanded of Junior.

"There's a farm pond a hundred yards down over the ridge." Junior pointed. The fireman left to help his colleagues flake out hoses.

The fire was so intense that Junior had to retreat. He was trying to decide if it was hot enough and going well enough that the firemen's efforts would be futile when he realized Arleigh Tate was standing beside him.

"You're going to lose a lot of tires, Junior," the sheriff said, speaking loudly so that he could be heard over the roar of the flames.

"Sure looks like it."

"Thousands of dollars' worth," Tate added.

"Hell of a note, ain't it?"

"Got any insurance?"

"Are you kidding? On a junkyard?"

Several more minutes passed, then Delmar Clay drove up in his cruiser. Come to think of it, Junior had passed Delmar as they were coming up the road. He was out of his cruiser picking up something from the brush along the edge of the road.

Now the deputy approached the sheriff, who was still standing beside Junior. "I know who did this," Delmar brayed.

Junior's heart threatened to quit on him, right there and then. He broke into a cold sweat and felt his knees get weak.

"Oh," said the sheriff, only mildly interested. Yet his eyes flicked to Junior's face, which in spite of the heat had gone dead white.

Caught already! Arch, I'm going to wring your scrawny neck, thinking we could get away with—

"It was the Barrow boys," Delmar announced triumphantly. "I passed them coming out as I was coming in. They were up here stripping cars and must have decided to torch that pile."

Delmar had something in his hands, and now he lifted it for them to see. "Here's a starter they threw down over the hill a ways. They threw out parts and tools all the way down the road. The stuff is all over. The fire must have got going faster than they thought it would, so they had to hightail it. Then they threw away the evidence."

Stunned, and vastly relieved at this extraordinary twist of fate, Junior still managed to mutter, "Well, I'll be."

"Those boys just don't have any luck at all," Arleigh Tate remarked to no one in particular as another portion of the tire pile exploded into flame. The remark hit Junior with the impact of a sledgehammer.

The sheriff hadn't bought Delmar's solution to this crime!

Crime! Prison! A cell! His mother would be devastated, his father ashamed . . . his life would be ruined. *Ruined!*

And Diamond . . . he would never spend another afternoon with her in the hayloft, never again taste those wild, wanton lips, never . . .

Arch Stehlik rolled up just as the firemen began to play the first hose on the raging inferno. "Did anyone bring marshmallows?" Arch asked loudly.

The emotional roller coaster was too much for Junior. Arch had done this to him. Betrayed him. His best friend. He launched himself at Arch with murder in his eye.

Fortunately he tripped over a fire hose and went sprawling.

Arch was there instantly to help him. "Hell of a fire, huh?" Arch whispered.

"You bastard! I'm gonna kill you." Still on the ground, partially stunned, Junior got one hand on Arch's arm and began squeezing.

"Let go my arm!" Arch hissed. "Let go! You're going to break my arm, you crazy idiot!"

"You did this to me. I—"

Arch, dear Arch, he understood. He had grown up with Junior, knew every quirk in his psyche, and he instantly understood. Fortunately he was positioned so that he could help poor Junior through this crisis, as he had so many others. With his free hand he grabbed a handful of Junior's hair, lifted his head as far as it would go, then slammed it into the ground. Junior went limp.

Arch looked around to see who had witnessed the knockout. Apparently no one. Everyone seemed intent on the fire.

The firemen had water streaming from a hose by this time. Squatting beside a sleeping Junior, Arch studied the process with interest. The fire hose was about as effective as an eyedropper on a volcano, he concluded.

Arch was feeling pretty good until someone spoke into his ear. "You ought to take him home to sleep it off. I'll help you load him in your truck."

Arch turned his head and looked squarely into the fleshy face of Arleigh Tate.

"Uh . . . yeah, Sheriff."

"I guess the excitement was too much."

Arch Stehlik gave the benediction. "So it was."

Junior woke up in the bed of Arch's pickup, which was parked behind Doolin's. He was dazed when he awoke, but when he sat up and saw the glow in the sky, the horror of the evening came flooding back—arson, jail, that idiot Arch . . .

His head felt as if it were splitting. He moaned.

"Hey, you're okay." Arch's voice.

Junior managed to turn his head. It *was* Arch, leaning against the bed of the pickup with a can of beer in his hand, watching the glow on the horizon.

"Tate knows." Junior had to say it three times before the words were recognizable.

Arch Stehlik looked as serene as a blue May sky.

"I'm telling you that Arleigh Tate knows. That you set that fire. That I knew about it before you did it." Junior spoke slowly, working to form the words around a numb, thick tongue.

"Has he got any proof?"

"Not that I've heard about," Junior admitted. "But he knows."

"What Tate has is a suspicion," Arch said, his voice very definite. "If he gets it in his head to do some checking, he's going to eventually find someone who will tell him that those tires were a twelve-thousand-dollar liability to you. That's bad. But the nearest thing he's got to an eyewitness is Delmar Clay, his very own deputy, who will run all over the county telling everyone he meets that the Barrow boys did the dirty deed. With his own eyes Tate saw you pounding a gavel at the Lions Club dinner when the fire started."

Junior nodded. The motion of his head made his jaw ache, so he rubbed it. Gently. It was very sore.

"The Barrow boys being up there in the junkyard stealing when that fire started was a lucky break for us," Arch continued meditatively. "Life's like that. Sometimes you get the breaks, sometimes you don't. This time we did."

"Tate knows," Junior insisted.

Arch didn't lose his patience. Junior's innocence always charmed him. He liked Junior just the way he was. Still . . . "June, my wife tells me that God is a woman. She is absolutely certain."

Junior was confused. "A *woman?*"

"Yep. God is a woman who don't take kindly to men who wear grease-stained clothes, drink beer, don't shave, and get their hair cut once a year. At first I thought she was just kidding, but now I think she really believes that. Believes it for an absolute fact, so she does."

"So?"

"That's what I said. So? And Arleigh Tate can believe anything he finds appealing. So what? All we need to worry about is what he can prove, which is nothing at all."

After pondering a bit, Junior said, "I think I see your point."

"Get on with life and stop worrying."

"You don't think God is a woman, do you, Arch?"

"He could be a big raccoon for all I know, but I'm sure He drinks beer every Saturday and likes a good football game. That's what I told my wife."

Junior lay down in the bed of the truck and thought about raccoons and fires and women. After a bit he asked, "What happened up there tonight, anyway?"

"There was a fire."

"I remember seeing you, and I got mad as hell and I started for you and . . ."

"And?"

"That's all I remember."

"You don't remember going berserk and shouting, 'We did it, we did it,' and me punching you out to keep you quiet?"

"Nooo," Junior said tentatively, almost inaudibly. "I don't remember that."

"That's good. 'Cause it didn't happen."

"What *did* happen?"

"You tripped over a fire hose and hit your chin on a rock."

"Oh."

"Funniest thing I ever saw. You went out like a light. Sheriff Tate helped me load you in the truck."

"Well, I'll be."

"They'll kid you about it for years at Lions Club. Maybe you ought to think about joining Rotary."

The volunteer fire department left the junkyard about four in the morning. They pumped water from the nearest farm pond onto the fire, pumped the pond completely dry, with no discernible effect. When the tires were consumed, the fire died. The firemen loaded the hoses onto their trucks and drove away, leaving the remnants of the fire smoldering. At ten o'clock the next morning the ash pile was merely giving off wisps of greasy, noxious smoke.

Junior stood at the edge of the acre-sized disaster zone surveying the damage. The sheriff's car was parked nearby, although the officer wasn't in sight. Still, he was around somewhere, so Junior bit his lip to suppress his glee. The fire had consumed every single tire, all eight thousand of them. Twisted, blackened steel belts were visible amid the foot-thick ash, yet even so, it was just about the cleanest job Junior had ever seen.

He was standing in the morning sun enjoying the grace that comes with relief from a heavy burden when the fire chief rolled up.

"Hey, whatcha doin'?" Junior called.

"Come to see how bad it was," the fire chief said. When he reached Junior's side he remarked, "Wow, you lost 'em all. Tough break."

Junior managed not to grin.

"Well, you'd better load these steel belts onto a truck and take them to the county landfill. They aren't worth anything to anybody."

"Think the landfill folks will take 'em?" Junior asked tentatively.

"I talked to the manager there this morning. He said to bring them over."

"I sure do appreciate that," Junior said with feeling. "It's terrific how everybody is willing to help out when disaster strikes. Renews my faith."

"Eden's a good place," the fire chief agreed. He held out his hand to Junior. "Sorry we couldn't do more to help last night."

"You did the best you could," Junior assured him. "The fire was just too far along."

"Nothing worse than a tire fire," the fireman agreed. "Sure hope they send those firebug Barrow boys back up the river." With that, he got into his car and drove away.

Finding footprints on a forest floor littered with newly fallen leaves is a tricky business. Even when wet, leaves don't take footprints well, and new leaves coming down soon cover what marks there are. Still, an experienced fellow with an eye for tracks and a practical knowledge of his fellow man can see things. Sheriff Arleigh Tate had more years of experience than he cared to admit, experience that had given him a rather clear insight into the ways of his Eden-country neighbors.

He idly noted the churned-up mess of the hillside where the firemen had strung their hoses to the farm pond, then moved slowly through the woods, looking.

He thought that if a cautious fellow were going to commit a crime in Junior's junkyard, he wouldn't drive up the main road bold as brass, do the deed, then drive out the same way. A fool might—and the Barrow boys were indeed fools—but not a fellow with a lick of sense. No, sir. A reasonable man with arson or larceny on his mind who didn't want to spend the winter in the county jail would probably park in Skunk Hollow, where there was almost no chance that someone would see his vehicle, then hike up the ridge to the junkyard.

Before he came to the junkyard this morning, Sheriff Tate had driven to Skunk Hollow. He found fresh tire tracks, all right, tracks left since yesterday's rain. And there were footprints in the mud. He lost the footprints in a briar thicket, so he couldn't say for sure they came up this ridge. Now he was looking at the other end of the trail.

Despite the shadows and subdued light amid the trees, he finally found what he was looking for: depressions in the leaves at regular intervals. Footprints. He moved to a place where he could get a better view. Yes, someone had descended the hill here, someone moving hurriedly—in several places he had slipped and left muddy slashes in the leaves. The trail went diagonally down the ridge in the direction of Skunk Hollow.

Arleigh Tate lit a cigar as he stood contemplating the tracks and puffed it meditatively. Finally he turned and followed the trail back toward the junkyard. The gentle breeze spread the cigar smoke into gossamer clouds that dissipated slowly.

When the sheriff came out of the woods he saw Junior greasing his front-end loader.

He merely nodded a reply to Junior's cheery greeting.

A moment later he muttered, "Amazing about those Barrow boys."

"Whaddaya mean?" Junior said, wiping the grease from his hands with a red mechanic's rag.

"How many years have they been stealing parts off you?"

"Ever since I opened this junkyard. 'Bout ten years, I guess. Except when they've been in jail or prison."

Arleigh puffed furiously at his cigar, which had been in danger of going out. With the tip glowing nicely, he removed it from his mouth and said, "It doesn't figure. This junkyard is their pantry. They swipe a starter or alternator, sell it for beer money, then come back next week for another one. They're like mice."

"Yeah."

"Then they burned down the pantry."

"The Barrows are crazy," Junior told Sheriff Tate. "Always have been. Like to do meanness when the mood gets on 'em. They enjoy it. And the cars are still here. They'll be back soon as God gives them a thirst."

Arleigh Tate leaned forward for a closer look at Junior's chin. "That's quite a bruise. Still sore, I bet."

Junior's conscience knifed him again. He was guilty, guilty, guilty. And the bruise—he remembered falling, and wasn't he grabbing at Arch when he passed out? Or was that later? It seemed foggy, as if . . .

The sheriff got into his car. He flipped a hand at Junior in farewell, fastened his seat belt and got the engine ticking over.

Junior went back to greasing the front-end loader. It would be prudent to load those steel belts on the truck and get them to the landfill before the manager there changed his mind. Yet when the sheriff's car was out of sight, he forgot about the grease gun. He sat hugging his knees, staring listlessly at the ashy devastation.

TWELVE

The wind blew down the last of the colorful autumn leaves in the Eden country. The temperatures dropped below freezing every night and rose into the fifties during the day. Yet the storms of winter didn't come; the skies remained clear. Autumn seemed reluctant to leave.

One day Anne Harris went to visit Ed's mother. She was now in a nursing home, had been for over a year. After her husband died, Ed found someone to stay with her, cook her meals, keep her clean, clean the house. As her condition deteriorated, her needs became too great for one helper to handle, so she was moved to a nursing home. By that time she didn't seem to care.

On the day they packed her clothes she had sat in the living room of the old house humming vacantly, lost in a world no one else could enter.

She was like that this afternoon, sitting in her room with a blanket arranged around her legs, facing the window, humming tunelessly, mindlessly. Anne sat in the visitor's chair and studied the older woman's face, watching how the sun smoothed the wrinkled skin and made her look younger. It was an illusion, of course, minimizing the irreversible damage done by that insidious, merciless villain, Time.

Ah, Time, you great deceiver, with your sweet, extravagant, shameless promises . . . then you pillage youth, ravage innocence, murder passion, corrupt health, and finally steal life itself, sneak silently and stealthily away

189

with that tarnished bauble in the dead of night after destroying everything that makes it precious.

Ed's father, Lane, had fought Time, fought with all his strength against the inevitable, until near the end. Near the end he surrendered. He hadn't surrendered that first day that Ed went up on the mountain after the deer, though.

Oh, no. She went into his bedroom with the soup and medicine that evening, just after dark, before Ed returned.

"He back yet?" the old man asked.

"No."

She had placed the soup on the stand, helped him with the pills, put pillows behind him so he could eat. Then he couldn't hold the spoon. She helped him with several bites. He refused more.

"Enough."

"You must eat."

"Food is another appetite that I've lost."

She moved the bowl away, straightened the bed. In a few minutes there was nothing else to do, but still she lingered. The old man had no wants, no little requests.

"Is there anything else I can do?" she asked finally, distractedly, her mind on her husband.

"Stop judging me, lady. But perhaps you can't do that."

"I'm not judging you, Father Harris."

"You can't lie worth a damn, either."

"Don't you think perhaps it's time to make your peace with me? With those of us you are soon to leave behind?"

The old man was in pain, obvious pain. He waited for a spasm to pass, then said, "How should I do that?"

"I don't know exactly," she retorted. "It does seem that you must be thinking of many things as you lie there. Thinking back, perhaps."

"The past is over, finished, dead," he shot back. "This minute I'm still alive. Hurting like hell, but by God, still alive. Without a future, with a dead past, with just this moment to live in."

"Is that all there is?"

"Fight it out with the preachers. Somewhere else. You go into the other room now and get on with living. Let me lie here."

As she was going out the door with the soup bowl, he said, "Send Eddie in when he gets back."

Ed came in a half hour later, long after the last of the twilight had faded. Snow covered his coat and hat and melted as he stood in the kitchen entryway warming up. He leaned the rifle in a corner and slowly peeled off his wet outer clothes. He sat down to take off his boots.

"Your father wants to see you."

"How is he?"

"Alert. Nasty."

"Did the doctor come today?"

"No. I talked to him by telephone. He'll be by in the morning after he finishes his hospital rounds."

"Mom?"

"I don't think she understands what's happening."

"Sis?"

"Sat in a bedroom upstairs and sobbed all day."

"I'll go see them in a bit. How about something to eat? Something hot. And a drink of whiskey."

He went to his father's bedroom carrying his drink in his hand, still wearing his hunting pants, his face still flushed with cold. Anne put the pot of soup on the stove to warm. The refrigerator held the remains of a roast, so she warmed up some of that, too.

Ed spent almost a half hour with the old man. He was still with him when the night nurse arrived, muttering about slick roads. Anne briefed the nurse, who went in to see the patient while Ed was still there. When the nurse returned she took dinner to Mrs. Harris and Ed's sister, Sarah.

Finally Ed returned to the kitchen. "He wanted a minute-by-minute account," he told Anne as he sat down to eat.

"He's crazy," she said curtly.

Ed drank another slug of whiskey and attacked the food.

"You're crazy, too, to go along with this. Hunting, for Christ's sake."

Ed ate in silence as she busied herself cleaning pots and pans; then he went upstairs to see his mother and sister. When he came back downstairs, Ed put his boots on the hearth to dry and stretched out in his father's easy chair. By the time Anne and the nurse finished preparing another round of medication for the old man, Ed was asleep.

She put a blanket over him finally, then sat staring into the fire. The wind rattled the single-pane windows and howled around the chimney. Once she crossed the room and spent a few minutes watching snow falling into the tiny circle of light that escaped the window. Occasionally she added logs to the fire.

She was exhausted, but she didn't think she could get to sleep. She was wound too tightly.

If life is a journey, and it seems to be, why does it have to end here, like this? Answer me that, God.

After all the twisty parts and dry stretches and long hills, you get to the end of the road and find a senile wife, a worthless daughter, and a son who scampers into the forest so he won't have to watch.

She pitied Lane. And she hated him.

This mess was partly his fault. He raised an incompetent, incapable daughter, he sent Ed away today, and he chose to do his dying here, in this ramshackle old farmhouse on the ragged edge of nowhere, when he should have had the common decency to die in a damned hospital like everyone else.

The old man was going to be a selfish, chauvinistic curmudgeon right to the bitter end.

Finally Anne poured herself a drink and tossed it off. She stretched out on the couch so the night nurse could wake her if she needed help, pulled a blanket around herself, and went to sleep listening to the wind.

When she awoke, the night nurse was washing dishes in the kitchen.

"Where's Ed?"

"He went out fifteen minutes ago. I fixed him some eggs and toast, and he put some sandwiches in his pocket."

"What time is it?"

"Six-thirty. Almost dawn. There's fresh coffee in the pot."

Although she knew the answer, Anne asked anyway. "Did Ed wear his hunting clothes?"

"Yes."

She went to the kitchen door and threw it open. She stepped out onto the porch, reeling from the bite of the cold wind. Ed wasn't in sight. Tracks in the snow led off into the gloom. *Damn him!*

She went back into the kitchen, closed the door against the cold and stood with her back against it.

"Mr. Harris is sleeping just now," the nurse said.

"How is he?"

"A day or two. Three, perhaps—I don't know. Not long, though, I think."

Anne was in the kitchen washing dishes when the doctor came. He was a big man, in his fifties, with an honest, cheerful face. Half the people in the county called him their doctor, and they called him every time they got the sniffles.

She was still there when he came out of the patient's bedroom. "I'll take a little shot of that coffee," he said.

As he leaned against the counter sipping the beverage, he asked, "So how are you holding up?"

"Okay, I guess."

"Feel like hell?"

"Yes."

"Where's Ed?"

"Hunting."

The doctor nodded and met her eyes, and his features softened. "Lane's got a lot of pain," he said, "and we're medicating all we can. If he wants whiskey in the evening, give him a couple of ounces."

"He asked for it last night."

"The danger is that the booze will react with his medication and kill him." He shrugged. "If he wants it, let him have it." The doctor finished the coffee and set the cup in the dishwater. "When I get to the office I'll see about getting a nurse out here in the daytime, too. I think you've had enough."

"Thank you."

Going out the door he told her, "You know my number. Call me anytime. I can be here in half an hour."

The contrast between the doctor's comment and Ed's blithe odyssey in pursuit of a deer hit her hard. Her stomach felt as if it contained a rock. A large, cold rock.

Ed's sister, Sarah, came downstairs around ten o'clock and helped herself to toast and coffee. Although she had been named after her grandmother, Anne mused, never were two women more unlike.

Sarah sat next to the fire nibbling on the toast. "Oh, this weather," she said at last, to break the silence.

Anne grunted.

"You must think me a terrible daughter."

The temptation to say something polite tripped across Anne's synapses, which irritated her. Sarah was a miserable human being; everything she did and said rubbed Anne the wrong way. Here she was now, pleading for sympathy! Well, she would get not the tiniest smidgen from her sister-in-law.

Sarah sighed audibly.

Anne got a firm grip on her lower lip with her teeth.

"Oh, I do wish William were here." William was her husband. Sarah always called him by his Christian name, although everyone else who knew him more than ten minutes called him Bill. "He wanted desperately to come but couldn't get away."

"Umm," Anne managed. She had met Bill on only two occasions, both mercifully short. He was a lost-in-cyberspace technoid, a chubby, bald man with sweaty palms and a florid complexion that hinted at a future of heart disease who had created and sold several computer games to a major manufacturer. He was reputedly rich, about ten million dollars' worth. Anne idly wondered what grotesque flaw in Bill's character made Sarah attractive to him. If she was. Perhaps he was having a wild fling in California just now, celebrating a few days' reprieve from Sarah's limpid company.

After a while Sarah said, "I suppose I should go to see Father." She glanced at Anne, who bit so hard on her lower lip that it hurt.

"It's so difficult," Sarah explained. "I want to remember Dad as he was, not sick and helpless and——"

"Dying?"

"Dad certainly wouldn't want us to remember him——"

"You make me want to puke," Anne snarled. She marched into the kitchen, then decided she had had all of this house she could stand. She threw open the kitchen door and went out into the snow.

Her tears felt like icicles as they slid down her cheeks. She swabbed at them angrily.

The snow had stopped. Patches of blue were visible between dark, ragged clouds. Every now and then a sunbeam hit the snow with a brilliant light that hurt the eyes. The wind was still strong, and cold.

Shivering, her tears stanched, Anne went back inside. Sarah wasn't in the living room, she noted with relief.

The old man's voice came through the open bedroom door. "I do not want to talk to a minister. If you get that windbag out here I won't see him."

"You are a nasty old man," Sarah said belligerently.

"Daughter, I do believe that is the nicest thing you've ever said about me. Certainly the truest."

"You should have stayed in the hospital."

"Perhaps," Lane Harris said gently. "How is your mother taking all this?"

"She's very upset."

"And you?"

"Oh, Daddy, it's very hard seeing you like this." The sound of sobs came through the doorway. Anne stepped into the bedroom to catch the performance.

Lane put a stop to it. "I'm tired," he said. "Take care of your mother, Sarah. And let me get some rest, please." He closed his eyes.

Sarah went upstairs, still sobbing. Anne checked the patient, then closed the door behind her.

An hour later when she returned to the bedroom with more pills, Lane was awake. His eyes followed her around the room. "Want to tell me what's on your mind, too?"

"No."

"Maybe you'd better get it said. There isn't much time left."

"It doesn't matter."

"Very few things do. If we only talked about things that mattered, we wouldn't ever say much."

"Okay," she said, making up her mind. "Okay, I'll say it. You sent Ed to hunt that deer. To shoot it. To kill it. That deer must die because you're dying. God, that is foul."

"You don't understand anyone but yourself, Anne. You never did."

That comment cut her to the quick.

"Sorry," he said. "Didn't mean to hurt you. No call for that."

She struggled to maintain her composure. "I certainly don't understand you," she murmured finally.

"The problem is that you're too smart. I told Ed you were too smart before he married you. He did it anyway. Guess I knew he would."

"Thanks for trying," she said acidly.

"Only two kinds of men marry women smarter than they are: damn fools and men with so much money they don't give a rat's patootie. Ed didn't have that much money, and I never really thought he was a damn fool."

He fell silent. She said, "If you expect me to comment on that crack, you can forget it."

"A man in my condition can't afford expectations."

"This is a silly conversation," Anne said starchily. "Your son loves me. Just because you wouldn't have picked me to marry doesn't make Ed a mystery."

"Made him happy, have you?"

"Twenty years of marriage is certainly not a weekend fling or a passing fancy."

"Statistics don't impress me, lady. Hell, lots of people stay married until the day they croak because they're too lazy to get a divorce. Or too scared. Too something." He paused for a bit, then added, "Too many people settle for less than love."

"Ed and I haven't."

Lane Harris seemed not to have heard. His gaze went from the ceiling to a picture on the wall, then to a framed photo of his wife taken years ago. "Life's a gift," he said finally, "like a sunset, a butterfly, a drop of rain. It doesn't *mean* anything. But it has to be lived, every hour."

After some thought he added, "Life is what you don't understand, woman. By all that's holy, I've lived mine. Lived it to the hilt. Loved a good woman, had some kids, built something to leave behind . . . *savored* all of it. And I'm going to live every minute I have left. Right to the end."

He tried to turn so that he could see her face, but the pain got him bad. When it passed he said, "If I could get out of this damned bed I'd be up there on that mountain, feeling the cold, the snow, the wind, looking for that big buck. But I can't. I do the next best thing. I lie here thinking about it."

The speech was a huge effort, so he closed his eyes and rested. When he opened them again, Anne was still there.

"Don't expect you to understand. Women never do. Not even the smart ones. That's been my experience. Don't know why. But they never do."

He took three deep breaths, then whispered, "Leave me now. Please. Let me think about the mountain."

Anne went.

———

That had been almost two years ago. Today, sitting beside Ed's mother, basking in the sunlight streaming though a large exterior window of the nursing home, Anne thought about Lane Harris' comment that life is like a sunset. What else did he add? A butterfly and a drop of rain.

She could remember every word she and Lane had said to one another that week, which was one of the benefits of having a terrific memory. Or one of the drawbacks.

She recalled with a flash of discomfort her statement to the dying man that she and Ed were happy. The implication that Ed was merely enduring marriage to a smarter woman had infuriated Anne, caused her to make an assertion that she would never have made if left unprovoked. Her relationship with Ed was certainly none of Lane Harris' business. Nor anyone else's, for that matter.

But was it true?

What is happiness, anyway? The young think it is joyous ecstasy, every day like Christmas morning—nothing less will do. Lane Harris knew better, and so did Anne.

She was thinking about happiness, about Ed, about the raindrops and sunsets they had spent together, when she felt a caress on her cheek. It was Mrs. Harris, wiping away a tear with a fingertip. She wore the gentlest smile.

"Oh, Mother Harris, God bless you," Anne said, and reached to hug the lady. It was then that she understood why Lane Harris had loved his wife.

THIRTEEN

Junior Grimes was changing the spark plugs in a pickup when his mother came to the door of the garage and told him, "J. S. Kline called. He wants you to bring the roll-back up to his place."

Junior straightened. A frown crossed his face. "Is it his tractor or pickup?"

"He didn't say. Just wanted you to come by."

His mother didn't know how to take messages, Junior fumed, not for the first time. He prided himself on his quick response to problems with working equipment. If old man Kline's tractor broke down while he was in the middle of a job, Junior would hurry up there with an assortment of parts that would probably allow him to repair the tractor on the spot.

Calling Mr. Kline back was likely not worth the effort. Farmers who lived alone weren't usually sitting by the telephone sipping coffee.

Junior finished installing the spark plugs and replaced the ignition wires. Then he started the vehicle and backed it out of the garage. Ten minutes later he was on the road to Canaan at the helm of the roll-back.

Junior liked to drive. He found that thinking went better when he was behind the wheel of something. He had a lot to think about these days. Sheriff Arleigh Tate had not spoken to him since the "great tire fire," as it was being called by the Edenites. Nor had the sheriff questioned Arch Stehlik. For reasons that he couldn't pinpoint, this bothered Junior. Alas, he had never before been seriously troubled by a burdened conscience. Oh, he had been in trouble on occasion—with Arch around, little difficulties were bound to crop up from time to time, difficulties with his mother, his girlfriend, and the law—but he was usually caught fairly quickly, so his conscience didn't fester.

Deputy Delmar Clay was ostentatiously investigating the Barrow boys, who apparently had never in their lives suffered from conscience pangs. The chances that Delmar would manage to do more than annoy the Barrows were, of course, very slim. Still, that was the one bright spot on Junior's horizon.

His girlfriend, Diamond, was being distant and uncommunicative. At first Junior attributed her mood to a female problem, but in his experience female troubles didn't last more than a few days, and Diamond's sulks had been going on—what? Two weeks? More?

Junior hoped it wasn't the marriage thing. Why do women always mess up a good romance talking about marriage?

Maybe she was in a snit over his request for help with Billy Joe Elkins' problem. Billy Joe and Melanie Noroditsky's. Arch had tactfully pointed out that this was a possibility, but Junior had difficulty understanding why this might be so. He who was always willing to help anyone who needed it couldn't quite see that everyone else didn't feel similar obligations to his fellow man.

J. S. Kline was sitting on his front porch when Junior rolled in.

"You showed up mighty quick," Kline said as Junior walked over.

"Thought you might need a little help. Be broke down or hung up somewhere."

"Nope." Kline nodded toward the Camaro on blocks. "Want you to haul that out of here."

Shocked, Junior tilted back his cap and rubbed his forehead. He scrutinized Kline's face. The man appeared serious. His flinty eyes didn't waver from Junior's.

Junior turned to survey the Camaro. "Hadn't considered that," he admitted.

"It's been sitting there long enough. Take it to the junkyard."

With his hands buried in his pockets, Junior Grimes strolled over to the sedan and peered in through the broken windows as he considered the ins and outs of this unexpected turn of events. J. S. Kline followed him.

"Can only give you a hundred and fifty for it, Mr. Kline. Ain't much, I know, but the engine is about the only thing that's worth any—"

"Ten years ago you offered me a hundred for it."

Actually the car had no value today except as scrap metal, about two cents a pound, and Junior had to bear the expense of hauling it to the junkyard to recover that. The engine was undoubtedly beyond salvage. Junior's cash offer was merely window dressing to ease Mr. Kline's pain. Afraid that the old man would see that, Junior blustered, "Things has gone up in ten years. It's worth a little more now."

"Well, I'm not selling it. I'm giving it to you. Put it on the roll-back and haul it anywhere you want."

"I know what this car means to you, Mr. Kline. I don't want to take it if you're going to miss it or regret that you gave it to me."

Kline's face got colder. "Think I don't know my own mind?"

"Oh, no, sir. Nothing like that. It's just . . ." Junior took a deep breath. "Thing like this is important. Seems like a mighty big step to me after all these years, that's all. Mighty big step."

Kline remained silent.

"Knew your boy," Junior added. "He was about ten years older than me. Bought stuff down at the store and took me hunting a time or two . . . hell of a football player, so he was. I wanted to grow up to be just like him."

"Talked to that new woman preacher," J. S. Kline said. "Carcano. She made sense."

"Uh-huh."

"She's pretty smart, and she knows things."

Junior waited expectantly for more, but Kline apparently thought he had said enough. He stood for a while longer looking at the car, then abruptly turned away. He tossed over his shoulder, "Get it out of here."

Junior watched him go.

"Mighty big step for a Wednesday," Junior told the trees and weeds and whoever else might be listening. "So it is."

J. S. Kline was sitting at the foot of an apple tree near the top of the orchard when Junior drove away with the Camaro securely chained to the bed of the roll-back. As the sound of Junior's diesel engine faded, the reaction set in.

His son was gone and his wife was gone. The car had been his last link with them, with the past and all that could have been and never was. Now it, too, was gone.

He felt empty. Profoundly empty. As if he were dead. Truly, he wished he were. Wished he were beyond all caring, beyond the remembering and the pain and the love he felt for his son and had never shown.

The preacher had sensed that. Mrs. Carcano. "Did you ever tell him how much you loved him?" she asked, gently, with that soft, knowing voice.

"No," he admitted, ashamed of the truth yet not willing to lie to a preacher.

"That was what the car was for, wasn't it?"

"Yes."

"And your wife knew that."

"Said the car was a waste of money."

"Because your son knew you loved him. Your wife knew that. Knew that a gift wasn't needed to tell him what he already knew in his heart."

He had broken down then. Told the preacher of the boy, told how the pride in that boy—and the love—used to flood through him so strongly he couldn't speak, confessed to her that it had been impossible to tell the boy how he felt. Oh, his words sounded so silly now, a generation after the boy was dead. And his mother was dead. Silly words of loss and pain from an old, old man with much to regret.

Mrs. Carcano had listened. No words of comfort or advice. Listened and nodded. That was all.

Then she went away.

That was two days ago.

He had thought and thought, then called Doolin's and left word for Junior to bring the roll-back.

His son was truly gone and would never be coming home. With the car sitting by the mailbox, waiting, he had never had to accept the finality of that brutal fact. Now the car was gone.

He sat in the orchard as the sun sank toward the horizon and the shadows lengthened, watched the sunset, watched the dusk creep over the land.

His wife had known. And he didn't listen to her.

All these years of pain, and he hadn't listened.

His refusal to face the truth had hurt her deeply. She, too, was gone forever, had been gone for many a year.

Maybe God knew how he felt. Knew how much he had loved them both, still loved them both.

A jay scolded him from a branch. Probably wanted to roost in this tree for the night.

"All right," he said to the bird, and got to his feet. He walked down through the orchard toward the house he had shared with his wife for forty years, the house the boy had been born and raised in.

The house was dark.

He would turn on a light.

In a night this big, there should be a light.

"So I kissed Mom good-bye and shook Dad's hand," Verlin Ice said. "He gave me twenty dollars, and off I went on the bus, all the way to Fort Knox. It was my first big adventure, and I'll admit it here today, I was more than a little tense. Scared, to tell the truth.

"Everything went okay until they made us take off all our clothes and get in line, then they ran us through this medical building like cattle through a chute. Shots in both arms at the same time—and I hated needles. Still do. Don't know why I didn't pass out. The sergeant told me not to tense up, but

I did, gritted my teeth and trotted through that line naked as the day I was born while fellas on both sides jabbed and jabbed."

Verlin Ice shook his head at the memory. "I figure there ain't a disease in the world that could get me now. No, sir. I'm immune to just about ever' bug there is. Ever'body else gets 'em, but not me."

Here Verlin paused and launched a dark stream of tobacco juice into the dirt floor of the barn. His audience of hound and state trooper waited patiently for the monologue to continue. Verlin munched on his quid a little and wiped his mouth.

"I was doing okay at that army business there for a while. Got so I could march pretty good, say yessir and nossir and salute pretty tolerable . . . and I always could shoot. Can shoot just about any rifle made pretty darn good, if I do say so myself. I was banging away with the best of those army fellas back then. The sergeants said that I had a talent, said I had a future in that outfit."

He thought about that a bit, about those strange days when he was young. Finally he said, "Also had a cousin who was a bigwig there at Fort Knox, though I didn't know it at the time, which was a shame, 'cause he could probably have pulled some strings and got me out of all that marchin' and salutin' and runnin' and gettin' inspected.

"But I guess it worked out. I was doing just fine until I sort of had a heart attack on bivouac. The captain came into the hospital where they had me and told me he'd sure like to keep me 'cause I'd make a good soldier, but he had to send me home.

"It was a hell of a thing. Haven't had another heart problem from that day to this. Sorta suspect all I had was indigestion from eating too much rich food—the army was sure a good feeder—but a fella never knows. Awful hard to argue with a doctor. I do sort of wonder sometimes, though, what my life might have been like if I hadn't had that attack. Might have been a top sergeant or general or something. Do you ever wonder about what if?"

Sam Neely had been waiting patiently for an opportunity to nudge the conversation toward where he wanted it to go, and this looked like it. "I do," he said fervently. "A fellow tries to steer his life, but there are times when it seems to go in a certain direction whether he wants it to or not. Take women, for example. You get a certain woman on your mind and there's nothing in the world you can do to get her out of your thoughts."

Verlin Ice nodded his agreement. "Down at Fort Knox there was this gal in the pay office," he said, "with yellow hair. She always gave me a big grin when she saw me, batted her eyes in that way that yellow-haired gals have—"

Sam Neely wasn't the least bit interested in Verlin's romantic adventures. He interrupted. "Truth is, I'm interested in your daughter Crystal."

"Huh!"

"Yep. She is a fine woman."

"Crystal, you say?"

"Crystal," Sam Neely said firmly.

"There's a woman I could never figure out," her father mused. "Fine hunk of woman, but too smart. Always reading. She's looking for something but I don't think she knows what it is. Lot of women like that, though."

Neely opened his mouth to speak, then thought better of it.

"Of course," Verlin continued, "all women are hard to figure. Don't know that it does a man any good to ponder about what's in their heads. Any man who thinks he has women figured out is a fool. Men just sorta take life as it comes, if you know what I mean, but women want to make life into their idea of what it should be."

"Maybe—"

"Now, you take Crystal. Too smart for her own good, with a college education, working in Capitol City, not interested in any of the local boys—doesn't think they're good enough. Maybe they aren't." Verlin shrugged. "Now she's hanging around that writer fella, Hudson. Didn't know he was a writer. Writes books, so I hear. Now Crystal's talking about giving up her job in Capitol City. A writer!"

Verlin shook his head as he considered this amazing turn of events. "You just can't predict life," he said after some thought. "She went to see him again this morning, so she did. Diamond went, too. Said she wanted to meet this man."

"They're there now?" Neely asked sharply. "At Hudson's?"

"I suspect so. Unless they went someplace else. With women you never know. Those girls are so flighty that—"

He fell silent because he lost his audience. Trooper Neely had walked out of the barn, and the hound hadn't been paying much attention. Verlin addressed his next comment to the dog anyway. "Funny thing—Crystal didn't want Diamond to go."

Verlin got up from the feedway where he had been sitting and walked to the door of the barn, where he could see Neely getting into his cruiser. "Nice fella, but he's got it bad, I think."

Sam Neely crossed Hudson's porch and knocked on the front door.

At the third rap the door flew open and Crystal charged out, almost into his arms. She had a book in her hands.

"Hello," he said, not emphasizing it, because he had a suspicion that what was coming was not going to be pleasant.

"Where are they?" Crystal demanded.

"Who?"

"They went for a walk," she said, partially answering her own question. She galloped to the end of the porch and scanned the plowed earth behind the house. Then she trotted back to the front door and went into the house.

Since she left the door standing open, Neely followed. "I hope you don't mind the intrusion, but I—"

"Did you know?" she demanded, shaking the book at him.

"Know what?"

"That he's Rip Hays?"

Neely felt as if he'd arrived in the middle of the movie. "I thought his name was Richard Hudson."

"It is! But he's Rip Hays, too."

"Are you sure that——?"

She thrust the book at him, holding it so he could see the cover. Depicted boldly on the dust jacket was a sun-bronzed weight lifter in a loincloth swinging a large sword. "Hudson's Rip Hays!" she exclaimed. "It's a pen name, like Mark Twain. *He writes Prince Ziad!*"

"Look, Crystal. I——"

"I'm not Crystal. I'm Diamond."

Neely felt dizzy, light-headed. "Didn't you and I . . . ?"

"Oh, yes. But it didn't mean anything. Two healthy people, we needed each other. Then. That was all it was. Purely physical. Just a roll in the hay."

"In the leaves."

"Whatever." She made a dismissive gesture.

"But you're Diamond. We had never even met."

"Oh, that. So my sister and I look a lot alike. We're identical twins. Not really identical, but almost. Don't feel bad. You're not the first boy who made that mistake."

"And how long is that list?" Neely asked bitterly.

Diamond ignored the question, if she even heard it. "He's Rip Hays!" She hugged the book to her bosom. "Oh, my goodness. I had no idea. Crystal has been mooning over him for weeks and I thought she was just off her rocker. But he's *Rip Hays!* My heavens. Imagine that!"

"I haven't read any Rip Hays books," Neely said simply. The truth was, he had never even heard of the man.

"Prince Ziad is simply the most magnificent man in the universe. He's handsome, kind, intelligent, brave, he *understands women*——"

"I certainly don't," Sam Neely said with conviction. "I confess, I don't know what the hell is going on here."

"*He* understands. And Richard Hudson is the man who wrote him. Don't you see? Richard Hudson is Prince Ziad!"

This was too much for Neely. He found a chair and lowered himself into it.

"Crystal didn't want to tell me," Diamond explained, continuing to hug the book. "Wouldn't talk to me about this man she was spending all this time with. I couldn't understand it. That isn't like her. Then when they took a walk a short while ago, I started looking. Found all these Rip Hays books, looked in his desk drawers—oh, I know that I shouldn't have, but still . . . You understand, don't you?"

Neely was beginning to get a glimmer.

She put down the books and knelt on the floor beside him. "Oh, you poor man. I'm sorry. You're in love with Crystal, aren't you?"

"I sorta thought I was . . ."

"You poor, poor man. She's thrown herself at Rip—Richard, I mean. It's really obscene. She's such a leech. It's obvious that he doesn't want her, but she refuses to face it." Her voice hardened. "Don't worry—I'll pry her off, then you can have her."

"Why would you—"

She bounced up and almost skipped across the room to look out the window. Then she turned to face him, wearing a radiant smile. "I'm going to take him."

"Richard Hudson?"

"Rip Hays. Prince Ziad."

"They are figments of the man's imagination," Neely objected reasonably. "They don't exist. Richard is a pleasant little fellow who just wants to be left alone so he can dig up arrowheads and write."

"I've read his books," the lady said in no uncertain terms. "This man is searching for love. I have looked into his soul and he has looked into mine—he knows every nook and cranny. We were born for each other."

"Umm."

"He just doesn't know it yet."

"I see." Neely rose from the chair and settled his hat onto his head. He stepped tentatively toward the door.

"We'll be so very happy," Diamond assured him. "You'll see."

"I do see. But I thought you and Junior Grimes . . . ?"

"Junior? Hah! He doesn't want to leave his mother. Never has and never will, not for any woman alive." She glanced out the window again.

"There they are!"

She bolted for the door.

Diamond Ice was bounding like a young deer across the plowed furrows as Neely dived behind the wheel of the cruiser. He got the motor spinning and backed out smartly onto the Vegan road.

As he was driving away he got a glimpse of Goofy on his cinder blocks with his nose pressed against one of Hudson's windows.

When he arrived at the state police office in Indian River, Sam Neely found two people waiting for him, a man and a woman, both gray-haired. They came into his small office and sat in his two visitor's chairs.

"What can I do for you?"

"My name is John Morgan Ramsey. This is my wife, Flora. We've come about the Barrow boys."

Neely pulled his yellow legal pad into position and armed his pen. "What have they done this time?"

"We were on the road between Canaan and Goshen, just driving along, when they passed us in that old car of theirs. They hollered a bit going by, then slowed down in front of us until they were barely moving. When we got close behind them, they spun their wheels and showered our windshield with rocks."

"Which one was driving?"

"Looked like Bushrod to me—they call him Bush—but I couldn't say for swearing to. He and Coonrod look a lot alike, so they do, and I don't know 'em that well. Don't want to know 'em no better, neither."

"I see."

"Well, they did that rock trick to us twice. The second time the windshield cracked. The third time I wouldn't pull up behind them close enough, I guess, so they parked their car and came walking back. Leaned in my window, called me some names, said I better quit messing with them if I knew what was good for me."

"Called John some pretty dirty names," Mrs. Ramsey said.

Mr. Ramsey continued his narration. "Then they got back into their car and drove away laughing. I was pretty hot about it, so I came here."

"When did this happen, Mr. Ramsey?"

"About an hour ago, more or less."

"Did anyone else witness this incident?"

"Well, not that I know of."

"Are you willing to sign a complaint?"

Here John and Flora Ramsey looked at each other. Neither seemed in a hurry to speak. Neely suspected that they had thoroughly discussed this aspect of the matter during the drive to Indian River.

"They know who we are," John Morgan Ramsey said finally. "We have a farm near Goshen, keep about a hundred and ten head of stock. The Barrow boys have been known to sit out on the road and shoot cattle. Just shoot 'em and watch 'em drop. To get even with people. And nobody ever sees who did it, so the law can never touch 'em."

"Without a complaint, Mr. Ramsey, there is nothing that I can do."

"I told you he'd say that," Flora Ramsey told her husband.

"It seems like there ought to be something," Mr. Ramsey said stoutly. "The Barrows are outlaws who don't play by anyone's rules. Yet we have to."

"I'm sorry."

"Those cattle are our living."

"If you should change your mind about signing a complaint, please come back."

Sam Neely ushered the Ramseys from the room and closed the door behind them. Then he went back to his chair and sat looking out his window at the alley behind the courthouse.

After a while he decided to get on record with his own complaint. "If You'd put Your mind to it, God," he said aloud, "seems to me that You could have done a little better job of putting this world together."

FOURTEEN

Elijah Murphy was in Indian River when he fell off the wagon.

He awoke that fateful morning clean, sober and hungry. He fixed a little something to eat, waved at the widow Wilfred when she swept her porch, and hummed pleasantly to himself as he swept out his shack. His woodpile was huge, the junk was gone from his yard, he had some groceries laid in, and his new bathroom was coming right along. This would be a good day, he decided, to go to the hardware store in Indian River. He made a mental note of the bathroom fittings he needed and did some measuring. Then he pulled on his coat and set off.

He walked to the hard road and hitched a ride to town. The farmer who gave him a ride dropped him right in front of the hardware store. After he purchased his fittings, he stood on the sidewalk looking the town over.

Elijah Murphy hadn't taken a really good look at this town in years, probably because he was always drunk or suffering from DTs when he was there. This morning he strolled the sidewalk looking in store windows and examining facades, marveling at changes both large and subtle that had occurred over the years without his notice.

Somehow he found himself in front of the Paris Saloon, a lowlife dive about as far as one could get from Gay Paree on this side of the Atlantic. Why he found himself staring through the dirty windows of this beer joint at the drunks inside holding up the bar is one of life's great mysteries, one that was certainly beyond the ability of Elijah Murphy to wrestle with at that moment. All he knew was that he was thirsty and there was beer right through that door.

He had been doing very well sober, but he didn't think about that now. He had also been making excellent progress with the widow Wilfred, which was a bright spot in his life. He liked her immensely and she seemed to like him. Alas, he wasn't thinking about that good lady when he pushed open the door to the Paris Saloon and strolled through.

She popped into his thoughts for a fleeting moment as he stepped up to the bar, however. Murphy knew precisely what she would say if she saw him in here.

"Just one beer won't matter," he told his conscience, and meant it.

"Murphy, where have you been?" the bar slattern said. "Our profits went off the cliff when you stopped coming. We thought you had died."

"I'm healthy and thirsty, honey," replied Elijah Murphy, man of the world. "Gimme a cold one."

"We don't serve 'em warm, Murphy," the girl said. As the barflies tittered, she added, "This is a high-class joint."

"A draft."

"You got it."

That first sip was the high point in Elijah Murphy's life. Never had anything tasted so good. It was as if he had emerged from a desert after an eternity without water, and into his parched, burning mouth flowed the tangy, bubbling, foaming essence of all that was good and desirable in life.

Fortunately more than one sip was available; he held a cold, dripping, brimming glass of this marvelous elixir right in his hand. So he had another sip. And another.

When the glass was empty, he called for more.

———

Junior Grimes was in the garage working on Harley Martel's '57 Chevy Bel Air when Sam Neely came storming in. The scene yesterday with Diamond at Richard Hudson's house had been festering for almost twenty-four hours and he was looking for someone to shout at. For reasons he thought excellent, he had settled on Junior as that someone.

"How come," Neely demanded, "you didn't tell me that Crystal and Diamond Ice are identical twins?"

Junior extracted his head from under Martel's hood and turned in amazement. The state trooper standing there in a towering fury irritated Junior somewhat. "Say what?"

Neely belligerently repeated his question.

"Everybody knows they're identical twins," Junior said.

"*I* didn't."

"They're not exactly identical; pretty close, though. Once you get to know them, you can tell them apart, no problem."

"I didn't know that!" Neely howled.

"Do I look like an encyclopedia? How am I supposed to know what you don't know?"

"You—of all people—*you* should have told me."

"What else don't you know? Quality folks use toilet paper. Women shave their legs. Brassieres come in sizes, and the hooks are in the back. Don't eat yellow snow or pick your nose in church. Okra tastes like—"

"Of all people, *you* should have told me."

Junior threw his wrench. It made a clang as it hit the floor. "Okay, I'll bite. Why should *I* have told you?"

"Because I was interested in Crystal."

"So?"

"You dummy!" Neely roared. "You big, blind jackass. I wound up in bed with Diamond!"

After that statement, the garage was profoundly quiet as Junior Grimes stared at the trooper in stupefied amazement.

Neely recovered first and broke the silence. "It wasn't bed, actually. It was a pile of leaves on a ridge. Gorgeous evening. I thought—"

What he thought had to remain unsaid, because just then Billy Joe Elkins came rushing into the garage from the store.

"Junior, I have got to talk to you." He glanced at the uniformed trooper, who turned and faced a girlie calendar advertising socket wrenches.

"It's urgent, Junior," Billy Joe whispered.

Junior Grimes took three or four deep breaths and shifted gears. "Aren't you supposed to be in school right now?"

"I cut French class. I had to talk to you."

"Well, what is it?"

The young man's eyes flicked toward the trooper. "Couldn't we go someplace and—"

"Whisper."

"Okay." Billy Joe dropped his voice and moved closer. "Delmar Clay stopped Melanie last night. Pulled her over. Told her he had some interesting pictures."

"He's lying. I told you that Arch and I went to Benny Modesso's drugstore and took Delmar's roll out of the bag."

"I know, Junior, I know. But he says he has pictures and he wants Melanie to meet him on Saturday night or he'll mail the pictures to her dad."

"She should tell him to go screw himself."

"Hey, Junior! Look at the position she is in. If he just talks to Frank Naroditsky, she's dead. She can't tell Delmar anything."

Junior Grimes used his shirttail to wipe his forehead. "Okay, okay."

"We have got to do something about Delmar Clay."

"I'm working on it."

"Like quick, Junior. This jerk could ruin Melanie's life."

"Go back to French class. Let me work some more on it."

With a last glance at Sam Neely's back, the boy bustled out. Junior retrieved his wrench from the floor and arranged himself under the Chevy's hood.

After a bit he heard Neely say, "I didn't know it was Diamond, of course."

"Are you still here?"

"Didn't know then. I found out yesterday when I talked to her at Richard Hudson's house. Hudson's a writer, you know."

"Oh."

"She's fallen for Hudson. In fact, both the Ice sisters have. Crystal and Diamond."

This was too much for Junior. He gave up on the Chevy's plugs and backed out so that he could see Neely. "Are you crazy? That little bald fat guy?"

"Yep. Hudson. That little bald fat guy. Both the Ice girls are nuts over him."

Junior tossed the wrench again, then sat heavily on a box of something or other that he had propped against a wall. He put his head in his hands.

"Mr. Elkins, your senior wife called and wants you to call her back when you have a few minutes." Hayden Elkins' secretary delivered this message in a cool tone, with one eyebrow raised.

"For two cents I'd fire you, Harriet," the prosecuting attorney said to his loyal government employee. He had been putting up with her sarcasm for weeks.

"You can't fire me, Mr. Elkins," she replied with simple dignity, "without a majority vote of the county commissioners. Our civil service system is designed to protect government employees from the arbitrary, capricious whims of elected officials. Remember?"

His life was completely, totally out of control. Everyone in the county snickered at the sight of him, the courthouse crowd guffawed, the judge laughed uproariously in his face . . . his secretary made his life miserable, his wife—make that wives—took malicious delight in drawing blood drop by painful drop . . .

There were moments when he just wanted to cry.

It wasn't fair. That was the galling thing. Of course he made a pass at Anne Harris. He didn't rape her, for heaven's sake. She *welcomed* his advances. They had sex. Once. Was that so terrible? And now people regarded her as a tragic figure, sympathized, took pity upon her.

Even his wife, Matilda, did. That was the unbelievable part, the part Hayden Elkins found impossible to understand.

He picked up the telephone and dialed. Matilda answered.

"It's me," he said.

"Dear, I want you to stop by the store on your way home. Pick up some artichoke hearts for the dinner salad."

"You don't like artichoke hearts."

"Oh, I don't, but Anne does. She dotes on them. Be a dear and bring some home."

He put the instrument back on the receiver and sat staring at it with distaste, unwilling to believe what his ears had just heard.

Amazingly, it was true. Matilda and Anne were becoming best friends.

They sat and chatted by the hour, did the housework together, compared recipes and cooked up gourmet delights shoulder to shoulder, attended social events together; they were becoming inseparable. "After all," Matilda told him last night, "we have so much in common."

Hayden ignored that remark. He was getting in the habit of ignoring remarks. "We've got to send her home, Matilda. She must leave our house."

"But where will she go? She can't go home. Ed won't let her. And she doesn't want to. We can't just put her out"—here Matilda gestured vaguely at the trackless wilderness that lay beyond the door—"with winter coming on. Surely you see that?"

"Are you off your nut? That woman owns half the bank! She has more money than we do! She's probably one of the two or three richest people in the county. She could buy any house in this state that's for sale."

"She doesn't want to live alone."

"She could live in a hotel. A hotel in New York. Or Paris. She could tour Europe until that idiot husband of hers recovers his senses or she decides to divorce him."

"She doesn't want to divorce him, dear."

"Matilda, that isn't our problem. And providing housing for her isn't our problem."

"Anne is a friend," Matilda explained patiently. "She's a friend of yours and a friend of mine. In addition to friendship, there is the obligation of Christian charity. Remember the good Samaritan. She may stay here as long as she wishes, as long as she needs to."

"That is *precisely* my point, Matilda. Dear! The woman doesn't *need* to stay here."

"But she wants to. And I want her to. So I don't want to talk any more about it."

That was the conversation last night.

What were his options?

Divorce. He could divorce Matilda. File the action in Lester Storm's court and listen to that judicial monstrosity laugh, chuckle, wheeze and snort through hearing after endless hearing.

Chuck the whole scene and run away. Change his name. Get a job dealing cards in Vegas; move in with an exotic dancer with artificial boobs. Forget the past. Start life over.

That option certainly seemed to have its attractions, but it also had a rather obvious downside. Matilda would find him, would hire private detectives to ferret him out if it took every cent she could lay hands on. Ferret him out to punish him. A month ago she wouldn't have dreamed of doing that to a wayward husband, but now she would. He sensed it, knew it to a certainty.

Suicide. He could shoot himself. Actually that option was not all that ridiculous. His life was becoming a living hell and there looked to be no end to the torture.

Gun, rope or gas?

He would have to think about it.

Oh, my God, look at me. Contemplating suicide. After one very short adulterous incident.

And it was the last sex he had had. Maybe the last sexual encounter he would ever have. In his whole life. Things were certainly shaping up that way. He had tried making advances to Matilda and had been unequivocally rebuffed every time. "I'm not emotionally ready," she told him gently but firmly. He could sense the cold steel in her voice under that ladylike demeanor, and it made him shiver.

He had gotten so frustrated that he even made another pass at Anne, who looked at him as if he were a dung-eating beetle in search of a meal.

"I take it you aren't romantically interested just now," he said, trying to keep it light.

"Touch me and I'll cut it off."

"If you change your mind . . ."

"If I took up streetwalking I still wouldn't let you touch me."

"You did once."

"Don't ever mention that incident in my presence again for the rest of your life."

"Perhaps some other time."

You couldn't let them know they were getting to you. Or shouldn't.

Lord knows they *were* getting to him. All of them. It was as if everyone he knew had written him out of the human race. He was a pariah. Even his own son didn't want to be seen with him.

"It's not that I'm not proud of you, Dad," Billy Joe had explained. "But people get this funny look and point and whisper. I'm not up to dealing with it."

"And I am?"

"You're tough, Dad. I know you can take it. But I'm still young, just a kid, really. It's not fair for the sins of the father to be visited upon the son."

"Sins?"

"Give me a break, Dad. Cut me some slack. I don't want to talk about it."

Somehow he managed to get his mind off his personal problems long enough to read the police report on his desk. It was signed by that half-wit deputy, Delmar Clay. Claimed that the Barrow boys had torched Junior Grimes' junkyard tire pile. The only basis for this accusation, as far as Hayden Elkins could determine, was Delmar's personal statement that he had witnessed the Barrow boys fleeing the scene of the crime. There was no evidence tying them to the purchase of arson material, no hint of a motive, not a single, solitary additional witness, not even a whiff of a suggestion that any fire official would get on the stand and swear the blaze was arson. The entire case for the prosecution would consist of putting Delmar Clay on the stand, eliciting his testimony, then resting.

Lester Storm would have a conniption fit if Elkins wasted his time with a farce like that. Who would blame him?

No wonder the Barrow boys rarely got convicted of anything. With Delmar Clay hot on their trail, the state was hopelessly handicapped. Of course, Arleigh Tate could have taken a hand in this investigation to see that it was developed properly or buried. Apparently he hadn't, which was curious.

Elkins reached for the telephone to call Arleigh, then slowly withdrew his hand. Better leave well enough alone. He sighed and threw the file carelessly onto the large pile in the corner behind his desk.

The Ice girls arrived at Richard Hudson's house in midmorning. They began by cleaning the kitchen and preparing a sumptuous lunch. Hudson ate alone, trying to decide what to do. As he ate, he listened to the washing machine and clothes dryer, both located in a nook just off the kitchen. The machines were running full tilt. The women had decided to wash and iron every stitch he owned and were now hard at it. He could hear them upstairs in the bedroom, where they were sorting the clothes in his closet.

As Hudson ate, Goofy watched him through the kitchen window.

Hudson got up, fixed a big sandwich for Goofy, opened the window and handed it out. He also passed Goofy a cup of hot coffee because it was downright chilly outside. "Sure you don't want to come in?"

Goofy shook his head no, accepted the sandwich and coffee and began eating, still standing on his cinder blocks. Hudson closed the window to keep the heat in and went back to his lunch on the kitchen table.

How was he ever going to get any writing done? Looking for arrowheads was one thing, but actually getting his head into a story and stringing words together in the midst of domestic bedlam was something else again.

Two women! How did the old Mormons manage?

He bolted the last of his food and went back to the mud. When he tired of walking and looking, he found a stump to sit in front of and lean against. Goofy sat on the other side of the stump. Hudson examined the points he had found that day and stared at the house and watched the shadows lengthen.

From where he sat he could see Goofy's cinder blocks under the kitchen window. Of course he was wondering what the Ice sisters were doing in his house. Finally the thoughts coalesced—thoughts do that sometimes. He rose, dusted off his jeans and marched for the house with Goofy trailing along behind. He arranged the blocks just so, then climbed up on them and looked into the kitchen.

The sisters weren't there. He carried the blocks around to the study. There they were, looking at his books. He could even hear what they were saying.

They were arguing about the literary merits of his various tales. He watched them for a minute or two, then sat on the cinder blocks under the window. He could still hear them plainly.

As he listened he became more and more irritated. According to Crystal and Diamond, he was an extraordinarily gifted writer who could see inside human hearts. Yet here he sat under his study window on a chilly evening listening to two dingbats who had taken over his house and refused to leave. Gifted? Hell, he was an idiot.

"What do you think we should do, Goofy?"

This was actually the first question he had addressed to Goofy in the course of their acquaintance that required a considered answer. Goofy was a little surprised, and he studied on it for several seconds before he answered. "Cold. Time them take me home."

"Of course it is," Richard Hudson agreed, and rose from his perch. He handed Goofy his cinder blocks, then headed for the front of the house, followed by Goofy. Up the stairs, through the door, into the study.

"Goofy is cold and tired and wants to go home. I suggest you two take him—now. I am also cold and tired. I want some peace and quiet in my own house."

By God, it worked! The two women got in their respective cars—Goofy got in with Crystal—and away they went. Richard Hudson carefully locked the front door, then went to the kitchen to fix himself a drink.

It was close to 9:00 P.M. when a car pulled up in front of the open door to the garage bay at Doolin's. Junior was sweeping the garage. Normally at this time of the evening he would be helping Mom close the store or watching television or hanging around Verlin Ice's, but tonight he wanted to be alone.

A woman got out of the car, saw him, and walked in his direction. He recognized her when she came into the light. "Evening, Mrs. Carcano."

"Good evening, Mr. Grimes. Are you alone?"

"Yes, ma'am. As a matter of fact, I don't think I've ever been more alone in my whole life."

Mrs. Carcano turned and gestured toward the car. "I picked up a man just outside of Indian River who said he wanted to come here. Unfortunately, he's drunk."

Junior strode for the car. No one was visible in the front seat, so he opened the rear passenger door. Elijah Murphy was lying on the backseat. The odor of vomit washed over Junior like a wave.

"Don't worry, Mrs. Carcano. I'll clean this mess up." He grasped the comatose man by the back of the shirt collar and his belt and lifted him from the car. Junior carried him across the asphalt and into the garage, where he stowed him under a tool bench. Then he bent down. "Hey, Murph! Murphy! It's me, Junior. How you doin'?"

"You got any beer, Junior?"

"Are you going to be sick again?"

"I don't think so."

"If you are, say so. I'll get you to the bathroom."

"Okay."

"Just stay there and keep quiet. I've got to clean out the preacher's car."

He put water in a bucket, added detergent, found a sponge, then went over to the car. Mrs. Carcano stood nearby and watched. As he was sponging up the mess, she said, "I appreciate this."

"Nice of you to give ol' Murph a ride. Going to get cold tonight. Too cold for a drunk to sleep outside."

"Does he come here often?"

"Oh, he's been here a few times. More than Mom knows about, that's for sure. I put a blanket over him and he sleeps under the tool bench. If he's sick it's easy to hose away."

Junior had about got the mess removed from Mrs. Carcano's car when he said, "Don't think Murph had a drop for about six weeks. It's a real shame he lost it. He wasn't going to drink anymore. Was courting the widow Wilfred. When she hears about this, that'll be all over. She doesn't hold with drinking."

"A social drink is one thing, Mr. Grimes. Falling-down, puking drunk is something else."

"Better call me Junior. Everyone else does."

"What's his name? Murphy?"

"Elijah Murphy."

"Mr. Murphy is a drunk."

Junior finished cleaning and closed the car door. He checked the window of the store to see if his mother was watching. Apparently not. "Yes, ma'am. He's surely that. Been one for a lot of years. Spent most of his life drunk and I suspect he's gonna die that way. Not that he really wants to. He really wants to sober up. You don't get everything you want in life, though."

He carried the bucket back into the garage. Mrs. Carcano followed, so he kept talking. "Funny thing. When he's drinking, Murph doesn't get mean like a lot of fellas do. Never gets nasty or says hateful things, would never hurt anyone. When a man gets stinking drunk, he forgets all his manners and inhibitions, and you can see what kind of a man he is all the way through to the backbone. Way down inside Murphy is a good man. Now that won't get him into the widow Wilfred's bed or into your church, but I suspect it's good enough for the Lord. He'll probably be standing out there at the Pearly Gates with Saint Pete to welcome ol' Murph when the time comes."

"And you, Mr. Grimes? Are you a good man?"

That stumped Junior. Never in his life had he wondered if he was good or bad. So he chewed on the question a moment before he said, "I just hope Murphy puts in a word for me, ma'am. So I do."

"Junior," Elijah Murphy croaked from under the tool bench, "I think I'm gonna be sick again."

Junior lifted the drunken man with ease—the back of the collar in his left hand and the belt in his right—and draped him over the restroom commode as if he were a sack of grain.

He was holding Murphy when Lula Grimes came into the garage. She went by Mrs. Carcano without nodding and looked to see what was going on in the restroom. The sound of retching was quite plain.

"Junior, is that Murphy?"

"Yeah, Mom."

"Did you give him beer?"

"No, Mom."

"Where'd he get it?" Lula Grimes demanded suspiciously.

"Indian River, I believe," Mrs. Carcano said. "I picked him up on the edge of town. He was hitchhiking."

"Junior collects things," Lula told the preacher. "Birds with broken wings, orphan fawns, heartsick boys, brokenhearted girls . . . and drunks."

"I brought Mr. Murphy by a few minutes ago, Mrs. Grimes. I'm sorry. I asked for Junior's help. If he would bring Mr. Murphy over to my house in the morning, I would appreciate it." With that Mrs. Carcano walked out of the garage, got into her car and drove away.

Lula Grimes shook her head in frustration, then went back through the side door of the garage into the store.

Elijah Murphy spent the night in his shack. He slept on the floor and Junior Grimes sacked out on the bed. Murphy didn't care a whit. He was too drunk.

Junior fully intended to let Murphy sleep it off under his tool bench in the garage—Murphy had slept there on several winter nights in the past— but his mother returned to the garage and put her foot down. "I own half this place. You are not going to turn it into a shelter for wandering drunks. Not while I'm alive, anyway."

"Yes, Mom."

"That preacher wants to see Murphy in the morning."

"I'll get him there," Junior said.

"A total waste of time. The man is hopeless."

"It's her time."

"No, Junior. It's *your* time. You have to clean up after him, you have to look after him tonight, you have to get him to the preacher's tomorrow. Preachers get paid to wrestle with the sins of weak men—you don't. You get paid to fix cars. The next time Murphy staggers in here blind drunk, I hope you remember this evening."

Junior nodded. He had learned years ago that arguing with his mother wasn't worth the air it cost.

"You can't make pets of people, Junior. Aren't you ever going to learn that?"

Junior loaded Elijah Murphy into the cab of his roll-back and took him to his cabin. Junior didn't think like his mother. He knew that but never mused about why she felt as she did. He accepted a great many things in life without trying to figure them out; his mother was one of them.

He built a fire in the stove, cleaned Murphy up a little bit, then got the already sleeping man arranged in a corner with a blanket over him and a pillow under his head. As the fire in the stove made popping noises and heat seeped into the room, Junior took off his boots and stretched out on Murphy's bed.

His mind turned to Diamond Ice. Like his mother, Diamond was one of the phenomena in his world that Junior didn't normally ponder about. But Diamond and Sam Neely—now that was galling.

Hard to blame Neely, of course. Claimed he didn't know Crystal from Diamond, and Junior could see how a newcomer to Eden could make that mistake. The girls bore a startling physical resemblance. Diamond, on the other hand, didn't have an excuse: Sam Neely didn't look a bit like Junior.

All that talk of marriage, then she takes Neely up on a ridge . . . in the leaves . . .

FIFTEEN

The next morning rain fell steadily from a slate sky. Junior stoked the fire in the woodstove and cut up four potatoes that Murphy had in his cabinet. Murphy awoke while he was frying them.

"Better get yourself cleaned up," Junior said. "You got to go see the preacher in a little while."

"What preacher?"

"Mrs. Carcano."

"I ain't going to chin with no preacher. No way. Got this far without being prayed over and I'll just keep going down the trail without it."

"You're goin', so I don't want to hear any more about it. She brought you out from Indian River last night."

"Mighty steep price for a ride." Murphy was so stiff and sore from sleeping on the floor that he couldn't stand without holding on to something. And he felt sick, really sick. "Guess I was pretty drunk last night."

"You were plastered, all right, but it wasn't pretty."

"Don't remember much about it."

"If you want to break up with the widow Wilfred, why didn't you just tell her so?"

"She doesn't know, does she?" Murphy hitched himself sideways to a window and peered over at Twila Wilfred's house.

"Women know everything," Junior said gloomily. "Better wash and put on clean clothes, some that don't stink. These potatoes will be ready in a few minutes."

"I couldn't eat."

"A few bites will make you feel better."

Elijah Murphy sank onto the one chair he owned and stared morosely at the wall.

Junior dropped Murphy in front of Mrs. Carcano's house and watched as he walked slowly across the lawn, oblivious to the rain. He climbed the stairs to the porch as if he were scaling Mount Everest. Standing in front of the door with his shoulders hunched, a wizened little man in grubby clothes, Murphy looked so forlorn that Junior almost called to him to come back to the truck. He managed to restrain himself.

Instead he turned off the engine. He wasn't going anywhere until Murphy was in that house, with the door closed. He knew Elijah Murphy too well. The instant Junior was out of sight Murphy might rabbit for the woods. Not that Junior blamed him. A root canal without anesthetic would be preferable to a one-on-one session with a woman preacher with your sins as the main topic of conversation. Oh, well, Murphy had gotten himself into this mess; he had to take his medicine.

Finally Murphy lifted his hand and knocked on the preacher's door.

Junior started the roll-back. When the door opened and Murphy disappeared into the house, Junior lifted the clutch and fed gas.

"How do you like your coffee, Mr. Murphy?"

"Don't matter."

"Strong and black, then. Please come into the kitchen—we can talk there."

Murphy followed Mrs. Carcano and took a seat at the kitchen table. He took off his old cap and sat twisting it in his hands as she rattled cups and saucers. When the steaming black liquid was in front of him, he couldn't help himself. He put the cap in his lap and used both hands to lift the cup to his lips. His hands were shaking again.

"Do you really want to stop drinking?" Mrs. Carcano asked over her shoulder. When his answer didn't come immediately, she paused and turned to face him.

"I don't know," Murphy said when he got the cup back into its saucer.

"Won't be easy."

The coffee perked Murphy up. "Praying about it ain't going to help, I don't figure."

"I couldn't agree with you more. The strength and determination must come from within."

"What would you know about it?"

Mrs. Carcano took a seat across from Murphy and sipped her coffee before she answered. "I'm an alcoholic," she said softly. "I can't even drink cough syrup with alcohol in it."

"Ahh . . ."

"It's true, Mr. Murphy. I'm an alcoholic. I managed to stop drinking just before it killed me. I started drinking as a teenager, stayed drunk from the time I was fifteen until I was twenty-four. Flunked out of college, my first husband divorced me, my family disowned me, I lost my self-respect— basically I lost everything. I gave it all up. So I could keep drinking. I knew the costs and drank anyway."

"What made you stop?"

She got up from the table and went over to the window. With her back to him she said, "I woke up one morning in the Tombs. That's the jail in New York City. I had been arrested for prostitution. I had a venereal disease, the DTs, I hadn't eaten in days, my teeth were loose from malnutrition, and I didn't have a cent to my name. Not a person on this earth gave a damn about me, because I didn't give a damn about myself. That morning in the Tombs, sitting in my own filth and surrounded by the dregs of humanity, I hit rock bottom. I was so ashamed of myself I couldn't even cry. I decided I would never drink again, would try to make something of the years I had left."

"Why are you telling me this?"

She turned to face him. "Life is only what you make it, Mr. Murphy. You put nothing in, you get nothing out. You're going to have to decide."

"I tried. I tried to stop. But yesterday, standing in front of that beer joint, thinking about how good that beer would taste—"

"No, Mr. Murphy. You can't sell me that lie. I've wallowed deeper in the slime than you'll ever get. What you were thinking about was how good that alcohol high would feel. That is what you are addicted to, Mr. Murphy. That is what I'm addicted to, and that's why I can't touch anything with alcohol in it. Just one little alcohol kick and I won't be able to stop."

"Did you ever fall off the wagon?"

"Yes."

"But you don't drink now?"

"Not for fifteen years."

"Could I have some more coffee, Mrs. Carcano?"

When the thick envelope addressed to Anne Harris arrived at the Elkins house, Matilda gave it to Anne, who recognized Ed's handwriting on the address. Anne took it to her bedroom to read.

Dear Anne,

You asked why I went hunting those days before Dad died two years ago. I have thought about it a good bit these last two weeks, so I will write my thoughts down for you. I don't know that you will understand, because I am not sure I did myself at the time. Even now, I am not sure I have it right.

The first morning hunting I thought mostly about pending matters at the bank. Almost two years later, confessing that makes me blush. With Dad dying and Mom getting senile, walking through the deep woods in sleet and snow, getting wet and cold, my mind was on the bank—interest rates, personnel problems, a couple of pending loans, and a loan that looked as if we would have to call it. It takes a lot to get me out of my rut.

Finally I began to think of other things, about Dad, his life, Mom, that part of their journey that I accompanied them on, the road still to travel . . . Gradually, looking at the gray trees and the snow and the low clouds, listening, listening to the silence, waiting for that flash of movement that oh so rarely comes, even the folks faded. Sometime that afternoon—I am not sure when—up there on that mountain there was just the winter forest and the elusive deer, and me. Me, this little blob of bone, muscle, sinew and digestive tract that the world knows as Ed Harris, a mortal man with at least half his life already past.

I didn't wear enough clothes that first day, so I had to keep moving to stay warm. Couldn't stand or sit for more than three minutes. Finally my coat began to absorb water and my feet got cold and my fingers got numb. I kept moving around Panther Lick, which is the head of the Indian River drainage.

A family farmed this high mountain meadow around the turn of the last century: they died or moved away in the '20s. They merely eked out a poor living on thin, rocky soil, and the young people were probably glad to go. The land was sold for taxes during the Great Depression. The man who purchased it on the courthouse steps by paying the delinquent taxes merely let the trees grow. Dad bought it about 1960 and cut the timber three or four years later.

Panther Lick is becoming timber again. The ruins of the old house are still visible amid the weeds and brush, and you can see the foundations of the well house. Every now and then you find a locust fence post still standing—there are not many of those. Everything else that man made is pretty well gone except the logging road, which is badly washed out in places.

Ed Harris, cold, shivering middle-aged banker, thought some about the family that lived there all those years ago, thought about who they were, what they might have wanted from life, what they wanted for their kids. Wondered why they picked this place, isolated, up here in the forest on this mountain.

I was on a tip of a ridge that comes down off the main ridge and overlooks the meadow where the house stood, idly turning these questions over, when I found the cemetery.

I hunted all over that area as a youngster, even before Dad bought the land, and I didn't know the graveyard was there. It is merely a dozen or so stone slabs amid the trees. No doubt the ridge was meadow or pasture when the bodies were buried, but after the family left, it went back to trees. The stones—slate, I think—have some carving on them. That first afternoon I could read the carving clearly in the diffused half-light; the next afternoon, with the sun shining, I could only see scratches—the names and dates were impossible to make out.

I didn't see hide nor hair of that big buck the first day. I don't think I did, anyway. I jumped several deer, but they bounded off through the trees so quickly that I couldn't see if they were does or bucks.

Not that I cared.

My being up there wandering around was enough to satisfy Dad. He thought I was hunting. That was enough. My only regret was that I hadn't worn enough clothes, so I had to keep moving, which cost me a lot of energy.

That evening I was so tired, yet I had to tell Dad what I'd seen. I wanted to know how he was feeling, how his day had gone, but he didn't want to talk about that. He wanted to hear about the hunt, about Panther Lick.

I had seen a couple of deer, sex unknown. He assured me again that the big buck was up there, told me about watching him for almost an hour one afternoon.

I asked him about the cemetery.

"You didn't know it was there?" he replied.

"No."

He lay there silently for a moment, then said, "All of us are going to be forgotten eventually, like those folks up on that mountain. When the people who loved you are gone, you're gone."

That was all he said about the cemetery. He talked some more about the buck, told me what he looked like and where he had seen him and where he thought I might find him. He spent the rest of our time together on that subject.

When I left him I was too exhausted to talk to you, too tired to keep my eyes open. I remember collapsing in the chair by the fire.

The next morning I awoke about five. You had put a blanket over me and were asleep on the couch.

Dad was sleeping fitfully, and every now and then he would exhale, then not inhale for the longest moment. I asked the nurse about it. She whispered that often they go like that, exhale and never inhale again.

Standing there in the doorway of the bedroom in those moments before dawn, waiting for Dad to breathe again, I felt so helpless, realized how little I knew of life, of its processes and profound mysteries.

I hope there is a God. Don't know that there is, and maybe that skepticism is widely shared these days. I flat don't know.

But I hope He exists. And I hope He cares.

You were stretched out on the couch sleeping deeply. I decided not to wake you. Wish now that I had. Wish I'd kissed you and told you I loved you. But I didn't; like so many of life's chances, that moment is gone forever.

The porch thermometer read seventeen degrees. Wind blowing, snow coming down but not sticking, the ground frozen . . . I had a lot more clothes on than the day before but still the cold wind cut through.

When you first feel the winter wind's bite there is a moment of doubt, a moment when you don't know if you will be able to make the journey. The trail will be long. The path ahead is unknown, fraught with perils both real and imagined. Will you be strong enough, tough enough? Can you endure?

There were a couple of deer in among the old apple trees behind the barn, and I heard them scamper away. Didn't see them, not in the snowy darkness that precedes the dawn. I kept walking. I was going pretty good when the gray dawn came and was almost to Panther Lick when a break in the clouds admitted a little sliver of sunlight. Just a sliver, then it was gone.

I guess that even then I didn't believe in the big buck Dad had talked about. The deer had no reality, no substance. Somewhere between nine and ten that morning, that changed. The snow had become flurries, and the Lick cleared momentarily. I was on the ridge at the head of the drainage working my way along it when I saw him, five or six hundred yards away, trotting across the old meadow behind the cabin site. He was following two does, had his head up. His coat was a dark gray, nearly black, and he was huge, almost twice the size of the does.

Even now, as I write this, I can see him trotting along, sampling the wind, his enormous antlers carried high, a legend become flesh. Until I saw him, I didn't believe. Oh, I heard and nodded and knew Dad was telling the truth, but I didn't believe.

I was too far away to shoot, of course. With open sights at that distance, I didn't have a chance.

Suddenly I wasn't tired. Wasn't cold. Wasn't depressed about Dad and Mom and the absence of hope. And the bank was gone—interest rates, bad loans, everything—washed away as if it had never been.

I walked ever so carefully through the woods, easing along, knowing that the three deer were somewhere in the timber ahead, and if luck or fate or God willed it, somewhere, sometime, I would be close enough, would get a shot.

Every sense was alert. I could hear every dry leaf rustle, hear the trees popping and snapping from the cold, hear my footsteps, my breathing, my heart. At moments like that, your eyes become attuned to catch movement and you peer between trees and around rocks as you sneak along, trying to breathe shallowly, make no noise, become one with the forest.

I walked like that for hours . . . and didn't see the buck again that day. Looked and looked amid the cold wind. The sun came out and fine, frozen snow that didn't accumulate kept falling, but I couldn't find the buck or his does.

When I stumbled into the farm that evening, I was whipped. I told Dad about seeing the buck, which perked him up. He seemed to become more alert for a while as we talked about the woods, the wind, the snow and freezing cold, about the buck and where he might be tomorrow. For a few minutes his mind was clear, he talked in complete sentences, then he drifted off.

I forced myself to take a shower, then I collapsed. Slept without dreaming.

Anne put down the letter and went to the window. She, too, remembered that evening two years ago. She had had to call the doctor, and he had arrived around nine. Ed had already fallen asleep on the couch. After the doctor examined the patient, he sipped coffee in the kitchen while Sarah wandered about like a lost soul.

"Won't be long," the doctor said. "His heart could quit anytime. To-night, tomorrow night . . . I'll be amazed if he's alive a week from now."

"I see."

"The nurses doing okay?"

"Yes."

"And you?"

"I suppose."

"Get plenty of rest. Give him pain medication when he needs it."

"Is it always like this?" Sarah asked. She had drifted into the kitchen.

"Death, you mean?" When Sarah didn't answer immediately, the doctor added, "Or life?"

"I don't know."

"I don't, either. Bodies wear out so differently, people are so different in their attitudes toward death . . ." He shrugged. "Death is a natural part of life, yet people confound their physicians every day. They die when they should have lived; they live when the medical journals say life is no longer possible. You figure it out. By the way, this is good coffee."

He left soon afterward, as Ed slept. Poor, lonely Sarah went back to her aimless trek back and forth through the drafty, cold rooms and hallways.

The snow was sticking the third morning. It came in flurries. When the flurries were thickest, visibility was reduced to about a hundred feet. I thought the deer would be lying in, so I kept moving, hoping to jump them out. I confess, by then I wanted that buck badly.

It seemed to me that conditions were ideal, or close to it. If I could get that big buck moving, I could track him, which would have been impossible the previous two days. If I could get on his trail, I could keep him moving, and finally he would tire, would let me get closer and closer before he moved on. Then I would get a shot. If I didn't wear down first.

But I felt good. Confident. The previous two days of hiking had taken the soreness out of my muscles and inured me to the cold and wind. It seemed to me that I had a chance.

Most of life's opportunities are like that; all you get is a chance. And you can easily blow it.

I wanted that deer. I wanted to go back and tell Dad that I got him, tell him how it was. This I could share with my father. He wanted to share it with me and I with him. That was important that morning as I walked up the mountain in the snow. Now, two years later, I'm not sure that I understand. But it was important then.

I jumped the buck and two does just behind the old farmhouse site on the meadow at Panther Lick. I got a glimpse of his antlers, saw brown hide, then they were gone. I didn't have a shot. They left nice tracks, though, and there was no doubt which set belonged to Old Buck. His were almost twice as big as the ladies'.

With the snow falling I couldn't dawdle. My tactics were useless if I followed too slowly and allowed the deer to rest. And the accumulating snow was merciless; if it wiped out the tracks I was finished.

Still I felt optimistic. This was only the second time I had seen him in three days, and I felt the conditions had given me an edge. I moved right along as quickly as I could.

I was soon sweating. Now I had on too much clothing. I took off a sweatshirt and tied it around my waist, let the coat hang open.

Sure enough, on the side of the mountain I jumped them again, only they were so far ahead I only saw their white tails in the snow. They went up over the ridge behind Panther Lick, then went along the side of Laurel Mountain to where it drops off into the upper reaches of the Little River Basin. This was perhaps five miles from where I jumped them the first time. I could tell from their tracks where they slowed, stopped to listen and look back, browsed, even laid down once until they heard or saw me coming. Then they bounded away, finally slowing to a walk again.

Somewhere above the Little River they began to circle back. Went across Laurel Mountain and started back toward Panther Lick.

It was darn near noon by then, and I was beat. I figured I had done six miles through snow and thickets, six miles over logs, up hills and down . . . I was so tired. If only I had known how tired I was going to get.

Six miles out, six miles back. The snow let up some that afternoon—it seemed there was about six to eight inches on the ground then. The tracks were easy to follow. Finally it dawned on me that I wasn't far behind the deer.

They were moving slowly by then. The hike had taken a lot out of them, too. They needed time to browse, to rest, and I was insisting they burn calories.

About two o'clock or so I got a glimpse of them again, got the rifle on the old buck and actually snapped off a shot. After the silence of the woods for the previous two days, the boom of the report seemed extraordinarily loud, like a cannon.

A .25-35 doesn't kick much, but it kicks a little, enough to raise the barrel so that your target is momentarily obscured. When I got the barrel back down, the deer weren't in sight.

I charged over to the place where they had been. No blood. I could see where their sharp hooves had dug deeply into the snow and leaves that lay underneath. At the crack of the gun they had accelerated to great, leaping bounds.

At that time I believe I was three miles from Panther Lick, which is, as you've heard, a mile or so above the farmhouse. I confess, at that moment I believed the hunt was hopeless. I was so exhausted that I wanted to lie down in the snow and sleep for a week, and the deer were running strongly . . . there was just no way.

The only bright spot was that they were running in the direction of Panther Lick, and I had to go that way in any event. I think that if they had been running in any other direction, I would have let them go.

Perhaps.

Oh, I don't know.

Certainly at that point I didn't realize how close to collapse I was, how much energy it was going to take to walk the miles back to the farm. As it was I almost didn't make it, but looking back, I am not sure I realized how perilously close to the edge I was at that time, after I shot and missed.

So I followed them. Followed the trail through the trees, up on the ridge behind Panther Lick and along it toward the west.

I was still thinking then, wondering why they didn't go on down into the Lick. Didn't understand. The answer, as it turned out, was that the snow was deep on the north side of the ridge, really deep, and the deer were staying on the ridge so they wouldn't have to fight through it.

They were wandering, going down off the crest, then coming back up, trying it again a little farther on.

I began to move straight along the ridge. I was doing that when I saw them.

A doe was in the lead. Saw her first. Then the doe behind.

The distance was less than a hundred yards, maybe about seventy-five or eighty. There were lots of trees, lots of blown-down timber, so I was just getting glimpses.

I steadied the rifle against a tree, cocked it and held my breath.

Sure enough, the buck came into view. I saw him as he passed between two trees, but he was gone before I could shoot. I shifted the rifle . . . and he came out from behind a big tree and paused, looked back over his shoulder, back the way they had come.

I shot him then. The bullet knocked him down. He got up and I shot him again. That time he stayed down.

He was dead by the time I got to him, thank God! Both bullets had hit him in the chest—one apparently went through his heart.

I collapsed in the snow.

I wasn't elated. I wasn't anything, as I recall. Just bone-weary tired. So tired . . .

How long I sat in the snow I don't recall exactly. It couldn't have been over ten or fifteen minutes. I was soaked with sweat and began to get cold, deathly cold, and that hard reality got me up and moving.

First I had to gut the deer. Hot blood, steaming in the cold—it was then that it sank in that I had killed a living thing. That was what I had been trying to do, of course, and I knew when I was pulling the trigger and the rifle was booming and bucking that I was trying to kill, but the visceral reaction didn't set in until I was pulling guts out of his body cavity and the slippery, hot blood was warm on my hands and steaming in the snow. Red snow . . . I can still see it as I write these words.

And yet I didn't feel guilty. Every living thing is condemned to death at the moment of its birth. That's been said so often it is trite, yet until you come to grips with that extraordinary fact at a gut level, you cannot cope with life. You fear it, shrink from it.

Luckily I had the foresight, years ago, to put a length of rope in the pocket of that hunting coat. I got it out, tied it around the antlers of the deer, picked up my rifle, and started pulling. Downhill.

Downhill seemed best, toward the old homestead on Panther Lick. I figured I was about a half mile above it.

The problem was the snow. It was nearly two feet deep on the side of that ridge, which was why the buck and does had gone along the top of the ridge instead.

Pulling that dead deer through the snow, struggling to move my feet, falling regularly over buried limbs and tree trunks, I quickly expended what energy I had left. I was facing absolute exhaustion when I got down to the edge of the old meadow, a couple hundred yards from the ruins of the farmhouse.

I could not drag the deer another step.

I decided to hang it in a tree, come back for it tomorrow. In those temperatures the carcass would keep nicely.

The problem was getting it into the tree.

Rope over a low limb, pull and lift. Tug, strain . . .

I dropped the deer twice. Finally got its feet up a few inches above the snow, but I could get it no higher, pull as I might on the rope.

I think it was then that I realized that I would be fortunate to get back to the house that night. And if I didn't make it I would freeze to death.

Unbelievable! A middle-aged banker goes hunting just a few miles from his father's house, and he is in danger of dying from exposure.

I don't remember knotting the rope or retrieving my rifle, any of that. What I remember now is staggering along the old logging road toward the house, trying to keep my eyes open, trying to keep upright. The temptation to lie down for just a few moments was so very strong; the light was fading fast, the air was getting colder.

Just a little farther, a little farther. I kept telling myself that.

I don't remember much more than that about the walk home.

Somehow I made it. I remember coming into the kitchen, the light, the warmth, you standing there looking at me.

I remember going in to see Dad, trying to tell him I had gotten the buck, trying to tell him how it was up on the mountain in the snow, and I remember waking up in the chair in his room when the nurse was fussing around him. I don't know what time that was—maybe three or four in the morning. Dad was in a deep sleep by then and never woke again. As you recall, he died six or seven hours later.

I don't know whether he understood that I had gotten the deer, or whether he cared by that time. Perhaps it doesn't matter.

In the end, nothing matters. And yet we deny our humanity if we fail to understand that our obligation to the living is the only thing that does matter. To us.

Ed

SIXTEEN

Diamond Ice saw the flashing light in her rearview mirror, distorted by the drizzling rain that coated the glass. She glanced in her left side mirror. Police.

At first she thought it was Trooper Sam Neely in the state cruiser, and she had half a mind not to stop. She wasn't up to coping with his broken heart this morning, not after Richard Hudson had thrown both her and Crystal out of his house the other evening. No, she wasn't ready for Neely's earnest lapdog mooning.

When she heard the moan of the siren she knew it probably wasn't Neely. She slowed and found a place to pull off the road.

Why was she being stopped? She wasn't speeding . . . well, only five or ten miles per hour over, but that shouldn't be a problem. Hadn't run any red lights in the last ten minutes or blasted through any stop signs.

She stopped the car and rolled down the driver's window.

Delmar Clay came marching up, accoutered for a downpour in raincoat and Smokey Bear hat with plastic cover. He hove to abeam the window and adjusted his gunbelt under the rain gear. He was one of those rare men who could strut standing still; he did a little of that now for her benefit.

"How are you doing this morning, Diamond?"

"What are you going to allege I did this time, Clay?"

"Diamond, baby, you know I don't give beautiful women tickets unless they deserve them."

She fished in her purse for her driver's license and vehicle registration, then stuck them out at Clay. "Go write the ticket. Unless you want to stand there all day looking stupid."

He took the documents and headed back to the cruiser.

Damn! She certainly didn't need any more points on her license, and a fine would play havoc with her tiny checking account. She rolled up the window.

The windshield wipers slapped occasionally while Clay bent over his paperwork in the car behind her. She turned on the radio, listened for ten seconds, then snapped it off. She drummed her nails on the steering wheel, checked on Clay in the mirror.

Then she remembered Junior's request. Well, this was a golden opportunity. And Delmar Clay richly deserved it.

Of course, it was over between her and Junior. Finished, dead, cold as ashes. Junior would never leave his mother, never marry her. The time had come when the truth could be ignored no longer, and a miserable, rotten truth it was: Junior Grimes was never going to grow up. He had had thirty-six years to perform that feat. It was dead certain now that he wasn't going to get it done if he lived to be a hundred.

Richard—now there was a man. Sensitive, intelligent, articulate, a man who knew people.

She and Crystal had come on too strong. Well, Crystal had, pestering the man for weeks, making his life a misery. Poor girl, too stupid to see that he didn't want her.

The trick was going to be to make Richard want the other Ice girl, Diamond. Crystal had certainly put the fear in the poor man, but Diamond liked a challenge. At least, she always told herself she did.

Here came Clay. She lowered the window again.

"I just wrote you a warning. Speeding. Sign it at the *X*."

He passed a small clipboard through the window. Her license and registration were under the metal clip.

"Golly, you are about the prettiest thing in this county," Delmar said as she signed her name.

Up until that moment she had been undecided. Delmar's comment pushed her over the edge. *Okay, Junior, this one's for you.*

As she passed the clipboard back to Delmar, Diamond Ice gave him her best grin. "Thank you."

Delmar strutted, smiled, hunted through the attic for another compliment. Before he could find one that looked promising, she added, "You're pretty good-looking yourself."

Delmar almost dropped the clipboard.

Like shooting fish in a barrel, Diamond told herself. To Deputy Clay she said, "You're not the kind of man who kisses and tells, are you?"

A huge grin split his face, exposing every tooth in his head. "Why do you want to know?"

"Oh, a girl likes to know these things. For future reference, you understand."

"I do indeed. To answer your question, I am not. I never tattle. I believe a kiss is a very private thing, just between two people. That's my philosophy."

Diamond's mind went blank for a second. To think that there were women alive today who fell for this bull! Groping, she replied, "I like men who have a philosophy. They're just so hard to find these days."

"That isn't all I've got," said the suave, debonair man of the world. "I'd sure like to show you my assets sometime."

Diamond had to turn her head away and bite her lip. When she had her smile glued back on, she turned to him and said, as sweetly as she could, "I'd really like to, Delmar. You have a certain unique charm."

"I do?"

"You're direct. I like a man who knows what he wants. But if Junior ever found out . . ."

"That muscle-bound meathead? He'll never know anything! And if he gives you a hard time, I'll take care of Mister Junior Grimes!"

"Would it be okay if I called you sometime?"

"Not at home. But you could call me at the office." Delmar leaned down and rested an elbow on the top of the driver's door, which placed his head perilously close to hers.

"Oh, you're *so* sweet! I'm going to do that, I really am."

"I've liked you for a long, long time, Diamond."

"I know, and I think you're going to like me a lot more." With that she winked, pulled the transmission into drive, and left the poor dumb snook standing there in the mist wearing a wide grin on his homely, lecherous face.

When she was around the first curve she shouted, "Yuck, I can't believe I did that." She felt dirty, as if she needed a bath. "You owe me, Junior be-a-friend-of-man Grimes. You owe me big-time, buster."

Diamond Ice called the garage.

"This is Junior."

"This is Di."

"Hey."

"Do you still want Delmar Clay's head?"

"Yes. Want it bad."

"All I have to do is call him and give him the time and place."

"It's got to be daytime, the closer to noon the better. The weather is supposed to be good tomorrow. About one o'clock tomorrow afternoon at the old Varner place?"

"I'll pack a lunch. But this is the very last thing I'm ever going to do for you. It's over between us."

Junior didn't say anything.

"Delmar expects women to fall at his feet," Diamond continued. "He's my candidate for the Stupidest Man Alive Award. Amazing as it sounds, he's even stupider than you are. And he's slimy, like pond scum. Letting him touch me will be the vilest thing I've ever done."

"Close your eyes and pretend he's Sam Neely," Junior shot back, then hung up the telephone.

To pull this off, Junior realized, he was going to need expert help. Fortunately he had access to the perfect individual, a man with a quick mind and an enviable grasp of human psychology, a man who could be relied upon to keep his head in dire, desperate situations, a man who never allowed the subtler nuances of legal or social responsibility to get in the way of what needed to be done. So Junior called Arch Stehlik.

"We're gonna have to get Arleigh Tate in on this," Arch advised after listening to Junior's summary of preparations to date.

Junior was appalled. "But he knows we did the tire fire," he objected. Since the fire, Junior had been assiduously avoiding Sheriff Tate. He couldn't avoid him at Lions Club, of course, so he had tried to do the next best thing: act innocent. Alas, he had this horrible feeling that Sheriff Tate knew the precise extent of his criminal responsibility and was planning an excruciatingly public humiliation. A guilty conscience was a burden almost too heavy for Junior to bear.

Arch didn't suffer from Junior's affliction. "I'll call him," Arch said mildly. "I'll invite him to dinner tonight at the restaurant. We can talk afterwards in the garage."

Full of chicken-fried steak, mashed potatoes and gravy, corn, three rolls, a piece of blueberry pie with ice cream and three cups of coffee, Arleigh Tate was in a benign mood when he followed Junior and Arch through the restaurant kitchen into the store. From her stool behind the counter, Lula Grimes was sparring with miser Hardy.

"I wouldn't count your chickens before they hatch, young man," Lula told Mr. Hardy, who had logged at least seventy-five years on this planet so far. Tate, Junior and Arch drifted toward the conversation.

"I don't think it was very nice," Mr. Hardy said, oblivious of his growing audience, "what you said about my mother."

"All I said was that your father will probably leave his money to your mother, and you won't get any until she passes away. I'm sure she'll do the right thing by you when the time comes."

"Yes," Hardy said slowly. "I'm sure of that. She loves me, so she does."

"How is her health these days?"

"Mighty fine. Right pert, she is."

"But your daddy is feeling down?"

"That he is. Of course, he's been that way for years and years. Got a lot of money, though. A lot of money." Miser Hardy fell silent as he thought about the money.

"That'll be sixteen cents, please," Lula reminded him.

Mr. Hardy counted out sixteen pennies and arranged them in a row on the counter.

"When you come into that money, you come back and see me," Lula Grimes told Mr. Hardy. He nodded and went on out the door.

"Flirtin' with the customers again, Mom?" Junior asked after the spring pulled the door closed.

"Just working on finding you a new daddy, son. Mr. Hardy thought I ought to know that he's coming into some money one of these days."

"Got his eye on you, does he?" Sheriff Tate asked.

"All the men do. They think that if they could latch on to me they could eat free in the restaurant, and they know that my boy Junior will work cheap."

"And how is Moses' health?"

"He's in bed with a cold.".

"If it turns into pneumonia, I might start courting you myself."

"You'll have to get in line. Some of these old men would gag a maggot, but some of them are pretty good prospects."

"Oh, Mom!" Junior protested. "You shouldn't say things like that."

"I don't want you to ever be an orphan, Junior. A mother has to think of these things."

"What did Mr. Hardy buy?" Arch asked curiously.

"A cigar. Cheapest brand we have."

"I didn't know he smoked."

"He doesn't. He cuts the cigar up and chews the pieces. Says it's cheaper than chewing tobacco or cigarettes."

When the men got to the garage, Sheriff Tate lit his own cigar. His was not cheap; the sheriff enjoyed a few of life's little pleasures.

"What are you two innocents up to these days?" he asked Arch and Junior after he got his stogie drawing properly.

"The time has come," Arch said, "to help you solve your biggest problem. Fortunately we are in a position to be of some assistance."

Tate seemed amused. His eyes twinkled as he asked, "And just what might my biggest problem be?"

"Delmar Clay."

Tate took three or four short, quick puffs on the cigar, then removed it from his mouth. The twinkle had disappeared from his eyes, which were narrow now, and hard. "And how do you propose to do that?"

Arch started from the beginning, explained about Billy Joe Elkins and Melanie Naroditsky, about the photos, about how he and Junior had substituted the film, about Delmar stopping Melanie and threatening her. He covered these points while Junior scuffed at the concrete with the toe of his boot and looked everywhere but at Sheriff Tate.

Finally Arch explained about tomorrow, about how it would work. Then he covered the denouement, which Junior thought showed a keen appreciation for the political realities that kept Arleigh Tate in office.

During this recital Tate puffed on his cigar and said nothing.

When Arch was finished, the sheriff sat down on one of Junior's boxes of motor oil. He eyed the two standing men speculatively. "Well, it might work." He nodded grudgingly. "It just might, at that." Tate sighed. " 'Course, if it doesn't, I'm going to have to arrest you both for attempting to compromise an officer of the law. Don't know exactly what the charge would be, but I can probably find something in the code that covers the case."

Junior looked as if he were going to be sick.

"This will work," Arch said with conviction.

"It'd better," the sheriff said bluntly. "It'd better work a lot slicker than the tire fire. Half the people in the county are wondering when I'm going to arrest you two jaybirds for that shenanigan."

Junior charged for the bathroom and upchucked his dinner. He was cleaning himself up when he heard the sheriff tell Arch, "Had a visit from some EPA weenie the other day. He talked on and on about evildoers who pollute the air. I told him to come back when he had some evidence."

Junior almost lost it again.

"This will work," Arch insisted.

"It might if the Ice girl doesn't lose her nerve."

"She's got a lot of gumption. She can handle it."

"Okay," said Arleigh Tate. "We'll go up there in the morning. I'll stop by here with the cameras at eleven."

"Thanks, Sheriff. You won't regret this."

"If I regret it, you will, too, Stehlik. You and Junior. I promise."

The sheriff was gone when Junior came out of the bathroom looking a little green.

"Something you ate?" Arch asked solicitously.

"I *told* you he knew."

Arch Stehlik laughed, a loud, honking belly laugh.

Junior crawled under the tool bench. He pulled the blanket around him that he had arranged over Elijah Murphy and told Arch, "Go away. Leave me alone."

"See you tomorrow, June."

After a while Junior felt better. This thing tomorrow would work, then Billy Joe and Melanie would be off the hook.

Tomorrow night he would have a long chat with Diamond. Get her mind off Richard Hudson and Sam Neely. As this thought went through the gray matter, his conscience zinged him. Again. The truth was, he had been neglecting her lately. That poor girl, listening to every man who sweet-talked her . . . and they didn't care about her, not like he did.

First things first. This thing tomorrow . . .

Maybe he should call Billy Joe. The boy could whisper something to Melanie, put her mind at ease.

Junior crawled from under the tool bench. He folded the blanket and stored it on the shelf, then looked up the Elkinses' number in the telephone book.

The rain stopped that night. The next day the sun was out, and the morning warmed nicely. Junior, Arch and the sheriff walked in to the old Varner place from the hard road, about a quarter of a mile, and were in position by noon. Then they settled down to wait. By then the temperature was in the sixties.

Junior began fretting. The fact that the leaves were down meant that everyone was well away from the location where they hoped Delmar would park his car.

They had discussed it, picked positions that covered the most likely place.

Arleigh Tate had shown up in Sam Neely's state police cruiser. Neely was driving and didn't look at Junior when he got into the backseat with Arch. Neely did glance at him, though, when he let them out to walk in to the Varner place. Sort of a casual, hope-you-don't-have-any-hard-feelings glance, Junior decided, thinking about it now.

Well, he did have hard feelings. Neely had no business sniffing around the Ice farm like an old hound dog, looking for something to get into. Wasn't gentlemanly. Wasn't right.

Junior swatted at a late-season bug.

There was nothing to do but lie there and think. And the thoughts were not pleasant. Understandably enough, Junior tried not to think.

The minutes crawled by.

————

Billy Joe Elkins pulled the Jeep off into the brush and killed the engine. He got out and stood listening to the silence.

He had left school when the lunch break started. He was going to miss most of the afternoon; when he returned to school, he would go straight to the principal's office and report himself. The principal would give him a lecture and several hours in detention hall. Perhaps the principal would write a note to his parents. Billy Joe didn't care.

Satisfied that no one was around, Billy Joe reached into the Jeep, unzipped the gun case lying on the floor behind the driver's seat, and extracted his shotgun. He worked the action a few times.

The gun was an old Model 97 Winchester twelve-gauge pump, with a hammer. It had belonged to his grandfather Elkins and had been given to Billy Joe when the old man died.

The boy took four shells from his pocket and fed them into the gun one at a time. Then he pumped a round into the chamber and lowered the hammer to half cock.

He made sure the keys to the Jeep were in his pocket, then closed the driver's door and ensured it was latched. After checking his watch, he started up the ridge he was facing. If he had his geography right, the old Varner place was at the head of the hollow on the other side of this ridge.

Even though the ridge was steep, Billy Joe went up it at a rapid pace; he was young and in excellent physical condition. The wet leaves made little noise under his feet.

Somewhere off to his right a squirrel chattered. Billy Joe didn't look. A doe jumped out ahead of him and scampered away along a contour about fifty feet, then paused and turned to look the man over. He kept going up the ridge and the doe pranced away with her tail in the air.

Going up the ridge with the gun heavy in his hand, Billy Joe had a sense that he was taking an irrevocable step, doing something with unpredictable consequences that could never be undone.

He tried to remember if he had ever done something like that before. Not knowingly, he decided.

Well, perhaps it was time.

About 12:30 Diamond Ice arrived in her Ford Mustang. She parked in front of the ruin of the Varner farmhouse, got out and stretched. She was wearing jeans and a sweater, neither of which did anything to disguise her excellent figure.

She looked so good standing there with the breeze whipping her hair that Junior stood up and waved. She turned her back on him.

"Hey, Diamond!"

She had to have heard him, although she didn't turn around.

She opened the trunk of her car and removed a picnic basket. Then she spread a blanket beside the car and proceeded to unpack the basket. Junior watched enviously from his hiding place fifty yards away.

He was tempted to go to her, to tell her he loved her, to thank her for her help, but he couldn't. Delmar Clay would be along at any second; if he saw Junior the game was over. So Junior stayed hidden, fidgeting, fretting, wondering where Delmar was.

The minutes dragged. Junior had about decided that Delmar had chickened out when he heard the sound of a car engine coming up the dirt road. He looked at his watch. Delmar was ten minutes early.

The deputy parked the cruiser behind the Mustang and hopped out. He didn't even look around, just strutted over to the blanket and sat down beside Diamond.

Clay said something to her, and she laughed. She handed him a plate heaped with food and a bottle of beer. Junior was close enough to see their lips moving, but he couldn't hear a word. The temptation to worm closer gnawed at him. Diamond had never fixed a picnic for *him!* He thought about that omission as he lay on his stomach in the grass watching Delmar Clay eating a fine lunch, watching Diamond run her hand through her hair to show off her breasts and laugh at everything that fathead had to say, watching and watching . . . and couldn't hear a thing except his own heart breaking.

She even had pie in the basket! She sliced it, cutting a piece for each of them, and put the wedges on plates. Fished in the basket for clean forks, handed one to Delmar.

They each took a bite, and giggled and giggled.

Finally Delmar's hormones got the better of him and he reached for her. She slapped his hand away, put down her pie dish, then slowly and languidly pulled her sweater off over her head. She wasn't wearing a bra.

"Gawd!" Junior said under his breath.

A minute went by, then another as Diamond Ice finished her pie with a fork, chewing and savoring each bite, while the breeze made her long blond hair dance on her naked shoulders.

Finally she stood and took off her shoes one by one. The jeans came last. She peeled the blue denim down over her hips, then stepped out of each leg. She wasn't wearing panties.

There she stood in front of Delmar, facing toward Junior, fluffing her hair, naked as the day she was born. She looked right at Junior and gave him a big grin.

Junior came out of his hiding place like a halfback charging at the snap of the ball. And promptly tripped. Fell flat on his face.

When he looked up, Delmar was standing and taking off his gunbelt.

Wait a minute, Junior! Let the guy get naked. That was the plan, wasn't it?

Junior prayed that Arleigh Tate and Arch Stehlik were getting this on film. The sheriff had supplied two cameras with telephoto lenses. The two men were up in the edge of the woods to Junior's right and left, each snapping away, or so Junior hoped. With two cameras at different angles, it figured that some of the pictures would be decent.

Delmar finished taking off his uniform and reached for Diamond again. She waggled a finger at him, then led him over to the police cruiser. She opened the rear door and climbed in. Delmar bent to get in with her.

Junior charged.

He had covered about five yards when he heard the shot, a clear, sharp crack that echoed through the little valley.

Delmar straightened abruptly.

Another shot.

Delmar screamed. He hopped around holding his ass screaming at the top of his lungs.

He was still in full cry when he saw Junior closing at a dead run. That silenced him.

He tried to set himself to receive Junior's charge, but he was a split second too late. Junior Grimes flattened him with a haymaker to the chin as he went by.

Diamond smiled at Junior as he skidded to a stop. "You okay?" he demanded.

"Of course. Did you shoot him?"

"No."

"That poor man! So near and yet so far."

Junior bent over to examine Delmar, who was out cold. Junior rolled him over. His buttocks were peppered with red pinholes. Birdshot! From the small of the back down to his knees. Maybe a hundred pellets.

Billy Joe Elkins! Must have been. Calling him last night was a major uh-oh.

Junior straightened and looked around to see if he could spot Billy Joe. No.

Diamond was standing beside him now, still naked, not attempting to hide a thing, her skin golden in the sun. She inspected the victim. "He is sorta cute," she said, then went over to the blanket and pulled on her jeans. Then her shoes.

With the sweater in her hands she said to Junior, "This is your last look, too, lover boy. Better enjoy it."

Taking her time, she inserted one arm into the sweater, then the other, raised them over her head and languidly worked the sweater down over her body.

As Delmar Clay lay comatose, she carefully repacked the picnic basket and put it in the trunk of her car. She folded the blanket and stowed it, then snapped the trunk lid closed.

As she was getting in the car she said to Junior, "Don't ever call me again. And have a nice life."

Junior watched her drive away. When the car was out of sight, he checked on Delmar. Still out cold as a Christmas turkey. The pellet holes in his butt were leaking blood, but not a copious amount. His jaw didn't seem to be broken.

He looked up to see Arleigh Tate walking through the grass toward him. Arch leaped the creek, camera held high.

After he inspected the victim, Arleigh leaned into the cruiser and flipped on the radio. He reached for the mike. "Sam, are you there?"

"Yes, Sheriff."

"Come get us."

He turned the radio off and replaced the mike in its bracket.

As Arch examined Delmar's behind, he said to Junior, "I thought you were going to act outraged and run him off?"

"I forgot."

"We shouldn't leave him like this," Arch remarked without a great deal of conviction.

"He might catch cold," Junior added, not that he cared. Getting Delmar shot wasn't part of the program, and he had been the one who telephoned Billy Joe Elkins. Sheriff Tate eyed him speculatively as he stripped the cellophane off a cigar and felt for his matches.

"Oh, I think Delmar will be all right," Arleigh said offhandedly. "Hot as he was, it'll take a while for him to cool down. And there isn't anything around here hungry enough to eat him."

He arranged his camera on the strap around his shoulder, lit the cigar and took a few puffs. After a last glance at his still-sleeping deputy, he set off down the dirt road. Junior and Arch fell in behind.

"Was it Billy Joe?" Junior whispered to Stehlik.

"Yeah. I saw him leave. So did Tate."

"You two can stop that damn whispering," the sheriff barked.

Junior and Arch quickened their pace and caught up with the sheriff. After they had walked a couple of hundred yards in silence, Tate rumbled, "I'll say this, Junior. That is one hell of a fine hunk of woman. Let me know if you two ever call it quits."

Then Arleigh Tate started to laugh. He was ha-ha-ha-ing at the top of his lungs when Arch and Junior could stand it no longer and joined in.

SEVENTEEN

Elijah Murphy held the board in place with his left hand and wielded the hammer with his right. He got the nail going straight and hammered until the head was flush with the wood. Then he pounded some more. Pounded and pounded until his wrist and arm ached.

The weak autumn sun warmed his face and arms, but the hammering was what he needed. He got another nail from the sack, made sure the board was in the right position, then got the nail started. He beat on the head of the nail with all his strength. The whamming of the hammer made the hollow ring.

His visit with preacher Carcano kept running through his head, things she said, in no particular order. Funny, he had spent over an hour with a preacher and she hadn't once offered to pray over him. Come to think of it, she did mention prayer, though. Told him if he was going to get anything out of it he was going to have to do it himself.

Hell of a thing for a preacher to say. That's what Murphy told himself now as he beat nails into submission. He had never met a preacher like her, that was certain. Never in his life.

Elijah Murphy knew precisely what she had been talking about when she spoke of waking up sick and shaking in jail. He had been there, more times than he could count.

But jail was not a regular thing with him, really. Usually he awoke in a vacant lot or an alley—lots of times in the alley behind the Paris Saloon—or alongside roads all over this end of the county. In fact, he had probably spent more nights outside sleeping it off than he had spent in bed these last ten years. No, twenty. Well, twenty-five. Okay, thirty. Nearly thirty years.

When he awoke it always took a while to figure out just where he was. Jail he knew: The bars were a decorator item you rarely found other places. And the alley behind the Paris Saloon—he had slept there so often he always recognized it in short order.

But when he woke up beside the road someplace, well . . . there was always a period of time when he didn't recognize anything, couldn't remember how he got there. Sometimes he wondered if he were dead and in the Hereafter. He would get up, which made the top of his head feel like he had been scalped, wander along, looking about through bloodshot eyes, trying to find something familiar, a house or a barn or a road sign—something!

One time he wandered for a day without seeing a single, solitary thing he could recognize. Someone, perhaps the Barrow boys, had rolled him into a ditch two counties away. He was three days getting home that time and still had only the haziest idea of where he had been.

That was when? Two, three years ago?

He paused in his hammering and tried to recall just when that odyssey had been, then gave up. *Doesn't matter,* he thought.

He had lived the last thirty years in a drunken stupor. Most of it just ran together in his mind, and none of it was of any importance.

It . . . is . . . important. I matter. To me. This . . . is . . . my . . . life . . . and . . . I . . . am . . . not . . . going . . . to . . . throw . . . it . . . away. He hammered the message on the board.

"Aren't you going to use nails, Mr. Murphy?"

He turned. Mrs. Wilfred was standing there looking at him quizzically with a pitcher of water in one hand and a glass in the other. She repeated her question.

He had forgotten the nails, was just hammering.

He tried to grin at her.

"Some water, Mr. Murphy?"

"I got drunk the night before last, Mrs. Wilfred. Fell off the wagon."

"I heard. Won't you have a drink of water?"

"Thank you. I will."

He cleared a place for her to sit, sipped at the water. His right arm felt like rubber. He rubbed it, drank some more water.

"You've been wasting your life, Mr. Murphy."

"Yes," he said.

After a bit she remarked, "Sometimes the people who appreciate life the most get it taken away, and people who don't value it at all get lots of it. It seems that way sometimes. I've never understood that."

"Hard to figure."

They sat looking at the bare trees in the cool sunlight. Mrs. Wilfred pulled her sweater tighter around her shoulders, but she stayed seated.

"I think you are strong enough, Mr. Murphy."

"We'll see," he said. He didn't want to make any promises. Not to widow Wilfred, not to preacher Carcano, not to himself.

"But you're going to try?"

"Yes."

"I think you can do it."

"I don't know, Mrs. Wilfred. I really don't. I never did much figuring on life, about why things are like they are. Never spent time fretting on it. I'm not really sure why I drink. I want to quit, but it's going to be real hard. Mrs. Carcano told me I'm going to have to fight it every day for the rest of my life. I think she may be right. So the battle will never be won."

"It'll be won a day at a time."

"That's what Mrs. Carcano said. That's the way she said we have to live it."

"What else did Mrs. Carcano say?"

"This and that." Elijah Murphy was unwilling to repeat Mrs. Carcano's personal history. If the preacher wanted it to become public knowledge, she could tell it herself.

Mrs. Wilfred took his silence with good grace. When he had finished two glasses of water, she stood and retrieved her pitcher. He handed her the glass.

"Have a nice day, Mr. Murphy."

"Thank you. I'll try."

"Use nails. The job will go faster."

Murphy nodded solemnly.

Arleigh Tate was in his office addressing an envelope to the state crime lab when he heard a rapping on the door. "Come in."

His secretary opened the door and leaned in. "Sheriff, I just got a call from the hospital. Deputy Clay checked in there a while ago. They say he's going to be there for a few days."

Tate didn't even look up from the envelope. "What's wrong with Clay?"

"Hemorrhoids."

"Those can be painful."

"They want someone to come over and retrieve the cruiser. The receptionist has the keys."

"I'll walk over in a moment or two."

"Should I call Mrs. Clay?"

"I suppose."

When the door was closed again, Tate put the two rolls of film in the envelope and sealed it. Might as well mail this on the way to the hospital.

He was whistling as he walked past the secretary with the envelope in his hand.

Richard Hudson sat in front of his computer staring at the blank screen. He was ready for the final dash to the climax for his latest Prince Ziad novel, but the words wouldn't come. He needed a hundred pages of manuscript to finish the thing. One hundred pages—twenty-five thousand words of deathless prose that would neatly solve all the prince's problems and give the gallant warrior time to recuperate for his next adventure.

But it wouldn't come. Richard Hudson's mind was as blank as the computer screen. Nothing. *Nada*. Zilch.

The cursor sat in the upper left corner of the screen blinking at him.

True, he hadn't been doing much thinking about Prince Ziad lately. A writer must think about his characters, must see and hear them on the stage of his mind. Only then can he write them. It's a very simple process; think about what's happening to them, watch them react, listen to what they say, then write it.

The only prerequisite is that you must clear your mind of extraneous matters.

Richard Hudson hunched his shoulders, stared at the blank computer screen, and thought about the Ice sisters. Two women—well, there was no other way to describe it—throwing themselves at him. How in the world had this happened? To him, of all people, the last man on earth interested in a breeding partner? Or partners. Who would have predicted that the liberation of women would lead to predatory females stalking harmless, balding, fat male writers?

He was pondering the perverse ways of fate when he heard knocking on the front door.

He panicked. He had managed to run them off only an hour ago. Made them take Goofy home, insisted rather rudely that they both must leave.

His first impulse was to ignore the knocking. Maybe they would think he'd gone somewhere. Drat, his car was still in the driveway.

"Go away," he shouted from the safety of the living room.

"I need to talk to you, Mr. Hudson." A man's voice.

Hudson scuttled to a window and peeked around the curtain. By putting his face almost against the glass he could just see the figure standing in front of the door. That state policeman. Neely. Alone. No women in sight. Perhaps they were hiding behind the bushes.

Aaagh, the paranoia has begun. Next will come madness, then jibbering fits, a complete separation from reality.

Steeling himself, he went to the door, unlocked it and pulled it open.

"I need a few minutes of your time."

"What about?" Hudson was in no mood for chitchat. Unable to help himself, he scanned the yard to ensure the women weren't rushing the open door.

"It's personal, not official."

He gave in and took the trooper to the living room. Then he went back to the door and locked it, just in case.

"I'm sorry to bother you this evening, Mr. Hudson, but I wanted to stop by and talk to you about Crystal."

"I asked you to remove her from this house, and you refused."

"I remember. But there was no way to do it unless I physically carried her out. You saw that, didn't you?"

"Now it's Crystal *and* her sister. I don't know what I'm going to do."

"They're both in love with you."

Richard Hudson goggled. "Oh, my God," he moaned. "What *am* I going to do?"

Perhaps he could sell the house, move someplace else. Tell no one where he was going. Slip out in the dead of night and drive away, write to the real estate agent later listing the house. Have his agent mail the letter from New York. He could change his name. He could—

"I don't know just how to say this, Mr. Hudson, but I was wondering, since there are two of them, could you . . . ?"

"What?"

"Could you . . . tell Crystal there is no way, that you aren't interested in her?"

"You idiot! I've told her that. Over and over. It's like talking to a stump."

"You should not have led her on," Sam Neely said, "given her encouragement at the beginning of your relationship. Obviously she doesn't believe you now." His tone implied that he didn't, either.

"I didn't encourage either of them," Richard Hudson wailed, deeply offended. "And I don't know how I could make my feelings any plainer. I used English, no big words, spoke slowly in simple, declarative sentences. They won't listen. They *refuse* to listen."

Neely twisted his hat in his hands. "But you must be giving Crystal some reason to hope, Mr. Hudson, or she would have gone away. Heartbroken, of course—that's unavoidable. Perhaps—"

The writer scowled. This simple fool thought he, Richard Hudson, had some control over this mess. "Perhaps what?" he demanded.

"Perhaps if you told her that Diamond is . . . your choice. That Diamond is more suited to your—"

"Are you crazy?" Hudson raved. He jabbed his fist into the air. "Are you out of your mind? I was happy with my life as it was. What's so bad about that? Happy! Do you understand, you hormone-drenched nincompoop? I don't want either of those oversexed women! And I am not about to encourage one to discourage the other. Not in a million years—"

A knock on the door interrupted this tirade.

"See who it is," Hudson snarled at the trooper. "Don't let those women in! No women at all." He scampered for the study.

When he heard male voices, he peeked into the living room. Junior Grimes was standing there looking about suspiciously. Neely was still twisting his hat.

"Hey there, Hudson," Junior said, and took a seat.

"Hello."

"Whatcha doin'?"

"Discussing the state of the universe with Trooper Neely."

"I came over to have a private chat with you about a personal matter," Junior said, looking pointedly at Neely. "Are you leaving soon?" he asked the cop.

"If the personal matter is one of the Ice girls, or both of them, the answer is no," Hudson said. "I am not about to pick one in order to get rid of the other."

"You want them both? Like Hayden Elkins?"

Richard Hudson couldn't believe this was happening in his own house. Before he could reply to that outrage, Junior continued, "There's only so many women hereabouts. I don't think it's right for a fella to go hoggin' more than his share. Now if we had a lot of extras—"

"I don't want either of the Ice sisters," Hudson explained with as much patience as he could muster. "I have been trying to explain that basic fact to Mr. Neely. I want rid of both of them."

"Oh."

"Which one are you interested in, anyway?"

"Diamond."

"If you two weren't such dismally poor suitors, I wouldn't be plagued by these women. You are miserable specimens of the male gender, but better women have accepted worse. You could have tried a little harder. It's outrageous that your innocent neighbors have to bear the burdens caused by your romantic failures. Outrageous!"

"I did try, Mr. Hudson," Junior assured him warmly. "The very best I know how. Diamond is a tough woman to please, and—"

"Excuses" was Hudson's bitter retort. He collapsed into a chair. "What am I to do?"

A heavy silence descended on the room.

"Maybe you should talk to Mrs. Carcano," Junior suggested finally.

"The new minister?"

"Why not? She's mighty sharp. What do you think, Neely?"

"Couldn't hurt," the state trooper admitted.

The conversation petered out there. No one had any other ideas. After a while Sam Neely and Junior Grimes left. Hudson locked the door behind them.

They stood in the yard and argued a bit, but the conversation stayed on a high, intellectual plane; neither threw a punch. Then they got into their separate vehicles and went their separate ways.

Richard Hudson returned to his study and sat staring morosely at the blinking cursor on the black computer screen.

Anne Harris and Matilda Elkins had become good friends in the last two weeks. They approached each other tentatively at first, with chitchat that avoided The Situation, but they found that the ground between them was surprisingly firm. The conversations broadened, deepened, and each had grown comfortable with the other.

"We weren't really friends in the past," Matilda said one day. "Just acquaintances. I seem to have a lot of acquaintances and very few friends."

Anne wondered if men had the same problem with same-sex relationships. What was the pull that attracted Ed and Hayden to each other, and why was that relationship so weak that Hayden made a pass at Ed's wife? She didn't have an answer to that question and finally dropped it.

To understand that there are portions of the human experience that are beyond your ken, that you will never be able to fathom, was the beginning of wisdom, she mused. And yet the need to understand the motivations of your fellow man was the very essence of being human.

This afternoon the two women were sitting at the kitchen table eating cookies right from the oven and drinking milk when Anne said, "I'm leaving tomorrow, Matilda. It's time."

"Are you going home? To Ed?"

"No. But it's time I left here. I've intruded upon your hospitality long enough. I've been a royal pain; I've put you through grief that no woman should have to endure. I've come to really know you these last few weeks, and I'm ashamed of myself. I'll never be able to make it up to you."

"You should stay here, Anne. At least until you decide what to do."

"I'll get a place of my own. An apartment or a house. Something month to month."

"Anne, dear Anne. I've come to know you, too. A place by yourself alone wouldn't be good. You need people around you. You need a friend."

"Matilda, I've been such an ass. I'm sorry."

Matilda Elkins went to the coffeepot and poured two cups. When she placed them on the table she said, "This experience has been good for me. I've learned about myself this past month, about what I want out of life, about how to go about getting it. This may sound strange, but I've become a stronger person, a better person. And Hayden is learning some lessons, too; he may actually turn into a human being worth loving. I might, too." Her shoulders moved, hinting at a shrug. "In the long run this experience may strengthen our marriage." She snorted derisively. "I needed a miracle, and I got one. You made it happen. Thank you."

"Me?"

"Yes. Thank you."

"I really should leave."

"You really shouldn't."

Anne began to chuckle. Then she laughed. "I wonder what Ed and Hayden would say if they heard this conversation?"

Matilda hooted. They made the kitchen ring with laughter, then helped themselves to more chocolate chip cookies.

"It feels good to laugh again," Anne mused.

Five days after Delmar's misadventure, Billy Joe Elkins was enveloped in the gentle folds of a great calm. He sat through his classes, strolled the halls with his books, and talked to friends and acquaintances wearing a gentle smile. He looked out the windows at the shifting shadows cast by puffy clouds that hurried through the restless November sky and knew in his heart of hearts that all was right with the world. It was a rare feeling for him, so he savored it.

Football season was over. It had been fun and he had done well, not well enough to get an athletic scholarship to college, but well enough that high school football would be a pleasant memory in the years ahead.

His parents and Anne Harris—the terrible threesome—were merely a source of amusement, not embarrassment. Their problem was theirs alone, and he no longer gave any thought to how they were going to solve it. Or if they were.

Nor did he dwell on the possible consequences of shooting Delmar Clay. If the law wanted him, Sheriff Tate knew where to find him: He was going to be right here until graduation in May. And if Delmar wanted a pound of flesh, he was welcome to try to take it. Not that Billy Joe was concerned about Delmar; he suspected that he and Melanie had heard the very last of Deputy Clay.

When he thought about Melanie a smile crossed his face. She was a dear, sweet girl, a warm, bright place in his life. Just thinking of her made him fill his lungs with air and exhale slowly.

While he hadn't had a chance to use that condom, the urgency was gone. Someday, with the right girl . . . and that someday would be soon enough.

Despite the warmth and affection he felt for her, he was not sure that Melanie was that girl. He didn't fret it, didn't worry over it, just accepted it the way he accepted his parents and the possible consequences of pulling the trigger on Delmar.

The view of Delmar's naked behind over the silver bead on the shotgun barrel was still fresh enough to recall clearly. Billy Joe had been very calm then. Surprisingly so. He had intended to shoot only once, but after the first shot he automatically pumped another shell into the chamber, and good ol' Delmar obligingly held the position—probably too frozen with shock and pain to comprehend what had just happened. So Billy Joe made him a gift of another ounce and a quarter of #6 birdshot.

Now Billy Joe realized that the hike over the ridge and through the woods to the Varner place with his shotgun in hand had been some kind of crossing, a bridge from one phase of his life into another. He had walked away from the problems of his youth into an unknown future, and he went knowing full well that this future was dangerous, fraught with unknown peril. He had gone anyway. He had already crossed that bridge when he pulled the trigger the first time.

The significance of that passage was nebulous, but instinctively he knew he couldn't go back. He couldn't undo what he had intentionally done, couldn't cease being the person he had become. Even if he wanted to, and he didn't.

He was thinking about the future when he met Melanie at her locker after school.

They had met the evening after Delmar's accident, and he had told her everything: about Diamond Ice naked and graceful in the sun, about Arch and the sheriff taking pictures, about shooting Delmar . . . They had discussed the incident from every angle and agreed not to discuss it again, with each other or anyone else. They hadn't. Billy Joe's role in Delmar's hospitalization for hemorrhoids—the kids here at school had heard and were snickering about it—was their secret.

Somehow Melanie sensed the subtle change that had occurred in Billy Joe. He was steadier, she thought, more confident these last few days, and now when his chums roughhoused in the hall he stood and watched instead of joining in. He smiled more now, too, she noticed, and she took pleasure in that.

Yet she felt a distance between the two of them that hadn't been there before, which troubled her. At first she couldn't put her finger on it. She thought Billy Joe might be worried about being arrested; gradually it came to her that he wasn't. He truly didn't care. That puzzled her.

Yesterday afternoon he had gotten out the college brochures that had resided in his locker unread all fall and spent thirty minutes with her looking them over. He thought he would like to become an engineer, build things, he said, and he wanted a college with a first-rate engineering department.

Melanie understood then. Billy Joe was growing away from her. He was going forward into a future where she couldn't follow. It was bittersweet and tragic, and yet . . . and yet it was inevitable. There was nothing on earth she could do about it. Watching him walk through the hall today toward her with a smile on her face, she felt her heart fill almost to bursting. *I know I am going to lose you, Billy Joe, but today we have each other.*

"Let's go get a Coke," he said as he hefted her book bag.

"Lead on, Mr. Elkins. I want to walk beside you for a little while longer."

"Pick your side, my lady. Right or left?"

She pretended to consider carefully, then chose his right side. Off they went, holding hands.

Melanie thought of the idea while scrunched beside Billy Joe in a booth at the Teen Shack as a pop tune blared from the jukebox four feet behind them. She broached it to Billy Joe as a "Wouldn't it be funny if—"

To her surprise, he took it seriously. His eyes twinkled as he thought about it, and those eyes made Melanie's knees feel watery. He was just so darn cute, so masculine, so very adorable. She leaned over and kissed him.

"That's an interesting idea, Mel. I like it. Let's go outside and talk it over."

In the Jeep they discussed it. "We should invite everyone," he suggested. "All their friends and all the neighbors, everyone who knows them."

"This will kill or cure, Billy," Melanie said soberly. "Think this through before you commit yourself."

"Let's go ask how long it will take to have the invitations printed."

"Okay."

At the print shop the lady behind the counter was aghast. "This is a secret," Billy Joe cautioned her, and his seriousness convinced her.

"We won't tell."

"How long?"

"One hundred printed invitations and matching envelopes—I can have them for you in four days." She offered him a form and a pencil. "Write out exactly what you want the invitations to say."

"Let's do it," Melanie urged.

Billy Joe took a deep, deep breath and exhaled slowly as he considered. "Okay," he said, and reached for the writing materials.

EIGHTEEN

Junior was pumping gas for a customer when Verlin Ice's pickup rolled into Doolin's with the windshield shattered and the headlights broken. Verlin got out slowly. His nose was bloody.

"What happened?" Junior demanded, and looked inside the vehicle at Mrs. Ice. She had her head buried in her hands.

"The Barrow boys," Verlin said. "Spun their tires and threw rocks all over the windshield and broke it all to hell. I leaned out and shook my fist at 'em, so they stopped, came back and punched me."

Junior led Verlin to the bench near the door and made him sit. Then he went into the store looking for his father. "Dad, you'd better get out here. The Barrow boys smashed Verlin Ice's windshield and punched him."

When Junior and Moses Grimes got back outside, Lula was already helping Minnie from the truck. She issued orders to the men. "Take Verlin to the restroom and clean him up. We'll be in the restaurant."

Ten minutes later over coffee, Verlin told them what had happened. "Just meanness," he said after he had covered the facts. "Bullying people. Those Barrows like to strut and act tough. They're the most worthless two humans on the face of this earth. Got no respect for age or women. Cussed right in Minnie's face, so they did."

"Which one hit you?" Junior asked.

"I thought it was Coonrod, but I can't be sure. Hadn't seen 'em up close in years, not since that arson trial when Lester Storm sent 'em up."

"You were on the jury, weren't you?"

"That's right. But, you know, I don't think they remembered that today. I figure I'd be lying out there in the road bleeding to death if they had remembered."

"It's too bad they can't remember what prison was like," Lula Grimes said with steel in her voice. "It looks like they're bound and determined to get back there one way or the other."

"Lester Storm will send them back," Moses told Verlin, "if you'll sign a complaint. They're just out on probation now."

Verlin dabbed at his nose with a wet rag and said nothing.

"Let me call Arleigh Tate or Sam Neely," Moses pleaded. "Let's get the law down here to look at your truck. They can fill out the complaint and you can sign it."

"No."

"Verlin, somebody has got to—"

"The Barrows burn houses, burn barns, shoot cattle. Now, if they shoot a few of my cows, that wouldn't be a disaster because Minnie and I have our Social Security. But what if they burn the barn? Burn my house? Attack my daughters? Go up to my boy Jirl's and shoot up his house when he's got children living there? Or shoot some of his steers? No."

"I understand," Moses Grimes said.

"I hope you do. Honest, I hope you do. Don't think less of me because I'm not willing to put my family at risk."

"I don't, Verlin. I've known you too long."

Moses Grimes patted his friend on the shoulder, then walked through the kitchen into the store. He sat behind the cash register staring through the plate glass window at Verlin's truck. Junior was out there now, changing the headlights.

He called the state police office, got Neely and told him about the Barrows and Verlin Ice.

"This is the fourth incident like this that has been reported," Neely said sadly. "But no one will sign a complaint. Everyone is afraid of them. Without a complaint, there is nothing I can do."

"I'll sign a complaint."

"You know you can't do that."

Arleigh Tate told Moses the same thing. It was maddening.

Junior came into the store and caught the last of his father's conversation with Sheriff Tate.

"Don't worry, Dad. Arch and I will take care of those Barrows."

"No, you won't. You two have been in enough trouble lately. There is a limit on how much Arleigh Tate will ignore, and you're there or thereabouts." He ran Junior out.

But if the law won't do anything, self-help is the only remedy remaining. It's time to settle the Barrows' hash, Moses told himself. Past time. He picked up the telephone and dialed the number for Information in Capitol City.

When Sam Neely came into the restaurant the next morning for breakfast, Moses and Junior Grimes were seated at the table in the back of the room talking to two men in army camouflage outfits. Careful to avoid looking at the wall mural, Sam went back to join them.

The conversation died as Neely approached the table. He got the impression that the discussion had been serious—no one was smiling. Junior looked up as he approached and averted his eyes. Moses gave him a grin and a welcome, however. "Sam, pull up a chair. A couple of fellows I want you to meet, friends of mine from Capitol City. This is Otis Hammond and Sherman Fisher. Fellows, meet Sam Neely, our local trooper."

"Glad to meet you." Neely shook hands, then pulled a chair around. Hammond and Fisher, he noted, were perhaps the fittest men he had seen in years. Both had wide shoulders, flat stomachs and muscular arms. Neely could just see a portion of Fisher's upper right leg, the thigh so big the trouser leg was stretched drumhead tight.

"What kind of work do you fellows do?" the state policeman asked curiously.

"I own the Capitol City Karate Academy," Hammond said. "Fisher is my head instructor. He used to be an unarmed combat instructor for the FBI."

"So what brings you to our corner of paradise?"

"Otis and Sherman are going crow hunting," Moses said, and gestured toward the camouflage clothes.

"I thought camos were just high fashion these days."

"Moses has been bragging on the Eden-country crows all summer," Hammond said with a smile. "We had nothing to do today, so we decided to come see if he's been blowing smoke. He's bet us that we get shots at a dozen birds or we get a free dinner tonight."

"Steak dinners," Moses said, nodding in affirmation.

"There's a lot of crows this year," Junior said. "I've sure been seeing them. Up to J. S. Kline's and around by Jared Kane's, down by the old Varner place, up to Lyle Samples' . . ."

"We'll find them," Hammond said. "If Fisher doesn't swallow the crow call, we should get those shots." The conversation drifted into the intricacies of crow hunting.

Neely was still eating his breakfast when Hammond and Fisher departed. He watched them walk toward the register at the front, coordinated and light on their feet despite the weight of the muscles they carried.

Moses finished his coffee and left, but Junior remained behind. "Are you and I going to be friends or what?" Junior asked Neely.

"Which would you prefer?"

"We could go out back and have a little tussle and see if that clears the air."

"I'm on duty."

"When you're off."

"If that's what you want, it's fine with me."

Junior frowned into his coffee cup. "I don't want that, I reckon." He had learned his lesson years ago. After every schoolboy fight, win or lose, the remorse had been almost more than he could handle. Long ago he resolved never to fight again. There were times, though, when that resolution slipped his mind.

"June, you know I wouldn't have . . . with Diamond . . . if I had known it was Diamond. I thought she was Crystal. She said she was."

"It was her fault, huh?"

"Well, I don't like to blame women, but the honest fact is I thought she was Crystal, and she knew I thought that. Maybe she wanted to make you jealous."

"I am jealous," Junior growled. "Don't do it again, okay?"

"Why don't you marry the woman?"

"Who are you to ask that? You came trotting into my garage to break the news that you've had a roll with my girl—she tricked you into it, you say—and now you advise me to take her to the altar?"

Sam Neely threw up his hands. "Forget I said it."

"You'd better forget more than that!"

Neely stood and dug into his pocket for a tip. He grabbed his hat and check. "If you change your mind about that tussle, give me a call. I'd enjoy rearranging your face."

With that he walked out.

Hammond and Fisher cruised the gravel road toward Vegan. Fisher was behind the wheel of the Jeep Cherokee paying attention to the road, but Hammond was looking around at the farms and checking the hills for crows.

"What did Moses say they were driving?"

"Old blue Chevy sedan, two-door, with peeling paint."

"Just because they live at Goshen doesn't mean they'll be there."

"I'm aware of that. We'll play it by ear."

"What if they aren't home?"

"Then we'll drive around until we find them. That'll be more fun than hunting crows anyway."

"I have a dollar that says they're home."

"I'll take that bet."

Going through Vegan, Fisher said, "I've never killed a crow in my life. And I feel like an idiot in this camo outfit."

"The trooper bought it. Crow hunters wear this stuff."

"Go over it again, how we're supposed to blow that crow call."

Otis Hammond got the call from his pocket and gave some experimental toots. Fisher rolled down the windows in the Jeep to lessen the pain.

Hammond was calling lustily between glances at the sky for big, black birds when Fisher said, "There they are." He pointed. The blue sedan was coming toward them from Goshen; it had just topped the ridge a half mile away.

"You sure?"

"Another dollar. Old blue clunker sedan."

"Well, stop this thing. Turn around. Hurry."

Fisher found a place and turned the Cherokee. Then he started creeping back the way he had come, toward Vegan and Eden.

"Not here on the crest of this hill. Go over the rise, down about a hundred yards on the other side."

"Okay." Fisher fed gas. "Looks like they graveled the road this summer."

"That undoubtedly inspired the Barrows."

Sherman Fisher had the Cherokee creeping along, barely in motion, when the Barrow boys came flying over the crest behind him in their old blue Chevy and slammed on their brakes. The Chevy careened toward them in a cloud of dirt and small gravel.

The sedan was just behind the bumper, barely moving, when Fisher jammed the gas pedal to the floor. The rear tires spun madly and he sawed at the wheel to keep the Cherokee going straight. Flying dirt obscured the rearview mirror.

Hammond was looking back over his shoulder. "That's enough, I think."

Fisher took his foot from the gas pedal and applied the brakes.

They sat there, both men looking over their shoulders, waiting for the dust cloud to dissipate. The Chevy was fifty yards behind them. Even from this distance, they could see the cracks in the windshield.

The Chevy began moving. Someone was leaning out the passenger window, shaking his fist, jabbing his middle finger up and down.

Fisher waited. The battered old sedan came to a stop twenty feet behind the Cherokee, and both doors opened.

"Back up and give it to them again," Hammond said.

"This is fun," Fisher said with a grin as he pulled the transmission into reverse.

This time they heard screams as the dirt and rocks flew.

"Think we got them?"

"We got something. Why don't you park here and let's walk back and see?"

"Okay."

As they walked toward the Chevy, the Barrows ran to meet them. "You bastards! What in hell do you think you're doing?" the driver yelled.

Hammond pointed toward the rear tires on the Jeep. "New tires," he said conversationally. "We were testing them. Didn't know you were back there. Sorry."

"Jesus!" one Barrow said to the other. "Look at the clothes on these dudes." He sneered at Fisher and Hammond. "Where did you faggots come from?"

"Now is that a nice thing to say?"

"Look at our windshield. You bastards did that! You owe us! It looks like it's been sledgehammered."

"Doesn't look fresh to me," Hammond said, peering at the windshield. "I think you fellows broke that windshield weeks ago, and now you are trying to take advantage of a minor road incident to line your pockets."

"Are you calling me a liar?"

"Yes. Most certainly. And I would bet money that your parents never saw the inside of a church."

"Why, you—" Coonrod Barrow drew back his right fist and fired it at Otis Hammond's nose. It never arrived, of course. Hammond grabbed the wrist and threw a hip, and Coonrod flew like an eagle for about twelve feet. He landed on his face in the hard-packed gravel, groaned once and lay still.

Meanwhile Bushrod had similar notions. Sherman Fisher deflected the blow with his left and smashed a short right into Bushrod's nose. Blood flew.

Wild fury registered on Bushrod Barrow's face. He opened his mouth to roar something, but he never got it out. His opponent kicked him in the balls. He collapsed in the dirt. Fisher bent down and grabbed a handful of hair. He lifted Bushrod's head free of the ground. "Have you ever flown?"

"Uh . . . uh . . ."

"Today you're going to solo."

Fisher grabbed a wrist and ankle and began to spin. On the second revolution he released his hold. Bushrod went up and over the rail fence beside the road. He landed with a sickening splat fifteen feet beyond the fence, in a cow pasture. He didn't get up.

"Help me get this other one off the road," Hammond said.

"You need help?"

"Not really, but I think teamwork has a certain artistic charm."

They each grabbed an ankle and wrist and tossed Coonrod over the fence. He landed in a heap near his brother.

Fisher walked back to the Chevy. The doors were open, the engine still running. He merely looked inside. "They do have a rifle," he announced. He pulled it from behind the driver's seat. "Old army rifle," he told Hammond. He opened the bolt and a shell flew out. He toggled the bolt release and pulled the bolt free of the action. Then he threw it as far as he could.

Just off the road close to the fence was a large stone. Fisher held the rifle by the barrel and swung it like a baseball bat. The stock shattered. He tossed the barreled action, now free of the stock, into the backseat of the car.

"You going to leave that car running?"

"Yep."

"How do you suppose that guy knew that we were gay?"

"He didn't. He was just trying to insult us."

"Maybe he could tell. You've been looking a bit effeminate lately. Maybe that tipped him off."

"I have not."

"I think it's the way you move your hips when you walk. Gives me the hots."

"Oh, shut up and get in the Jeep. I'm in a mood to kill something. Let's go find a crow."

"You think we ought to leave those clowns just lying there?"

"They're over in the pasture with the rest of the manure. That's a good place for them."

The Barrow boys staggered into the state police office in Indian River about lunchtime. Sam Neely couldn't believe his eyes. One of them had his nose smeared across his left cheek and blood dripping off his chin. He hugged himself as he took small, mincing steps into the office and collapsed into a chair.

The other one had almost no skin left on his face. He wasn't bleeding much, but lots of dirt and gravel were visible in the deep cuts and vicious scrapes.

Neely had seen their mug shots so many times that he felt sure these were the Barrow boys. Of course, in the condition they were in it was impossible to be certain.

"Car wreck?" Neely asked solicitously.

"No. We—"

"I've never seen anyone that looked as bad as you two do. Oh, I've seen automobile accident victims that looked worse, but they were dead. You're the first living humans I've ever seen this torn up. Hold still and let me look."

They remained silent while he closely inspected their wounds, shaking his head sadly and tut-tutting. Finally he straightened and crossed his arms. He sighed. "What is it you want?"

"We want to make a complaint."

"You've come to the right place." Sam Neely seated himself at the desk and arranged his legal pad just so. He got out his ballpoint pen and made sure the point worked. He moved around to settle his fanny. "Shoot."

"Two dudes beat us up. After they rocked our windshield with their tires and smashed it real bad. Big dudes. City types. Wearing funny army clothes."

"Only two?"

"There might have been more, but we didn't see them."

"Get their license number?"

"Things happened so fast we couldn't get it written down."

"That's a disappointment. Names, please."

"We don't know their—"

"Not their names. *Your* names."

"Barrow. I'm Bushrod. This is Coonrod."

"Your mother was long on imagination, wasn't she? Better spell those for me."

Bushrod did so. Slowly, because Neely made him go slow.

"Okay, where did all this beating up happen?"

Coonrod answered that one. "One of them threw me on my face in the road, and they kicked Bushrod in the balls and smashed his nose and—"

"In this county?"

"Yes."

"Where in this county?"

"Up above Vegan. About halfway to Goshen."

"You sure about that?"

"Well, I kinda think it was—"

"I must have the exact location."

It took the Barrow boys almost thirty minutes to get all the details out to Neely's satisfaction, and only then did he type up the complaint and let them scrawl their signatures.

"You fellows should go to the hospital and get those injuries looked at. Bushrod—it is Bushrod, isn't it?—has bled all over my floor. The next time someone beats you up, I suggest that you go to the hospital first, then come here to do the paperwork after the bleeding has stopped."

"We want you to get out there, find those guys. Arrest them."

"You bet. They're wearing army camouflage clothes and driving a Jeep Cherokee?"

"A red Cherokee. Late model. Nearly new."

"Well, without a license number, I doubt if the prosecutor will be interested, but I'll do my best. Meanwhile you fellows go to the hospital and show them how you can bleed. Oh, by the way, you'd better get your windshield repaired. I'd hate to have to write you a ticket for having a defective windshield. It's a safety item, you know, and we're real sticklers on traffic safety."

"We want to be safe," Coonrod mumbled.

Neely shooed them out, put on his hat, turned off the lights and locked the door.

The last thing in the world the policeman wanted was to stumble across Otis Hammond and Sherman Fisher in their shiny red Cherokee with an unknown license number. They were hunting crows in the southern part of the county; that was where they collided with the Barrows. It seemed likely they would stay in that vicinity. Consequently Sam Neely drove north out of Indian River. He drove all the way to the northern end of the county— chuckling all the way—and parked the cruiser beside the road sign. If those suspects came by here, he would stop them and get their story. If not . . .

NINETEEN

Richard Hudson drove by the house three times before he decided to stop. He could have called ahead, of course, and asked if he could drop by, but then he would have been committed, and at some point in the conversation he would have had to give a reason for his visit.

When he parked the car, he told himself that he still had all his options. This could be just a social visit, a welcome-to-the-neighborhood kind of thing.

He sat in the car with the engine off staring at the house, another ramshackle Victorian. Okay, he admitted to himself, he was nervous. Very nervous. He told himself that was because the lady was a minister. Funerals were the only occasions in his adult life on which he knowingly conversed with rabbis and ministers. As a general rule, members of God's squad made him uncomfortable, although he had never bothered to try to figure out why that was so.

Aggravating his historic queasiness around the clergy was the fact that this minister was a woman. The truth of the matter was that he didn't like women much, either. Oh, he talked to them, of course. Women were ubiquitous in American society; there was just no way to avoid them unless you lived in a cave in Arizona or an igloo in Alaska. Yet his contacts with them were superficial, in the line of duty, so to speak, and he liked it that way.

Perhaps that was why the Ice girls frightened him so. They were so . . . brazen, so up-front with their femininity. The "I woman, you man" approach gave him cold chills.

He wouldn't go into that with Mrs. Carcano, of course. The problem, if he decided to discuss it, was how to get the Ice women out of his life. Without bloodshed.

Actually, shooting them wasn't a bad idea. He would write in prison. A nice cell, peace and quiet, a computer . . .

And it might come to that. If Crystal and Diamond couldn't be induced to leave him alone, it just might.

He whacked his head twice against the steering wheel.

Get a grip, man!

Okay. *I'm a sane, sober, middle-aged misogynistic slob with a female problem. Two problems. I have been referred to you for consultation and advice. If you have any advice. If you don't, forget I was here and have a nice life. See you at a funeral. 'Bye.*

He opened the door and got out of the car. Closed the door. Marched through the gate and up the walk, climbed the steps, went across the porch and rapped sharply at the door. Like a house-siding salesman making a cold call, he thought.

He heard footsteps coming toward the door, which sent chills up his spine. His knees felt watery.

The door opened—and revealed a pleasant, well-scrubbed woman somewhere between thirty and forty, probably closer to forty than thirty, brown hair in a sensible style, wearing a dress. Don't see many dresses nowadays. "Good morning. May I help you?"

"Uh . . . Mrs. Carcano, isn't it?"

"Yes."

"My name is Hudson. Richard Hudson. I live . . . uh"—he turned and gestured vaguely—"up the road. I was talking the other day with some friends—uh, acquaintances, actually—about a personal problem—uh, two problems, in point of fact—and they . . . uh . . . recommended that I stop sometime to see you and discuss . . . ." He ran out of steam there.

"Come in, Mr. Hudson." She opened the door wide.

"If you're busy I could come back some other time. That might be best. An appointment for sometime . . . next week?"

"I'm not busy. I'll be delighted to spend a few minutes with you now. Come in."

So he went in. Against his better judgment. Actually entered the house of a woman of the cloth for the express purpose of talking about his personal problems. Both of them.

"I can't believe they've reduced me to this," he muttered to himself.

"I'm sorry. What did you say?" She was leading him along a hallway. The kitchen was visible at the end of it.

"Nothing important. Just mumbling. I do that from time to time."

"Will you have some coffee or tea?"

"Why not?"

"Which would you prefer?"

"Whatever you are having."

"Please sit down." She indicated a chair at the kitchen table. He slid into it. Looked around the room. A white room, white paint over wainscoting. Old, neat and clean.

She puttered with cups and saucers and the coffeepot.

He reviewed how he intended to approach this consultation: tell her what he did for a living—after all, everyone else knew—and why he needed his privacy, then get delicately into the problem of the affectionate sisters. No gory details, of course.

She still had her back to him when she said, "Richard Hudson . . . There is a novelist by that name who writes science fiction. *The Voyagers* and *The Survivors* are his most famous works." She turned and started across the room bearing coffee cups. "By any chance, are you that Richard Hudson?"

He cleared his throat. "Yes."

She seated herself across from him and smiled. "I enjoyed both those books. I've read several more of your stories, but I can't recall the titles."

"You're not a sci-fi fanatic, are you?"

"Alas, no. I read science fiction from time to time, but I read other books, too, books from many genres."

"That's good. You should read widely, good books on many subjects." Listen to him, yammering away as if he had known her all his life.

"Tell me about writing, about how you do it."

"There's nothing esoteric about it. I dream up a story, figure out how it will go, create the characters necessary to tell the tale, find a starting place and begin. Then I improvise as I go along."

"There must be more to it than that."

"No. All one needs is a half-decent imagination and the storytelling skills. The skills are the craft, acquired through study of successful, skilled writers, and practice. Lots of practice."

Away he went, talking about the one great passion of his life. She filled the coffee cups; he talked on and on.

He heard a clock chime somewhere in the house and glanced at his watch. He had been here almost forty-five minutes, he realized with a jolt. "I'm sorry I've taken up so much of your time, but I must tell you why I came," he said, and tentatively began explaining about the Ice sisters, the near-fanatical hero worship that threatened his solitude and his writing. "I hate to say this, Mrs. Carcano, but I need help. I've got to do something."

"Are they interested in you romantically?"

"Yes." He blushed.

"My suggestion, Mr. Hudson, is that you tell them flatly and unequivocally that you aren't interested."

"I've tried that."

"Then put them to work."

"They jump in without my saying anything. I've got the cleanest house in the county."

"Do you like chicken salad?"

"Uh, yes, but don't—"

She was already up and moving. As she took things from the refrigerator and bread drawer, she kept talking. "The other thing you can do is develop a romantic interest of your own, with someone else."

"Well, I'm not interested in that. I like the way I live."

"I know how you feel. I like the way I live, too."

"I've never been married, you see. Always lived alone. Wouldn't want to start courting when I know I don't want it to go anywhere. That wouldn't be fair." Why did he say that?

He realized with a start that this woman was dangerous. A few minutes with her and he was ready to tell her everything.

"I was married," Mrs. Carcano volunteered. "Twice. My first husband left me, and my second husband died, about two years ago."

"I'm sorry."

"Life goes on, Mr. Hudson. Life is for the living." She smiled wryly. "That's a platitude. But it does reflect, I think, an underlying truth. We cannot live in the past. We must come to grips with it, then go on living."

The chicken salad sandwiches were good, the milk cold and delicious. Richard Hudson ate two sandwiches and drank two glasses of milk.

She had a way of looking at him that was almost hypnotic. She kept her gaze firmly on his eyes. Sooner or later he would look away, but when he looked at her again, her gaze was still on his eyes. She had good eyes, wide and brown. They looked through your eyes and saw . . . Richard Hudson shivered involuntarily.

It was unconscious with her, he decided. She was interested in the human she was talking to, so she looked intently at the face, absorbed all the cues, heard what was said and saw what was meant.

She was dangerous—his first reaction was correct.

And yet . . . and yet Richard Hudson had the feeling that she wasn't. The impression began to grow that she was one of the gentlest, kindest people he had ever met. Her aura surrounded him, warming him in a way that no fire ever had.

"It's a sin to eat too much," he said. "That's one of my many sins."

She smiled.

"How do you stand on sin, anyway?"

"I'm against it, Mr. Hudson, but I'm not bigoted about it."

Hudson laughed, the first laugh he had had in weeks.

"That's not original with me," she confessed. "Damon Runyon said it first, about lawbreaking, I believe."

"Damon Runyon, an American original."

Hudson reluctantly said his good-byes and departed. And to think he almost didn't stop to talk!

Her advice was sound. Tell them the truth and put them to work.

He whistled all the way home, vastly pleased with the world and his little place in it. Life is good, he told himself. You just can't let the little problems get you down.

He walked through his front door and stopped, facing the Ice girls. "I am not in love with either of you and will never fall in love with either of you. You are not welcome here. If you won't leave, stop sitting here like guests and clean the place up. Run the washer, do the ironing, clean the windows."

Crystal and Diamond Ice gaped at him.

He went on to the study and closed the door behind him. He flipped on his computer. Okay, Ziad, time to cut and slash. He was tapping away when he heard the vacuum sweeper roar into life in the bedroom over his head.

Sheriff Arleigh Tate locked his door before he opened the large manila envelope from the state crime lab. Hoo boy, those telephoto lenses gave you a ringside seat on the action, and the lab technicians had blown up the photos into eight-by-tens that were so hot they almost sizzled.

Diamond Ice—now there was a woman! Too much woman for Junior Grimes, Arleigh Tate felt, and about fifty times more woman than Delmar Clay could handle on the best day he ever had. She was something to dream about.

Tate went through all the photos, examining each one, then went back through the stack again, separating it into two piles. Finally he took the more promising stack and examined each photo closely with a magnifying glass. When he was finished, he had settled on six pictures. The ones he chose had at least two things in common: Diamond Ice was totally nude, and Delmar Clay was easily and positively recognizable, beyond a shadow of a doubt. In two of the shots Delmar was partially clad.

From his desk drawer he selected a black magic marker. He used it to black out Diamond's face in the six photographs. While waiting for the ink to dry, he consulted the telephone book. When he found the listing he wanted, he copied the address onto a large white envelope using block letters, inserted the edited photos, and sealed it.

He didn't want to hand the envelope to a postal clerk who might remember it, so he rooted in his drawer until he found some stamps. He wasn't sure how much postage would be enough, so he licked ten first-class stamps and glued them in place. That should do the trick, he hoped.

Sarah Armbrecht was remembering snow. The breeze had a bite to it that made her think of snow under a cloudless blue sky, the chill wind coming in gusts and whirlwinds that picked up the granules and swept them along in waves only inches deep, like sand in the desert. The wind sculpted the snow, made ridges and depressions and hummocks that looked so perfect that you sighed over the beauty of it. And the impermanence.

She wished she could see it again, could watch the winter wind play with the snow just one more afternoon. Just one. But she couldn't see very well anymore, hadn't been able to see much for years.

She had so many memories, so very many. Of winter, spring, summer, and her favorite season, autumn, when the leaves turned. She hadn't seen much of this past autumn, either.

Trapped in this old, old body, blind, frail, with only her memories, there wasn't much left to live for. Not that she was ready to go, because she wasn't. She loved life too much. Loved it, savored it, reveled in it. These young people who still had perfect health, many of them saw life as drudgery, as something to be endured, which was so very sad.

The key, she decided, was perspective, a proper perch from which to view life's parade. The view Sarah's ninety-five years gave her was rather extraordinary, although lonely. There weren't many people to share it with.

She remembered her great-grandfather, an old man with a long white beard and only one arm; a minié ball had shattered his left arm near the crest of Missionary Ridge during the battle for Chattanooga. The surgeons amputated the limb at the shoulder. That was in November of '63—1863. Yet Sarah Armbrecht could see the old man and hear his deep voice telling her of the battle as if she were again ten years old and had seen him only yesterday.

He never forgot the experience that turned out to be the high point in his life, an epic day of fear, exhaustion, nervous energy, shooting and killing and running, tidal waves of noise, men screaming, shouting, taking bullets, stabbing, crying, laughing, dying . . . He never forgot the blood or the pain, the nearness of death and the exhilaration of life. So sixty years later he could tell youngsters who gathered to listen, tell it as his eyes danced, his voice rising and falling like a musical instrument, tell it as if he had lived it just yesterday. The events of his youth became the children's reality and now, eighty-odd years later, were an essential part of Sarah Armbrecht's past that somehow defined who she was and how she ordered her life.

She was letting her mind drift, watching that young man who would become her great-grandfather as he scrambled up the steep side of Missionary Ridge with Rebel bullets whistling around his ears, when the day girl said, "Mrs. Armbrecht, shouldn't you come in? There is a definite chill in the air."

"A little longer, dear. The porch season is about over. Let me enjoy it while I can."

"Ring your bell when you're ready."

"Yes."

The porch season, life, the sweet and not-so-sweet moments, all would end too soon. If only these young people knew.

When she heard the car coming, she rang the bell. "I'll see my guest in the living room," she told the girl.

The caller was Cecile Carcano, who introduced herself to Mrs. Armbrecht as the new pastor of the Eden Chapel. "I'm calling on my parishioners whom I haven't yet met, Mrs. Armbrecht. I haven't seen you in church."

"I don't get there often, I'm afraid. Too much trouble for an old woman."

They were sitting in the living room drinking tea. Mrs. Carcano said, "One of my parishioners, Mr. Junior Grimes, has offered to transport people who need some assistance to church on Sunday mornings. Do you know him well?"

Mrs. Armbrecht chuckled softly. "You may find this hard to believe, Mrs. Carcano, but Junior calls on me regularly to check up, see how I'm getting along. Comes sometime during the first week of every month."

"I didn't know that."

"I'm not the only elderly person Junior visits. In fact, I do believe he calls on everyone in the area who has trouble getting around. After every snowstorm he plows my driveway. And he runs errands. On several occasions he has picked up prescriptions and done some postal business for me. He knows I can afford to pay; indeed, I would prefer to, but he refuses to accept a penny. Ah, yes, I know Junior Grimes."

"I saw some entries in the church ledger, gifts from you in Junior's name."

"Sssh! That's a secret. Junior would be embarrassed if he knew."

Mrs. Carcano smiled. "As you can see, I am still learning my way around my parish, still sorting out the personalities."

"You will find them no better and no worse than people anywhere else," Mrs. Armbrecht said. "They struggle to earn their livings, to do what they believe to be right, to raise their children properly, just like people everywhere."

"Tell me about yourself, Mrs. Armbrecht. I would like to know you better."

The old woman laughed and asked the day girl to bring more tea.

Cecile Carcano was ready to leave a half hour later when Anne Harris arrived. "Anne is my grandson's wife," Mrs. Armbrecht explained to the minister. "Marrying her was the smartest thing Ed Harris ever did."

"Pleased to meet you, Mrs. Harris," the minister said. After a few pleasantries, she brought up another subject. "We're having a meeting tonight at the Eden Chapel, Mrs. Harris, and I wonder if you could come? The hymnals are wearing out and need to be replaced. Perhaps you could help us with some ideas on fund-raisers for that purpose?"

Anne Harris agreed to come. Cecile Carcano kissed Sarah Armbrecht, then shook Anne's hand.

When she and Sarah were alone, Anne said, "You didn't have to say that, Granny Sarah, about Ed. You know I'm not living with him right now, and you must be loyal to your grandson."

"I am loyal to him," the old lady said firmly. "I was simply telling the unvarnished truth. At my age, I've found that people expect it."

"I hadn't met Mrs. Carcano before."

"I like her. She asked if I would like to join her in prayer. I told her yes, if it wasn't too long. So we said the Lord's Prayer together. I thought it very touching."

A few moments later Anne got around to the point of her visit. "The last time I was here you asked me why Lane gave me half the bank stock, and I didn't know. I still don't, though I have been thinking about it. Would you care to hear my thoughts?"

"If you wish to share them."

"I think Lane liked me, but he also pitied me."

"Pity?"

"He didn't think I was very resilient. Or not resilient enough. I believe that he thought I didn't understand life very well, so I was probably not going to do a very good job living it. Consequently he gave me the bank stock so I would have something to fall back on."

"I see."

"One can never be sure, of course," Anne mused. "But looking back from this vantage point, I think that is what motivated him."

"Was he correct?"

"There is some truth in all opinions."

"The battle to understand is never won," Sarah Armbrecht said. "Take me, for instance. Last week I had the strangest dream. My mother came to me, sat beside my bed and talked to me. I haven't dreamed of her in, oh, so many years. She died when I was just fifteen. She was in her thirties then, a beautiful woman. Naturally I got over the loss as the years passed and other things filled my life.

"Then last week she came to my bedside. Her hair was done up the way they wore it back then, and she was wearing a long, ivory-colored dress that came to her ankles, long sleeves with lace, a high collar . . . I can still see her, even now."

"What did she say? In your dream."

"I can't recall exactly . . . now. She sat beside my bed, my mother, young and beautiful as I remember her, and I was old, very old, and we talked and talked . . . of woman things, I believe . . . I am not sure, and perhaps it doesn't matter. But she was mother and I was daughter, although she was young and I wasn't."

Anne Harris realized the old lady was weeping.

In a moment Sarah spoke again. "Here I am, all these years later, a great-grandmother many times over, and I miss my mother."

Later she whispered, "Life is too complex to understand completely. Too rich."

When the driver unloaded the horse from the trailer, Jirl Ice's heart sank. He had paid a thousand dollars for the horse—a gentle, sixteen-year-old chestnut gelding that would make a good riding horse for his daughters—three days ago, and he looked fine then.

He didn't look good now. His head was down, he showed no curiosity in its new surroundings, he refused handfuls of sweet hay—in short, he just stood listlessly, like a sick horse.

Jirl telephoned the seller, who sounded surprised. "The horse was fine when he left here an hour ago. Maybe he's carsick. He'll probably snap out of it in a few hours."

Jirl wasn't so sure.

"Wouldn't hurt to call a vet," the seller suggested. "But he's your horse now. It's up to you."

A thousand dollars was a thousand dollars, so Jirl Ice called the veterinarian, who arrived in the late afternoon. The horse looked no better, Jirl thought.

The vet examined the horse in a stall in the barn. "This animal is sick, Mr. Ice," she said. "I'm going to give him an antibiotic and take some blood samples, but I'm not optimistic."

"How sick is he?"

"Very sick. A horse this old . . ."

"How old?" Jirl asked suspiciously.

"Twenty-two or -three, I should say."

A thousand dollars gone, poof, just like that. Plus the vet's bill . . . Jirl Ice was so depressed that he could scarcely eat his dinner.

"Go to church this evening," his wife advised. "The new minister is holding a meeting about the hymnals."

"I don't have money to donate for hymnals."

"It'll take your mind off the horse. Go."

So at seven o'clock Jirl was sitting in the Eden Chapel with a dozen or so other people listening to Cecile Carcano talk about hymnals. She passed the books around and asked people to carefully examine the bindings and pages.

"We will need five hundred dollars to purchase new hymnals," Mrs. Carcano said. "The suggestion has been made that we hold a raffle. What do you think?"

They discussed it. Naturally the question became, What would be the prize of the raffle? It was here that the idea occurred to Jirl Ice. At first he dismissed it as foolish, but when no one offered to donate something of value as the raffle prize, he scratched his head and pondered and finally gave in to temptation. "What about a horse?" he asked.

"A horse? That would be good, if we had one."

A murmur of approval greeted this remark, and all eyes turned to Jirl.

He cleared his throat before he spoke. "I have a horse. He's a gelding, chestnut, very gentle, and he's worth a thousand dollars. I'd be willing to donate half his value, but I'd need five hundred for him."

More discussion. A horse would certainly be a nice prize, everyone agreed, but the mechanics of funding a payment to Mr. Ice merited some thought.

Mrs. Carcano cut through the controversy with her usual aplomb. "Perhaps we can sell a thousand tickets for a dollar each. The first five hundred dollars in sales will go for hymnals. All the money in excess of five hundred will go to Mr. Jirl Ice in partial payment for his horse. Would that be acceptable, Mr. Ice?"

Feeling more than a little guilty, Jirl agreed to this proposal. Several people shook his hand after the meeting. Mrs. Carcano gave him a warm smile.

"Very generous," Richard Hudson told him at the door as he shook his hand. "I'm going to buy a hundred dollars' worth of tickets myself, even though I don't need a horse."

"I don't need him, either. But he's a good horse."

"I know your sisters very well, Mr. Ice."

"Hmm," said Jirl, who was anxious to be on his way.

"Too well," Richard Hudson muttered, and glanced back over his shoulder at Mrs. Carcano, who was talking to Anne Harris and Matilda Elkins.

After Jirl departed, Richard Hudson waited alone outside the chapel in the hope of getting a few minutes alone with Mrs. Carcano. She was deep in conversation with Anne and Matilda. Richard Hudson walked to his car lost in thought.

TWENTY

The next morning Richard Hudson came home whistling. Earlier, when Diamond and Crystal arrived, he had put them to work cleaning bathrooms. Then he drove over to Mrs. Carcano's house, picked her up, and took her to Doolin's for coffee and rolls. After a very pleasant hour, he was home again.

He strode into his house still whistling and went to his study. He flipped on the computer, then took off his coat and hat and hung them on the rack. He flexed his fingers while he thought about Prince Ziad. He saw the story now, saw his characters, the situation, how the action had to go, saw precisely how he could bring this tale to a smashing climax that would leave the readers gasping.

Whistling aimlessly, he dropped into his chair at the desk and started tapping the keys.

He was hard at it some time later when he realized Diamond Ice was standing behind him reading over his shoulder.

He pushed a button to save what he had written. She put her hands on his shoulders and began a slow massage.

He pushed her away. "We need to have a serious talk."

"So talk, sweet man."

"You, Crystal, and me. In the living room. Would you ask her to come, please?"

When they were seated in the living room facing him, he dropped the bomb. "There is another woman."

The sisters looked at each other, then fastened their gaze upon him, dumbfounded.

His announcement was a bold stroke. Daring, even. And he had thought it up himself, a fact of which he was rather proud. He had cleared it this morning with Cecile—he called her that now, at her request. "I have a very large favor to ask of you," he told the minister on the steps of her porch when they returned from Doolin's. "With your permission, I want to tell the Ice sisters that I have fallen for you, so there is no hope for them."

Surprise registered on Cecile Carcano's face. "You understand," she said, "that tidbit will become the talk of the county?"

"Which is precisely why I have come to you for permission before I tell them. I don't want to compromise you in any way, nor to damage your reputation. You can always deny that you have any interest in me, truthfully deny it, so it will appear to our many curious neighbors that I am a frustrated suitor." He smiled hopefully.

When she didn't reply immediately, he added, "There are a lot of frustrated suitors in Eden, so I'll be in good company. These people have raised romantic frustration to a high art. Believe me, they understand it, though they understand little else."

Cecile Carcano seated herself on the top step as she considered his request. "The only problem I see, Richard, is that you are compromising your personal integrity."

"I don't think a little white lie is going to scar me," he said lightly. "After all, I am a professional liar. I tell lies for a living."

"A personal lie is not fiction written to entertain," she replied. "And a lie about a matter of the heart is the worst sort of lie. Only you know what you deeply feel. A lie like that will haunt you."

Richard Hudson didn't want to hear this. "Let's concentrate on the effect on you," he said. "I have a major problem that I hope this will help solve, yet I don't want to injure you in any way."

She ran her fingers through her hair. "I don't suppose anyone will be shocked. We are both mature adults, both single, and neither of us has any other romantic attachments."

"Precisely. That is why I thought of you."

"But are you sure there is no truth in it?"

"It's just a ploy, Cecile, although I'll tell it in such a way that Crystal and Diamond will believe it."

"I see," she said, and rose from her seat.

He nervously shifted his weight from foot to foot. "May I say it, then?"

"If you believe it will help you."

"Thank you. You are a very nice lady." He skipped back to his car and paused by the door to wave.

Now he was using his little tale. The silence grew and grew as the Ice sisters digested the first bite. Crystal was the first to speak.

"Who is it?"

"Mrs. Carcano."

"The woman preacher?"

"Yes. I have fallen for her. I don't think she returns my affection, but I have fallen head over heels. She is so wonderful, so decent, so pleasant, so very, very wise . . . All in all, she is the woman I have looked for all my life. I have finally realized that and, in all honesty, felt that you two should be the first to hear."

"Doesn't she know?" Diamond demanded.

"Yes, she does. I have discussed my feelings with her. But . . ." He let the "but" hang in the air, twisting slowly.

"You can't control your heart," Diamond said thoughtfully, hugging herself.

"I hoped you would understand," Hudson told them warmly, sensing victory. "You are two wonderful human beings, caring, sensitive, with hearts full of love to give, but . . ." The first "but" worked so well, he decided to loft another.

"I don't think that I am in love with you, Richard," Crystal said. "I like you, care for you greatly, and admire you ever so much. Your stories have moved me deeply. I guess I hoped my admiration would grow into love. On my part and yours."

The bubbling, efflorescent optimism that had fired Richard Hudson all morning vanished in a twinkling. "I don't want to hurt you," he murmured. "I've always been afraid of that. I don't want to hurt anyone, and I don't want anyone hurt over me."

Diamond rose from her chair and reached for her coat. "I think you are also afraid of being hurt, Richard. You think that when a woman sees who you really are—sees the man who hides behind all the words—she will lose interest. That *you* will be the one in pain."

She pulled on her coat, then knelt in front of him and placed her hands on his knees. "I don't think you've ever been in love before, Richard Hudson. Love is an opening of the heart, and when the heart is open, it can be hurt. That is the way of it. Nothing can change that reality. Finally, you have opened your heart to Mrs. Carcano, which is good, but you must be brave. Be brave, Richard! Have faith in this fellow human being."

They left him then.

He wandered around the house feeling so very alone, so guilty. They were two good people and he had hurt them.

He was standing looking out the window when he realized that Cecile Carcano had been correct: He had compromised his integrity. How blithely he had told her that the lie wouldn't scar him! He recalled those words with bitterness now. Three people had been hurt because he had been willing— eager—to tell a lie: the Ice sisters and Richard Hudson.

He stood staring at the clouds building over the mountains on the horizon thinking about these things.

The ringing telephone brought Sheriff Arleigh Tate out of his doze. He reached for it, but he still had his feet on the desk, and with his ample tummy, there was no way. He got his feet onto the floor, then went for the instrument.

"Sheriff Tate."

"Sheriff, this is Rose Westfall in the circuit clerk's office. That civil matter you were waiting for has been filed. It needs to be served."

"Which lawyer filed it?"

"Hayden Elkins."

"Somehow that doesn't surprise me." He sighed. "I'll be right up."

He checked to ensure his shirttail was tucked in and his trousers were down over his boots, then opened his office door. Delmar Clay was behind his desk, sitting on two pillows, piddling over a report.

"How are those hemorrhoids today, Delmar?"

"Awful sore, Sheriff. Glad I got them doctored, though."

"Those things can fret a fellow for years if he doesn't bite the bullet and get them worked on," the sheriff said politely.

If Delmar attached any significance to the sheriff's macabre choice of words, he pretended not to. "Be back on patrol in just a few days, so I will."

Tate leaned forward so he could see Delmar's face better. "That looks like a nasty bruise on your chin, all purple and yellow. How did you get that?"

"Ran into a door."

"Oooh, I hope your luck changes soon," the sheriff rumbled. "It's good to have you back." And he strolled out of the office.

The circuit clerk's office was next to the courtroom, two floors above the sheriff's office. Tate went in, circled the counter and took the seat beside Rose Westfall's desk.

"Here it is," she said, and handed him a complaint and summons.

The sheriff scanned the style of the case. "Lucinda Beach Clay versus Delmar Eugene Clay, an action for the dissolution of marriage."

"There's a photo on the back of the complaint," Rose said. "First one like that that *I've* ever seen." A nervous giggle escaped her. "The clerk told us not to tell anyone about it."

Tate flipped to the back page, which was a black-and-white photocopy of a photograph of Delmar watching a woman with her face blacked out climb into the backseat of a sheriff's cruiser. Neither of them was wearing a stitch. The photocopy was marked EXHIBIT A.

"You know what they say about idle tittle-tattle," the sheriff cautioned Rose, who he knew to a certainty could be relied upon to broadcast the delicious news of Delmar's transgression to the farthest reaches of the county before dark this evening. "Still, it does look like Delmar has been sowing some very wild oats. And doing it in a county car, darn it. Guess I'll have to look into that."

He scrutinized the photocopy for a long moment, made a tsk-tsk noise with his tongue, and murmured for public consumption, "Poor Mrs. Clay."

"It's just amazing," Rose Westfall said with conviction, "the things that go on around here that a person never suspects!"

"Indeed."

"And this a Christian community!"

"Boggles the mind."

The sheriff got out his pen and went to work on the summons. *Let's see, I'll serve it in three minutes. So put that time in, the date, place will be the sheriff's office, person serving the summons will be Arleigh Tate, sheriff of Indian River County.* He scrawled his signature at the bottom and handed the summons to Rose, who witnessed his signature.

"Thanks."

"How did you know this complaint was going to be filed, Sheriff?" she asked as he rose from the chair.

The county's chief law enforcement officer held a finger in front of his lips and shook his head firmly from side to side.

He trooped down the two flights of stairs to the sheriff's department office. Delmar was still behind his desk sitting on his pillows.

Tate tossed a copy of the complaint and its lurid exhibit in front of the deputy. "You've been served," he said.

Delmar picked up the document and read the caption. His eyes widened. "What the—?"

"Looks like your wife wants a divorce, Delmar. Sorry to see it. These things happen in the best of families, I guess."

"Well, I'll be——"

"It's a shame. Really is. People change as time passes, and we must accept that reality. Probably the best thing for both of you, however. Little hard to see right now, I know, yet I think that you'll come to that conclusion later. Life marches on."

Delmar had been scanning the document, and now he arrived at the final page, the photo. His mouth fell open as he stared at it.

"One more thing, Delmar," the sheriff continued. "It's obvious from Exhibit A that you've been misusing a county car. You're fired. Give the secretary your badge and gun and be out of here in five minutes. Don't forget to take the pillows——you'll probably need them."

On that happy note Sheriff Arleigh Tate treated himself to a cigar and went home for the day. Although it was only three in the afternoon, he felt he deserved some time off.

"You were right," Hudson told Cecile Carcano. "I feel guilty."

The minister didn't reply. She was sitting at her desk in her tiny office, which had been tacked on to the back of the Eden Chapel several decades ago. In one corner a woodstove leaking smoke fought the chill.

Hudson warmed his hands over the stove as he told Mrs. Carcano about the confrontation with the Ice sisters. "They would probably have given up on me in a few more days. I should have waited."

"Perhaps," she said.

"Anyway, I'm sorry I didn't take your advice."

"Don't apologize to me. Apologize to the Ice sisters."

That option hadn't occurred to Hudson. "What in the world would I say to them?"

"The truth is usually best."

307

"You're a hard woman, Cecile."

"Sit a moment, Richard."

He took the only other chair in the small room, which was arranged beside the desk facing her. Her eyes were right there, looking straight into his soul.

"The other thing you can do is stop in the chapel and pray. I highly recommend that."

"I'm not very religious."

It was as if his face were clear window glass; she could see everything that went on in his mind with a pellucid clarity.

"God was here before you arrived, Richard, and He will be here after you are gone. He can give you the strength to bear any burden. He can certainly help you with your teaspoonful of guilt. Talk to Him. That is my recommendation, as a minister and friend."

He had to get away from those eyes. He stood. He found the paper bag he had brought with him and took out two books. "One's for you and one's for your daughter." He laid them on the desk and made his escape.

The little chapel was chilly and quiet. His breath made tiny clouds that hung in the air. The only light came from clear glass windows. His footsteps reverberated on the wooden floor as he walked the center aisle. When he reached for the knob on the double front door, Richard Hudson paused. He turned and slid into the first pew.

He sat listening to the silence, staring at the simple white cross behind the altar.

Anne and Matilda parked in front of Jirl Ice's house and climbed out of the car in high spirits. They had been out for a drive this afternoon and on a lark decided to see the horse that was being raffled off Friday evening at the Eden Chapel. Doolin's had been selling copious amounts of raffle tickets, as had several of the businesses in Indian River. Both of the women had purchased a pocketful.

The horse wasn't in the barn, and no one was in sight, so they went into the pasture and closed the gate behind them. The cattle looked at them suspiciously as they strolled along, then apparently decided the women were harmless and went back to the serious business of grazing.

Anne felt almost euphoric, filled with vigorous life. Her recent visit with Granny Sarah and her deepening friendship with Matilda were two of the key ingredients of her excellent mood, she thought. Another was Cecile Carcano. Strange, but after a few minutes of conversation with the minister— conversation on quite mundane subjects—Anne felt as if she were getting reacquainted with an old, treasured friend, one from the half-forgotten past. She never met Cecile before, and yet . . . There was something about her, something that implied shared experiences, shared emotions, shared dreams. She *was* a friend.

Anne paused and picked a dried wildflower, examined it closely, then sniffed it. The aroma was faint but delicious. She handed it to Matilda with a smile. "For the very good friend you turned out to be, Matty."

"We didn't really know each other, did we?"

As they crested the low hill, they saw something brown lying in the dried leaves near the fence, under a huge oak.

"That must be the horse, lying down."

They walked in that direction, savoring the tang of the autumn breeze.

"Oh, my heavens! How terrible!" Matilda exclaimed as they neared the horse, which was obviously dead.

They heard an engine noise coming toward them. Jirl Ice drove up in his pickup and parked.

"Your horse appears to be ill, Mr. Ice," Anne remarked.

Jirl jumped from the truck and strode over to the decomposing carcass.

"The poor creature," Matilda muttered.

"He's dead," Jirl said sadly, and turned to face the women.

Matilda turned her back on the animal. "It appears to have been dead for a day or two," she stated firmly.

Jirl tried to bluff his way through. "I'm as surprised as you ladies are.

Indeed, I am. Why, he was fit as a fiddle this morning, scampering around and kicking his heels like a colt full of milk. Darn if this isn't nasty."

Anne Harris laughed. She had a cold, hard laugh that she usually used on people who were trying to induce her to accept stupidity, incompetence or bumbling error as inevitable, but that wasn't the laugh she used this time. She felt too good to be irritated this afternoon. Her laugh rang forth as a merry peal.

Matilda took a good look at Jirl's reddening face and laughed, too. Together the two women walked back toward the barn, leaving Jirl with his dead horse.

Jirl watched them go with a sinking feeling. There went his five hundred dollars!

He threw up his hands in disgust and resignation, then said to the horse, "Poor ol' fellow, I know exactly how you feel."

Billy Joe and Melanie picked up the printed invitations, which came in a box that also contained envelopes. The Indian River library was the only place for a task this big, so they went there and spread the pile on a large table in the reading room. The local telephone book provided the addresses.

After they had the envelopes addressed, Melanie said, "Do you really think we should do this?"

"I called Ruth Harris last night, talked to her about it," Billy Joe told Melanie. "She said that her parents and mine are going to have to grow up sooner or later. Maybe this will speed the process along."

"I don't know her very well," Melanie said. "She's three years older than I am, I think."

"She's a kill-or-cure kind of gal. You'd like her a lot."

When they were finished stuffing the invitations into the envelopes and sealing each one, they put the envelopes back in the box. They bought stamps at the post office and sat in the front seat of Billy Joe's Jeep licking them and sticking them on.

"My tongue tastes terrible," Melanie giggled.

"A soda pop afterward," Billy Joe promised.

They dumped all the envelopes in the big blue mailbox outside the post office, then went off to find a soft drink.

Jirl Ice entered the social hall beside the Eden Chapel that Friday evening with a heavy, reluctant tread. He expected the crowd, which was substantial, to be buzzing with pointed comments about the health of the raffle horse. Yet as he moved along shaking hands and muttering greetings, not a word was said on that subject.

Yes, Anne Harris and Matilda Elkins were there, chattering with the minister.

Jirl wished the subject would come up soon. He had spent a miserable twenty-four hours dreading the inevitable crunch; the sooner it was over, the better. What greedy impulse induced him to volunteer a sick old horse for Mrs. Carcano to raffle off? Temporary insanity, he decided. Forlorn, awaiting the public humiliation that even now was being gleefully prepared by the ruler of the universe, the doomed man found a seat in a corner and tried to become invisible.

As was the custom at Eden Chapel socials, most folks had brought a covered dish of prepared food. They visited, spooned food from every dish on the table onto their paper plates, and ate noisily, all the while circulating and gossiping with neighbors.

All this was new to Richard Hudson, who hadn't known that he should bring a covered dish. Still, someone thrust a paper plate and plastic fork at him, and he joined the grub line with everyone else. He paid little attention to the culinary triumphs of his neighbors, however. Cecile Carcano was very much on his mind. He maneuvered so that he could hear her voice, watch her gestures, catch a smile occasionally.

She was becoming an obsession. Just being around her made him tingle all over, as if he were being kissed by a thousand butterflies. A sensation of warmth and well-being suffused him and made all his other concerns fade to insignificance.

It seemed to Hudson, as he sat tonight with his plate on his lap half-listening to the conversation and watching Cecile go through the line, that he had lived his whole life to get to this moment. To see this woman. To hear her. To speak to her. To be on the receiving end of her smile.

He was losing his grip on his old life, his old existence. His future contained extraordinarily large unknowns. Amid the gloom of this misty future, strobed randomly by flickering lights, a myriad of strange, wondrous things could occasionally be glimpsed. He wanted to go deeper into this exotic, mysterious place. Indeed, he couldn't help himself. He was being drawn in.

The whole scene was a real mind bender.

He had just inserted a bite of potato salad into his mouth when he realized that he was probably falling in love.

Could it be?

If this fantastic glow he felt was love, it would be his very first voyage into the poet's realm. Love? At his age? Or a mutant virus?

And here she came toward him, carrying a plate of food in one hand and a drink in the other. He watched her come, mesmerized, unable to believe his good fortune.

"May I join you, Richard?"

When he started to reply, he found he still had the potato salad in his mouth. He chewed furiously, made noises, and gestured toward the empty chair.

She seated herself, greeted the couple nearby, then remarked, "Isn't this a nice turnout?"

Hudson could only nod.

"I believe we have sold almost seven hundred tickets already. Thank you for buying a hundred."

He sat frozen, unable to speak, unable to do anything but stare at the goddess beside him.

She spoke in a low voice, just loud enough for him to hear. "We really need new hymnals, and I think Mr. Ice needs the money for the horse. It died, you see. Don't mention it—we might embarrass him."

Richard Hudson managed to whisper, "The horse is dead?"

"I'm afraid so. You didn't want a horse, did you?"

He shook his head no.

"I don't think anyone else did, either. People who want a horse already have one, and those who don't have one really don't want one, even if they think they might. A dead horse may be the perfect raffle prize."

The writer's eyebrows knitted as he tried to follow her logic. Seeing his expression, she continued between bites, "By buying tickets you contribute to a good cause—two good causes, actually—dream about being the lucky winner, and fantasize about riding a horse into an endless meadow under a golden sun. All that for just a dollar. And if by chance you do win, the fantasy will never be tarnished by reality."

Richard Hudson smiled. He knew a great deal about fantasies. A lot less about reality, he admitted candidly to himself. Still . . . "Reality doesn't always fall short of our expectations, Cecile. Sometimes it exceeds them."

"On rare occasions," she agreed. She finished her dinner in four or five bites.

He sighed deeply.

She glanced his way, and her gaze stayed on him. The faintest trace of a smile crossed her lips. "Have a good evening," she said, and rose from her chair.

Her daughter was on the other side of the room watching her, so she walked over. "Did you get enough to eat?"

"Yes, I did. Who is that man, Mother?"

"Richard Hudson."

"I think he's in love with you."

"He thinks so, too," Cecile Carcano said.

Moses Grimes got everyone's attention. "Folks, it's about time for the raffle. We have sold about seven hundred fifty tickets, so let's take a few minutes here and see if we can't sell the rest of them. Junior will circulate through the crowd with the tickets. Dig deep, everyone. Take a chance on a horse and help a worthy cause."

Junior walked around with a paper bag full of stubs and a roll of tickets. People bought a few more.

When Junior got to miser Hardy, the old man stared dubiously at the bag. "Come on, Mr. Hardy," Junior said. "You like to sing hymns, don't you?"

"I don't need a horse," Hardy declared. "A horse eats too much and I don't have a shed to keep him in."

"Don't worry. You won't win."

"Well, I might."

"If you win, we'll give you your dollar back," Junior told him.

"A very worthy cause," Cecile Carcano said. She was at Junior's elbow. Miser Hardy got out his purse and counted out four quarters, which he placed in Junior's hand. Junior scribbled Hardy's name on a ticket stub and dropped it into the bag. He handed the ticket to Hardy.

Jirl Ice watched this little procession coming his way and briefly thought of trying to escape. Mrs. Carcano had her eye on him, though. "I don't believe you have yet bought a ticket, Mr. Ice."

"That's true," he admitted, and dug into his pocket for a dollar. "But there's something I need to tell you, Mrs. Carcano. About the horse—"

She smiled gently. "You must have faith, Mr. Ice. I think the situation will work out nicely."

"Don't sweat it, Jirl," Junior added. He snagged the dollar and pressed the ticket into the reluctant purchaser's hand. Then, as Jirl and the minister watched, he wrote Jirl's name on the stub and dropped it into the bag.

When Junior and the minister had accepted all the money offered, the bag containing the stubs was handed to Moses Grimes. "Reverend Carcano, would you care to do the honors?"

She declined with a laugh. "No, Mr. Grimes, not tonight. Since you are chairman of our board of trustees, I think you should pick our winner."

With that Moses reached into the bag. He swirled his hand, dug deep, finally drew out two stubs. Without looking, he dropped one back into the bag and flourished the other. "Here it is, our lucky winner." He looked at the name on the ticket, then his eyes went around the room. "Jirl Ice!" he announced. He handed the stub to Mrs. Carcano.

Everyone applauded and several people slapped Jirl on the back. He didn't know what to say. He smiled as tears ran down his cheeks.

Later, as Jirl was leaving, Cecile Carcano caught up with him at the door. "Here is your money, Mr. Ice. We collected almost three hundred dollars more than we need for hymnals."

"Mrs. Carcano, I can't accept that."

"I don't see why not, Mr. Ice. A deal is a deal. You certainly didn't know that you were going to win the raffle."

"Amazing how that worked out," he replied. "But no. I think the good Lord smiled on me tonight, so I'd like to donate that money to the church. Something will come along that the chapel needs."

Cecile Carcano nodded and pocketed the money. "Thank you, Mr. Ice. We'll see you in church on Sunday. Please bring your family."

"I will," he said, and stepped out into the cool of the evening.

TWENTY-ONE

Mrs. Marple, the Eden postmistress, knew something was up on Saturday morning when the cream-colored envelopes, all alike, poured out of the mail sack from Indian River. She fingered them curiously, noted that just about everyone from Indian River to Vegan was going to get one, then began sorting them. When she found hers, she sat down to open it. This is what she read:

OPEN HOUSE

ANNE HARRIS AND MATILDA AND HAYDEN ELKINS

REQUEST THE PLEASURE OF YOUR COMPANY

AT A HOUSEWARMING

SEVEN P.M. NOVEMBER 10TH

AT THE ELKINS RESIDENCE.

PLEASE BRING A COVERED DISH.

"Good heavens!" Mrs. Marple exclaimed. "That's tonight!"

She went back to sorting letters, but her mind was on what dish she could prepare quickly when she went home that evening.

Mrs. Eufala Davis found her invitation in her box at the post office. She read it in stunned amazement. Then she showed it to the postmistress.

"Great Scott, Mrs. Marple! They've lost their minds at the Elkins household. Poor Matilda has been under a terrific strain; her mind must have snapped."

"Like a dry twig," Mrs. Marple agreed, shaking her head. "I'm thinking of taking a zucchini casserole."

"Oh, horrible! Horrible! Never in my life have I heard of anything like it! Man, wife and mistress—holding an open house to flaunt their sinful arrangements. A brazen, notorious, shameless *ménage à trois* right here in the Eden country! It is just too much! Too much!"

Ignoring the social commentary, Mrs. Marple asked pointedly, "Are you going?"

The question brought Eufala Davis back to earth. "I'll have to talk it over with Henry, of course. The invitation was addressed to both of us and I couldn't go without him. We may have to go, you see—it may be our Christian duty."

"I understand."

"Henry will know."

"I'll see you there, Eufala," Mrs. Marple said, and went back to sorting mail.

Eufala Davis had just gotten through the door of her house when the telephone rang.

"Eufala, this is Twila Wilfred. You will never believe what I received in the mail this morning!"

"An invitation to an open house at the Elkinses'."

"You received one, too?"

"Oh, yes. Isn't it dreadful?"

"Never have I heard of a man behaving like Hayden Elkins. And he looks so normal, so innocent."

"Oh, he's wicked, Twila. Wicked. He didn't just take a mistress, he acquired a *concubine*."

"I thought they did that only in China. Idol worshipers and such."

"And here, too, in Eden," Mrs. Davis boomed triumphantly. "Who would have thought Hayden Elkins capable of such depravity? You can never tell by looks, Twila," Mrs. Davis continued, answering her own rhetorical question. "Men can carry evil in their hearts for years, then suddenly, boom! Some little thing causes the foul seed to sprout. Something like a dirty picture. That's why I am so careful to keep suggestive movies and magazines away from Henry."

"You are so wise, Eufala. Are you going tonight?"

"I must talk to Henry and—"

"I'm going," the widow Wilfred said with conviction. "I'm going to ask Mr. Murphy to take me."

"Elijah Murphy?" said Eufala Davis, aghast.

"Yes, Eufala. Elijah and I have become friends."

Mrs. Davis spluttered, but finally she got it out. "But he drinks!"

"He has yielded to temptation in the past and may again in the future," the widow Wilfred admitted.

"Wallowed in it, you mean," Eufala shot back.

The widow Wilfred steamed on undaunted. "He's trying. And he's a gentleman at heart. I'll see you at the Elkinses'." She hung up then, leaving Eufala Davis so stunned that a long moment passed before she remembered to put the telephone back on its cradle.

She was trying to decide what dish she should prepare for the evening when it occurred to her that a food question would be an excellent pretext for a call to Matilda. If indeed the poor woman had gone off her nut, the paramedics might even now be taking her away in a straitjacket.

She dialed the telephone and waited expectantly.

"Good morning."

"This is Eufala Davis, Matilda."

"How are you?"

"Fine, thank you. I was wondering what dish I could bring tonight. Do you have any suggestions?"

"Tonight? What's tonight?"

"Why, the open house!"

"What open house?" The surprise in Matilda's voice seemed genuine.

"Matilda, don't tell me you don't know? I received an invitation in the mail this morning to attend an open house—a 'housewarming'—at your house. Tonight. Seven o'clock."

"We didn't send—"

"Twila Wilfred got one and so did Mrs. Marple."

Matilda was speechless.

"I'll have to discuss it with Henry," Mrs. Davis went on, "but I'm sure he—"

"This is the first I've heard of it," Matilda Elkins said. "I wonder who else got those invitations."

"Well, I'm sure I don't know. You might call Mrs. Marple at the post office."

"I believe I will. Thank you." And Matilda hung up.

Mrs. Marple's answer left Matilda Elkins gasping for air. "I believe almost everyone between Indian River and Vegan got them, Mrs. Elkins. There were sixty or seventy of those cream envelopes."

"Sixty—"

"Or seventy."

Matilda took several deep breaths while she processed the information.

"A covered dish affair tonight at seven o'clock," Mrs. Marple volunteered. "Didn't you send the invitations?"

"No, I didn't," Matilda replied, and reached a sudden decision. "But we'll see you tonight. You are coming, aren't you?"

"Well, only if—"

"At seven, then. Good-bye."

After she hung up the telephone, Matilda called loudly, "Billy Joe! *Billy Joe Elkins!*" Thank goodness it was Saturday and he wasn't in school. "Come down here *now!*"

The scion of the clan came into the kitchen wearing a sheepish grin. That look spoke volumes to his mother. "Want to tell me about it, or am I supposed to be surprised tonight?"

"Uh, tonight would be just fine."

"How many invitations did you send?"

"One hundred." When his mother reached for the counter to steady herself, Billy Joe added, "They won't all come, of course."

After a long moment and several deep breaths, Matilda asked, "How much money do you have in your bank account?"

"About three hundred dollars, I think."

"I suggest you withdraw it from the bank and use it to buy soft drinks for all these people. A half dozen cases should do it, I hope. Fortunately we have several cases of beer in the basement and some wine. We'll also need paper plates, plastic knives and forks, disposable glasses, napkins, and garbage bags."

"Okay, Mom."

"This wasn't a nice thing you did, Billy Joe."

"I think it's time you and Dad and Anne Harris got your personal lives straightened out."

"I think you are a foolish young man sticking your nose where it doesn't belong," his mother replied tartly. "But we'll discuss it later. Go to the bank, get your money and buy those things."

"Yes, Mother."

Eufala Davis settled on lasagna as her dish for the evening. After checking her refrigerator and cupboards, she donned a jacket and dashed across the road to Doolin's store. As usual, Lula Grimes was behind the register. When Eufala had selected the items she needed, she brought them to the counter.

"I haven't talked to Henry yet," she confided to Lula, "but I suspect he will insist we attend the Elkinses' open house."

"What open house?"

Eufala became flustered. "Why, I just assumed you and Moses were invited. I hope I haven't committed a social . . . Oh, there it is! In your mail."

She pointed triumphantly at the stack of mail lying on the counter near the register.

The postman had delivered the mail a few minutes ago. On top of the stack were two cream-colored envelopes, one addressed to Mr. and Mrs. Moses Grimes, the other to Junior. Lula picked up hers and tore it open.

"See!" Eufala said, greatly relieved. "I just knew that you would be included. So embarrassing . . ."

As Lula stared at the invitation, she only half-listened to Eufala prattling on, but when she heard these words, they sank in:

". . . so I called poor Matilda, and—this is so hard to understand—I do believe that poor, harried woman had no idea these invitations had been sent. I just can't imagine how they would have gone out—printed invitations, no less—without her knowledge. Why, I think the poor thing must have *forgotten!* Isn't that extraordinary!"

"*Junior!*" Lula roared.

The vocal blast stunned Eufala, who spilled the contents of her purse upon the counter.

Lula marched in the direction of the garage. "Junior Grimes! *Get—in— here—now!*"

She met him coming through the door from the garage and fluttered the invitation in his face. "Did you do this?"

"Do what?" Junior reached for the invitation and read it. He wasn't a fast reader, so this took a moment.

"Matilda Elkins didn't know about this. Did you and Arch cook this up?"

"No, Mom," Junior said. "Sounds like it's going to be a good party, though." He beamed at her. It was pleasant, for a change, to be wrongly accused.

Relieved, Lula Grimes sighed and marched back through the store.

"Can I go, too?" Junior called at her back.

"There's an invitation for you by the register." She heard him clumping along behind her, so she whirled about. "I expect you to be on good behavior tonight. Don't let Arch Stehlik talk you into anything."

"Mom, I—"

"Man the register for a moment while I speak to the cook. I'll have her prepare a couple of meat loaves."

"Sure, Mom," Junior said. He grinned broadly at Mrs. Davis, who was getting the last of her things repacked in her purse.

"An open house," he declared. "Sounds like quite a party. Guess we'll get the lowdown on con-jew-gal arrangements among the quality folk, eh, Miz Davis?"

The minister's wife flushed.

"Since I'm sorta short on girlfriends at the moment, I wonder if you would like to go as my date?"

"I'm married to a minister, Mr. Junior Grimes. I don't think that remark the least bit funny."

"Oh, Henry can come along, too, Miz Davis. It's the modern age we're living in."

The guests came all in a rush, a flood of people that milled through the rooms of the house and filled it to brimming. Billy Joe and Melanie acted as official greeters, standing on the porch welcoming people, who queued up with their food dishes to get through the front door. Ruth Harris was one of the first to arrive. She didn't go into the house but joined Billy Joe and Melanie shaking hands on the porch.

"Where's your dad, son?" Judge Lester Storm asked loudly as he climbed the stairs, bypassing the line of guests bearing food.

"He's in the den, I believe, sir."

"Into the sauce already, is he?" Lester said. He nodded at the ladies and went inside.

Melanie eyed the endless stream of cars creeping up the driveway and parking on the lawn with a growing sense of impending doom. Finally she said, "It looks as if everyone we invited is coming, Billy Joe, and they're bringing their whole families!"

"Looks like it. This will be the social event of the year."

"Oooh, we shouldn't have done this," Melanie said.

"Relax," Ruth Harris said calmly. "It will work out. Life always does. You'll see."

"Mr. Elkins is going to be so mad," Melanie insisted.

Billy Joe wasn't worried. "Hello, Mrs. Davis, Reverend Davis, Mr. Kline, come right on in . . ."

In the living room Judge Storm saw the very last person in Indian River County that he would have expected to find at a social event: Elijah Murphy. The little man was standing rather forlornly against one wall watching people file in bearing plates of food.

"Murphy, how are you?" the judge asked in his usual courtroom voice. He stopped in front of his perennial defendant.

"Dry, Your Honor. Desperately dry."

"Hmmm," said the judge, who noticed that Murphy didn't look as grimy as usual. His color was better, and . . . the judge realized with a start that Murphy didn't have a hangover. In fact, he was clean shaven and had even invested in a haircut at some time in the not-too-distant past. His suit wasn't from Brooks Brothers, but it was clean and pressed.

Judge Storm was so taken with Elijah Murphy's appearance that he reached out and straightened his jacket for him. "Murphy, you look so good that a fellow might think you're a candidate for office."

"I'm on the wagon, Judge. Only fell off once since you jugged me in September."

The surprise showed on Lester Storm's face. He reached for Murphy's hand and shook it vigorously. He was still pumping when a lady beside him said, "How are you, Judge Storm?"

"You know the widow Wilfred, don't you, Judge?" Murphy asked, pulling his hand from Storm's grasp.

The jurist surveyed the lady in wonder. "Why, yes. I believe I do. Mrs. Wilfred, good to see you again. Very good to see you again. Out and about on this festive occasion." He kept rambling because the widow Wilfred slipped her hand into the crook of Murphy's arm and stood smiling benignly, looking quite pleased with life.

"Extraordinary how life works out," the judge continued, still taking in the couple standing before him. "Astounding, really. The human parade never ceases to fascinate me, with all its infinite possibilities . . . and . . ."

"You must try the stuffed peppers I brought this evening," the widow Wilfred said as the judge ran down. "Elijah enjoys them immensely."

"She's a great cook," Murphy said.

"Yes, I'm certain of it." Lester Storm shook Murphy's hand one last time, smiled at the beaming widow, and moved on, in the direction of the den.

The house was not small, but the people filled it. They stood in the kitchen, the living and dining rooms, the stairs and hallways, the bedrooms, the basement, spilled over into the heated garage and the unheated porch, even the lawn. And they all seemed to be having a fine time. The crowd kept circulating past the dining room table, which had every square inch covered with dishes containing food. As fast as one dish emptied, Matilda or Anne shuttled in another from the kitchen, which was also full of people talking, laughing and visiting.

Diamond and Crystal Ice were standing together balancing paper plates in their hands when Richard Hudson found them. "I need a word with you ladies," he said over the hubbub, part of which consisted of music blaring from Billy Joe's sound system.

Neither woman smiled.

"I owe you both an apology."

"You don't owe me anything," Crystal said, and concentrated on worrying some meat off a chicken leg with a fork.

"I think he's changed his mind. He wants both of us," Diamond remarked, addressing her sister. "Or maybe only one. Shall we flip for him or fight a duel?"

"I guess I deserve this," Hudson said contritely.

Crystal worked on her chicken without looking up. "And we were desolate, heartbroken, wondering if it was worthwhile to go on living."

"Wondering if life held any tender thing to heal our rejected, scorned, scarred hearts."

"What would Prince Ziad do in this situation?" Crystal asked her sister.

"He would sweep the lady off her feet, kiss her passionately, and tell her that the gods have willed it."

"Really?"

"It always works. Passion sweeps away all vestiges of ladylike restraint."

"Perhaps that will work for you," Crystal said to Hudson. She laid her paper plate on the bookcase behind her and spread her arms. "Try me."

"I deserve that. I'm sorry. I fibbed to you the other day when I told you I had fallen for Mrs. Carcano. That wasn't really true. I—" He took a deep breath. "I lied."

Diamond's left eyebrow rose into an arch. Crystal lowered her arms and retrieved her plate.

Hudson continued, "But to tell the truth—"

"By all means. The whole truth and nothing but."

"The truth is that, since then, I have sort of . . . developed a very tender feeling for her."

Crystal giggled.

"Does she know?" Diamond asked.

"No," Hudson confessed, and blushed. He turned and looked shyly across the room at Cecile Carcano, who was standing with her daughter talking to Matilda Elkins. Diamond and Crystal glanced at each other knowingly.

Just then Junior Grimes joined the group. "Hudson, what are you doin'?"

"Nothing much, Junior. Nothing much."

"Like hell. You're breaking my woman's heart, that's what you're doin'. I oughta pop you one."

Diamond latched on to Junior's right arm. "Behave yourself, Junior Grimes."

"This man," Hudson said, "is the Prince Ziad of Eden."

"I know," Diamond replied, and grinned luxuriously. She reached up and rumpled Junior's hair.

"Who's this Prince guy? The rock star?" Junior asked.

"Junior's a real live hero and he's mine," Diamond said, and led him away.

When they were in a corner with no one obviously eavesdropping, Junior said, "I want to ask you an important question, Di, so I do. Real important. I been working up to this for a long time, but I'm not going to ask it if you're still moping over Hudson like a lovesick puppy, so I'm not."

"You may ask, my prince."

"Does that mean that you and he . . . ?"

"He's in love with Mrs. Carcano."

"Huh! I'll be . . ." Junior scratched his head, then brightened. "Don't that beat all! Well, she's a fine lady and he's a good fella."

"And you were going to ask . . ."

"Oh. Maybe it should wait. Tonight isn't—"

"*Now,* Junior. Or never."

It took him a moment to work up his courage, a moment during which his face muscles contorted spasmodically. As Diamond well knew, every emotion Junior ever felt shot from his brain to his face in a nanosecond, which was, she thought, one of his many charms. A poker player he would never be. Nor a liar.

Finally he got it out. "Will you marry me, Diamond Ice?"

"With a wedding, and flowers and music and a honeymoon and a home of our own?"

"Sure. All of that. Maybe even a rug rat or two. I always thought you'd make a fine mother if you put your mind to it."

She lowered her head a moment, and when she raised it to face him again, she said, "You aren't the smartest man I've ever met, Junior Grimes, but I think you have the biggest heart. I have never met a man who cared more about other people than you do. I will be honored to be your wife, and I will love you all my life."

Junior let out a shout. When everyone turned to look, he laughed and pointed to Diamond. "She said yes," he announced loudly. He lifted her from the floor and kissed her.

When they broke for air, Junior suggested, "Let's go see when Mrs. Carcano can tie the knot."

"Looks as if you are gaining a brother-in-law," Richard Hudson said to Crystal, who winked at him and grinned broadly.

Sheriff Arleigh Tate found Hayden Elkins in the den sharing a drink with Judge Lester Storm, who had apparently already had two or three. "It's my very favorite officer of the law," the jurist declared. "Welcome to the inner sanctum. Close the door, Tate, and tell us about crime."

"What will you have, Sheriff?"

"Bourbon on ice, Hayden. What about crime don't you know, Judge?"

"I heard a rumor, Tate. Strictly a rumor. Don't know that there's a word of truth in it, but I heard that Delmar Clay was mired in the quicksand of a delicate situation before you fired him."

Arleigh Tate tested his drink, then settled into one of the prosecutor's overstuffed chairs. He flipped a hand in acknowledgment.

"Don't really want to know all the official details, of course," Judge Storm continued. "Some of these people might be in front of the bench one day. I'll weigh the evidence then as it is presented. However, I think that tonight, with just the three of us sharing this fine whiskey, we might in good conscience indulge ourselves with a few unsworn, unsubstantiated, vicious idle rumors."

"Sounds safe enough," Arleigh Tate agreed. "Heard any lately?"

"Well, like I said, I have heard this tale about your boy Delmar, the most hated man in the county. I heard that someone caught him in flagrante delicto with a woman not his wife and shot him in the ass. You heard anything along those lines, Sheriff?"

"I'm not strong on Latin," Arleigh Tate said cautiously. "But I did hear that Delmar was caught with his pants down, so to speak, and suffered some birdshot damage to his derriere."

"French, no less," the judge said gaily to the prosecutor, and held out his glass for more whiskey. "The thing I find uncanny, Hayden, is that Tate knows literally everything. Everything! He is everywhere, sees everything, hears everything—he's sort of an unfrocked angel, if you will. For example, let me ask him this: What is the name of the lady with whom Delmar was dallying?"

"Strictly rumor, Judge. Don't want to compromise a lady's reputation, you know."

"I understand completely. You're among friends, and your words will not be repeated, so rumor away."

"Diamond Ice."

"Verlin's daughter?"

"One of the twins."

The judge sipped and pondered. After a moment he asked, "And which of our local gentlemen stroked the trigger?"

Arleigh Tate looked quizzically at the prosecutor. "Have you heard anything about this, counselor?"

"I represent Mrs. Clay in her divorce action. I knew there was another woman, but Mrs. Clay didn't know who it was. This is the first I've heard about a shooting."

"You didn't hear it here. Promise me."

"We're just discussing rumors."

"No, I need a promise. When you walk out that door, you haven't heard this."

"All right."

"Your son shot Delmar."

Hayden Elkins' glass, which thankfully was nearly empty, slipped from numb fingers. He didn't seem to notice.

"Billy Joe? Are you sure?"

"I was there. Saw him do it. Shot Delmar twice, as a matter of fact, when he was naked as a jaybird on a Sunday morning in May. Bang, bang, right in the gluteus, where it would do the maximus good."

Lester Storm lost himself in laughter. When he regained control, he apologized. "This is my last drink, gents. Go ahead, Arleigh, tell it all. I'll try to keep a grip."

Sheriff Tate settled himself deeper into his chair. "This incident started some weeks ago when Billy Joe and his girlfriend, Melanie Naroditsky, decided the time had come to consummate their relationship . . ."

"Would you care to dance, Mrs. Wilfred?"

"I didn't know you danced, Mr. Murphy. When did you acquire that skill?"

"Oh, way back there, years and years ago. They say it's something you never forget, like riding a bicycle."

The dance floor was the living room. Billy Joe, Melanie and Ruth had pushed back the furniture, and now Billy Joe was playing slow tunes on his sound system. Elijah Murphy led Mrs. Wilfred out into the middle of the area, where he slipped his right arm behind her and took her hand in his. "Where did you learn?" she asked.

"My mother taught me."

"Did you love your mother, Mr. Murphy?"

"Oh, yes. Desperately. In fact, I think she was the only woman I've ever loved."

"If a boy doesn't love his mother, he can't love another woman, Mr. Murphy. That's a natural fact."

"How much longer are we going to keep calling each other Mr. Murphy and Mrs. Wilfred?"

"I don't know. I sort of like it. It's formal, polite, very how-do-you-do. Do you think we should drop it on informal occasions, Elijah?"

"I do, Twila. On most occasions."

"You're a good dancer, Elijah."

"My mother called me Eli."

"Eli."

He smiled at her. He had a fine smile, she thought. She rested her head on his shoulder and concentrated on the music.

Across the room Junior was breaking the news to his future mother-in-law. "Diamond finally broke down and agreed to become an honest woman, Miz Ice. The preacher lady says she can tie the knot three Sundays from now."

"You're sure now, are you, Junior?"

"Yes, Miz Ice, I think I know my own mind. Just had to work my way up to all the responsibility. That can take some doin', you know."

"If you make her as good a husband as Verlin has been to me, she will be truly blessed."

"I'll try my best, Miz Ice," Junior said humbly. "I really will."

In the den, behind closed doors, Arleigh Tate was winding up his story. "The problem, of course, was always Mrs. Clay's extended family, to whom I had made numerous promises in return for political support. Their enthusiasm for Delmar evaporated when Mrs. Clay told them about the photographs and announced she was divorcing him."

Hayden Elkins had listened to Sheriff Tate's recitation in silence. He sat now contemplating his shoes and thinking about his son, Billy Joe.

Arleigh Tate seemed to read his thoughts. "Your son is growing up, Hayden."

"Yes," the prosecutor answered absently. "Yes, I think he is."

"At some point in every man's life," Arleigh continued, "he must learn to stand up for what he knows to be right. We all make mistakes, and Billy Joe has probably made all the mistakes you and I made when we were his age. Yet he decided that *he* was going to ensure Delmar got precisely what he deserved, and he didn't much give a damn who found out about it. The boy knew I was going to be there—Junior told him. He went anyway. He dusted Delmar's butt with a twelve-gauge when opportunity offered. Then he stood, put the gun over his shoulder, and walked back across the ridge as if he were just out for a stroll in the woods. I could almost hear him saying, 'If you want me, Sheriff, you know where to find me.' I liked that, Hayden. Liked it a lot."

"He *is* growing up," Billy Joe's father agreed.

"I'd take him any day for a son of mine. The boy has class."

"Yes," Hayden agreed thoughtfully. "Perhaps more class than his father does."

"There's something in the Good Book," Judge Storm said slowly, "about the children teaching the parents."

"The truth is," the sheriff said, "I should have fired Delmar Clay several years ago when I found out what a poor law officer he was. Shouldn't have waited for Diamond Ice to do me a favor, shouldn't have let Delmar make a boy feel that he had to shoulder a gun to protect a girl's honor. We all live and learn."

"I've changed my mind, Hayden," Judge Storm rumbled. "I will have one more drink."

"Mom, Diamond is going to be your daughter-in-law" was the way Junior broke the news to his parents when he found them in the kitchen talking to J. S. Kline.

"When, Junior?" his mother asked. "I've waited a good many years on you and I don't know if I have much more wait left in me."

"Three Sundays from now. Mrs. Carcano is going to tie the knot in the Eden Chapel."

Lula Grimes seized Diamond and hugged her fiercely as Moses Grimes pounded Junior on the back and shook his hand. J. S. Kline reached in for a hearty handshake, too.

"You did it!" Lula whispered to Diamond. "You did it!"

"I'll be a good wife, Mother Grimes."

"I know you will, Di." She faced Junior. "I want grandchildren, son of mine. Girls and boys. Especially girls." Her face clouded up. "I think I'm going to cry."

"Not now, Mom," Junior told her, and gathered her into his arms. "Do it at the wedding. You and Miz Ice can bawl your hearts out then if you want to."

"I'll bring along plenty of hankies," Moses Grimes said, and threw back his head and laughed.

The party was in full swing when Ed Harris arrived. He managed to squeeze through the front door. The crowd inside was elbow to elbow. There were so many people that it took him a few moments to spot her. She was behind the dining room table, which was still heaped with food. She was talking to someone—and looking straight at him.

He moved, sliding between people, murmuring greetings, nodding, here and there shaking a hand, yet whenever he looked, she still had her eyes on him.

He bumped into someone and mumbled, "Excuse me."

"Is that the best you can do, Dad?"

"Ruth! What are you doing here?"

"I received an express invitation from the organizers of the party, Billy Joe and Melanie Naroditsky. I was so excited about the prospect of seeing Mom's new home that I dropped everything and rushed over."

"And how is everything at the university?"

"I need some money. That is the other reason I came."

"What do you spend it all on, anyway?"

"Women today pay their own way, Dad. It's sexist to expect the man to pick up the check. And I have an active social life. Very active."

"Hmm." Anne was still watching him. Her eyes met his whenever people moved out of the way.

"Will you dance with me?" his daughter asked.

"I'd be delighted."

The dance floor was crowded, with five or six couples dancing to Sinatra. Ed and Ruth joined them.

"Remember when I taught you to dance like this?"

"For my fourth-grade Christmas party. After you sent me to bed, you and Mother danced for hours."

"How do you know that?"

"I watched from the stairs."

"I love you, Ruth," he told her.

"I know you do, Dad. And I love you."

When the music was over, Ed Harris kissed his daughter on her forehead. Anne's eyes were still locked on him.

He walked toward the eyes, which never wavered. "May I have the next dance?"

She smiled and gave him her hand.

As they danced she murmured, "Here to check out the ladies?"

"Since I'm semisingle, I thought I should get back into circulation. Are there any semiattached females here tonight to whom I should pay particular attention?"

"Only this one."

It was good to be holding her again, good to smell the aroma of her cologne, feel the firmness of her back, feel her warmth, the touch of her hand, her presence, bask in her aura. When the first tune was over, he held her lightly until the next one began. And the next. And the next.

Finally he said, "Are you ready to go home?"

"Yes," she whispered.

They didn't even stop to get their coats.

"Hello, I'm Ruth Harris." She stuck out her hand.

Trooper Sam Neely took it and told her his name.

"You're new around here."

"Got here in September. Just getting to know people, trying to remember names."

"If you'd like to know me better, you could dance with me."

"I don't know how to dance," Sam Neely confessed.

"It's easy," Ruth assured him, and led him to the center of the living room. After a few minutes he seemed to have the box step mastered to the point that he could talk and dance, too, so she asked, "Which of the local girls do you have your eye on?"

"You're a very forward young woman, aren't you?"

"I'm a child of our age, Mr. Neely, liberated from the dull, stale, tired conventions that frustrated women throughout history."

"How do you know they were frustrated?"

Ruth laughed. "That is the weak point in the argument, isn't it?" She pressed herself a little closer to him and examined the way his eyes crinkled when he smiled.

A warm feeling had flooded through her a few moments ago when she watched her parents slip away. And they thought no one was paying attention. Loving your parents was painful when they had their rocky episodes—and so delicious when life went right.

Ah, she thought, if only I can find a man who loves me as much as Dad loves Mom. If only . . .

"I believe Goofy is outside looking in the window," Cecile Carcano whispered to Minnie Ice. She had found the lady at the breakfast nook in the kitchen and slid into the booth beside her.

"He does that," Mrs. Ice said solemnly. "He can't help himself. It isn't Christian, I know, but I don't think he does anybody any harm."

"Why don't you bring him inside?"

"We did, when we came tonight. He slipped away from me and went out. He feels more comfortable outside looking in, I guess."

"What is Goofy's last name, Mrs. Ice?"

"Well, I don't rightly know." Minnie lowered her voice so much that it was almost lost in the hum of conversation washing over them. Cecile Carcano had to lean close to hear.

"When he was born I put Verlin's name down as the father, but he wasn't. It was a fellow selling lightning rods. I ran off with him and came home pregnant, and Verlin pretended it never happened. He lets everyone think that Goofy is his boy by some woman he had an affair with. But he never had an affair."

She looked at Mrs. Carcano. "There, I've told it. Never could for all these years. Been wanting to tell someone who would understand. I can't take it to the grave by myself. Someone else has to know."

Cecile Carcano touched Minnie's cheek. "Verlin always knew," she whispered in Mrs. Ice's ear. "And he forgave you. Surely God will be as understanding as your husband."

"I don't know. Verlin loves me. Always has."

Junior found Arch Stehlik in the front yard under a large pine tree watching snow fall into the lights. Goofy was standing on his cinder blocks looking into the living room window.

"Nice party, eh?" Junior said.

"I saw the Harrises slip out a minute ago. They left together in Ed's car."

Junior felt good, very good. He slapped his arm around his friend's shoulder and stuck his tongue out to catch a snowflake.

"Remember that Weingardt girl that lives on Clover Lick?" Junior asked. "Her daddy works for the county?"

"Sort of heavy, not too bright?"

"Yeah. She stopped by the store the other evening, and I got to thinking—"

"Maybe you should give that up."

"—Got to thinking that she's actually kind of cute in a chubby sort of way. I kidded her a little, and she admitted that she doesn't have a boyfriend."

"Oh, no! Don't start that again!"

"Ol' Goof needs a girlfriend, Arch. We could—"

"Of all people, June, you should know—women put a terrific strain on a man's nervous system. Goofy might not be able to handle it."

"Life's a dangerous business, Arch. This is worth a try. After all, he's going to be my brother-in-law."

"You're kidding!"

"Nope. I proposed and Diamond accepted, so she did. Three Sundays from tomorrow. Circle it on the calendar and get your suit cleaned. You're going to be the best man."

"What is the world coming to?"

"Anyway, I thought maybe a triple date: you, me, Goofy and the girls. What do you say?"

Hours later, after Matilda had said good-bye to the last of the guests, she found Hayden in the kitchen cleaning up. "It was a nice party, wasn't it?" she said.

"Our neighbors are good people," Hayden agreed. He finished the pot he was washing, then turned toward her as he dried it. "I've been a real horse's ass the last few months, Matilda, and I owe you an apology. Thanks for sticking by me when I didn't deserve it."

He dried his hands and put down the cloth. When he reached for her, she got in close and hugged him. "I love you, Hayden."

"I love you, too, Matty. I'm sorry I hurt you."

"Let's finish cleaning up in the morning."

After they turned off most of the downstairs lights, Hayden opened the front door. He and Matilda stood arm in arm watching the snow fall.

"Hey, douse that light."

"Billy Joe? Are you out here?"

"Yeah." He and Melanie were sitting in the swing with a blanket around them. "Did you enjoy the party?"

"Indeed we did," his father said. "When are you taking Melanie home?"

"In a few minutes."

"When you get back, please lock the door and turn out the rest of the lights."

"Good night, Mom and Dad."

"And Billy Joe?"

"Yes?"

"Thanks for everything."